Praise for the novels of Brenda Novak

"*The Perfect Couple* was fast-paced
and extremely engaging from the very first page....
Once I started, I couldn't stop! Definitely, most definitely
add *The Perfect Couple* to your reading list."
—*True Crime Book Reviews*

"Novak delivers another expertly crafted work
of suspenseful intrigue heightened by white-knuckle danger
and realistically complicated romance."
—*Booklist* on *The Perfect Couple*

"I guarantee *The Perfect Couple* will keep readers
on the edge of their seats."
—*Romance Reviews Today*

"Realistic and gritty, this story grabs the reader by the throat
on the first page and never lets go."
—*RT Book Reviews* on *Watch Me*

"Gripping, frightening and intense...
a compelling romance as well as a riveting and
suspenseful mystery...Novak delivers another winner."
—*Library Journal* on *The Perfect Liar*

"A chilling, sensual tale that features a host of skillfully
developed characters and intricate, multilayered plotting.
Sacramento-based Novak writes gripping romantic thrillers."
—*Library Journal* on *The Perfect Murder*

"As always, Novak's plotting is flawless,
and her characterizations are rich and multilayered.
What sets this story apart from the rest is the intensity
of the romance between the two wounded protagonists—
it simply sizzles. A keeper." (4.5 stars, Top Pick)
—*RT Book Reviews* on *The Perfect Murder*

"It's hard to go wrong with a Brenda Novak novel."
—*Book Cove Reviews*

BRENDA NOVAK

BODY HEAT

MIRA®

MIRA®

Recycling programs
for this product may
not exist in your area.

ISBN-13: 978-0-7783-2803-2

BODY HEAT

To Bradley and Audrey Simkins at Booklovers Books...
I love coming into the store and seeing gigantic posters
of my novels covering the wall. Thanks for hand-selling
so many of my novels. Thanks for coming out to any
event where I need a bookseller. Thanks for doing the
BBQ at my launch party each summer (no one can BBQ
like you!). And thanks for constantly reminding me,
just because of your own passion,
how much I love everything about books.

Dear Reader,

It never fails. With each new set of books (I've been doing three per summer for a few years now) I seem to choose a favorite hero. One always intrigues me or resonates with me more than the other two, and this summer that's the hero of this novel, Roderick Guerrero. Rod's a character who has triumphed over a great deal of adversity. Instead of letting it break him, he's used it to make himself wiser and stronger. I like people who've survived a few bumps. They're always more textured, more interesting.

The research for this novel took a little more time than usual, but I was glad of the opportunity. I learned a lot about Arizona and the area along the Mexican border. Although Bordertown is a fictional place, there are many towns similar to it, with lots of atmosphere and challenges. I think challenges make a place more interesting, too.

I'd like to extend a special thank-you to Debbie Berke and Grant Noyes. Their names show up as characters in this novel because they were generous enough to purchase the privilege to help me support worthy causes such as fundraising for my children's high school and diabetes research. To me, these are real heroes.

I love to hear from readers. Please feel free to write me at P.O. Box 3781, Citrus Heights, CA 95611, or visit my Web site at www.brendanovak.com, where you can enter to win monthly draws, read samples of other books I've written, download a pdf list of all my titles or check out my annual online auction for diabetes research, which includes *so* many cool things. So far, together with my fans, friends and publishing associates, we've raised over $1 million for this cause. My youngest son is a Type 1 diabetic, so I live with it up close. A cure is my fondest dream.

Love is the key!

Brenda Novak

1

Racism is man's gravest threat to man—the maximum of hatred for a minimum of reasons.

—Abraham J. Heschel,
rabbi and philosopher (1907–72)

Benita Sanchez was almost as afraid of running into a rattlesnake as she was U.S. Customs and Border Protection. The CBP would send her and her husband back to Mexico. But a snake… The way José said she should creep across the ground—always staying low, *very* low—made her feel so vulnerable. Snakes came out at night, when the temperature cooled. She could easily stumble into one. Maybe they'd hear a brief shake of the rattle, but they'd never see its beady eyes or sharp fangs before it struck. Since they'd lost their coyote, or smuggler, they had only the moon to help them. And it was barely a sliver—a sliver that looked like a tiny rent in a gigantic dome of black velvet, which was slowly turning purple as the night edged toward dawn.

Although they'd crossed the border with thirty-one other Mexican nationals, they were now alone. Everyone had scattered when the border patrol spotted them more than twenty-four hours ago. Had any of those people made it safely back to Mexico? Or were they in some holding cell? She and José had escaped "La Migra," but she was no longer sure she considered them lucky. Did José actually know where he was leading her? He said he did. He'd come to America once, but that was five years ago. And their coyote had promised they'd have only a six-hour walk. Even if she deducted for the time they'd spent sleeping, they'd been on their feet for eighteen.

As they came to a cluster of mobile homes, José whispered to circle wide and crouch lower. He'd once told her it was easy to sneak across *la frontera*. But it hadn't been easy at all. Although he'd insisted she wear several layers of clothing, the thorny plants that scrabbled for purchase in the rocky soil still managed to sink sharp spines through the fabric or scratch her somewhere she wasn't covered. Add to that the hunger, thirst, homesickness and fear— fear of snakes, dogs, drug-runners, thieves, unfriendly Americans, La Migra—and it was almost unbearable. The whole world felt hostile.

Tears began to burn behind Benita's eyes. She wasn't sure she could go on. She hoped the presence of these trailers meant they were on the outskirts of a town where she could at least get a drink of water, but even if they were close, two miles seemed like fifty when you were walking through the desert.

"José?" She could hear the determined crunch of his footsteps in front of her.

At the sound of her voice, he stopped. "You must be quiet," he replied in rapid Spanish. "Do you want the people in that trailer to hear you? If they do, they'll call the border patrol!"

The mobile home they skirted was one of the nicer ones she'd seen, a double-wide with a yard and everything. But its white paint seemed to glow in the dark, making it look like a giant ghost with flat, empty eyes. This was a soulless, godforsaken land. How could it be the paradise José promised?

"Maybe we could drink from the hose," she suggested.

He hesitated and finally agreed. He had to be thirsty, too. But as they drew close, a dog began to bark, so he grabbed her hand and yanked her away.

"*Agua!*" she begged.

"We can't risk it."

"Then let's try another place. Maybe the next one won't have a dog."

"We're almost there."

He'd been saying that for miles. Unable to believe him anymore, she stopped walking. "I'm scared. I want to turn back."

"*¿Estás loca?*" he said, instantly angry. "We've come too far. We can't go back."

"But…" She swallowed hard. "How much longer?"

"We'll be there soon," he promised.

But would she be any happier after they arrived? They were going to a safe house and then the home of his cousin, Carlos Garcia. She'd met Carlos on two different occasions and didn't like him. He enjoyed playing the big shot, pretending to be something he wasn't. She didn't want José to become like him….

"Hurry!"

Her husband was getting impatient. Benita knew how much this trip meant to him. He'd talked of it the whole time they were dating, painted appealing pictures of the opportunities to be found in America. But…

Gathering her courage, she started after him again. She

wouldn't be a disappointment, wouldn't make him regret marrying her. Besides, as he said, they'd come too far to turn back. Surely the number of mobile homes meant they were indeed close to the safe house. Bordertown was as far as they had to go tonight. It was all arranged. They'd rest, then they'd call Carlos and he'd pick them up and take them to Phoenix. There, they'd live with him and two other roommates and, hopefully, find work so they could help pay the mortgage until they'd saved enough to afford their own place.

"Aren't you worried about snakes?" she grumbled.

"Snakes will be the least of our worries if you don't keep moving."

Sighing, she tried to move faster, but with every step she wished she'd been able to talk José out of this. They were young and in love; they could make a living in Mexico *somehow,* couldn't they? She didn't want to go to America. Maybe he could make more money here—big money, like he said—but would they ever be happy living in a foreign land? A land that didn't want them? And what if they were caught and deported after they'd begun to build a life here?

It was a risk Benita didn't want to take. "José, I really, really want to go home." The tears she'd been holding back began to stream down her cheeks.

He didn't even turn around. "You'll be glad we did this. Just…trust me."

She thought of the water bottle they'd finished hours ago. Would they find themselves lost in the desert when the sun came up in less than an hour? Would they stagger around in the one hundred and fifteen degree heat without food or water and eventually die a terrible death?

The mere possibility made her shudder. All she had

left was a pocketful of nuts. And they were covered with salt.

"We shouldn't have crossed," she said. "We should not have done this."

A gruff chuckle alerted them to the presence of a third party. "Well, well…what do you know? It sounds as if *someone* is coming to their senses."

Benita squealed, then clamped a hand over her mouth. A dark amorphous shape stood in front of them, blocking the faint light of the moon. She couldn't make out specific features, but she knew he was a stranger. And she was pretty sure he was wearing a cowboy hat and holding a gun. He had *something* in his hand….

Was he white? She might've thought so except he spoke perfect Spanish.

Her husband inched toward her, placing his body in front of hers, and she let him. She hadn't yet told José, hadn't wanted to worry him before their trip *el norte,* but she'd just found out she was pregnant.

"Disculpe, señor," he said. "We—we mean no harm. We are passing through, that is all."

The stranger switched to English, which seemed to come as naturally to him as Spanish. "What you're doing is illegal, *mi amigo."*

Although he knew bits of English, much more than Benita did, José wasn't fluent. He stuck with his native tongue. "But we are just visiting family. We mean no harm. We plan to go back to Mexico after two weeks. We stay only two weeks."

It was an obvious lie, and the man was far from fooled. "Shut up." Again he spoke in English but even Benita understood the meaning of those sharp words.

"*Señor,* please." José edged closer to her. "It is only me and my—my little brother. We have no drugs, nothing."

This time, the response came in Spanish. "Your brother."

He'd heard her speak, which made this another transparent lie, but Benita kept her mouth shut, in case he believed José. Some boys had high voices, didn't they?

"*Sí.* He—he is frightened. *Por favor…*please, do not hurt him."

Benita could hardly breathe. The stories of rape, beatings, robbery and other abuse that occurred during border crossings had circulated throughout Mexico. Parents used them to warn their children to stay home, as her father had warned her. But, other than to insist she chop her hair short and wear a baseball cap and men's clothing, José had shrugged off her parents' concerns. He said they worried for no reason and promised her everything would be fine.

"Stop groveling or I'll shoot you both right where you stand."

Those words and the disgust in the stranger's voice made Benita start shaking. Who was this man? What was he doing out here? If he was a border patrol agent, he would've told them by now, wouldn't he? Had they interrupted a drug run? Or was this a local farmer who didn't want them on his land?

"I—I have money," José said.

They didn't have a lot. It was Carlos who was supposed to pay their coyote once they'd made it safely across. But at this point Benita was ready to turn herself in to the authorities. She didn't care if he sacrificed every peso.

The man laughed. "You think I'm a dirty cop—like the kind you have in Mexico?"

José didn't answer. "Forgive me. I am not trying to offend you, *señor*."

"Your smell offends me, *amigo*. You being where you don't belong offends me. And the fact that every word out of your mouth is a lie offends me."

There was a click, and a brief flash of light. Benita covered her face, bracing for the worst. But he was only lighting a cigarette. She caught a brief glimpse of his chin, which was covered with dark stubble, before he closed his lighter.

"I'll make you a deal," he said, blowing smoke in their faces.

"*Sí*. Money. You want money?" José bent to get the cash hidden in his sock.

"I don't want your lousy *dinero*. You couldn't have enough pesos to buy me a new pair of boots, *amigo*. What I want is for you to undress your little brother here. I'll use my night-vision goggles to take a peek at his chest. If he is, as you say, a boy, I'll let you pass. You can head on to Tucson or L.A. or wherever else and bleed this country dry just like all your wetback relatives who've snuck over the border before you. But—" he took another long drag on his cigarette "—if she's got *tetas*..." Another blast of smoke hit Benita in the face, making her cough. "I'm going to punish you for being the lying sack of shit you are."

José didn't move. Benita could feel his tension, could tell he was weighing his options. What had the man said? She'd recognized only a few words. Would José decide to run? They couldn't. They'd be shot.

"Okay, I—I admit it. This is my wife, not my brother." José's voice was raspy with desperation. "But...she's barely twenty, *señor*. And she's frightened. Please, I beg you. Let us go. We will head back to Mexico. Right now."

The man took another drag. "Until next week or the week after. Then you'll come creeping across the border again." He switched to Spanish, no doubt to make sure she'd understand. "I read an article that said you wetbacks try at least six times before giving up. Takes some pretty big balls to be so bold, you know what I'm saying? Besides, someone's got to die. Might as well be you."

Die? Benita sank to her knees. "*No, por favor!* I—I didn't even want to come here. I'd rather go home. I'll *stay* home. Don't hurt us."

He made a *tsking* sound. "How could you put your wife in such danger, Pedro?"

He had never asked for José's name. He was using "Pedro" as a racial slur. She could feel this man's hatred as palpably as the heat of the sun when it beat down at midday. But she was glad José didn't complain. He squeezed her shoulder. Probably to comfort her. Maybe to convey an apology. *You were right. We should've stayed.* "I was just…trying to give her a better life," he said.

A light went on in the closest trailer. When the man turned to look, José grabbed a handful of Benita's shirt and jerked her forward. He wanted her to run, but she couldn't get up fast enough and they lost the precious second that might've allowed them to escape.

The cowboy swung back, and they both froze with fear. Thanks to the light coming through the trailer window, the barrel of his pistol was outlined in silver, and they could see that it had something on the end.

Benita knew what that something was; she'd seen a silencer before. Her brother hadn't always lived the kind of life he was living now that he'd settled down and had a couple of kids.

"Someone's awake," José said. "They'll see you. You'll get caught if you shoot us. Let us go."

The stranger didn't seem the least bit worried. Chuckling deep in his throat, he tossed his cigarette on the ground and fired so fast Benita didn't realize he'd pulled the trigger until José collapsed. Her husband's hand clenched, dragging her to the ground with him, so the shot intended for her went over her head. But that was all he could do to help. In the next second, he made a funny noise and went still, and she knew the man she loved, the father of her unborn child, was dead.

"You killed him!" she wailed, crouching over his body. "You killed him!"

"Hey, what's going on out there?" A woman had opened the door of the trailer and called out in English. Although Benita couldn't understand her words, she thought the interruption would make the man run away. But it didn't. With a curse, Cowboy brought up his gun and aimed again.

"This oughta teach you spic cockroaches to stay in your own damn country," he ground out, and pulled the trigger.

Benita felt a flash of pain between her eyes. Then she felt nothing at all.

2

The sun was just beginning to creep over the horizon when Sophia St. Claire brought her cruiser to a skidding halt at the dusty group of drab to not-so-drab trailers a mile outside of town. She'd thrown on her uniform and dashed out of the house as soon as the call came in. But she was too late. The people who lived here had abandoned the comfort of their homes to gawk and were standing in the middle of the crime scene.

"There goes whatever evidence I might've been able to collect," she grumbled. But why get upset about it? If this was the work of the same killer she'd already been chasing, chances were he hadn't left any evidence to begin with. In the past six weeks, someone had killed ten—now twelve—people in three different incidents, all UDAs or undocumented aliens, and walked or driven off into the night. Whoever it was didn't attempt to bury the victims or hide their corpses, even when he had the chance. His earlier targets hadn't been discovered until more than a week after their deaths.

As she turned off the engine, the small crowd, all of whom had glanced up when she arrived, watched her with pinched and worried expressions. They were obviously aware of the gravity of the situation. But they didn't seem to realize that they should move away from the bodies. Maybe the *CSI* shows weren't always one hundred percent accurate on forensic procedures and techniques, especially when it came to timelines, but surely these people had seen enough TV to know they shouldn't contaminate the crime scene? It wasn't as if they lived in some bucolic *Mayberry R.F.D.* The people here, mostly Mexican Americans with some whites and a few American Indians thrown in, were as rugged as the land. What with drug trafficking, human trafficking, gangs who had ties to the Mexican Mafia, racial disputes and a local chapter of the Hells Angels roaring around, blowing through stoplights, breaking speed limits and looking for trouble, this was almost a war zone.

Catching a glimpse of two prone bodies, she winced and jerked her door open.

Debbie Berke, the woman who'd called to report the shooting, met her as she got out. "Sophia, they're dead," she said. "They were killed instantly. Wasn't no reason to get the paramedics out here."

Sophia wasn't surprised to be addressed by her first name. Only thirty, she hadn't been chief of police for very long. And most of these folks had known her since she was a baby. Debbie's late husband had been the veterinarian who'd operated on Toby, her family's dog, when Sophia was fifteen, and eventually put him down. "I understand. I've called the medical examiner."

"He's on his way?"

"That's what he said." But Sophia doubted he was in any kind of hurry. Some of the sentiments Dr. Sandy Vonnegut had expressed at the last crime scene led her to believe he didn't consider the death of illegal aliens to be much more distressing than roadkill.

She hollered for the crowd to step back at least twenty paces.

With their brown skin and inky black hair, the victims were, as expected, Mexican. One was a man, the other a woman. The male victim lay facedown in the dirt. They both had on several layers of clothing—long-sleeved shirts with dirty work pants—and tennis shoes, all secondhand quality at best. Sophia couldn't see where the man had been shot; any blood was hidden beneath his body. It was the woman who gave away the manner of death. She lay on her back, staring up at the sky with a perfect hole in her forehead. That hole oozed a slim trickle of blood. The woman's heart had stopped almost immediately....

They were young. Too young to die. Especially like this.

Sophia crouched next to them, checking each for a pulse. It was a pointless gesture. They were both dead; that was obvious. But she went through the motions, anyway, hoping...

Finding Debbie to be absolutely correct, she stood and studied their surroundings, searching for anything that struck her as odd or out of place. An object left behind. An object taken. Tire tracks. Except for the fact that this incident had happened much closer to town, the scene looked exactly like the two she'd visited during the previous month and a half. The killings had occurred on a barren patch of desert too rocky to reveal tire tracks or footprints. And from what she could see so far, the perpetrator had left nothing behind but the bodies.

"What do you think?" Debbie murmured over Sophia's shoulder. The expectation in her voice suggested she believed Sophia could pull the killer's name out of thin air.

With a sigh, Sophia took a pad and pen from her shirt pocket and guided Debbie away from the bodies. She wanted to talk to her and anyone else who might've seen or heard something. She also needed to enforce the perimeter she'd created and, as long as she stood close to the victims, the others would come closer, too. "Can you tell me what happened?" she asked.

"I heard a—a noise."

A siren wailed in the distance. One of her two deputies, Grant—who'd been on duty last night—was on his way, bringing the yellow police tape he'd accidentally put in his car instead of hers the last time they'd been through this. "What kind of noise?"

"At first, I thought it was a wounded animal." She paused. "I know there've been other murders like this. Everyone's talking about them. But you just never imagine—" she shrugged helplessly and tears welled up as she gazed at the corpses "—you just never imagine it can happen right outside your door."

Sophia laid a comforting hand on her arm. "It might be easier if you don't look," she said, and shifted positions to block Debbie's line of vision. "Take a minute, if you need to. We can continue whenever you're ready."

Dashing a hand across her cheeks, Debbie struggled to control her emotions. "I heard a cry. It frightened me, so I got up and walked through my house. Everything seemed fine. I peeked out the window, but it was too dark to see, and I didn't want to go outside. I told myself there wasn't anything to worry about and started back to bed. But then I heard voices. They seemed to be arguing. One belonged to a woman." She lowered her voice. "That made me think Earl and Marlene had had another fight." She jerked her head to indicate a couple standing in their bathrobes staring, in a dazed fashion, at the lifeless bodies, but it wasn't necessary for her to point out who the Nelsons were. Sophia knew them by name. She knew almost everyone who lived in the mini trailer park. Although her financial circumstances had been much better, she'd grown up less than a mile away.

"They haven't been getting along so great since he lost his job," she explained, after which her volume edged up to normal again. "Once I thought I knew what the problem was, I lost my fear and stuck my fool head out to see if I could get them to settle down. That's when I heard two thumps, right in a row. A woman cried out in Spanish and I knew it wasn't Marlene."

"You couldn't see anything?"

"Nothing. It was pitch-black out here. And I had the lights on inside, which didn't help."

Sophia wanted to groan in frustration. Why couldn't they catch a break? "Can you remember what the woman said?"

"I don't speak Spanish. You know that."

"What did it sound like?"

"To me, it was gobbledygook."

As long as Debbie had lived in Bordertown she hadn't been able to pick up *any* Spanish? That should've surprised Sophia, but it didn't. For the most part, there were clear lines of demarcation between the two nationalities, despite almost constant contact. "So then what?"

"I ducked back inside, called Earl and grabbed my shotgun. I keep one in the closet in case I need to scare off a mountain lion or a javelina or what have you. But by the time Earl rolled out of bed, and I found ammunition, whoever had killed these poor people was gone."

"You didn't see *anyone* in the area?"

"No."

Damn it! "What about a car or truck?"

She motioned around her. "Just what you see here."

"Did you *hear* a vehicle?"

She shook her head. "But I wasn't listening carefully because I was so frantic to find my ammo."

"Do you think whoever did this could've left on foot?"

"I figured they must have. So I jumped in my old truck and drove around for a bit, but I couldn't see a soul. And I'm sort of glad," she admitted, tears filling her eyes again. "I wouldn't want to come face-to-face with the kind of man who could do this."

Sophia was thinking they probably bumped into him on a variety of occasions. Bordertown had shrunk drastically from its former silver-mining days. Now it had a population of only three thousand. And, judging by the location of the other murders, which were all in the surrounding desert, she guessed the killer lived nearby.

"Why would anyone do this?" Debbie asked.

That was the one question Sophia found easy to answer. "Hate."

"But who could hate enough to kill absolute strangers? I mean, yeah, maybe these people were breaking the law. I get tired of the situation with the illegals, too. We all do. But some of them are just plain…*desperate*. You can hardly fault them for wanting to be able to put food on the table!"

"This killer feels justified." Sophia could sense it in the way he left the bodies. He didn't rape or rob or beat them. He didn't touch his victims at all. He exterminated them like vermin. And the fact that he didn't bother to even throw some brush over their bodies told her he was proud of his actions.

"It must be someone new to the area," Debbie guessed.

She couldn't imagine a friend or acquaintance committing such a heinous act. But Sophia wasn't so sure. It didn't have to be a stranger. She'd witnessed enough racism to understand it could be anyone. Or maybe this wasn't what it appeared to be. She had plenty of political enemies who wanted to discredit her—one man in particular. Creating a high-profile case like this, a case she couldn't solve fast enough to defuse the ticking time bomb of public sentiment, would be one way to do it. There were plenty of other possible scenarios, too. Although she'd previously considered border patrol a federal issue and hadn't gotten too deeply involved in it, she knew the ranchers and farmers in the area were angry about the damage caused by the droves of illegal aliens who crossed their land.

"I don't think he's new." Something about the confidence with which this killer acted made Sophia believe he'd been around for a long time, that he was intimately familiar with the region and its politics, and that his hatred of illegal immigrants had recently been honed and sharpened. Which was why her thoughts again turned to the man who'd most like to see her fail. Leonard Taylor. Because of a situation with a Mexican woman, a UDA—or undocumented alien—Sophia had the job he felt should be his....

"You're saying it's someone from around *here?*" Debbie gasped.

"I'm saying it could be. Maybe the killer had a run-in with a UDA that went badly, or he was robbed by one, or his wife left him for a Mexican or cheated on him with one. He might even have lost his job to someone who wasn't supposed to be in the country." Or he didn't become chief of police as he'd always hoped thanks to an illegal immigrant who claimed he'd raped her.

"Anything could be a trigger," she added. Because of their random nature, hate crimes were some of the most difficult to solve. That meant she had to do the nearly impossible—before this killer could strike again. Lives depended on it. Her job could depend on it, too.

Douglas was larger. Why couldn't all of this have happened fifteen miles to the east?

"I hope you're wrong," Debbie murmured.

"Thanks for your help. You think of anything else, give me a call."

Determined to take a closer look at the ground on which they lay, Sophia returned to the bodies. Although the perpetrator had collected his shell casings when he'd killed before, she doubted he'd done it here. Now that she'd spoken to Debbie, she figured he wouldn't have had the time. He'd shot these people knowing there was a trailer forty feet away with an occupant who'd just called out to him.

The fact that Debbie's shout hadn't saved their lives showed a distinct lack of fear and no respect for law enforcement. That was another reason she thought Leonard, or one of his supporters, might be involved. This killer definitely wasn't worried about any threat *she* might pose. He was bold. And he was growing bolder by the day.

Suddenly, she saw it. The glint of metal in the dirt.

Cautioning everyone not to move, she jogged back to her squad car and got the small forensics kit she kept in her trunk. Then she used a pair of metal tongs to gently lift a spent shell casing from the small rocks that'd previously concealed it.

"Handgun," Earl volunteered.

Sophia hadn't realized he'd stepped up behind her. She shaded her eyes. "Looks like it." It was the right size for a semiautomatic. And there was a distinctive bulge in the web area forward of the extractor groove. She was no ballistics expert, but she knew any deformity might tie it to a specific gun.

After dropping it in a small paper sack, she managed to find two other casings that had fallen into some thorny mesquite. She'd expected a total of two, but this proved there were three shots. All the casings had the same defect; they'd come from the same gun.

She was closing and marking the bag when Officer Grant Noyes, a twenty-three-year-old fresh out of the academy in Phoenix, arrived with the crime-scene tape. He blanched when he saw the bodies and turned a bit green. He had a weak stomach. But he had to learn to deal with the pressures of the job. She needed his help.

"Set up a perimeter," she said.

Another car came toward her, this one a black sedan. The Cochise County medical examiner. Apparently, Dr. Vonnegut had decided to show up without making her wait too long.

While the M.E. parked and climbed out of his car, Sophia got her measuring tape, her video camera and her digital camera. She needed to take photographs and a video of the bodies before anyone touched them. She needed to take photographs and a video of the whole area. And she needed to include a scale so prosecutors could recreate the scene, if necessary. She didn't have the forensics team a larger city might have. She had her two deputies, and until the FBI officially responded to her request for help, she had the assistance of a detective from the Cochise County sheriff's substation in Douglas. Dinah Lindstrom lived in Sierra Vista five miles away, but she'd been raised in Bordertown. Sophia hadn't yet notified her that there'd been another killing. The intentional oversight wouldn't improve their relationship, which was strained at best. But Sophia worked for city council, not the sheriff's office. And considering the fact that Dinah Lindstrom had been one of Leonard Taylor's biggest advocates, she couldn't be sure the detective was really on her side, even now.

"What've we got?" Vonnegut, clearly unhappy, frowned as he trudged toward her. Fortunately, unlike Lindstrom, he didn't seem to have any particular affinity for Leonard, or none that she knew of, anyway. It wasn't as if she and Vonnegut had ever been enemies. But no matter how many times she dealt with him, they never became friends, either. He seemed a little too proud to be accessible. At the very least he was impersonal.

"Two vics, both dead," she replied.

"Same killer as last time?"

"Same M.O. UDAs shot in the desert and left where they fell."

"What's with the guy who's doing this?" he grumbled when he was close enough that he couldn't be overheard by the others.

"Seems to me he's dissatisfied with the immigration problem."

"But if he gets caught, he'll go to prison. What's the point? For every one he shoots, there are thousands who'll cross the border right after. Patrols pick up six hundred a day. Even conservative estimates suggest they miss twice that many."

"Hence, his frustration." Frustration that could easily cause Taylor's anger at what his victim had cost him to boil over. Considering that anger, she'd often feared he might try to hurt *her*. But if anyone else wondered about Leonard's culpability, she hadn't heard, and she hadn't mentioned it herself. First, she needed proof. Otherwise, she'd be criticized for having some sort of vendetta against him. His friends had already accused her of making up the rape she'd reported on behalf of the illegal alien who would never have come forward without her—all to "steal his job."

After telling Grant to keep the bystanders out of the way, she walked Vonnegut over to the bodies.

"Maybe it's not an American who's doing this," he said as he knelt next to the male. "Maybe it's a Mexican drug lord settling old debts with poor mules or runners who tried to sell the dope they carried and keep the money."

"That's highly unlikely."

"It's possible."

She wasn't optimistic about his theory. Except for the fact that the couple had been killed execution style, the murders didn't suggest it. As far as she could tell, this wasn't Mexico's problem. It was *their* problem. "There's no evidence to support it. The victims all crossed the border from Mexico, but that's about the only thing they have in common. Most of the people we've identified came from different regions and had no contact with organized crime. All the indications are that they didn't previously know one another, either."

"I'm *still* hoping it's a drug lord," he muttered. "Because if this is a vigilante, it's going to get ugly around here."

Sophia grimaced. "Take a look. It's already ugly."

"Yeah, well, unless you can stop this guy, it'll get worse."

"Thanks for stating the obvious."

He rolled the male onto his back. The victim had a goatee and the tattoo of a cross on his neck. A bloodstain indicated he'd been shot in the chest, but he hadn't bled much more than the female.

"Son of a bitch knows how to make quick work of it."

Vonnegut was talking about the killer, of course. Sophia had noticed that, too, but she wasn't impressed. "A bullet at point-blank range is pretty effective."

Crouching beside him, she began to search the victim's pockets. Sometimes UDAs carried voter registration cards. These cards seemed to hold more significance to Mexicans than the same thing did to Americans. Maybe because they included a photo, in addition to the standard name and address.

Unfortunately, this guy didn't have any ID. Sophia found five hundred pesos—roughly the equivalent of fifty bucks—tucked into his right sock, as well as a piece of paper with a phone number that had a Tucson area code.

Suddenly light-headed, she swatted at the flies buzzing around the bodies and rocked back to fill her lungs with air that wasn't pregnant with the smell of stale sweat and unwashed clothing. She hadn't searched the woman yet, but she needed a moment to recover or she was going to be sick. Judging by the nausea roiling in her stomach, she was as pale as Grant had been the first time he saw one of the bodies.

"Why do you live here?" she asked Dr. Vonnegut while watching Grant finish with the yellow tape.

He was busy getting a body temperature. "What'd you say?"

"Why do you live near the border if you hate Mexicans?"

"I don't hate Mexicans. I just want them to stay in their own country. Besides, my wife is from around here. And I like to be able to golf year-round."

"Makes sense."

"What about you?"

Breathe. Mind over matter. Do not embarrass yourself. These are not *dead humans. These are…objects.*

Squeezing her eyes closed, she turned her face up to the sun. "I've got family here, too," she said, but she wasn't talking about her mother and stepfather or her older brother. He didn't live there anymore, anyway. She was thinking about Starkey. These days, she hated the Hells Angels and everything they stood for, hated that she'd ever had anything to do with them. She and Starkey had gotten together her junior year in high school, when her stepfather had moved in. Since her mother wouldn't believe her complaints, and her older brother was away at college, Starkey had provided a deterrent to her stepfather's advances. No one dared mess with her once Starkey came into her life. They knew there'd be hell to pay. She'd enjoyed the protection, as well as rolling on his Harley and wearing all that leather. But the longer she'd stayed with him, the more certain she was that she didn't want to be an "old lady," as the Hells Angels referred to their women. Determined to become a full patch member, Starkey was getting more and more committed to the club, which was so involved in drug and gun trafficking that she faced a different kind of risk from the one posed by her stepfather.

So she'd broken free, moved out on her own and migrated to the opposite extreme—law enforcement. After feeling so vulnerable, both at home and with Starkey's pals as she became more aware of what they were really like, being able to protect herself had meant everything to her. She loved being a cop. But there was one person from the Starkey era she couldn't let go of, and that was Starkey's son, Rafe. She didn't care that he wasn't technically hers; she'd taken care of him those three years she'd been with Starkey—especially the two years she'd lived with him—and she wouldn't walk out on the boy. His real mother was a crackhead who'd sell her soul for another bump. In many ways, Sophia was all Rafe had.

And she loved him. It came down to that.

"Someday I'm going to move," she added, and forced herself to search the dead woman. There was nothing in her pockets except some nuts and a folded piece of paper with several words written in Spanish.

Sophia expected it to be a paper prayer. A lot of illegal immigrants carried them. But it wasn't. It was a love note.

Although Sophia wasn't fluent in Spanish, she could read and understand most of what she heard. She'd taken two years of Spanish classes in high school and she'd come into contact with it almost constantly since, via the ranch hands who frequented her stepfather's feed store and the Mexicans she apprehended. Fortunately, that was enough to be able to decipher the few sentences she saw written there.

"You're beautiful. Will you marry me? I love you. José."

This woman had left behind everything she owned except this note? That meant it had to be important to her. She was wearing a thin gold band. It wasn't very expensive, but it was a wedding ring all the same. Obviously, she'd said yes to that proposal.

Tears welled up in Sophia's eyes. Trying to hide her reaction, she ducked her head, but Dr. Vonnegut immediately caught on that something was wrong.

"Hey, you okay?"

She averted her face. "Fine. Just doing my job. Why?"

"You're acting strange."

Was it so strange to experience grief for these people? To feel that their deaths mattered?

She swallowed in spite of the lump clogging her throat. "I think the guy's name was José."

"José what?"

"That's what I have to find out. And this—" she gazed at a face that, in life, would've been as pretty as the note suggested "—this was his wife."

"Dumb wetbacks," he mumbled.

Sophia whirled on him before she could stop herself. "Shut up!" she shouted. "Just…shut up!"

Anger quickly replaced his initial shock. "You're not cut out for this job. I knew it when they hired you," he said. Then he got up, removed his plastic gloves and stomped away, leaving the bodies to the boys from the morgue, who put bags around the victims' hands, in case they could recover some sort of trace evidence, and began wrapping their corpses in clean white sheets.

Ignoring the stares of the people who'd been looking on, Sophia pinched the bridge of her nose and struggled to compose herself. She had to be careful. There were enough sexist jerks in Bordertown who thought her job should've gone to a man—even though the only viable candidate was a criminal himself.

Her cell phone rang. As she pulled it from her pocket, she hoped it might be Rafe. He'd give her something good to hang on to, help her get through this. But it was too early for him to be up. And as soon as she saw the incoming number, she knew a bad morning was about to get worse: It was Wayne Schilling, the mayor.

3

The voice on the other end of the phone stopped Roderick Guerrero in his tracks. Because he hadn't recognized the number, he'd been curious enough to answer. But from the moment he'd heard the word *hello,* he'd known it was his father, although they hadn't spoken in years—ever since he'd graduated from BUD/S training and received his Naval Special Warfare SEAL classification. He still couldn't say how Bruce Dunlap had found out he was graduating, or the time and date of the ceremony. Roderick sure as shit hadn't told him. But someone had. After all the years Dunlap had chosen to ignore him—even lied about their relationship—he'd flown to California to attend and looked on; acting as proud as any other parent. The only difference was that his wife sat at his side, her lips pressed tight with disapproval. Edna was the kind of woman who walked through town looking down her nose at everybody. Roderick disliked her even more than he disliked his father.

He didn't know what to say and had no desire to say anything, so he hung up. He felt no obligation to Bruce. It wouldn't have mattered if Bruce had been calling to offer him a million-dollar inheritance. Roderick didn't want his father's money, his advice, his legacy or his love. His love least of all. He didn't even use his father's name. Legally, he wasn't a Dunlap, anyway. He was a bastard and as such had been an embarrassment to his wealthy white father all the time he was growing up. As soon as he was old enough to contest his mother's wishes, he'd taken her name instead. She hadn't been happy about that. He was related to the wealthiest man in town and she wanted everyone to know it. It gave her a sense of pride, a connection to something more through him.

Or maybe she enjoyed it for other reasons. Maybe she got some pleasure from knowing her son's very existence grated on Edna. But Roderick wanted to distance himself from the Dunlaps and all they represented as much as they wanted to distance themselves from him. He was satisfied with his mother's name. *Guerrero* meant warrior. That suited him better. He'd been fighting since the day he was born.

Milton Berger stuck his head out of the conference room a few feet down the hall. *"What are you doing?"*

Roderick had almost forgotten that his boss was waiting to be debriefed on his latest assignment.

"Nothing." He started to slide his cell phone into the pocket of his khaki shorts when it rang again.

"Can you shut that off and get your ass in here? I don't have all day!" Milt snapped. As sole owner of Department 6, Milt couldn't seem to focus on any one thing longer than five minutes. He was too busy juggling. Always in a meeting or on a call, he wasn't an average workaholic; he was like a workaholic on speed. Roderick was beginning to think the fortysomething-year-old never went home at night.

But he didn't care what Milt did in his off-hours. Milt wasn't the kind of guy Roderick liked spending time with.

Milt had six operatives, and every single one of them thought he was a bona fide asshole. What did *that* say about a guy?

As his phone continued to jingle, Roderick's thumb hovered over the red phone symbol that would send the call to voice mail. It was his father again. Why the hell was the old man making an effort now? At thirty, Roderick was no longer a dirt-poor Mexican boy with no prospects and no family beyond a weary mother who'd come into the country illegally when she was barely twenty and cut lettuce in the fields of the selfish jerk who'd impregnated her. Whatever Bruce wanted, it was too late.

But Milt's impatience grated on Roderick almost as much as his father's untimely call, so he answered out of spite. *"How did you get my number?"*

"What the hell!" Milt complained.

Roderick ignored him.

"I've been keeping tabs on you."

The question that immediately came to Rod's tongue was why, but he knew his father's answer wouldn't make sense to him, and he wasn't sure he wanted to hear it anyway, so he went with "How?"

"Jorge mentions you from time to time."

Jorge was Bruce's overseer. He was also the closest thing Rod had to a grandfather and the only person in Bordertown Rod stayed in contact with. Jorge loved hearing about Rod's undercover exploits, so Rod humored him by checking in every few months and catching up. The old man had never told him that Bruce had expressed an interest. Maybe he hadn't; maybe Jorge was attempting to engineer some sort of reunion. It'd be like him. He'd always had a soft heart. Jorge was part of the reason Rod's mother had never left the ranch despite her difficulties. She knew he couldn't go anywhere else and make the money he made working for Bruce. And she, no doubt, hoped Bruce would eventually "come to his senses" and accept Rod. Mostly, she'd stayed to see her son eventually have more and be more than she could hope to give if she left.

"Since when did the two of you become friends?"

"Time has a way of changing things, Rod."

"And some things will never change. So are you going to tell me what you want?"

"To hear me out. That's all I ask."

Hoping his father was about to lose the ranch and needed a loan or something, Roderick decided to indulge him. To a point. "You've got three minutes. Make it fast."

"I'd like you to come to Bordertown."

This made Roderick laugh. "You're joking, right? I'd sooner go to hell."

"Rod, I think you might be able to help with a situation down here. If half of what Jorge tells me is true, I *know* you can."

The gravity of "a situation" should've piqued his interest. It didn't. "I have no intention of helping you with anything. Ask one of your lazy-ass white sons."

Dropping several F-bombs and claiming Rod's "ass was grass," Milt stormed out of the conference room, marched to his office and slammed the door. But Rod wasn't worried about his boss's reaction. It wasn't as if he'd be fired. He'd just busted a large child-porn ring in L.A., which was a major coup. Local law enforcement hadn't been able to accomplish that in more than a year, and he'd done it inside of three months. His stock at Department 6 had never been higher.

"This isn't for me," Bruce said. "This is for her, okay?"

Roderick gripped the phone tighter. "Who's *her?*"

"Your mother."

Now his father had his full attention. "My mother is dead. Partly because she wore herself out before she could reach forty. Partly because you ripped her heart out and stomped on it every chance you could get. *You're* the reason she's dead. You and *Edna*." He pronounced Bruce's wife's name with the disdain he believed it deserved.

"I'm not the one who encouraged your mother to come to America. That was her decision. And I never promised her more than I gave her. I provided work, that's all. It was as good a job as she could get anywhere."

"You gave her a baby, that's what you gave her," Roderick growled. "A baby she struggled to take care of, along with her little brother." That brother had returned to Mexico not long before Carolina's death. Roderick had lost touch with him, but he thought about Arturo often. From time to time, he considered looking him up. He would have done it, except he was afraid Arturo was dead from some drug deal gone awry. He'd caused a lot of trouble before he left. Chances were that if he'd survived, he wasn't on the right side of the law. He was one of those restless spirits who could never find peace. At least, that was what his mother had always said.

"I gave her some money...now and then," his father said.

Rod was surprised he didn't mention how hard he'd tried to persuade her to get an abortion. Or the money he'd offered her in those early years to leave the ranch, leave Bordertown. "So...what? You paid her medical expenses and gave her a few bucks to help feed the kid you fathered? That means you deserve a medal?"

"No, no, you're right. I—I didn't do enough. I'm sorry about that."

"Life's a bitch, Mr. Dunlap. Babies don't go away just because you regret making them." Especially if the mother refused to get an abortion and refused to give up hope that her child would someday be accepted.

"I don't regret *you*. I regret how selfishly I acted. I was…scared. I didn't want what I'd done to cost me my wife and family."

Roderick rolled his eyes. "Or your inheritance."

"My father wouldn't have been sympathetic. Times were different back then. I know it's hard for you to understand, but it's true."

Bruce, Sr., had never once acknowledged Rod, even when his mother made it a point to cross his path and say, "That's your grandpa." She was so proud of her son she couldn't understand why the male Dunlaps, at least, couldn't see things her way. It was the male Dunlaps who, in her mind, held the power and controlled the money.

"I wish I could go back and do things differently," his father said. "But it's too late for that. I don't expect you to forgive me."

Roderick glanced at his watch. "Then why are you calling?"

Bruce sighed. "Some racist son of bitch is killing illegal immigrants as they come over the border. Shooting them at point-blank range and leaving their bodies to rot."

"The only racist son of a bitch I know is you. Besides your father. But he's not around anymore."

There was a moment of silence. One that told Rod he'd hit his target. Then his father said, "I deserve that.

So would he, if he was alive. But this isn't about me. Or him. I think this case is more than the local police can handle. They don't have the funding, the manpower or the experience to deal with it. I'm afraid a lot of people will wind up dead if we don't get some help."

Noise, coming from the reception area, indicated the other operatives were returning from lunch, so Rod stepped into the conference room Milt had just vacated and shut the door. He was acting tough, but speaking to his father shook him, made him feel like a little boy again. A hurt little boy. And the hurt resurrected the anger he'd shoved down deep inside. News of the killings brought that anger back, too. He kept imagining women like his mother creeping across the border with the hope of being able to make enough to feed themselves and their families, and being murdered by some vigilante who felt he had the right to take the law into his own hands. It was so easy to feel self-righteous and superior when you had a comfortable home, a safe place to live and a full stomach. "What, exactly, do you expect me to do?"

"According to Jorge, you've got the skills to help. If you want to."

"I'll have to thank Jorge next time we talk."

His father ignored the sarcasm. "You won't believe this, but I'm proud of you."

"Like you were proud of me when I was cutting lettuce in your fields and you'd come by and completely ignore me?"

Bruce didn't respond to the jab, but the tenor of his voice changed, grew softer. "You could make a difference to what's happening here. I know it."

"Since when did you start caring about Mexicans?"

"I've been a member of this community all my life.

Do you think I want to see senseless hate crimes tear it apart? I'm not a monster, Rod. I may not be happy about droves of people entering this country illegally, but that doesn't mean I want to see them murdered."

"Yeah, where would you be if you had to pay for *white* labor?"

"I'm good to my workers."

It was true that he'd been more generous than some farmers. That was another reason his mother had stayed. She interpreted this generosity to mean more than it really did. But Rod didn't want to give him even that much. Besides, what was happening in Bordertown wasn't Rod's problem. He'd finally escaped. No way was he willing to let this draw him back. "I live in California now, Mr. Dunlap. Since my mother died, there's nothing left for me in Arizona." Except Jorge. But speaking to him on the phone and sending the occasional package was enough.

"I'll pay you," Bruce offered.

"Absolutely not." He rubbed his temple to relieve the beginnings of a headache. "I don't want your money."

"You took it readily enough when your mother died!"

Clenching his jaw, Roderick spoke through gritted teeth. "Are you kidding me? I was sixteen years old and had just lost the only person I had in the world. I couldn't have paid for a decent burial without that money, and you know it." That was the only reason he'd taken it. He would never have accepted it if it hadn't been for her. "Besides, I paid you back. I made a payment every month afterward, even if it meant I went hungry." He'd had a hard time surviving the next two years. He'd mostly drifted, taken odd jobs as a dishwasher or a field hand or a painter. He'd probably still be rambling around without tether or anchor if not for a certain navy recruiter who'd worked down the street from an office he'd been painting. After badgering him for weeks, Linus Coleman had talked him into getting his G.E.D. and joining the navy. Rod had signed on the dotted line mostly because he'd been promised a free college education. But his commitment to the armed forces had quickly evolved into much more than that. In the navy, he'd found a home, friends who were more like brothers, purpose in what he did, some self-esteem. But it hadn't been an easy road.

"I never cashed those checks, Rod," his father said.

"That's *your* problem. They were money orders. It's not as if you were doing me any favors by not cashing them."

"I thought there might come a time when you'd actually include a return address on the envelope so I could send them back. I brought them with me to your BUD/S graduation, but…you didn't give me the chance to pull you aside long enough to speak privately. I never begrudged you a cent of that money."

"You're the one who brought it up."

"I guess…I guess I was trying to point out that there've been times when I've…tried to help."

"If that's 'trying to help,' you're even more pathetic than I thought," he said, and disconnected as Rachel Ferrentino, a fellow operative and good friend, came into the room.

"Hey," she said. "What's up?"

She looked concerned, so he plastered his usual easygoing smile on his face. "Nothing. Why?"

"Milt's throwing a fit. Says you have no respect for his time."

"It's not just his time. I have no respect for *him*."

He expected her to laugh, but she refused to let him throw her off track. She'd figured out that something significant had occurred.

"That was important, huh?" She eyed his phone.

Trying once again to bury the memories conjured up by his father's call—and the pain associated with them—he drew a deep breath. "Not really."

Her eyebrows knotted with skepticism. "You're full of crap. You know that?"

"That's what I've been told," he replied, and sauntered past her, chucking her on the chin as if his heart wasn't racing like a rabbit's.

The air-conditioning at the station was working double time to counter the heat of another one hundred and ten degree day, but Sophia was far from comfortable. She knew Detective Lindstrom would be showing up any minute. Lindstrom had called while she was at the crime scene, almost as soon as she'd hung up with the mayor, which meant she'd had two agonizing conversations in a row. Lindstrom had heard about the shooting via her police radio and was furious that Sophia hadn't notified her. Sophia had used the excuse that she couldn't be sure this shooting was related to the others, not until she'd had a look, but that had—understandably—done little to placate Lindstrom. By the time she arrived at the scene, there'd been nothing left except the tape that cordoned off the area and a spot of blood from the male victim's body. Along with the limited artifacts found in the victims' clothing, Sophia had taken the spent shell casings, and the morgue had taken the bodies. Because they were dealing with homicide victims, there'd be an autopsy, but Sophia didn't expect it to reveal anything she didn't already know, at least about the manner of death.

Ironing out the sheet of paper with the phone number she'd found on "José," she picked up her phone. She needed to identify the victims so she could call the Mexican consulate and have them notify the families of the deceased. With luck, the person at this number would be able to help.

Six rings. Then a voice speaking English with a strong Mexican accent told her to leave a message.

She was about to do so, but hung up when Lindstrom slammed her way into the reception area. Sophia could hear the detective's shrill voice, demanding Grant get Chief St. Claire immediately.

Grateful that Christina, who did the clerical work and disliked Lindstrom as much as she did, was away on vacation, Sophia got up and opened her door. "Detective Lindstrom? Would you like to step into my office?" She almost smiled at Grant's obvious relief but the temptation disappeared the minute Lindstrom stalked past the three desks in the front lobby. Brown eyes sparking with indignation, she leaned forward as she charged ahead, reminding Sophia of a dog straining at a leash.

"What happened this morning is completely unacceptable," she said. "*Completely* unacceptable."

"So you've said." Sophia told Grant to go home. It was time for him to get some rest. Then she waved Lindstrom in and motioned to a chair. "Would you like to sit down?"

"No. I still can't believe you'd go out there without calling me. We're supposed to be working this case *together,* Chief St. Claire. How can we do that if you cut me out?"

Maybe Sophia wouldn't have tried to cut her out if she could trust her. But Lindstrom had been childhood friends with Leonard Taylor's sister, and she'd made it clear that she didn't think Leonard was guilty of wrongdoing. Besides that, the woman was a high-strung pain in the butt. With her red hair slicked back into an unforgiving ponytail, she even *looked* uptight.

"You're a bit too intense, you know that?" She closed the door. "Any chance you could calm down?"

Lindstrom's eyes widened despite the pull of that ponytail and her mouth opened and closed several times. "Calm *down?* How do you expect me to react to what you did?"

Pretty much the way she was reacting. But Sophia's first obligation was to bring a killer to justice, and she had to protect herself and her job at the same time. As much as she wanted to believe these murders weren't politically motivated, the possibility remained. From what she knew about Leonard and those who'd rallied around him, she wouldn't put it past Lindstrom to "miss" some clue or sit on a piece of evidence long enough to make sure she was publicly shamed, maybe even fired, before the case was solved.

"Look, we have a job to do, so why don't we get to it?" Sophia said.

"And forget about this morning?"

"Why not? It wasn't that big a deal."

"You know it was," she said. "But you won't have control much longer."

Sophia straightened. "What's that supposed to mean?"

"The FBI is putting together a task force. They won't tolerate anyone who plays the maverick."

Contrary to what Lindstrom seemed to believe, Sophia welcomed the help. In fact, she'd requested it. "You think I don't know they're planning to get involved? I just wish they'd hurry. Because of those shake-ups in the Sierra Vista Resident Agency, they haven't been able to get on it as quickly as I'd hoped."

"You want their help but not mine?"

"They're not good friends with my enemies."

"You're the only one who can't leave the past where it belongs. And I'm tired of you trying to stonewall me. Sheriff Cooper will hear about this."

"Fine. Call him right now if that's what it'll take to get you to focus on something else." Sophia wasn't too worried. She knew Cooper liked her. They'd already discussed her concerns about Dinah. He'd explained that he didn't have anyone else he could assign right now and asked her to have patience and do the best she could. He'd also said that he, too, had contacted the FBI.

She and the detective had a stare-down. Finally Lindstrom huffed, set her bag on the floor and sank into the worn seat opposite Sophia's desk. "What did you find this morning?"

Sophia took the brown sack containing the shell casings from her desk and handed it over.

Lindstrom opened the top and gazed down at them. "What's with the bulge?"

"I don't know, but a defect like that would be handy if we ever came up with the murder weapon."

"Looks like a .45 of some sort." There was still a sulky quality to her voice.

"I'm hoping a ballistics expert can tell us the make of the gun."

"Unlikely. There might be fingerprints, though. Have you checked?"

"I'm leaving that for the crime lab."

Lindstrom returned the sack with the shell casings. "Anything else?"

"Five hundred pesos. A love note. And a number." Sophia slid the paper she'd just used to make that call across her desk so Lindstrom could see it.

"That's not a lot to carry across the border."

"They generally don't have much, do they?"

Lindstrom frowned as she considered what she'd been told. "He should've had a lot more money on him, close to sixteen hundred dollars. People who cross the border don't pay their guides until they're safely across, and it's not cheap."

"This couple must've had friends or family waiting for them, someone who'd pay when they arrived."

"You don't think they were robbed?"

"No."

"Where was the money?"

"In the male victim's right sock."

"He could've been robbed," she insisted. "He might have started out with more. But considering the smell of these people after walking so long in the hot sun, I wouldn't want fifty bucks badly enough to fish it out of his sock, either."

"He wasn't robbed. I'd bet my life on it."

"Fine." Leaving the note on the desk, she leaned back. "Who's at the other end of the line when you call that number?"

"No one yet. I got voice mail. A man, someone with a strong Mexican accent says, 'Leave a message.' I didn't."

"Any idea what part of Mexico these people came from?"

"No, but I'm guessing they crossed via Naco. It's the closest port of entry."

"You could be wrong about that. With the current security measures, more and more coyotes are taking their patrons farther west, near Sasabe."

Sophia shook her head. "That's a forty-five-mile walk and can take several days. These people weren't on their feet that long."

"How do you know?"

"They weren't totally dehydrated."

Lindstrom's voice turned sharp again as she arched her eyebrows. "They've done the autopsies already?"

Once again wishing the FBI would hurry with their promised task force, Sophia grappled for patience. "Dehydration causes your blood to…boil, for lack of a better word. When people who are dehydrated die, even if they actually die of other causes, blood will often ooze from the orifices of the face. There was none of that with these two. They didn't have any water with them, so they'd been walking long enough to run out of whatever amount they'd been carrying—and I'm assuming they were carrying some because they'd be crazy not to. But they hadn't been out for days. They weren't severely dehydrated. They probably came through Naco hoping to reach Highway 90 where someone could pick them up, but somehow got off course."

"More guessing."

"Yes."

"So…are you going to contact the Mexican consulate? Or should I?"

"Go ahead." Sophia was pretty safe letting Lindstrom

handle that part. It required a diplomat more than it required a cop. She didn't see Lindstrom as diplomatic, but if it saved her from being the bearer of bad news—why not? "Tell them I think the first name of the male victim is José and the woman was his wife." She lifted a hand, explaining before Lindstrom could say anything. "José signed the love note, and the woman was wearing a ring."

Sophia held the note up for her perusal. Lindstrom studied it, gave a curt nod to signify that she was through, and Sophia put it back on the desk.

"Meanwhile, you're going to do what?" Lindstrom asked.

"I'm going to use a reverse directory to see if I can get a name to go with this number. If I can track down the owner, maybe he can tell us more about our victims. I'm also sending the casings to the state crime lab, as I mentioned. Then I'm leaving for Naco."

The last comment distracted Lindstrom, as Sophia knew it would. "Not on the Mexican side."

"Of course on the Mexican side. Isn't that where the coyotes are? I don't know very many people who are trying to sneak across the border *into* Mexico."

Lindstrom leaped out of her chair. "But you're not supposed to leave the country!"

"We have to take a few risks if we want to figure out who killed these people."

"You think it was a coyote?"

"Not necessarily." Sophia thought it was Leonard shooting these Mexicans, that he was completely cracking up. Considering the timing and the fact that all the killings fell within her jurisdiction, she didn't feel it could be anyone else. He was her only enemy, and he had a very good reason to hate UDAs. But logic suggested these murders could also be perpetrated by a renegade border patrol agent who'd grown a little too sick of his job. If that was the case, the UDAs who tried to cross but were caught, and people who worked in the smuggling industry, might be able to tell her more than anyone on the American side. Maybe they'd encountered an agent who was acting peculiar or who was particularly aggressive.

It was a long shot but, at the moment, long shots were all she had. "In any case, a new perspective can change everything."

"You won't have *any* perspective if you get yourself killed. My husband works for the DEA, Chief St. Claire. Trust me. It's dangerous down there these days. He tells me that all the time. You don't want to go to Mexico."

Was Lindstrom really concerned for her safety? Or was she afraid Sophia would solve the case and salvage her job? "Like I said, we have to talk to people on both sides. I need to figure out exactly where our victims came from and how they crossed, meet the people they met while there's still a chance they'll be remembered."

"You could get some, if not all, of that information from the person who has that number."

"Maybe, maybe not. At this point, I don't even know if I'll be able to reach him." She picked up the phone. "Hang on." She tried the number; again, there was no answer. But this time she left a message. Then she accessed a reverse directory via her computer to see if she could come up with a name.

"It goes to a prepaid cellular phone," she said. Which told her nothing. It wasn't even anything she could trace.

"Maybe he'll call back."

"Maybe he will. But I'm not going to sit around and wait."

"You can't go into Mexico," Lindstrom insisted. "What about the other victims? Surely there's more work to be done there."

The other victims didn't offer the same opportunity. By the time they'd been found, their bodies were severely decomposed, too decomposed for a photograph to help with identification or anything else. Documents recovered from the bodies had identified some, relatives who'd contacted a foreign ministry field office in Mexico had identified others, but she still didn't have information on three of them. And time was running out. Mayor Schilling had said so just this morning. He'd hinted that he was under a lot of pressure, that he didn't know how long he could keep the city council and Bordertown's most powerful citizens behind her. But he'd been hoping to replace her with someone "proven" from the beginning, even before they were dealing with a serial killer. To him, she'd always been a stopgap because of her age and now he was convincing others.

He didn't spell out exactly how much time she had left, but she knew it wasn't much. Soon she'd be fired. And then it wouldn't matter that she'd ousted an officer who was as bad as the criminals he went after and had become the youngest chief of police in the state. She'd be publicly shamed and out of a job, single-handedly setting back the cause of women in police work here, in southern Arizona, by a decade or more.

"The Mexican consulate already posted on SIRLI whatever we could supply as far as physical descriptions and came up with nothing," she said. SIRLI was the Spanish acronym for a computer system that allowed the Mexican consulate to upload information that could be viewed by staff at the Mexican foreign ministry offices—not only in Mexico but throughout the world. "Unless someone comes forward to say they're missing a brother, a father, a friend, we have little hope of determining the identity of those earlier victims."

"But we have the shell casings this time. That should provide at least some answers."

"We also have a fresh kill. If we can retrace this young couple's steps, we might finally be able to gain some traction in this case."

"Maybe you have a point." Grudgingly, she sank back into her seat. "But there's no way my husband will let me go with you."

Wouldn't you know it? The one time Sophia wouldn't have minded Lindstrom's company—*some* company, anyway. "Then I'll go alone."

4

"You gonna let me in? Or are you gonna keep standing there, glaring at me?"

Reluctantly, Roderick stepped aside. He wasn't sure he wanted to talk to Rachel right now. It was easy to be her friend when *she* needed to vent. But that didn't mean he wanted to be the one doing the talking. Examining what he felt was like probing a bruise. There was no point.

"Can I get you a beer?" he asked.

"No, thanks." She eyed the empty cans he'd thrown in the recycle bin. "Should I put on a pot of coffee?"

"Hell, no." This was the best he'd felt all day, ever since he'd spoken to his father. Why ruin it?

"That call you got at the office…"

He frowned in irritation. "What about it?"

Helping herself to some chips he had out on the counter, she took her time answering. "You want to tell me why it has you so riled?"

"Isn't your husband waiting for you to come home?"

She popped another Dorito into her mouth. "He knows I'm here."

"Why didn't he come with you?"

"Because he's filling out a report. And I told him we needed time alone."

"We don't need time alone," he said with a scowl. Although he and Rachel had once been close, they'd drifted apart since she'd married. Roderick didn't mind. Her husband, Nate, was another operative at Department 6, one he respected, and Rod had never had romantic designs on her. But there were days he missed the camaraderie they used to share so consistently. This was one of those days. Too bad he couldn't back up and change a relationship that had already shifted into something different from what it used to be.

She began rinsing off the dirty dishes he'd piled in the sink. "Tell me what's going on."

"Nothing's going on."

"It isn't like you to sulk, Rod."

"Quit doing my dishes," he said. "And who the hell said I'm sulking?"

She glanced pointedly around the room. "The TV is off. The stereo is off. The blinds are down."

When they weren't talking, only the whir of the air conditioner filled the silence. He hadn't wanted it to appear as if he was home, hadn't wanted his busybody neighbor showing up asking if he could fix her leaky faucet. He'd been trying to give himself some downtime.

And Rachel was making that difficult.

"So?"

"So Milt said you refused to talk to him earlier." She put the plate she'd just rinsed in the dishwasher. "He said you left the office without telling him when you'd be back."

"Too bad for Milt."

"He happens to be your boss."

"I'll check in with him later."

"He's worried about you."

"Bullshit. Milt doesn't worry about anybody but himself." Rod finished off the beer sitting on the counter and crushed the can before tossing it into the recycle bin.

"Okay, let me rephrase that. He's interested in protecting his investment. *I'm* the one who's worried."

"I'm thinking about taking a few days off, that's all." He lifted a shoulder to make the statement more nonchalant.

Silverware clinked as she dropped it into its plastic container. "A few days off."

"Yeah."

"To do what? Hang around here with the blinds down and drink yourself into oblivion?"

"No, smart-ass. To visit Arizona."

She hesitated. "Anyone in particular you want to see?"

He imagined his father and Edna. "Not really." Although there *was* Jorge...

"You must have *some* reason for wanting to go. You barely got home after being away for three months."

He'd never given her any details about his childhood. He kept it vague with everyone, merely saying that he'd come from a hellhole in southern Arizona and was glad to be out of it. But Rachel clued in fast. Holding her dripping hands over the sink, she measured him with her eyes. "Does this have to do with your past?"

"Maybe."

After drying her hands on a towel, she shut the dishwasher. "You're really going to hold out on me?"

He moved toward the fridge to get another beer, but she intercepted him. "Sit down. I'm making you some dinner."

"No, you're not. With you getting in my way, I can't go back to drinking."

"That's true. But as long as I'm here, you may as well talk to me."

He shoved a hand through his hair. "Shit."

"That's flattering. I'm glad I came over to help."

"It's not that I don't want you here." Actually, it was. But not because he didn't care about her. "It's just… I'm not sure what to do."

"About…"

"Going to Arizona."

She took two frozen chicken breasts from his freezer. "Something happen down there?"

"Some asshole is shooting illegal aliens as they come across the border, and I'm contemplating putting a stop to it. That's all."

"Local law enforcement can't manage?"

"Bordertown isn't exactly prosperous. It has a few wealthy ranchers but almost everyone else lives below the poverty line. There isn't a lot of money in the public coffers."

She put the chicken in the microwave to defrost. "The county or the state will help. Maybe even the Feds."

"Probably. But I wouldn't charge anything. I know the area. And I'm fluent in Spanish. I could float around, maybe pick up on a few things law enforcement might miss." He felt he owed it to his mother and her people. That was the most compelling reason, but he didn't say so.

"If it's that important to you, I'm sure you can get the time off from Department 6. You've got weeks of vacation coming."

"That's what I figured."

"So why are you fighting it?"

"You think I should go."

She laughed. "No. *You* think you should go. Obviously. That's why you're so conflicted. I'm just trying to tell you that drinking won't change that."

"My father lives there," he finally admitted.

Her steady gaze met his. "You told me you didn't have a father."

"I did?" He couldn't remember saying that.

"Yep."

"Well, that's essentially true. He never acknowledged me. He gave my mother money every now and then—as much as he could siphon away without risking the wrath of his wife—but nothing steady and only out of a sense of obligation. He had another family. The one everyone looked up to."

She pretended this was a casual conversation, but he could tell she was taking it all in. "Any siblings?"

"Two white boys. Mean sons of bitches, too."

"Older or younger than you?"

"Older." And stronger. At least back then. He had no idea what they were like now. He only knew they'd joined forces to beat the crap out of him on several occasions, usually because he'd come across them on their own property and refused to step out of the way. He'd been tired of seeing his father and everyone else treat them like little princes while he couldn't pick an orange without being accused of stealing.

"Your father didn't stop them?"

"He turned a blind eye. He knew it would get back to his wife if he did and cause an even bigger problem."

"Your brothers still live there?"

"Don't know. I've never asked anyone." Even Jorge.

"But I can't imagine they'd leave. They're eventually going to inherit a sizeable farm right outside of Bordertown."

"Where's your mother?"

"Buried in the town cemetery."

The microwave dinged but she made no move to recover the poultry. "What happened to her, Rod?"

"Lung cancer. Never smoked a day in her life, yet she died of lung cancer." He chuckled bitterly. "Doesn't seem fair, does it?"

"None of it sounds fair. But you're not the person you were then. You'd be going back as someone else. Someone to be reckoned with."

He cocked an eyebrow at her. "What does that mean?"

"It means you can handle whatever's waiting for you there—a killer who's shooting illegal aliens, two mean sons of bitches who might still benefit from a good ass-whopping, a father who must have been a fool not to love you…and the sight of a grave that will probably break your heart."

"See? This is why I don't talk to you," he said.

"Why?"

"You just don't understand."

Knowing he meant the opposite, she smiled. "When are you leaving?"

"I guess I might as well go tonight. Any chance you'll take me to the airport?"

"You think you can get a flight?"

"I doubt I can get into Tucson, but I should be able to reach Phoenix. I'll rent a car and drive from there."

Sophia's long hair was dark enough to blend in with that of the Mexicans she'd encounter, but the color of her eyes and her skin tone would give her away. Her light green irises drew attention wherever she went. People always commented on how startling they were. And, although she had a bit of a tan now that it was summer, her skin was most definitely that of a white person. But at least she wouldn't look any more like a cop than she would a Mexican citizen. She had the tattoo "sleeve" partially covering one arm to thank for that. It might be a remnant of her wild youth, but she still liked the symbols of good and evil portrayed there. They showed humanity at its most realistic—never wholly honorable and never wholly bad. Besides, those tattoos gave her the hard edge she sometimes needed, helped make up for the fact that she was only five feet five inches tall and one hundred and ten pounds.

She pulled on a tank top to go with her jeans and biker boots. Then she combed her hair into a thick ponytail and lifted her pant leg so she could strap her pistol to her right calf before hopping onto the stripped-down Harley she'd purchased last summer. Other than Rafe and her brother, that bike was her only true love. She'd bought it after a particularly painful breakup, at a time when she preferred being single for the rest of her life to trusting another man. She'd been without sex long enough to rethink that "never again" attitude, but the Harley was still a better companion than the boyfriend she'd had last summer. She ran into Dick Callahan every now and then—him and the teenager he'd knocked up while they were together.

"Bastard," she mumbled as she turned out of her drive. That was pretty much her reaction every time she thought of Dick. It didn't help that she'd trusted him a little more than she would have otherwise because he was the pastor at First Calvary Church. Instead of coming to her right away, he'd strung her along with *I love yous* until the girl and her parents had shown up on her doorstep and surprised her with news of the baby. They'd also asked her to step aside so Dick would be willing to make a home for their daughter and her child.

Sophia had thought they were crazy to push for a permanent commitment. He "did the right thing" only to save his position with the church. She doubted the marriage would last. But she'd done what they requested and removed herself from the situation. Dick and seventeen-year-old Zeba had spoken their vows five months ago.

Since Dick, Sophia hadn't really dated anybody. Living in a small town didn't provide her with a lot of options, and being a police officer narrowed the field even further, because she knew too much about everyone. Harvey Hatfield tried to ask her out now and then. But back when he was married and she was just a regular officer, she'd been to his house to settle a domestic dispute. His wife—former wife now—hadn't pressed charges, but Sophia had seen her face and believed her when she said it was Harvey who'd given her that fat lip. Knowing he could be violent didn't make Sophia too thrilled about going out for a drink with him.

Then there was Craig Tenney, a local dentist. He'd seemed nice enough until Alice Greville had come into the station claiming he'd touched her breasts while he had her under nitrous oxide. His other clients had rallied behind him, and Alice had never been able to prove her claim, but Sophia had started going to a dentist in Douglas.

And last but not least, Stuart Dunlap showed interest. On the surface he seemed like an ideal candidate. Other than a bar fight six years ago, he'd had no brushes with the law. Along with his brother, he stood to inherit the Dunlap ranch—something Sophia's mother constantly pointed out. Anne had no qualms about marrying for money. When her first husband filed for bankruptcy, she'd acted decisively to protect her standard of living. But Stuart walked around Bordertown acting as if he owned the place. Sophia couldn't stand his arrogance. She preferred his brother, but Patrick was already married.

The highway blurred beneath her front tire as she gave the bike more gas. She thought of Detective Lindstrom heading home for an enjoyable supper with her DEA husband and wondered if she'd complained to the sheriff about being left out of the action this morning. Sophia *should've* contacted her when the call came in. She'd guessed immediately that their killer had struck again. But knowing that the detective had ties to Leonard and wouldn't mind seeing her out of a job made Sophia leery. A few hours ago, Lindstrom had called to see if she'd gotten the shell casings off to the state crime lab. Sophia said she had, but she'd actually sent them to a private expert, one Lindstrom would have little chance of finding. She'd also kept the third shell casing, in case her package got lost. Maybe her caution was overkill, but she had no plans to live with regret.

Because it was growing dark, and it was a weeknight, only a handful of cars were waiting to gain entrance into Mexico. But, as usual, there was a long line of traffic stacked up to get out. Peddlers toted piggy banks, wool blankets, tooled leather wallets and purses as they wandered among the cars, hawking their wares.

Sophia watched various drivers and passengers roll down their windows to inspect these goods while inching forward. When it was her turn to speak with a border agent, she pulled under the overhang that announced

Bienvenidos a Naco, Sonora, México and showed a uniformed Mexican man her passport, which was now necessary to cross the border, although at one time a driver's license had been sufficient. She wasn't carrying her badge. As far as the officials along the border or anywhere else were concerned, she wasn't going into Mexico on police business, and she wasn't armed.

After a cursory glance at her passport, the man waved her through, and the engine thrummed between her legs as she guided her bike into Naco, Sonora. It was just on the other side of the border from its sister city but was ten times the size. With nearly eight thousand residents, it had housing, motels and grocery stores—and plenty of indigents who begged for money.

It also had more than its fair share of coyotes.

Sophia could see them lounging against buildings or loitering on street corners, talking with anyone who passed. Some stood off by themselves—smoking, eyeing the scene, searching for potential customers. For a moment, the babel of voices frightened her. She'd been to Naco before; she knew it well enough to feel as comfortable as one could in a foreign and rather dangerous place. But she didn't speak much Spanish. She was relying on the fact that many of the people here knew English.

A group of men clustered at the entrance to the ramshackle motel Su Casa watched her "unass," as Starkey would've described it. She wasn't sure why she suddenly thought of her ex-boyfriend. Maybe because she sort of wished she'd brought him with her. He was no pillar of the community, but she did enough for Rafe that he treated her cordially, and he could hold his own in the worst of circumstances.

Whistling and grinning as she removed her helmet,

the men made their appreciation clear. They also spoke to one another in Spanish, using words like *espléndido* and *atractiva*. Despite numerous attempts, Sophia hadn't been able to reach the person attached to the number she'd found in José's sock, so she still didn't have any identification. But, unlike the situation with the previous victims, she had pictures that showed an actual resemblance. She'd downloaded the photographs she'd taken at the scene and printed out several copies of the clearest ones before leaving the station.

As she approached the group, most of whom were in their mid-twenties, she took a photo of each body from her back pocket. "Maybe you can help me."

Several were dressed in dirty "wifebeater" T-shirts and plain gray pants with thin-soled black canvas shoes. Others wore jeans and various kinds of shirts. They'd all been lounging against whatever was close by—the side of the building, a pillar, a foul-smelling trash can—but once she addressed them they straightened and stepped toward her.

"Can you tell me who these people are?" she asked, holding the photos out for them to see.

The closest one took the pictures and stared down at José and his wife. Then he handed them back. *"No hablo Inglés."*

"Nombre." She pointed at the pictures again and gave them to someone else.

"These people are dead." The second man's English was heavily accented but definitely understandable.

"That's the problem," she told him. "I'm trying to figure out how they got that way."

"So…you're a cop?" He laughed, making his skepticism obvious. "You don't look like no cop."

She lifted her shoulders in a little shrug. "Right now I'm just a concerned citizen."

"A concerned citizen," he repeated, and squinted as he studied the pictures a second time. "These two were killed crossing the border, eh? Like the others?"

It was no surprise that he knew. The previous murders had been in the papers, and Naco was right on the border, only ten miles from where some of the shootings had occurred. "Yes."

"Who are you?"

The insolence in his eyes unsettled her, but she steeled herself against it. She'd hung out with enough Hells Angels to know better than to reveal vulnerability. "A friend. At least to them."

He rubbed his fingers together in the classic sign that he wanted her to grease his palm. "How much you willing to pay?"

In a town where men rushed to hold parking places or dashed into the street to wash car windshields, hoping for tips, she'd expected this and planned to use it to her advantage. "Fifty U.S."

"For…"

"*Información.* On either one of them. Or anyone you feel might've had something to do with their deaths."

"You pay first?"

She laughed as she shook her head. "Sorry, I'm not *estúpida,* eh? I'll wait in the cantina across the street."

"What do you want to know?"

"Where they came from, how and when they crossed the border, who they were with before they died, if anyone's seen or heard anything strange or out of the ordinary lately that might be related to their murder."

"That's a lot, no?"

"You gotta start somewhere."

He thought for a moment. "Job like that could take all night, *señorita*. In the end, I might have nothing to show for my time. How can you be sure they came through here?"

"I'm willing to bet on it. They didn't die far away. Find me their coyote, someone who saw them or knows them, anything you can. The more you tell me, the more I'll pay. *¿Entendido?*"

"*¿Cuánto más?*" someone else called.

They were asking how much more. Fifty dollars was peanuts compared to what they were paid for a successful crossing. But not every crossing was successful. "Up to two hundred dollars U.S.," she said.

The man who'd just yelled out wiped the sweat from his forehead. "And if we find *nada?*"

"Then you get paid *nada*." She had no choice. They'd lie to her if she gave them the slightest incentive.

"Nah." Shaking their heads, some of the men closest to her turned away. One addressed two women huddled next to a wheeled cart where an old man was selling drinks and corn. "Hey, you want a new life?" he asked her. "You want to go to America? I can take you there."

He spoke in Spanish but Sophia understood the gist of his message.

One of the women, obviously older than the other, scoffed. "You think I'm a fool? It's too dangerous."

"It's safe," he insisted. "And easy. I can get you there, no problem. My metal detector can find the sensors."

"And what about *that?*" She waved in the direction of the tall metal fence dividing the two countries, but everyone knew the fence was virtually nonexistent in some places.

"You're worried about three strands of barbed wire?"

"I'm worried about being forced into the desert," she cried. "Do you want us to die?"

Sophia saw no reason he'd *want* them to die. He didn't care one way or the other, as long as he got paid.

He rolled his eyes. "You won't die in the desert. I know a shortcut. It's an hour's walk."

"Don't listen to him," Sophia interrupted. "It'll take much more than an hour. It could take days. And border patrol agents aren't the only thing you have to fear. Someone is killing illegal aliens, shooting them in cold blood."

The woman didn't seem to understand English. But she recognized the pistol Sophia made with her thumb and finger. Muttering something unintelligible, she grabbed her companion's hand and scurried away.

The coyote whirled around to confront Sophia. "Hey, you're costing me money!"

"Twelve people are dead," she said. "Twelve of your countrymen and -women. If anyone gives a damn, it should be you."

The man who spoke the best English was openly scornful. "Why should we care? They're just wetbacks."

"You make your living off those wetbacks!"

He shrugged. "So?"

"If this killer keeps going, people will be too frightened to cross. Even with a reliable coyote."

Flexing, he looked pointedly from one bulging bicep to the other, showing off for her. "I can get anyone across. For the right price."

Since the U.S. had strengthened security along the Naco border, coyotes had a much more difficult job. They had to avoid the stadium lights that were spaced every three miles and equipped with cameras and infrared sensors monitored by agents at central command. They had to figure out ways to circumvent or slip through the Virtual Presence and Extended Defense System, which included the feared ground sensors. And they had to escape the notice of an additional two hundred agents posted at various lookouts. The services of a knowledgeable guide had gone from three hundred dollars to eight hundred dollars. Smuggling undocumented aliens was becoming so lucrative that the Mexican Mafia was beginning to traffic in humans, as well as drugs.

"Money is all that matters to you?" she challenged.

"That and a good fuck," he said, and everyone burst out laughing.

Sophia refused to flinch at his crude language. She was hardly impressed with his attempt to shock her; thanks to Starkey and his friends, and her job, she'd heard much worse. "Good luck finding a woman who's willing."

"Oooh…" his friends moaned, mocking him.

Eyes glinting with a dangerous light, he swept his gaze from her head to her toes. "Maybe I won't bother getting permission."

"You're not worth my time." Jerking the pictures out of his hand, she turned away as if he didn't scare her in the least.

She'd taken only two steps when a man from the same group hailed her. "I'll see what I can find, *señorita*," he said, and nodded respectfully when she gave him the pictures.

"*Puta,*" the other man spat.

Sophia felt like drawing her gun. The cocky, sexist pig deserved to have a woman get the better of him. But she wasn't in Mexico to start trouble. She was here to get answers.

She ignored him.

"Two hundred U.S.?" The one who was taking the assignment asked. Short and stocky, with a jagged scar on his cheek and an elaborate snake tattoo on his arm, he appeared to be much older than the others, probably in his late forties.

"If the information is accurate," she clarified, and with another nod, he strode off.

5

It wasn't a cheap system. What with all his money going to support his wife and kids—two households now—Leonard Taylor had had to sell his riding lawn mower and all his saws and power tools. That was the only way he could get enough to purchase the listening devices he'd found on the Internet. He'd spent nearly two thousand dollars at that spy site. But he was extremely happy with the quality of what he'd been sent. The UHF transmitter camouflaged as an outlet adapter looked just like the real thing. No way would Sophia or anyone else be able to tell it from any other adapter. And the two pens looked every bit as genuine. Even better, the receiver he'd bought, together with the transmitters, wasn't very big. He'd easily be able to carry it in his pocket or his truck, where he could hide it under the seat if he had to. By the time he finished placing the transmitters, he'd be able to pick up anything Sophia did or said, as long as he was within range, and she'd never have a clue.

He'd never dreamed he'd have such a golden opportunity to plant them. Detective Lindstrom had called him on her way home from work to complain about Sophia and to tell him she wished she could be working with him instead, and she'd mentioned that Sophia was going to Mexico tonight. The second those words were out of her mouth, he'd known that it was time.

Under the guise of saying hello to Officer Lawrence, who was dating a distant cousin of his, he'd stopped by the station first. He'd had to sit around shooting the bull with Grant for more than an hour before Grant finally excused himself to go to the restroom. Then he'd stepped into Sophia's office and set the pen on a ledge under her desk. Even if she found it, that pen would look as if it had somehow fallen out of one of her drawers.

Bugging her office had taken all of five or ten seconds. He was back in his seat before Grant could flush the toilet. When Grant returned, Leonard casually said he had to be at work early in the morning and should be getting home.

From there, he'd driven down Sophia's street to make sure her neighbors were in bed, parked a good distance away and walked to her house. He'd been prepared to break in; he'd brought the tools. But that hadn't been necessary. He'd found her spare key under a decorative turtle in her front planter. Maybe, because she carried a gun, a baton and a Taser, she wasn't as worried about safety as another woman might be. Or, more likely, she left that spare key where it was for Rafe's benefit. She loved Starkey's boy. He knew that from how much she'd talked about him when they'd worked together.

Now he just needed to figure out where to place the pretend plug adapter. He wanted it somewhere central. That would increase his chances of picking up most of her conversations. So, tempted as he was by the bedroom—simply because that seemed like even more of an invasion of privacy, which she deserved—he avoided it. The transmitter should go in the living room, he decided. The living room was between the kitchen and the bedroom, plus the screened-in porch at the back. He'd be able to listen in on more conversations there than anywhere else.

Turning in a circle on her living room rug, he searched for the outlet he wanted and spotted one behind a table that held nothing but framed photographs. If he had his bet, this outlet never got used. She'd probably forgotten it was even there.

"Perfect," he murmured once he'd had a chance to test the device using his transmitter. "And now for the car."

Striding into the kitchen, he checked the keys hanging on hooks near the cupboards, identified the set that went with the cruiser sitting out front and walked outside to unlock it and put the pen under the dash. This was the trickiest part, since he could be spotted by any neighbor who happened to get up for a drink of water, so he made quick work of it. Then he locked up and headed back down the street.

He was whistling by the time he reached his vehicle. Maybe it'd taken a while to collect the money he needed, and it had taken even longer to catch Sophia on a night when she was out of town…

But his patience had been well rewarded.

It was after midnight and the man who'd walked away with her photographs of José and his wife hadn't returned. Sophia wasn't sure how long she should wait. Had he given up and gone home? Was she sitting here, wasting time? If he hadn't been able to get any information, there was no guarantee he'd come back to tell her….

The cantina was beginning to empty, but the table at the front was still occupied. The man who'd called her a *puta* and one of his friends had followed her into the bar and seated themselves close to the door. They'd stayed there ever since, brooding, drinking and glaring at her. Sophia knew they were trying to intimidate her. What she didn't know was whether they'd act on the not-so-subtle threat in their eyes.

Feeling the pressure of her Glock against her calf, she glanced at her watch and decided to wait another fifteen minutes. Any longer was too dangerous. She didn't want to be the last to leave the bar. That would give her friends near the front an easy opportunity to get her alone. The gun made her fairly confident that she could defend herself if attacked. But she didn't want to shoot anyone, especially in Mexico. There was no telling how that would go down with the local police or the Mexican government. They might not believe she'd acted in self-defense, and the fact that she'd brought a weapon into the country wouldn't be a point in her favor.

Waving the waitress away when the girl circled back to see if she wanted another ginger ale, Sophia toyed with the change on the table. Why hadn't she asked Starkey to come down here with her? He would've loved the chance to play protector. He enjoyed nothing more than acting tough. He *was* tough. But she knew better than to accept any favors from him. That would only get his hopes up that she'd take him back, and she didn't need that right now, not after years of trying to convince him that they were over for good.

Still, giving him a call would help pass the time and take her mind off the two thugs at the door, one of whom had basically threatened her with rape. The way she'd spouted off about the money she'd be willing to pay for information made robbery another possibility....

She checked her watch again. The minute hand was

creeping toward 12:25 a.m., but there was no need to worry that she might wake Starkey. She'd never known him to go to bed before two or three. He partied with the other Angels almost every night.

Pulling her cell from her pocket, she hit the key for Starkey's number. She expected it to go through its usual speed-dial sequence, but she got an error message instead, warning her that she was out of network range. Because she was within twenty miles of the town where she lived, she hadn't realized her phone wouldn't work. But, of course, that made sense. She wasn't in the States, anymore.

"Oh, boy," she muttered, and put the phone away.

Ten more minutes passed before she stood. She'd promised herself she'd stay fifteen, but another four people had sauntered toward the exit, making her worry that she'd delayed her departure too long already. Bracing for what could happen when she passed that front table, she started to leave. But as she took a step toward the door, the man she'd been waiting for came charging into the cantina, along with two lanky companions. At least twenty years younger than their sturdier counterpart, they looked like identical twins—until they came close enough for Sophia to see that they were only siblings.

"*Señorita,* I have what you want," the man she'd hired stated proudly.

This was promising—if it was real and not something he'd concocted in an effort to get paid.

As she sank into her seat, she gestured for the men to join her.

They were short a chair, but borrowed one from an empty table.

"Juan can help you." Indicating the guy to his left, the

man who'd accepted her offer tapped the pictures. "He and his brother, they act as *polleros*...er—" deep groves lined his forehead as he struggled with English "—guides? *Sí,* guides, for these people. They take them across *la frontera.*"

"They're coyotes?"

"No. They work for a coyote who can no longer cross."

"Why can't he cross?"

"He get caught by La Migra? The CBP? He go to jail. You understand?"

"He's on the list. If he gets caught trying to cross again, they'll prosecute him."

He nodded emphatically. "*Sí.* These are his runners."

She pulled out a small pad of paper and a pen she'd shoved into her back pocket. "And who are you?"

"Enrique."

"Enrique what?"

"Castillo."

She wrote that down. "And your friends?"

"Juan and Miguel Martinez."

As soon as she'd recorded this, she eyed Enrique's friends. "Can you tell me who these people are?"

They looked confused until Enrique jumped in. "*Juan y Miguel no hablan inglés, señorita.* I translate. But first, we talk price. One hundred U.S." He tapped Juan's shoulder, then Miguel's and then his own chest to make sure she understood that they *each* expected one hundred American dollars.

Sitting back, she folded her arms. "That's more than I offered."

A frown tugged at the corners of his mouth. "We have to live, to eat. And we have to pay the police, no?"

Juan and Miguel seemed to understand that Enrique was arguing for higher pay. They made noises of agreement.

She arched her eyebrows. "You expect me to cover your bribes?"

"They have to be paid or we no work."

Some coyotes made several thousand dollars a week even after they shelled out the standard ten percent to the Mexican military and police. Many camped along the border, sometimes for days at a time, tracking border agent activity, searching for any vulnerability. Among other things, the bribes helped insure that the Mexican police wouldn't interfere with their reconnaissance. But if Enrique went to the extra effort of scouting the guards, Sophia had a feeling he wasn't too successful. "There are no snitches here to tell anyone about our deal," she pointed out. "Why get greedy?"

His pitiable expression changed to grave. "They will find out. *Soplónes*…snitches…they are everywhere."

An additional hundred wasn't enough to argue about, not when it was getting so late. Sophia calculated the amount of money she had in her pocket. "I have two hundred and fifty-three dollars. That's all. Take it or leave it. And I'll pay you only after you've given me what I want." *If* they could give her what she wanted. She had no delusions; these men would cheat her if they could.

They conferred and quickly agreed, as she'd expected them to. Everything in Mexico was negotiable. *"Gracias, señorita."*

"What can you tell me?" she asked.

"Nombres." Enrique nudged Juan, who pointed at the two pictures.

"José y Benita."

Sophia's heart began to race. She hadn't mentioned that

she knew the man's first name. Enrique wasn't trying to con her. He'd found the people she needed to talk to.

"Can you give me a last name?"

Her words made no sense to Juan, but Enrique explained.

"Sanchez" came the response.

"José and Benita Sanchez," she repeated. "He's sure?"

"*Sí.*" All three men nodded in agreement and apparent satisfaction.

"Does he also remember where they're from?"

Again, Enrique addressed his companions before responding. "Nayarit."

Sophia didn't recognize the location. Despite growing up so close to the border, she'd spent very little time in Mexico and hadn't studied it except as it related to basic American history. "That's a city?"

"A state."

"Where? Is it far?"

"*Sí,*" Enrique answered soberly. "It is south, near the ocean."

The two men at the front table leaned toward each other, talking. They paused every now and then, their eyes shooting imaginary daggers at Sophia. They weren't happy that she'd found the help she needed. But she ignored them. She'd decide what to do about them later. "How did they get here from so far away?"

"Probably by bus." He checked with Juan, who agreed. *Bus* was easy to understand in either language.

Juan's brother spoke up, and Enrique listened to what he had to say before passing it on. "Miguel, he go to meet them when they arrive."

"When was that? How long ago?"

There was more conversation between them, and Sophia heard the word *cuatro,* which made sense when Enrique answered, "Four days. They rest at hotel on Thursday. Friday, they wait for night. And then—"

"Which hotel?" she broke in.

"Hotel California. That way." He motioned to indicate south.

"And then what?" she asked.

"And then Juan and Miguel, they pick them up at—" there was a rapid burst of Spanish before he finished "—seven-thirty."

"Just them? Or were there others?"

This question was passed on before it was answered. "Many others. A…" He rubbed his hands together as he again struggled to find the right English word. "A…group. About thirty."

"That many?" she asked in surprise.

"*Sí. Mucho.* Is better."

Sophia could see that there might be some safety in numbers. She also knew that coyotes often sent out smaller groups as decoys to confuse the patrol officers. But if the CBP couldn't keep groups of *thirty* from crossing the border, America didn't have much hope of stopping illegal immigration. "Who else was in this group? Can he give me a list of names?"

The men discussed this but Enrique ultimately shook his head. "No, *señorita.* Some names, maybe. He take groups two, three times a week, you understand? He no remember every one."

"He remembered Benita and José."

"Because she was *muy bonita*—pretty, eh? And scared. He tried to talk to her, to calm her. And her *esposo,* her husband, he no like it."

Okay, so the Sanchezes' youth, looks and relationship had set them apart, made them memorable. That was encouraging. What else could she get from these men while she had the chance? Because of the language barrier, it wasn't as if they'd volunteer information. She had to ask for it. "Where did Juan and Miguel take this group? Where did they cross?"

"There is an abandoned cattle *rancho*. About *cinco* kilometers from here. They go there to cross, after the fence turns to barbwire." He walked two fingers across the table to make sure she understood that they went on foot.

Sophia tried to imagine what that day must've been like for José and his wife. Leaving their families, their home. Arriving in this dirty town from somewhere deep in Mexico, a place that was bound to be cleaner if not more affluent. Being met by Miguel and shown to a hotel to wait for night. Being taken to a ranch and herded across the border like cattle. Being chased by the CBP.

"If José and Benita left with thirty people, how'd they end up alone?" she asked. "How is it that Juan and Miguel are sitting here alive and well, and this couple is dead?"

"La Migra," he said simply.

"You're saying the CBP killed them."

"No, the…the sensors give them away."

He was talking about the Virtual Presence and Extended Defense System, technology that could detect pedestrians and vehicles, even differentiate between them.

"Sensors go off, but no one knows, eh? Only agents at the command. They call other agents." He pretended to be driving, closing in on a target. "Mexicans run." Making an explosion with his hands, he tried to clarify, and Sophia knew exactly what he meant. She'd heard border patrol agents use the term *going quail*. The CBP had shown up and everyone had scattered.

But the illegals didn't always run. Sometimes they were too exhausted. Apparently, this group had been found early enough that they still had the energy to make a break for it.

"And this couple?" she asked. "Did they return to Mexico?"

"No."

"Did Juan or Miguel see them leave with anyone else?"

He shook his head but checked with his companions to be sure. "He was running himself."

"What about everyone else? What happened to them?"

Enrique told her that some of the same people who'd been "VPed," or caught by the new security system and repatriated to Mexico, had crossed the border the very next night without a problem. But he had no idea what'd happened to the others.

"Is there any talk of this on the street? About a particular border patrol agent, for example?"

"Not a *particular* agent. They'd all like to shoot us."

"That's not true."

"You don't know what goes on out there," he said grimly.

She was beginning to learn. And she didn't like what she heard. Becoming familiar with the unvarnished truth made her uncomfortable because there didn't seem to be any way to solve the problem and still be sensitive to the needs of Americans and Mexicans alike. "So no one has any idea who's doing this."

"None. But it sounds as if you do. It sounds as if you think it's the CBP."

"That's *not* what I think. I'm just being cautious enough to look at every possibility. If it is a Federal agent, it's one random officer gone bad, which you can find in any organization." She certainly didn't mean to villainize the whole force. She knew too many of the officers, saw how hard they worked to maintain their humanity while fulfilling the requirements of the job.

"You ask me? They're *all* bad," he said. "At least half are the children of Mexicans who snuck across the border a generation ago. How does that make them any better than us?"

"You consider them disloyal."

"Sí."

"What about *your* part in all this?" she asked.

Confusion lined his forehead. *"Señorita?"*

"You don't feel guilty—bad—about the people who get hurt because of what you do?"

"I no shoot them," he said, pressing a hand to his chest.

"You're encouraging others to break the law. You're helping them do it, which is putting them in a very dangerous situation. If it wasn't for Juan and Miguel, José and Benita might not have been killed."

"Maybe. Or someone else might have taken them across," he said indifferently. "Maybe me. *Es sólo un trabajo.*"

If she understood him right, he'd said it was just a job. "Maybe that's how the Mexican-American border agents feel, too."

Unconvinced, he smacked the table. "They cannot

blame us for helping people do what their parents did twenty, thirty years ago."

Except that twelve people had been murdered in the past six weeks and these men were *still* encouraging illegal immigration. But there was no point in arguing. She wasn't going to change his mind, so she withdrew the money from her pocket and handed it over. "I guess we'll have to agree to disagree."

"Gracias." Enrique eagerly accepted the worn bills and the three of them hurried outside.

Sophia was putting away her pad and pen and digging out the key to her Harley when she realized the cantina owner was waving to get her attention. Speaking in Spanish, he made shooing motions toward the saloon-style door. He was trying to close.

Her eyes gravitated to the front table. It was empty. The man who'd called her a *puta* and his friend had already been asked to leave.

But they weren't gone. She could see them standing outside, waiting for her.

6

Sophia considered asking the cantina owner to walk her to her bike, but she doubted she could string together enough Spanish to make herself understood. Not only that, she couldn't think of any reason he might be willing to put his life on the line for some gringo he'd never met before. Maybe she was being ungenerous and her nationality wouldn't enter into his decision, but she knew it could. Racism cut both ways.

She thought about heading down the dimly lit hallway where a sign promised Los Baños. But even if the restrooms had a window through which she could crawl into a back alley, what good would it do? As soon as the man who'd called her a whore figured out that she'd given him the slip, he'd simply cross over to her bike. He'd seen her drive up, knew where she'd parked. It was only a stone's throw from where he and his friend were standing.

She couldn't use her cell phone to call for help. And she didn't know a soul here in Mexico that she could depend on. She'd already let Enrique and his friends leave without asking them to escort her safely to her Harley. But that wasn't necessarily a bad decision. As far as she could tell, they were friends with the loser who seemed so bent on harassing her and could just as easily come to his aid if forced to choose sides. No, she preferred to keep the numbers small and manageable. There'd be fewer variables.

Taking her gun from under her pant leg, she held it against and slightly behind her body as she strolled out of the bar. She had no idea whether these guys were armed, but she had to assume the worst. It was too dangerous to do otherwise. Their behavior was aggressive enough to suggest it.

The breath she held burned in her chest as she reached the man who'd been doing his best to make her uncomfortable. He'd stationed himself so that she couldn't avoid walking past him.

She was prepared when his hand whipped out to grab her left arm. Letting him jerk her around to face him, she brought up her gun, using the momentum of his own action to shove the barrel between his ribs. "Let go or I'll kill you," she ground out, teeth clenched.

Fear replaced the menace in his eyes. She'd gotten the drop on him. He hadn't expected her to be armed.

But, wary as he'd become, he didn't release her.

Adrenaline poured through her body, which made her feel a little shaky, but she had to sell her "hard chick" performance. His life, and possibly her own, depended on whether or not he bought it. "You have three seconds. I'll even count *en español, comprendes?*"

At first, he couldn't seem to decide how to react. But his friend scrambled away so fast he fell in his hurry to put some distance between them.

"Uno...dos..." She knew she couldn't pull the trigger, not at this range. Although she'd had to use her firearm twice in the line of duty, she'd never actually killed a man. Unless he did something more than grab her arm, something to prove his intentions were what she feared,

her threat was only a bluff. But she had the image she'd created with her bike, her tattoos and the swagger she'd learned from the Hells Angels working to convince him otherwise.

She prayed it would be enough.

Before she could get to three, he muttered what sounded like "fucking *loca*" and stepped away with his hands up. By this time, his friend had darted around the corner and was no longer in sight.

"That's it," she murmured. "Nice and easy. No need to make me nervous."

"Puta!"

"You used that one already."

Hatred glittered in his eyes. "You better not ever come back here."

She smiled. "But this is such a nice place to visit."

Keeping the gun trained on him, she backed across the street. Then she shoved her Glock into her waistband, where she could grab it again, if necessary, got on her bike and rode away.

Only when she was in line to get out of the country did she pull her shirt down to cover her weapon. And it wasn't until after she'd crossed the border and was nearly home that she put it back in its holster. Maybe she was safe from the man who'd scared her in Naco, but the area wasn't as empty as the dark streets implied. Even as she flew down the road, there were coyotes smuggling bands of illegal immigrants into the country—and there was a killer lurking somewhere, waiting to shoot the unsuspecting in cold blood.

Roderick felt like roadkill. Unable to get a flight to Tucson, he'd gone to Phoenix, but it'd been after eleven-thirty when he got in. Then he'd had to wait for his luggage and go through the tedious paperwork involved in renting a car before driving four hours southeast to Bordertown. Other than a fifteen-minute nap on the plane, he'd been up for nearly twenty-four hours.

But, tired though he was, he couldn't bring himself to pull into the Mother Lode Motel and get a room. The sun wasn't up yet. Arriving so early gave him a short window of time during which he could drive around unnoticed, familiarize himself with what had changed and reacquaint himself with what hadn't—all before having to face his father or anyone else he might know from those early days. For an hour or so, he wouldn't need to don the mask of indifference he'd soon wear, wouldn't need to pretend that what'd happened here didn't bother him anymore.

"Welcome home," he muttered as he passed the drugstore, the family-owned grocery, Serrano's Western Wear and the Catholic church his mother used to drag him to each Sunday. She'd insisted her younger brother go to church with them, but religion hadn't been enough to keep Arturo on the right track. Was he even alive?

Roderick stretched the tight muscles in his neck. Maybe, when he was finished in Bordertown, he'd head down to Mexico and look for Arturo.

Then again, it'd been so long, maybe he wouldn't. Some things were better left alone. He had no idea if the man he'd find would even want to be found.

When he reached the high school, he slowed to a crawl. The buildings had recently been painted; a new addition stuck out from the main hall like an extra appendage. Elmer's Burrito Stand, the same awful blue color it'd always been, huddled on the corner across the street. Roderick had to marvel at that. For twenty years Elmer had made his living selling burritos out of that little stand. Not many places lasted so long. But not many places served food as good as Elmer's, either.

In the very center of town, the buildings had the wood-plank sidewalks and overhangs reminiscent of the Old West. In an effort to save itself after the mine closed nearly a century ago, Bordertown had followed Tombstone's lead in vying for the tourist dollar. But Bordertown didn't have the O.K. Corral or any other real claim to fame. It had to rely on tours of the old mine, a string of souvenir shops and a few ranches in the surrounding desert that boarded tourists and offered an "authentic Western experience." Rod was pretty sure the town would've died a slow death if not for the artisans who'd moved into one section and made a name for themselves selling turquoise jewelry and western art.

A few of the dumpier buildings downtown had been cleaned up. A chiropractor's office and a veterinary office had received a face-lift and sported new signs. But a strip mall that'd been new the year he'd left was now weathered and worn-looking, home to a Laundromat, an electronics discounter and a liquor store. What Roderick remembered as an old thrift shop had been taken over by a salon boasting a full set of acrylic nails for forty-five dollars. At the Circle K, where half the high school had loitered late into a Friday or Saturday night, there was litter in the bushes and graffiti on the tan bricks facing the alley. And most of the houses on Center Street, those that hadn't been turned into businesses, had bars covering the windows and doors.

On the whole, Bordertown wasn't particularly attractive. It never had been. But there was a nostalgic quality that, for Roderick, coalesced into a combination of homesickness and regret. As he drove through the quiet streets, gazing at the buildings, many of which featured the typical desert landscaping, it felt almost as if his mother was sitting in the car beside him.

He considered going out to the cemetery to visit her grave. Now would be the time, when he could pay his respects in private. But the thought of standing there, looking down at that small mound as he had when he was only sixteen, brought back too much pain. He wouldn't go. Not yet. Maybe if he avoided the cemetery, he wouldn't miss her quite so poignantly.

Once he drove to the edge of town, he turned right and continued several miles before making a left and then another right. He was going to the ranch. He wasn't sure why. He didn't care what it looked like, didn't want anything to do with his father or his half brothers, but he was curious.

The arched Dunlap ranch sign came up more quickly than he'd expected. It'd seemed much farther from town when he was young, probably because he had to walk if he wanted to go anywhere.

Paloverde trees lined the drive to the mansion where his half brothers had lived with Edna, Bruce's wife, who'd prided herself on her taste and cleanliness. His mother could've experienced a better life if she'd been allowed to become one of the maids. Edna had several in those days. His father had once promised Carolina the chance to work inside, get out of the terrible heat. But Edna had refused. She couldn't stand to have Carolina in such close proximity to the Family. Knowing that she'd also had a son by Bruce, Edna had lobbied to have Carolina kicked off the ranch completely.

Fortunately, his father had never gone quite that far.

He'd tried to buy her off once, but she'd refused to leave Jorge. So Bruce had let her stay. She'd continued to work in the fields, as long and as hard as any man, and continued to live in one of the little shacks along the periphery of the South Forty. Roderick had worked beside her, trying to do more than his share in order to give her a break. Until that last beating from his half brothers. Then his father had insisted he find work elsewhere to resolve the constant conflict.

That was why he felt so compelled to come here, he realized. As much as he hated his father, this was home, the only home he'd known until his mother had died and some other farm laborer had moved into her shack.

The tires of the Hummer he'd rented crunched on gravel as he rolled slowly down the drive and turned into the compound. He didn't have much time. Already, a light shone in the grand ranch house. His father had always been an early riser.

Circumventing the nicer vehicles and farm equipment stored near a large silver water tank and a grain bin, he took the narrow road that led along the fence to the living quarters for the field help. The shacks were as tiny as ever—only two rooms. But they'd been painted. A satellite dish sat on the roof of the first one, with cables running to the others, and there were air-conditioning units in the left side windows. Conditions here had improved. When Roderick was a boy, they'd had no heat or air-conditioning, no electricity at all, and no plumbing. When he told other Americans he'd grown up poor, they had no idea he was talking about the kind of poverty found in third-world countries like the one his mother had escaped.

As he sat there, taking it all in, a door swung open and a stooped, withered Mexican stepped out. The man hadn't turned on any lights. He probably had family inside he didn't want to wake.

Noticing Rod immediately, he squinted to see who it was.

Roderick froze when he realized he was looking at Jorge. Boy, had he aged in the past fourteen years!

Their eyes met, and the old man's wrinkled mouth curved, revealing several missing teeth.

The urge to throw the car into Reverse suddenly gripped Roderick. As ashamed as it made him feel, he wanted to forget his roots, forget he'd ever lived here. But he didn't drive off. Jorge was already shuffling toward the truck at an eager gait.

Conjuring up a pleasant expression, Rod lowered his window. *"Hola, mi amigo."*

"Hola, hijo." Jorge's gnarled hand clasped Rod's forearm with affection. *"¿Cómo estás? Eh?"*

"Muy bien. Muy bien." Rod switched to English. He could speak without the slightest accent, which reminded him that he'd escaped his past. He had plenty of money and opportunities and people he cared about—a whole other life in California. "You're still here, old man?"

"Where would I go? I'm too old and ornery. No one else would have me."

After seeing what so many years of physically grueling labor had done to Jorge, Rod was surprised Bruce had allowed him to stay. Certainly he couldn't do all the work he'd once done. Maybe there was an element of trust between him and Bruce that made up the difference.

"What's our Navy SEAL doing these days?" Jorge beamed with pride. "Still catching bad guys for Department 6?"

"For now."

"Your father is so proud."

The smile slipped from Rod's face; he felt it go. "What's going on with him? Why is he contacting me all of a sudden?"

"With age comes wisdom, eh?"

"Sorry, not buying it. Something must have caused such a major change of heart."

"No, he's asked me about you for years. He knows what you are, can't deny that you're a good son, someone to admire."

Rod cocked an eyebrow at him. "Jorge? Cut the crap."

"Listen, *hijo*. He had a bad health scare eight years ago, a heart attack. He's been different ever since. I think he has realized what he's lost and wants to fix it if he can."

"And bringing me here to help solve the murders, that was just an excuse?"

"More than an excuse. He thinks you can help. If someone can kill at will and walk away, never to face punishment, it scares everyone, eh? Americans as well as Mexicans. The whole community. You remember what I told you about that rancher near Portal."

He was referring to a man whose family had lived in the area for fifty years. "He was stabbed to death on his own land last March."

"That's right. He'd just called in to say he'd found some Mexican nationals suffering from dehydration and was assisting them."

Rod stretched the cramped muscles in his neck. "Do you think there's any connection between that incident and what's been happening lately?"

"I don't know. But even if there isn't, what if illegals arm themselves? Try to retaliate?"

"We've got to make sure it doesn't escalate," he muttered.

Jorge nodded in satisfaction. "Yes."

That increased Rod's dedication to finding the person responsible for all the bloodshed, but it didn't change anything else for him, not where his father was concerned. He glanced toward the house. "I gotta be on my way. Take care of yourself."

"What? No! Stay. You don't have to go. Your father would be happy to see you."

"There's no need to upset Edna and her boys."

"Bah! Who cares about Edna?" he teased. "And those boys? They won't bother you these days. They'd be able to tell just by looking at you that it wouldn't be a good idea."

"It's not only them. Regardless of what Bruce might feel or what he's been through, I'd rather not see him," Rod clarified. "I don't consider him to be any relation."

The expression on the old man's face led Rod to believe he'd hoped for more. "Forgive him, Roderick," he said, grabbing his forearm again. *"Deja ir el pasado."*

Let the past go…. "That's what I'm trying to do. Only I want him to go with it."

"That's not what she hoped for you."

A pickup began to move in the clearing. Someone was starting work. Roderick couldn't put off his departure any longer without risking some type of confrontation. He didn't want to hear what Jorge was trying to tell him, anyway. Just because his mother wouldn't give up on Bruce didn't mean *he'd* hang on till the bitter end. "It was great to see you," he said, and covered Jorge's hand with his own.

Jorge nodded but seemed troubled as Rod backed up

and headed out. Fortunately, the person in the pickup had taken the opposite direction, toward the lettuce fields. Was it his father or one of his half brothers driving? Rod couldn't tell. He could see only the taillights, back bumper and the dust kicked up by the tires.

He imagined confronting Stuart or Patrick now that he was older. He wanted them to demand he step out of the way, willing to take them both on at once, just as they'd always preferred. But…what was the point? He wouldn't feel any better afterward. That wasn't the kind of man he wanted to be.

Forget them, he told himself. But he'd been telling himself that for so long, it'd lost all meaning.

When the phone awakened Sophia from a dead sleep, her heart nearly seized in her chest. She was sure it was one of her officers or county dispatch, calling to inform her that more people had been killed. But a second later, the sound repeated itself and she breathed a sigh of relief. She'd been dreaming. It wasn't the phone. Someone was at the door.

With a groan, she rolled out of bed and went into the living room of her little one-bedroom hacienda-style house. There, she leaned against the door, squinting to see through the peephole.

It was Starkey. As usual, he was wearing his leather vest—or cut as they called it—with the patches that held so much significance for him, jeans and biker boots. His blond hair and his mustache, which was a shade darker than his hair, were longer than when she'd last seen him. He'd also put on a few pounds—but he wasn't fat. His biceps bulged when he crossed his arms. And he had a new tattoo to add to the skull and all the others: FTW.

She didn't plan to ask what it stood for. She already knew she wouldn't approve.

"Give me a minute." She hurried back to her bedroom so she could grab a robe to cover her T-shirt and men's boxers. Then she let him in. "Hey, what's up?"

His eyes ran over her disheveled hair, her robe, which she'd had for so long he probably recognized it from when they were dating nine years ago, her bare feet. "You okay?"

"Yeah, fine. Why?"

"I got a call from you last night. I got three, actually. But no messages."

Three calls? She'd tried to reach him from Mexico, but she'd been out of network range…. "I was hoping to speak to Rafe, but—"

"At one in the morning?"

"No, earlier," she lied. "Your number was in my recent call history. I must've pocket-dialed you."

"Fortunately, I didn't hear it ring, or I would've gone nuts wondering why you wouldn't say anything. I was at a party and the music was too damn loud."

She was glad of that. If he'd been aware of her calls, he would've been waiting for her when she got home last night, and she might've had to arrest him for driving under the influence. If he'd been at a party, there was no way he'd been drinking soda.

"What did you want with Rafe?" he asked.

"Just checking in, seeing how the week's going for him." She didn't usually lie, and already she'd lied twice. But now that she was out of Naco, she didn't really want to explain that she'd turned to him in her hour of need, so to speak. He'd take that to mean more than it did.

"He's fine. At some camp with a friend. Won't be back for four days."

Some camp? He didn't know which one? This was part of her problem with Starkey. He was a loving father but he didn't pay much attention to the kind of details most parents considered important. "Which friend?" Did he know that much?

"Chase LaBreque."

Sophia had heard Rafe talk about Chase and wasn't so sure he was the best influence. But Rafe was being raised by a Hells Angel, so if she was worried about any example, it should be that one. Regardless, she had no right to complain. She was lucky Starkey allowed her to be involved with Rafe. He wasn't pleased that she'd gone into law enforcement, felt it put him at risk just to associate with her. The others in the club were obviously unhappy that she was part of his life. They, too, would've preferred Leonard Taylor to be chief of police. Leonard was one of the good ol' boys who turned a blind eye to certain activities Sophia was unwilling to ignore.

"Have him get in touch with me when he gets back, will you?" she said.

"Yeah. Sure."

"Thanks." She started to close the door, but he stopped it with one of his giant paws. "Hey, wait! Guess who I saw?"

Not particularly interested, she covered a yawn. "Who?"

"Roderick Guerrero. You remember him, don't ya?"

Of course she did. She immediately recalled the café au lait skin and dark eyes of the boy she knew in high school. They'd been in the same grade growing up. But when it came to girls, he'd always kept to himself, and she'd been more than happy to let him. He'd approached life with a belligerence that made her uncomfortable, frequently getting into fights.

But he'd surprised her once. It was during their sophomore year, his last year in school. Despite having a minimal relationship—she'd been in one class with him and knew he watched her a great deal—he'd asked if she'd go to the Homecoming Dance with him. He didn't generally attend school dances. For one thing, he couldn't afford it. And he didn't go that year, either. She agreed to go, then stood him up when she got a better offer and, thanks to one particular girlfriend of hers, word of that spread all over the school.

Sophia was still embarrassed about the fact that she hadn't even tried to contact him and that she'd humiliated him so publicly. She'd never apologized or offered any explanation, either. She'd been young and stupid and hadn't known how to approach it. But she'd never forget the way he looked at her when he saw her at school after that weekend. She'd thought he was too tough, too mean, to be hurt. That was what she'd told herself when she ditched him. But as soon as their eyes met, she knew she'd hurt him deeply....

Those weren't comfortable memories. Kids could be callous, and she'd been no different. Which was why she preferred to forget. But she was too curious about what Roderick might be like now to just let the subject go. "Seriously? It was *Roderick?* You're sure?"

"Positive. Spotted him coming out of Bailey's Breakfast Dive and pulled over to say hello."

"I didn't realize you even knew him. He's my age."

"He had an uncle who was a few years older—Arturo.

I hung out with him for a year or two before he skipped town."

"I never met the uncle."

Starkey whistled. "He was one bad dude."

Roderick hadn't struck her as much nicer. In those days, her father hadn't yet lost his business, his marriage or his life, so she'd been oblivious to other people's needs. She'd been living in the idyllic bubble that had burst soon afterward and thrown her into the arms of Starkey.

"What's he doing in town?" She definitely didn't need this. Life was hard enough right now.

Starkey grinned. "I was waitin' for you to ask me that. You ready?"

She tightened the belt on her robe. "Ready for what?"

"He said he's here to investigate the UDA murders."

Her mouth fell open. *"What'd you say?"*

He chortled at her reaction. "I thought you'd like that. He's an 'operative' for a private security company in California. Those guys are *bad* asses. And they get paid the big bucks." She couldn't miss the twinkle in his eye that told her he wasn't finished with her yet. "When I told him *you're* the chief of police, he looked about as stunned as you do now."

"So he's staying longer than a few days?"

"Few weeks, at least. Haven't you been listenin'? He's tryin' to steal your case."

She shook her head. "Oh, no. That's definitely *not* going to happen."

"Any chance you'd like to thank me for the notice?"

She narrowed her eyes. "Thank you in what way?"

He sighed. "Didn't think so."

Ignoring his reference to thanking him, she moved on to her next question. "Where's he staying?"

"Don't know. But it can't be far." He clapped his hands together. "Anyway, it's been fun but I gotta dash. Someone's waitin' for me."

She didn't ask who. She didn't want to know about Starkey's dealings because most of them were illegal. She was too preoccupied at the moment, anyway. "Right." She waved numbly but made no move to go back inside.

Several seconds passed before a neighbor called goodmorning and she realized she was still standing in the doorway, staring after Starkey.

With a polite nod for old man Phil, who shuffled past her on his morning walk, she went back into the house, trying to convince herself that Roderick Guerrero had forgotten all about that Homecoming incident. But the memory of returning home to hear from her mother that he'd shown up in a suit and was carrying a corsage made her groan.

Who was she kidding? He'd remember....

7

"Rod? You in there?"

It was his father. Already. Jorge must've told him. Or Starkey. Or someone else who'd seen him having breakfast at Bailey's.

Reluctant to be disturbed, he raised his head from the pillow. "I'm sleeping!"

"I brought you something" came the response.

"Whatever it is, I don't want it."

"I think you will. Open the door."

Rod muttered a curse. This was his own fault for driving out to the ranch this morning. But it didn't matter. His father would've learned of his presence sooner or later. Bordertown was too small for anyone to remain anonymous for long. "Will you go away if I do?"

There was a slight pause. "If that's what you want."

Kicking off the sheet, he rolled out of bed and yanked on a pair of shorts. "What now?" he demanded as he jerked open the door.

Bruce handed him a stack of newspapers. "These have articles about the killings. I thought you might like to read them. They'll give you a feel for what's happened and what's been done about it so far."

This was the one thing Bruce could've brought that Rod wouldn't be angry about. "Fine. Great. Thank you."

"And I wanted to tell you there's no need to pay for a motel. You can stay out at the ranch, if you like."

Rod leaned against the doorjamb. "What did you say?"

"I said you're welcome at the ranch."

"What—one of the shacks is available?"

Color rose in his father's cheeks. "No. There's plenty of room at the house."

His house? The rambling two-story pueblo-style structure with the red roof and the fountain out front? What Rod wouldn't have given just to *see* inside it as a child. "You're kidding, right?"

"Not at all. It's a big house, and it's mostly empty now that the boys have moved out."

But Jorge had said Patrick and Stuart were still at the ranch. "Where are 'the boys'?"

"Patrick is married and living in a house of his own at the other end of the property. Stuart has his own place, too, next door to his brother."

"Stuart's not married?"

"Nope. I'm hoping he'll be ready for that soon. I'd like grandkids someday and Patrick's wife doesn't seem to be in any hurry. She owns the nail salon in town and says she's too busy."

Rod had seen the shop. "So he married a business-woman."

Although Bruce didn't seem the least bit embarrassed, Rod doubted Edna would approve of having a lowly cos-metologist for a daughter-in-law, even if she was a hard-working one. "More or less, I guess. Anyway, the house is available, as I said, and it's comfortable, roomy."

Bruce was trying too hard, which made the situation even more awkward than it already was.

Determined not to succumb to his bitterness, Rod bit back the harsh retort that sprang to his lips. "No, thank you. I'm fine here."

The flatness of his response, and what it indicated, didn't seem to register. Bruce maintained his cordial cheer. "Well, keep it in mind. If this mess drags on, living in a motel might get old. And we'd love to have you."

Again, Rod was tempted to ask if he'd forgotten the past, when Bruce couldn't stay far enough away from him and his mother. But revealing his anger would make it look as if he cared. Why give Bruce, Edna and their sons the satisfaction of knowing they'd been so successful at making him feel inferior and unwanted?

For the second time, he managed to reel in a scathing comment, but only by ignoring his father's rejoinder. "Thanks for the papers."

Applauding himself for his courteous veneer, he started to close the door—then jerked it open again. "By the way..."

Obviously eager to prolong the conversation, his father stepped back to the door. "Yes?"

"Is it true that Sophia St. Claire is the chief of police?"

"Sure, why? You know her?"

He knew her, all right. He'd had a terrible crush on her when they were in high school and had screwed up the courage to ask her to Homecoming for their sophomore year. Elated when she accepted, he'd thought maybe he'd been wrong about Bordertown, about his chances of succeeding in this place. It was only a school dance, but it'd seemed like a promise of hope. Never had he been so excited about life, about change. He'd spent everything he had on a suit and flowers, and eagerly counted the days until the big dance. When he found out that she'd stood him up and gone with a more popular boy, he'd felt as if she'd made a joke out of the belief that he could be more than he was. It felt like the most personal of rejections. Somehow that had cut deeper than almost anything else he'd experienced, probably because he'd been young and vulnerable back then in a way he hadn't been since. He'd made sure of that. "We were in the same class. When I went to school, of course."

Unwilling to address the negative aspects of the past—or, it seemed, to even remember them—Bruce skimmed over Rod's reference to dropping out. "She's a beauty." He added a whistle. "Stuart talks about her all the time."

"His wife doesn't mind?"

"It's Patrick who's married, not Stuart. Chief St. Claire is single, too. For now, anyway. There're about a dozen men who'd like to change that."

Including Stuart, apparently. "Who's she dating?"

"She goes out with Stuart now and then, but I don't get the impression she's all that serious about him. She used to see Dick Callahan, the pastor over at First Calvary Church, but that didn't go anywhere, either."

What, he'd figured out that her soul wasn't worth saving? "Why not?"

"Got some young girl pregnant. It was a big scandal, as you can imagine—a church man sleeping with an underage member of his flock. To save face, and his job, he claimed to love her. And maybe he really does. Who knows? He married her. The baby's due anytime."

"Poor Sophia." Rod couldn't think of anyone who deserved to be jilted more but he tried to cloak the sarcasm

in those two words. Not because he cared whether or not
others found out he wasn't all that impressed with Sophia
St. Claire—he didn't want to give his father an excuse
to hang around by asking questions. "She any good at
her job?" He wanted to know what he had to work with,
whether or not she'd be a competent and cooperative partner in the investigation.

"Seems to be," Bruce replied. "But she's had a rough
few months. First, she had to deal with the people in town
who were opposed to seeing a woman take charge, a young
woman at that. If not for Paul Fedorko and a couple others
on the city council who were adamantly opposed to her
main competitor, she wouldn't have had the opportunity.
But she did. And she braved the backlash. Then these killings started. If she can't solve them in a relatively short
period of time, it'll give her opponents the leverage they
need to get her fired."

Hearing this, Roderick had half a mind to sit back and
do nothing, to wait and see if she could rescue herself.
He certainly wasn't inclined to do her any favors. But he
couldn't risk the lives of innocent people just to feed an
old grudge. She didn't matter. Maybe he'd once had feelings for Sophia, but he hadn't thought of her in years.

Well, not in the past few months, anyway…. For whatever reason, no other woman had ever affected him in the
same way.

"Do you think she'll be willing to work with me on
this?"

"I don't see why she wouldn't. Someone with your reputation. I'm sure she can use all the help she can get. Last
I heard, the sheriff had assigned a detective to the case,
but he should've assigned two or three."

"She's got a lot going against her."

"Exactly."

Rod remembered what she'd done to him well enough that this news didn't make him entirely unhappy. He'd been so thrilled, as that naive teenager who thought he finally had a chance with the girl he'd always wanted. But she'd set him up, probably so she and her friends could have a good laugh. "I'll pay her a visit."

"It'll relieve the city council to have you involved in the investigation."

And Rod definitely wanted to please the good ol' boys on the city council. He swallowed a pained sigh. He hated small-town politics, but this dynamic would work in his favor so he didn't complain. Frightened of losing her job and in need of help, Sophia would be much more likely to cooperate with him. Experience had taught him that local cops with less incentive could be very stingy with information. "Glad to hear it."

His father didn't seem to pick up on his lack of enthusiasm. "You need an introduction or anything else, you let me know."

"Yeah, sure."

Again, Bruce seemed to miss the dry note that should've told him that Rod had no intention of coming to him for anything.

"By the way, I brought you something else."

Now what? Rod stretched up and gripped the top of the door frame with his fingertips. "Are you going to tell me what it is?"

"I'll get it." He walked to the passenger side of his big gray double-axle pickup truck and retrieved a manila envelope.

Rod dropped his arms to his sides but didn't comment as he accepted it. Opening the flap, which was unsealed, he withdrew a stack of money orders—the ones he'd sent at sixteen and seventeen, when he was trying to pay off his mother's funeral. He didn't want them, but he wasn't going to argue over them, either. He'd done what he could for his mother. He'd repaid the debt—whether Bruce allowed him to or not.

"I don't want these, and you know it."

"I'd appreciate it if you'd take them. I can't explain why, but…it's important to me."

"Whatever." Rod was about to close the flap and toss the envelope onto the small table by the door when his fingers encountered something with an entirely different texture. What was this?

When he pulled it from the envelope, he saw a snapshot of him and his mother standing outside their shack at the ranch. Carolina, young, beautiful and still healthy, was wearing one of her inexpensive cotton shirts, a wide-brimmed hat to protect her from the sun and a pair of jeans that had been cut off at the knees and rolled up a few inches. She was smiling and hugging him close.

Rod was maybe three or four, too young to remember having the photo taken. "Where did you get this?"

It was harder now, harder to keep the anger under control. Looking at Carolina, he could understand why Bruce had been attracted to her. She was beautiful. But that didn't make Rod willing to forgive him for taking advantage of her, not when Bruce already had everything a man could ever want.

"I took the picture myself." His father must've known from Rod's expression or the tension in his body that it was time to leave because he mumbled a quick goodbye and walked away.

Rod didn't respond. He could no longer speak or move.

All he could do was stare at that picture as memories of his mother crashed over him.

Sweat rolled between Sophia's shoulder blades, making her feel sticky and uncomfortable in her uniform as she went from trailer to trailer, getting formal statements from everyone who could have heard the gunshots that killed José and Benita Sanchez. Three shots had been fired. She knew that from the spent casings. But only one person—Debbie Berke, in the closest trailer—had heard enough noise to get her out of bed. Mac White, who lived next to Earl and Marlene, said he "might've" heard something. He told her he'd been awakened but shrugged off whatever had disturbed him. He was too used to Earl and Marlene's fights to worry about a little yelling. Randy Pinegar said he had a sleep disorder for which he'd taken a sleeping aid. But everyone knew he was an alcoholic. Sophia guessed he'd been in a stupor. And Ralph Newlin, the only other neighbor in that circle of trailers, had been in Phoenix, picking up his daughter from the home of his ex-wife. He was still gone, on his way to Disneyland.

Planning to ask Debbie a few more questions about the "thumps" she'd heard, Sophia had just stepped onto the landing when her cell phone rang. According to caller ID, it was Detective Lindstrom.

She nearly ignored it. But Councilman Fedorko had called this morning and added even more pressure to what she was already feeling. He'd told her the other city council members were getting nervous, that they were wondering if she had the experience to get the job done. He implied that there were two members, in particular, who were talking about replacing her. He claimed Mayor Schilling was even lamenting the fact that they hadn't promoted

Leonard. Paul seemed to believe that, questionable character aside, Leonard would have a better chance of catching the UDA killer. Sophia knew it was fear that was making the city council second-guess their decision. They were scared that someone who wasn't a UDA would get shot and a battle would erupt between the two factions. But she didn't appreciate their lack of faith.

Bottom line, she had to cooperate with Lindstrom, had to trust the detective despite the warning bells in her head and the sick feeling in her gut. She couldn't do this alone. There was too much work.

She hit the talk button. "Chief St. Claire."

"You identified the victims?"

She'd left Lindstrom a message to that effect after her chat with Fedorko. "I did."

"How?"

"Naco was worth the trip."

"I let the Mexican consulate know about the murders. You might want to alert them to this new development."

"I already did."

"Who'd you speak with?"

"Same guy you did. Deputy Consul Rudy Ruybal." He'd been their contact from the beginning.

"I pushed him to do the DNA testing for Philip Moreno. Did he say anything about it?"

Philip Moreno was among the victims in the second incident. They'd identified him via SIRLI, by posting a picture of the unusual eyeglass case found near his body and the logo on his T-shirt. "He didn't mention it."

"I can't believe they're dragging their feet on this."

"It's expensive. Rudy needs approval." When there was no other way to be sure of a deceased UDA's identity, the consulate had Baylor University do a DNA test, hoping to match the body with relatives back in Mexico. But it was a time-consuming and expensive process that had to be approved by the foreign ministry's headquarters in Mexico City, and the government wasn't too thrilled about doing it unless they were fairly sure it would be successful. Just in the past decade, thousands of illegal immigrants, many of them unidentified, had died in the Southwest. The logo on Moreno's T-shirt was the only thing they had to indicate he was from Durango. But if they could confirm his identity, it might help them identify the female who was traveling with him. Sophia suspected they were the brother and sister the Moreno family in Durango had reported missing.

"Did he seem upset?" Lindstrom asked.

"Definitely. He requested a meeting."

"You don't think he'll try to make us look bad by going to the media, do you?"

Fedorko had been worried about the same thing. He said any negative press would work against her, because it would give the mayor the ammunition he needed to bring the council to a consensus. "He will if he thinks it's in his country's best interest. But I don't think he wants this to turn into a war any more than we do."

"I want to be present at the meeting." Lindstrom sounded as if she was prepared for an argument, but Sophia was certainly willing to let her deal with Deputy Consul Ruybal.

"No problem. It's at two. When you go, please tell Rudy I'm busy with the investigation and couldn't get away."

There was a long pause. "You set me up."

"You set yourself up," Sophia said. "There's no reason for both of us to be there."

"Fine. Whatever. Tell me what happened in Naco. I

want every detail, everything you know, so I can show him we're doing all we can and that we're making progress."

"The Sanchezes came by bus from Nayarit to Naco, where they crossed on Friday night along with thirty others. They were led by two runners—Miguel and Juan Martinez. According to Juan, they were an hour or so into the walk when they were spotted by the border patrol and everyone scattered. José and Benita struck out alone."

"Then there's no way to track who saw them last," she complained. "Their killer could be anyone who came across them."

"Anyone with a silencer," Sophia said.

"You think the culprit used a silencer?"

"I didn't realize it right away, but it occurred to me that those shots would've disturbed more people if they'd sounded like regular gunfire."

"Silencers aren't easy to come by."

"It's not as tough here as it is in some states."

"I'll check with the Bureau of Alcohol, Tobacco, Firearms and Explosives to see if anyone in this area obtained one through legal means in the past year or so."

Sophia doubted it would be that simple. This guy was too smart. But they had to eliminate whatever possibilities they could. There were fewer silencers on the market than guns. "I know someone who might have a bead on the black market. I'll ask him to poke around, see what he can find." She didn't add that her contact was also an ex-boyfriend, who just happened to be intimately acquainted with that sort of thing.

Debbie Berke came to the door even though Sophia hadn't knocked yet. "I thought I heard your voice."

Sophia held up a finger to indicate she'd be with her in a second. "While you're talking to ATF, see if they have any undercover agents working in the area that we might be able to speak with. Maybe they've heard something about the sale or trade of a silencer."

"That's not a bad idea. So when's the autopsy?"

"Hasn't been scheduled yet. I'll let you know when I hear."

"Sure you will," Lindstrom said, and hung up.

Sophia was about to turn to Debbie to ask whether the shot she'd heard might have been fired through a silencer when a Hummer drove up and a man got out. The glare of the sun made it difficult to see him clearly, but the moment she raised a hand to shade her eyes, Sophia realized it was Roderick Guerrero.

Roderick hadn't expected to find Sophia here. He'd merely come to take a look at the crime scene. Since everyone in town was talking about the murders, it hadn't been hard to learn where they'd occurred. But there she was, standing in front of a heavyset woman Roderick was sure he'd never met. This grouping of trailers had been here when he'd lived in Bordertown, but he'd never associated with the people inside them.

The older woman watched him curiously. He could've ignored her and gone about his business. But now that Sophia had seen him, he had no choice except to confront her and explain his presence.

She tensed as he approached. Did she recognize him? He didn't see why she would. She hadn't considered him good enough to notice. She'd dated wealthy ranchers' sons, not illegitimate half-breeds who lived in shacks with dirt floors. The one time she'd agreed to go out with him, she'd made him a laughingstock to his two half brothers.

"Chief St. Claire?" he said.

"Yes?" Suspicion lit the eyes he remembered so well. Framed by thick black eyelashes, they were a very pale green. As a boy, Roderick had thought they were the prettiest eyes he'd ever seen and he had to admit that nothing in the past fourteen years had changed his mind.

"I'm Roderick Guerrero." He wasn't planning to mention that they'd once known each other. That wasn't significant. "I work for a company called Department 6."

"Isn't that the outfit that sent a couple of operatives to Paradise last summer to investigate the Covenanters?" the woman with Sophia chimed in.

"It is," he replied, and offered her a polite smile. "We do a lot of undercover work, mostly for the DEA, but I know my way around an investigation."

Sophia reclaimed his attention. "And you're here because…"

"Bruce Dunlap called me about the recent shootings. He said you don't have a lot of experience with this sort of thing and he asked me to come down here."

"He's paying you?"

"No, I have a…vested interest in seeing this solved."

"You don't think that'll happen without you."

He couldn't help reacting to the edge in her voice. "You said it. I didn't."

She pressed her lips so tightly together, all the color disappeared from them. "So we're going to pretend we've never met?"

"It's been years," he said calmly. "And it was such a minor acquaintance I didn't expect you to remember."

"Minor. I see."

The other woman was listening so avidly her mouth hung open, but he refused to pay her any heed. Pushing his sunglasses a little higher, he gestured at the markers that had been placed at the crime scene. "What'd you find out here?"

Sophia folded her arms. "And now you're assuming that my answer is yes."

"I'm assuming you're smart enough to realize when you're—"

"Looking at the solution to all my problems?" she broke in.

He felt a muscle tic in his cheek. "Getting something for nothing."

"You've got to be kidding me. You have no official right to be here. This is like some spectator going to the coach in the middle of a game and saying, 'Here, let me take over.'"

"If that coach is losing, it might serve him well to listen to that spectator."

The woman behind her snickered, but Sophia didn't even glance at her. "What if I don't want your help?"

Rod couldn't believe this was the girl he'd once admired. A cop was the last thing he'd expected her to become. He'd thought she'd grow up to be another Edna—a wife and stay-at-home mom who doted on her children, played bridge, went shopping and contributed to charity events. But here she was, wearing the typical police uniform— blue shirt and pants, heavy utility belt, gun, badge and shiny black shoes. There was some grit beneath Sophia's beauty that hadn't been there before. But he didn't like this version any better. Not after what she'd done.

"The color of my skin might allow me more freedom of movement among certain people. I speak Spanish. I know this area. And I'm offering you my time and expertise. Why would you say no?"

"You mean besides the fact that you're not here in any

kind of official capacity? The FBI is putting together a task force. I won't need you."

"What would it hurt to take all the help you can get?"

"I don't want you in my way, and I don't see how you can avoid it with an ego the size of yours."

He removed his sunglasses. "I can have myself assigned if you insist on being—" he wanted to say "a bitch" but choked it back "—*difficult*." Milt was an asshole on most counts, but his contacts and money—and the reputation of Department 6—could open doors. Rod had little doubt that someone with sufficient power would see his involvement as a good thing, especially if he was offering his services for free.

"By whom?" she scoffed.

"The governor, if necessary."

"Oh, yeah? Then I'll wait for his call," she said and motioned for the woman she was with to precede her into the trailer.

8

"Are you sure you don't want Mr. Guerrero's help?" Debbie asked as the door banged shut behind them.

"Positive," Sophia replied. "With the size of the chip on his shoulder, it'll be a miracle if he can stay out of his *own* way. This investigation is difficult enough as it is." She was thinking of Lindstrom and the possibility of Leonard Taylor's involvement. Having grown up in the area, Leonard had friends and family everywhere. Even the judge to whom she had to appeal for various warrants was related to him. As far as she was concerned, she was already surrounded by people she couldn't trust.

Debbie frowned. "I don't know. He seemed pretty confident. And if it could save lives…"

"I don't need him." Sophia wasn't going to cooperate with a man as arrogant as Roderick Guerrero. The FBI would be getting involved any day. He couldn't offer more than they could.

"You said something about knowing him." Debbie knelt on the couch to peek through the curtains, which she tended to keep closed against the hot sun. "But I've never seen him around."

"We went to school together. Until his mother died. Then he dropped out. He's Bruce Dunlap's bastard." It wasn't the kindest way to explain Rod's situation, but Sophia was still fuming over his "now that I'm here, everything will be okay" attitude.

"Of course! Edna nearly has a coronary whenever anyone mentions him."

Sophia didn't comment. Had he really threatened to go over her head?

"You'd think I would've remembered him," Debbie continued, still gazing out the window. "You don't run into a man who looks like *that* very often."

"He wasn't a man when he left. He was a sixteen-year-old boy." And he hadn't always looked as good as he did today. He'd been skinny in high school, with hands and feet too large for his body and a sullen expression that was as effective as a Do-Not-Approach sign. The fact that he was usually in need of a haircut and a change of clothes gave him a wild air that was just a little frightening. Coming upon him had been like encountering a lone wolf in the desert. Mangy, battle-worn, distrusting. Those were the three words Sophia would've used to describe him.

But this Roderick was completely different. For one thing, he'd finally grown into his hands and feet. At least six feet three inches tall, he had to weigh two hundred and twenty pounds. No longer resembling a mangy wolf or mangy *anything,* he had a soldier's powerful body. His hair, as black as ever, was cut short enough to suggest he'd been in the military. With beautiful coppery skin and teeth that were white and straight, he'd improved physically in every area except one—the wariness that used to lurk in his eyes had been replaced with contempt.

Debbie shifted positions. "He's not leaving."

"I don't care, as long as he doesn't cross my tape."

"He hasn't yet. But..." Debbie glanced back at her. "What would you do if he did?"

"I'd arrest him for interfering with my investigation!"

"Really?"

"Really."

She opened the drapes a little wider. "Then you might want to check this out."

Sophia joined her on the couch, where they both watched Roderick duck under the tape, walk around and then suddenly kneel on the ground several feet from where the bodies had fallen.

"No freaking way!" she cried, and marched to the door.

Roderick knew Sophia was coming but he didn't look up. He'd uncovered something with his foot that might be important. Carefully slipping it into one of the side pockets of his khaki shorts, he turned just as she came close enough to speak.

"What the hell do you think you're doing?" she yelled.

"Nothing." After stooping to clear the tape, he strode past her on his way to the Hummer.

"Don't you dare walk away from me!" She came charging after him. "You're under arrest!"

He ignored her.

"If you don't stop, I'll draw my weapon."

"I wouldn't, if I were you," he said over his shoulder. "That might be a bit difficult to explain when the governor calls."

Thanks to a much shorter stride, she was forced to take two steps to his one. "No, it won't. I'm well within my rights. You're a civilian who's interfering with a police investigation. You took something. I saw it. What is it?"

His flip-flops made flapping noises as he walked. "Evidence you should've claimed yourself. You can explain that when the governor calls, too."

She spoke louder. "Whatever it is, you'd better turn it over to me."

"I'll tell you what I learn from it. Maybe that'll start us off in the right direction."

"Don't bet on it. *We* won't be heading in any direction because you'll be in jail."

To let her know he wasn't worried, he didn't even bother to look back at her. "And who's going to put me there?"

"I am!"

"Good luck with that."

It was this statement that seemed to infuriate her more than any other. "This is your last warning," she said. "If you don't hand over what you took, you're going to need a very talented lawyer."

Reaching the Hummer, he opened the door. "Do yourself a favor and leave me alone, okay?"

She'd drawn her gun as promised and was aiming it at him. "Freeze, or I'll shoot."

Whirling, he wrenched the weapon from her grasp. The way her eyes flared in alarm told him he'd surprised her, but he didn't return her firearm. He shoved it in the waistband of his shorts.

"Next time you threaten a man, make sure he can't disarm you," he said. Then he got in his vehicle and drove away.

Sophia had never been angrier or more embarrassed in her life. She hadn't been afraid of Roderick Guerrero, so she hadn't taken the proper precautions, and he'd made a fool of her.

Debbie, standing halfway to the trailer, was trying not to laugh. "Did he just take your gun?"

"Yes!" she snapped, and jumped into her cruiser. Flipping on the alarm and the siren, she peeled out of the dirt drive and went barreling down the road.

The Hummer was about a mile ahead of her, so she gave the cruiser more gas. She wanted to close the gap and apprehend him before they got to the edge of town. But she didn't catch up to him until he'd stopped at the first of Bordertown's three traffic lights.

Even then, he didn't pull over. As soon as the light changed, he drove on as if she wasn't following him with her siren wailing and her flashers on. He actually led her through town twice by driving in a big circle.

He was toying with her, which only infuriated her more.

Finally she got out her blare horn and began shouting at him. "Pull over!" She repeated those words several times, but it didn't make any difference. He wouldn't cooperate.

At last he seemed to grow bored with the game and drove to the Mother Lode Motel, where he parked and got out, acting as though he hadn't spent the past thirty minutes evading capture.

"You are *so* screwed!" she cried as she scrambled out of her car.

He turned and sent her a smile, but she could tell there was no enjoyment in it. "Then I hope you screw better than you do everything else."

Using her open door as a shield, she grabbed her shotgun from the car. "Give me my Glock!"

He removed his sunglasses and started toward her.

"Don't you *dare*," she said, and this time he must've realized she was ready to blow a hole through him because he stopped.

"Look, I'm setting your gun on the hood of my car. I suggest you put it in your holster and get back to the business of taking care of real criminals."

Returning the gun wasn't enough of a concession. "Give me what you took from the crime scene, too."

"Sorry. Can't do that. But if you'll call me when you're capable of being reasonable, we can talk about it," he said, then walked inside.

Sophia nearly squeezed the trigger. But as much as her temper egged her on, she couldn't shoot a man for picking up something she'd missed at a crime scene. And for all she knew, he was bluffing and had a rock in his pocket.

"You turned out to be such a…a jerk!" she yelled after him.

The door remained shut. The curtains didn't even move. He'd dismissed her and didn't seem to care what she thought.

Leland Jennings, the hotel manager, stepped out to see what all the fuss was about. "Everything okay, Chief?"

Taking a deep breath, Sophia holstered her Glock and put away her rifle. "It's fine."

Her clipped response brought another question. "Anything I can do?"

"No, thanks," she said, and climbed into her vehicle. As far as she was concerned, Roderick Guerrero had no authority in Bordertown, no right to insert himself into her case, and she wouldn't let him get away with it. She couldn't expect her detractors to respect her if she couldn't maintain control of her own investigation.

She'd wait until nightfall and approach him again. Hopefully by then he'd be willing to cooperate.

And she'd be prepared in case he wasn't.

Roderick paced in front of the TV until Chief St. Claire left, then headed out again. He wanted to go to the post office so he could send the cigarette butt he'd found at the crime scene to the lab he worked with in San Diego. He wasn't sure if that butt had belonged to the killer. It'd been buried in the dirt and had only been churned to the surface by his footsteps. It could've been tossed there by a neighbor several days ago. But other than the expense, which he was happy to cover, Rod couldn't see how it would hurt to create a DNA profile. The profile wouldn't have much significance right now. But if they could come up with a suspect, it might prove invaluable. And if it proved invaluable, Sophia would have him to thank for the link.

Remembering her impotent rage, he grinned. It was probably the first time she'd ever been denied. At least by a man.

He'd just climbed into the Hummer when a truck exactly like his father's, except that it was red, pulled up behind him and boxed him in. It was one of his half brothers. With the glare of the sun, he couldn't see the driver's face well enough to tell which one. But exact identity was irrelevant; he hated them both equally.

Refusing to act as if this affected him one way or the other, he turned on his engine while waiting to catch a glimpse of his visitor in the rearview mirror. He couldn't imagine either of the Dunlap brothers trying to start trouble without the other's support, but adrenaline pumped through him all the same, preparing him for a fight. It was a triggered response. Sometimes the Dunlaps had surprised him by striking out at the most unlikely moments.

The truck door opened and the elder of the two brothers stepped out. Rod recognized Patrick easily, even though he'd changed quite a bit in the past fourteen years. His dark blond hair, which used to be long and a little curly, was trimmed above his ears and his clean-shaven face had grown fuller. To most women, he was probably still more handsome than not, but now he carried a spare tire around his middle.

He'd gotten married and gone soft....

Rod left his motor running to show that he didn't plan on wasting much time on this but got out, too. He didn't want to be stuck inside the vehicle if it came to a fight. Not that he was terribly worried that this would erupt into blows. He could take Pat, especially this Pat turned pudge-boy. Hell, without Stuart there, Rod wouldn't even have to break a sweat.

Looking a bit unsure of himself, Pat stopped about five feet away and cleared his throat. He had on a pair of leather work boots, as if he'd been out on the ranch, but his jeans were clean, and his golf shirt was more preppy than Western. "Dad mentioned you were in town."

That was it? That was his lead-in after everything he'd had to say when they were kids? The statement sounded so innocuous.

Rod made his contempt plain. "So? I've got as much right to be here as you do."

"I'm not saying you don't."

"Then what do you want?"

"To tell you that...I'm glad you came."

Rod barked a laugh. "You've got to be kidding, right?"

Pat hooked his thumbs in his leather belt. "Maybe you can stop what's happening around here before it gets any worse."

"I'd say it's already pretty bad for the Mexicans. But you wouldn't care about that."

He lowered his voice. "Things change, Rod. People change."

"Not that much. So what's the real story?" He glanced around the lot, checking the other cars as if he expected an ambush. "You waiting for your brother?"

Pat kicked a small rock across the pavement. "No."

"I've got a cell phone, if you'd like to give him a call." Rod held out his phone, but Pat didn't accept it.

"He already knows you're in town."

"And he didn't come to the party? Two on one—you always liked those odds before."

Sucking in his stomach, Patrick puffed out his chest, but there was no hiding that extra twenty pounds. "I didn't come here to start a fight."

"Too bad," Rod said, and part of him meant it—the part that was still looking for a way to vent the old anger.

His half brother shoved his hands into his pockets and the gold wedding band on his left hand disappeared from view. "I made some mistakes. If you want to hear me say it, I will."

"I don't want to hear you say it. I don't want *anything* from you, not even an apology."

"Of course not. Your pride would never allow you to reveal weakness. I guess you're the one who hasn't changed. That's just what you were like as a kid."

Here was a little of the old Pat. Feeling more comfortable with the familiar, Rod relaxed. "Is that how you sleep at night?" he asked. "By telling yourself I deserved those beatings?"

Patrick's voice turned slightly sulky. "No, but it didn't help that you were always challenging us."

"By being *alive?*" he said with another laugh. "I'm the product, buddy, not the cause. Your father's the one who was taking advantage of the migrants who worked for him."

"I think he cared about your mother."

"He had a damn fine way of showing it."

"What happened was as hard on him as anyone."

"Forgive me if I don't get all misty-eyed over *his* pain. I don't know how many times I'll have to say this, but I don't give a shit. I'm not here to see you, your father or your brother." He motioned toward the truck. "Do you mind?"

Tension filled Patrick's face, evidence of some emotion. But whether it was embarrassment or regret or perhaps frustration Rod had no idea. "It's not like I was offering you a damn olive branch."

"Great. Move your car."

"I had another reason for coming by."

"I'm waiting."

"I have information on the murders of those, er, Mexican nationals."

Rod leaned against the Hummer and crossed his feet. "Since when did you become so politically correct? Don't you prefer the term *wetbacks?* I believe that's what you used to call me. You even made up a song about the wetback bastard with brown eyes the size of saucers. Remember? It was a catchy tune. Made all your friends laugh."

Pat flinched. "Yeah, well—" he rubbed his neck "—I

hope I've grown up a bit since then. My, um, wife's half Mexican."

If he thought that would give them common ground, he was sadly mistaken. "And she's living with *you?* God, she has my sympathies."

"She's a good woman. Better than I deserve."

Carolina had been a good woman, too, yet they'd called her a spic and a whore and did everything they could to make her life miserable. One day she found that someone had gotten into her lunch box—most of the workers left their food in the shade while they worked—and replaced the meat in her sandwich with dog shit. No one came forward to take responsibility for that, but there'd never been any question in Rod's mind that it had been one or both of his half brothers.

"I'm happy for you." He made the words a meaningless platitude by adding a careless shrug of his shoulder.

"I'll bet you are."

"Listen, you have nothing to fear from me. You *or* your brother. I'm not after your father's love, attention or money, if that's what you're worried about. As soon as I solve this case, I'm gone."

"Fine, forget it." He pivoted to go, but Rod stopped him.

"You said you have information on the murders."

He paused, deliberated and eventually blew out a sigh. "I heard Leonard Taylor talking in the barbershop the other day."

"Who's Leonard Taylor?"

"Moved here about ten years ago from Douglas, when he was hired as a police officer."

"What'd he have to say?"

"He was going on and on about the killings, which isn't

so unusual. Everyone has something to say about them and how we should prepare to retaliate. It was the way he was talking that got my attention. It was completely callous. He seemed almost…gleeful. He's hoping this case gets Sophia St. Claire fired."

Rod felt a flicker of guilt. He probably hadn't helped Sophia's situation when he'd made her look inept during that merry chase through town. But he didn't owe her anything. She wasn't any better than his half brothers. "Why would he want to see her fired?"

"She took his job. Before the previous chief retired, he had two officers under him—her and Leonard. Leonard had a lot more experience and was the most likely to succeed him. The council was all set to promote him when Sophia came forward with an illegal immigrant who claimed he'd caught her in the desert south of town and offered her a deal."

"What kind of deal?"

"Sex in exchange for her freedom."

"That's some deal. Did you say he's related to your father?"

Pat ignored the insult. "It caused a pretty big stink with just about everyone in town choosing sides."

"How did Sophia find the woman? Did she come in to the station or—"

"No, some Mexican guy she'd thrown in the drunk tank was talking about how the police had done his sister wrong. No one else paid him any mind, but Sophia followed up on what he said and tracked the woman down. Sure enough, she claimed it was true."

"Did this asshole—this Leonard Taylor—lose his job?"

"No. The Mexican woman and her brother disappeared

soon after, and without either of them, the D.A. couldn't build a case. Taylor's reputation was damaged, and he lost the position as chief to St. Claire, but he could've stayed on. It wasn't like they'd proven anything. There was just the accusation."

"Only then he'd have to work for his nemesis."

"Exactly. His ego couldn't tolerate it, so he quit. Went back to working with livestock. Actually, that's what he did in Douglas before he entered the police academy. Now he manages a chicken ranch."

Taylor was definitely someone Rod needed to speak with. "Where does he live?"

"On the edge of town, not far from the intersection of Ray and Saguaro. That's also where he supposedly had sex with the Mexican woman—in his own backyard."

"You don't believe it?"

"I don't know what to believe. Seems unlikely a police officer would do a thing like that...but if he thought he could get away with it, I suppose anything's possible. Leonard's wife was in Albuquerque at the time, at a craft fair. She makes dolls. His older daughters were at sports camp. The smallest girl was the only one home with him. She said she heard daddy making funny sounds out in the trees, and he shouted for her to stay away when she tried to find him, but you can't convict a man based on a five-year-old's testimony of grunting and 'don't come out here.'"

Rod folded his arms. "So this man would've been chief of police if not for Sophia St. Claire."

"That's right. To top it all off, his wife left him and took the kids. She's living with her folks in Prescott."

Rod straightened. "I'll pay him a visit this afternoon."

"Be careful. I think he's got an arsenal out there," he said, and walked back to his truck.

Rod told himself to let the encounter go at that, but he couldn't. "Why did you tell me about Leonard?" he called out.

His half brother turned. "Isn't it obvious? He might have something to do with the murders."

"But everyone already knows his story. Chief St. Claire or someone else would've told me about it."

Patrick stared at his feet before meeting Rod's eyes. "My wife sent me over here," he admitted. "She wanted me to invite you to dinner."

Rod wondered about the conversation Pat must've had with his wife. "She *is* better than you deserve."

He squinted against the sun. "That's still a no, isn't it?"

"I can't imagine Stuart would be pleased about my coming to your place for dinner."

"Doesn't matter. As my wife says, you're my brother, too."

Rod had never dreamed he'd hear those words from Patrick. He wasn't sure how to react now that they'd been uttered. Why was Patrick's wife getting involved? Rod had never even met her. "Tell her she's worrying for nothing. Everything's as it should be."

"She won't believe it, not as long as we're enemies. I'm telling you, I married Mother Teresa."

"I guess that's one way to gain a conscience," he said and climbed into the Hummer while waiting for Patrick to move his truck.

9

Kevin Simpson owned thirty-five thousand acres along the border. Together with several of the ranchers from Douglas, he and his son and wife had taken to patrolling their own property in an effort to stop the illegal immigrants from cutting through. His son even had a blog on which he claimed that together they'd detained more than twelve thousand UDAs in the past ten years, which they'd turned over to the border patrol.

It was a staggering number, but only a fraction of the people who came through. Sophia had heard that the border patrol had apprehended twenty-three thousand UDAs on another ranch in one month. That was one ranch, and since they caught maybe one in five, a lot more made it through. As she stood next to Kevin and James, his son, who was holding the reins of the horses they'd ridden to this remote location, she saw what they'd brought her here to see—the highway of garbage that'd been left behind.

"Look here." A cowboy hat shaded Kevin's weathered face as he pointed to the water bottles, T-shirts, toilet paper and food wrappers that littered the hillside. "This is just from the past few months. I've about given up trying to keep it collected. Doesn't do any good. As soon as you pick it up, more of 'em come through and toss *their* garbage on the ground."

"And a cow's stupid enough to eat anything." James, dressed in Wranglers, cowboy boots and a Western shirt like his father, pushed his horse away from the thorny bush it was trying to nibble.

"So it's dangerous for the cattle." She knew this, of course. They'd been trying to get her out here to see it since she became chief of police. But they'd been very vocal in supporting Leonard Taylor, despite his corruption, so she hadn't been in any hurry to let them cry on her shoulder, especially because there was little she could do. This was a federal problem. She'd told them to take it up with the border patrol. Since the killings, however, she had a different perspective. She wanted to keep the Simpsons talking, hear what they had to say about illegal immigration and the damage it caused.

"Costs us several head a year," James said.

"And that's not all," Kevin added. "They break our pipes, and the water can run for a day or two before we catch it. They knock down fences. The cattle don't like having people come through, so they move around more and end up weighing less. And last year illegals slaughtered two of our calves." He pulled out a cigarette and, after lifting his eyebrows to make sure it was okay with her if he smoked, he lit up. "It's probably cost us five million over the past several years, but it's a losing battle. No one on this side of the border will even believe it's this bad unless they come out here and take a look."

Sophia had seen pictures of the mess on their blog, but the Simpsons were right—it made a much bigger impact in person.

Kevin adjusted his hat. "Our lawmakers say they're

gonna to do something about it, but they're too busy kissing Mexico's ass to take a stand."

She noted his tone. He was aggravated, angry, bitter. But did those emotions run deep enough that he'd resort to murder? He certainly had a motive. His property was being ruined and he wasn't receiving any redress from the government. He also had plenty of opportunity, weapons and years of experience tracking illegal immigrants.

"What's that?" She pointed to a white fleck way off in the distance.

He used the binoculars hanging around his neck to have a look, but his son answered before he could get them focused.

"She's talking about the water tank."

Kevin nodded. "Yeah, that's a water tank. Some idiot put it out there, thinking he's saving lives. Instead, he's tempting more hapless souls into the desert."

It was hot, more than a hundred degrees. Sophia couldn't imagine walking through the Sonoran Desert with less than a gallon of water, which was what most UDAs carried. "Why don't you take it down?"

James patted his horse's nose. "It's not on our land."

She accepted the binoculars Kevin handed her; through them she could easily see the water tank. "Your neighbor put it out there?"

"Hell, no. That's federal land. It's someone who doesn't have a clue about what he's doing. Someone who doesn't worry about the garbage left behind. Someone who feels no responsibility to clean up the mess. Someone who might even provide a safe house for the ones who cross."

"Those safe houses aren't cheap," James chimed in. "They charge five dollars a night for nothing—a square of cement to sleep on. Food and water are extra. That's a lot of money for the people who come through here."

Kevin jumped in again. "You might think the guys who erect water tanks are being such humanitarians." He laughed without humor. "In most cases, that isn't true at all. It's good old-fashioned self-interest at work. They want to make it easy for illegals to cross so they can sell them life's necessities."

James waved his hand, which was gloved in leather. "It's a real racket."

Sophia took the pictures of José and his wife from her pocket. She hadn't asked about them yet. She'd said she was here to talk about the border problem. She'd been trying to figure out just how much Kevin and his son hated illegal aliens. And they'd made that clear. They were so upset with UDAs they were happy to have someone listen to their complaints, even someone who couldn't do much about the problem except support politicians who promised tougher immigration enforcement. "Any chance you were out patrolling last Friday or Saturday night?"

James patted his horse's nose. "I did a cursory run. Didn't find anyone. But that doesn't mean they didn't come through. I do what I can, but I can't sit out here night after night. Why?"

"That's when these people crossed." She showed Kevin the pictures. "I need to come up with a suspect, and I'm thinking those who saw them last might be able to help." That included the border patrol agents who'd encountered them, if the Simpsons could help her narrow down which ones they were.

Kevin handed the photos to his son. "I *thought* that's why you dropped by."

She knew they had to have considered it. "These victims bring the total to twelve."

"Poor bastards," James muttered.

Kevin took exception to his son's sympathy. "I don't feel sorry for them." He climbed onto his horse. "They had no business breaking the law in the first place."

Sophia squinted up at him. "We're talking about murder, Mr. Simpson. As bad as the situation may be, becoming a vigilante isn't the way to solve it."

He stiffened in the saddle. "Which is why *I* haven't become a vigilante, Chief."

She took the pictures back from James. "You have friends who are border patrol agents, isn't that right?"

"Most people in this area have friends in the CBP."

"Since you and the agents are both trying to stop these people from breaking the law, you probably have more than most."

"Maybe. I have enough interaction with them, I guess."

"Have you heard any talk?"

Kevin squinted at her despite the shade provided by his hat. "What kind of talk?"

"About killing Mexicans. Bragging. Someone who seems to be losing it or is especially angry or bitter."

"No. None."

"You haven't noticed anything odd or unusual."

Both men spoke at once. "No."

"Would you tell me if you had?"

Kevin used a bandanna he pulled out of his pocket to mop the sweat from his forehead. "I'd like to say I would. But I'm guessing you'll ask the border patrol agents the same thing about us, and I'm hoping they don't see anything I've said or done as 'unusual,' either. Besides, the government's never been much help to me. I'm not sure I'd be too eager to bend over backward now that the shoe's on the other foot."

"We're not talking about the government. We're talking about a very tense situation that could blow up in our faces." Sophia turned to James. "What about you?"

"I haven't heard a thing, and have no idea who's killing these people. But…"

"But?" she echoed.

"I'd be lying if I said I wasn't glad *someone's* finally doing *something*."

"Even if that something includes murder?"

"If people were punished for breaking the immigration laws, maybe we wouldn't have such a terrible problem to begin with." He swung into the saddle and reached down to help her up behind him.

These men, who in most ways seemed like such decent, hard-working citizens, were definitely jaded by what they'd experienced. Were they really telling her everything they knew? "Who else should I talk to?"

Kevin merely shrugged and trotted on ahead of them.

But when they arrived at the ranch and James helped her down, he whispered, "Try Charlie Sumpter. He said he called the border patrol on a pretty big group that came through his property last weekend. He hates them as much as we do, especially since his best friend was murdered by illegals."

"Last I heard, that hadn't been proven."

"The poor guy had just called to say he'd stumbled upon a group of Mexicans and was found dead an hour later. Draw your own conclusions."

Was that the start of all this? She couldn't picture

Charlie as dangerous, but she knew how he felt about UDAs, particularly after Byron Gifford's murder six months ago.

Leonard Taylor's trailer looked empty and probably was. It was midafternoon. Chances were he was at work.

Roderick stood on the landing and leaned over the railing to see through the kitchen window.

A cat jumped onto the counter, startling him, but that seemed to be the only movement—other than the dog chained up under a tree in a fenced-off section of yard. He'd been barking ever since Rod drove up.

"Shut up already," Rod grumbled when the dog kept at it, and walked around to the back. He had no right to snoop, but he wasn't a cop, and that allowed him a little leeway. That leeway could get him into trouble, and did on occasion, but Milt was pretty good about bailing him out of jams. Rod was beginning to rely on it.

"Mr. Taylor? Anyone home?" He knocked at the back door, then tried the knob. Open. Taylor didn't have much worth stealing and, after losing his family, he obviously didn't care enough about what was left to bother protecting it.

From the looks of the trailer, anything of value had already been carted off by Mrs. Taylor. Leonard had an old TV he'd probably pulled out of some landfill, and a recliner that could've come from the same place. The rest of the furniture was gone. Pictures had been stripped from the walls, and area rugs had been taken off the floors, which was easy to tell because of the rectangles of cleaner carpet beneath. Instead of feeding the cat in a bowl, someone had simply ripped open an entire bag of the dried stuff and left it spilling out on the linoleum.

"Wow, buddy. You're living in a world of hurt." Rod picked his way through the mess. He was particularly interested in finding the "arsenal" Patrick had mentioned. He'd bet Mrs. Taylor hadn't taken her husband's guns.

Turned out he was right. In one bedroom wallpapered with pink roses—what had most likely been one of the daughters' rooms—Rod found a Czech .32-caliber pistol, a Rohm .22-caliber revolver, an F.I.E. model A27 .25-caliber pistol and a Ruger .22-caliber rifle sitting on the top shelf of the closet.

If Leonard was becoming as dangerous as it seemed, his wife had been smart to take the kids and get out.

After using his cell phone to snap a picture, Rod moved into the master bedroom. There, he saw a mattress lying on the floor, with clothes piled along the periphery. Even the shower was missing its curtain, but there was enough hair in the tub to suggest Leonard was using it.

"Pathetic." With a grimace, he turned away from the filthy bathroom. He needed to leave. It was getting late enough that Leonard could show up at any moment—and he wasn't in a good mental state. But then a splash of red caught Rod's eye. Something was taped to the back of the bedroom door.

Closing it the rest of the way, Rod pulled out his cell phone again. He had to take a photograph of this. Chief St. Claire was staring back at him from a newspaper clipping. The headline below read Sophia St. Claire Named Chief of Police. Her lips were curved in a gorgeous smile. But that wasn't why he wanted to record what he'd found. Leonard or someone else had written with a red marker across her face: *Die, Bitch!*

* * *

It was time for Rod Guerrero to realize he couldn't flout her authority simply because she was a woman.

Sophia thought about calling one of her officers in for backup. She would've felt more comfortable with re-inforcements, even if they consisted of a twenty-three-year-old man who was probably a bit too gentle to be in law enforcement and a thirty-nine-year-old who'd come to the job later in life and was too heavy to run or fight. But, for some reason, it was important to her that she be able to solve this problem all by herself. He'd never respect her if she didn't. She'd never be able to respect herself, either, because this went deeper than just a pissing con-test between her and an old classmate. She had to handle this little problem as decisively as any man. Maybe she didn't have Rod's brawn. But she had a brain, and she was going to use it to insure that she gained possession of the evidence he'd taken. If he refused to give it to her, she'd arrest him, but she hoped it wouldn't go that way.

There was only one small problem. While she was getting gas, she'd run into Stuart Dunlap, who'd been in the foulest mood she'd ever seen. He was complaining that his father had coaxed Rod ("the dirty bastard") back to Bordertown for no good reason except that he'd been obsessed with him ever since Rod had become a Navy SEAL.

Stuart's jealousy didn't matter to Sophia. She didn't like Stu all that much, and she didn't feel sorry for him, either. He'd been handed just about everything and seemed to expect the gravy train to go on forever. But learning that Rod had once been a SEAL was definitely a concern. Was she crazy for standing up to him?

Maybe. But she didn't really have a choice. As the chief

of police, she was in charge of an important investigation, and she couldn't lose control of it. Rod had taken something from the crime scene, essentially breaking the law, and he'd disarmed her and resisted arrest.

It was after midnight as she entered the parking lot of the Mother Lode Motel and paused in front of the small office. A vacancy sign glowed in the window, but the lights were off and the front desk was empty. Bordertown didn't have that many visitors, especially in the height of summer. Leland Jennings lived with his widowed mother. They went to bed every night around ten and came out of their small apartment only if someone rang the buzzer. Sophia knew because she often cruised by to make sure Hillary Hawthorne, a wayward teenager with an insatiable craving for sex, wasn't turning tricks here again.

Glad she wouldn't have a witness after what he'd done to her in front of Debbie Berke this morning—she drove through the empty lot and parked a few spaces from Rod's Hummer. Then she got her Taser gun and her battering ram and climbed out of the cruiser. She had to have some way to enforce her demands. She knew he wasn't going to simply give her what he'd found unless he had to, just as she knew she'd never shoot him, so there was no point in drawing a gun. A Taser was the only thing that might provide the force she needed without doing permanent damage.

She'd used it before—once to break up a fight and once to take down a guy who was so high on PCP he was a danger to everyone around him. She was very aware that for a man of Rod's age and in his physical condition, she'd be lucky if the effects lasted ten seconds.

But she was as ready as she'd ever be. Except for a racing heart and an abundance of nerves.

Calm down. You can do this. It's textbook police work.

The battering ram was heavy, but she'd used it before and knew she could do it. The door would break and the city would have to pay to fix it, but she wasn't about to announce her presence by knocking on the door. He'd refuse to open it. Then she'd be trying to get in while he was up and fully alert.

She'd have a much better chance of a successful arrest if she could confront him without that door between them….

Adjusting her bulletproof vest to make it as comfortable as possible, she situated herself outside the door, where she stood for several seconds, listening for movement. There wasn't a single sound. Even the TV was off. He had to be sleeping.

This was it. Taking a deep breath, she studied the lock. She had to hit it directly and with as much power as possible. If it didn't pop open on the first blow—

She didn't want to think about what might happen then.

Willing herself to remain calm and strong, she began to count. *One…two…three…* Then, putting everything she had into it, she swung the battering ram, using her body weight to lend it more power.

"Police! Open up!" she shouted, but her words were drowned out by splintering wood as the door crashed against the inside wall.

She was in. She almost couldn't believe it. Dropping the ram, she fumbled for her Taser gun and managed to aim it in the direction of the bed, where the lights from the parking lot revealed a surprised and disheveled Rod, pushing himself into a sitting position.

"Freeze! I'm here to collect the evidence you took from

my crime scene. Provide it and I'll forget what you did this morning. But if you don't..."

He didn't give her time to finish. Lunging for her, he grabbed her left hand, trying to get to the Taser in her right.

Before he could disarm her as he had earlier, she used a move she'd once learned in a self-defense class and succeeded in breaking his hold—but only because he wasn't completely awake and the tangle of sheets around his lower half hampered his movements. He kicked free of the bedding so he could come at her a second time, but the slight delay enabled her to regain her balance and her determination.

If he wouldn't cooperate, she had no choice but to insist. As he leaped out of bed, she pressed the button on her Taser.

The two probes shot out. They didn't need to come into direct contact with his skin. They merely had to land within a few inches for the electrical current to arc over. But, from his grunt, she was pretty sure she'd actually hit him.

The Taser affected only the muscles between the two probes. Rod jerked as he should have but seemed intent on fighting through the shock. She must not have hit him very effectively. And no doubt he knew that if he could get hold of her it would all be over.

She had to shock him again. But she didn't have the seconds she needed to reload. Pressing the handheld portion of the gun to whatever part of him she could reach, which turned out to be his stomach since he was on his knees, she used the Taser like a stun gun.

The second jolt stopped him cold. Although she couldn't see him clearly in the dark, she could tell he was in pain.

He fell as he was getting off the bed and writhed on the floor at her feet.

"Hold still or I'll shock you again!"

He stopped moving, but the fury that rolled off him in waves terrified her. She was tempted to hit him with a third jolt, just to make sure he wouldn't recover quickly enough to harm her when she cuffed him. She didn't really know him, after all. But she couldn't bring herself to do it. Seeing the results of what she'd already done made her cringe.

He asked for this, she reminded herself. She'd given him the chance to comply, provided a peaceful option.

But that didn't make her feel any better.

Hurrying to finish before he could move, she put the Taser on the dresser, pushed him onto his stomach and secured his hands behind his back.

Once the cuffs snapped into place, she was shaking but breathing a lot easier. Now she just needed to get him into her car. The prospect of jail time would convince him to hand over that evidence; she felt sure of it. But she wasn't sure how to go about getting him to the station. She couldn't pull him to his feet. He'd curled up and was too heavy. The motel was empty enough so the noise hadn't drawn anyone's attention. But that meant she couldn't ask anyone for assistance. And he hadn't yet regained control of his body.

"You gonna make it?" She tried to sound tough, but inside she was nervous. Tasers were a useful tool, one that helped her avoid lethal enforcement. She'd even been hit with a Taser when she was in training and knew they rarely caused lasting damage. But the publicity surrounding the cases that did go awry certainly came to mind....

When he didn't answer, she bent close to see for herself

and got a razor-sharp glare for her efforts. He was okay. She just needed to get him to the station and behind bars before she lost her nerve.

Using the threat of her Taser to make him move, she waved him to his feet. And that was when she realized she had another problem, one so apparent now that she couldn't believe she'd missed it before—despite the darkness and the adrenaline rush.

She'd expected to see a lot of bare skin. Most people didn't sleep fully clothed. But Rod wasn't even wearing boxers.

10

Sophia had to get him dressed, and she had to start with underwear. But she needed to find a pair, and that meant turning on the light and going through his luggage.

Roderick's jeans, shorts and T-shirts were neatly folded in a leather duffel bag sitting on the suitcase stand, his tennis shoes and suede flip-flops positioned directly beneath. A laptop sat on the nightstand, as if he'd set it aside just before bed.

As she sorted through his clothing, she could smell his fabric softener. If he washed his own clothes, and he probably did, he seemed to do a good job. But Roderick seemed to do a good job at everything. It was his military training, she supposed.

Had she been too impetuous when she rejected his offer of help? If so, it was too late to second-guess herself. She didn't need him. The FBI would be getting involved soon.

"Do you have a preference on what you'd like to wear *to jail?*" she asked.

He didn't answer. He was standing, but from the muscle that jumped in his cheek, he was angry enough to spit. And he didn't make any attempt to hide his nudity. There wasn't much he could do—not with his hands cuffed behind

his back—but he hardly seemed self-conscious about it.
Maybe he was taking some sort of perverse pleasure in
knowing she was discomfited by finding him this way.

It'd been a long time since Sophia had seen a body like
his. Actually, she'd never seen one quite so toned. Starkey hadn't been flabby, but his build was bulkier, much
less sculpted. His skin wasn't as nice, either. Rod had
the smoothest, softest-looking skin she'd ever seen on a
man and only one tattoo—a rose with a ribbon that read
In Loving Memory on his chest. In an attempt to avoid
staring at a certain asset, she focused on his tattoo.

"Fine, if you don't have a preference, I'll pick," she said.
"I think you'd look nice in red." She selected a T-shirt and
the khaki shorts he'd had on earlier. Then she dug deeper,
for underclothes. His boxers were in the bottom of the
bag.

She pulled out a pair that had a pattern of four-leaf clo-
vers and managed a smile. "Look. Lucky underwear."

Resentment simmered in his eyes, making her hesitant
to move close enough to dress him.

"You're going to cooperate with me while I help you get
these on, aren't you?" she asked. "Because I don't want
to have to shock you again."

That was true. She hadn't wanted to shock him the first
time. If only he'd agreed to turn over the evidence, this
would've gone down very differently.

Again, he didn't respond, but his expression wasn't
promising docile cooperation.

"Are you unable to speak?"

He finally broke his silence. "I'm afraid of what might
come out of my mouth."

Apparently, all his faculties had returned. "I don't think

it's fair to hold a grudge over this," she said. "I gave you a choice. And I'm just doing my job."

"*Excuse me?* Finding the man who's been killing people in the desert would be doing your job. This is a waste of time and effort. This is about assuaging your wounded pride!"

"You took something from the crime scene."

"Which I'm having analyzed in hopes of creating a DNA profile."

So it *wasn't* a rock…

"I was going to share the results with you," he added.

"And I was supposed to take that on faith?"

"But now that you've shot me with that damn thing," he went on, as if she hadn't spoken, "you can kiss my ass."

To give him what privacy she could, she kept her eyes averted. "I don't think you want to take that attitude."

"Or what? You'll shoot me with your Glock next time?"

"Maybe."

He shook his head. "You're nuts."

Her actions had seemed rational enough *before* she'd busted into his room. Why was she suddenly wishing she hadn't?

His nudity was part of it. Having his "equipment" staring her in the face made this so uncomfortable—far worse than a run-of-the-mill arrest.

Leave it to someone like Roderick to sleep nude. Everything about him was edgier, riskier, *wilder*.

"What did you take from my crime scene?" she demanded.

"A cigarette butt, okay? I took a cigarette butt, hoping there might be some of the killer's DNA."

She'd missed that? How? After she'd hung up with the

mayor and Lindstrom, she'd done a grid search. But she'd been upset, overwhelmed and distracted by the mayor's call. She'd also been working fast, hoping to finish before Lindstrom arrived. She'd felt lucky to have the shell casings and hadn't expected to find anything else. In the past, the killer had been too smart to leave that kind of evidence behind.

Were the long hours and the pressure starting to get to her? She was afraid they were....

It became harder and harder not to look south. The more Sophia told herself not to, the more that particular part of Rod's anatomy acted like a high-powered magnet. "You shouldn't have interfered," she said.

"I told you I was here to *help* you. That's not interfering!"

She couldn't stop herself; she glanced down. She quickly brought her gaze back up, but she'd seen enough to make her blush. "And I told you I didn't want your help. That's my decision to make. A civilian can't just insert himself into a police investigation. I was in the right."

"We'll see."

"Fine. We'll see." Shoving aside the exhaustion that threatened, and the disappointment and frustration she felt at missing evidence as important as a cigarette butt, she picked up the Taser and took a step toward him, carrying his underwear. She had to get him dressed before he noticed the extent of her distraction.

He didn't move as she approached, didn't flinch, but the way he ground out his next words told her he was clenching his jaw. "You shoot me with that thing again and I swear—"

"You do anything, anything at *all* to endanger me, and I *will* shoot you again," she cut in. "Do you understand?"

He snapped his teeth at her, which scared her. But she was so reluctant to shoot him that she merely jumped back and didn't fire.

"A little spooked?" he taunted.

"I don't know what you're capable of."

"That's right. And you'd better hope you never learn."

She lifted the Taser, threatening him.

"Do it."

"Do you really want this to go down the hard way?" she asked, angry herself now. "You asked for this when you took my gun, ignored my commands, refused to do the lawful thing. So if you really want more, I'll accommodate you."

He glared at her.

"Which is it?"

"Just get me dressed." He suddenly sounded bored. "I'm not going to touch you. Now that I know you need to be relieved of duty, I'll let the higher-ups take care of the problem."

He thought *she* was the problem? "You believe you can get me fired?"

"I plan to make it my life's mission."

"Then you'll have to get in line." She held his underwear so he could step into them, but it was difficult to appear dignified when pulling them up meant stretching the elastic waist over certain parts.

"For the record, I never dreamed you'd be naked," she mumbled.

"For the record, I consider this assault."

"You broke the law. Now it's my job to arrest you."

"I don't give a shit about your job."

His anger was chilling. She felt as if she had the

Tasmanian Devil of cartoon fame in handcuffs—or some other dangerous and unpredictable creature it was safer to avoid.

"If you play by the rules, we'll get through this just fine." Sophia helped him into his shorts and tossed his flip-flops at his feet. She wasn't about to uncuff him long enough to let him don his shirt. She figured she'd bring it with her and give it to him once he was behind bars.

"After you," she said with exaggerated courtesy, and waved toward the door.

The jail consisted of two cells at the back of the police station. Sophia generally used them for drunken and disorderly lockups. Rarely did she have to worry about incarcerating a serious criminal. The border patrol took care of any illegal aliens causing problems, ATF and the DEA handled a large percentage of the drug- and gun-trafficking infractions and the county dealt with the rest. Until the murders, which fell inside city limits, her job was mostly about keeping the peace.

Fortunately, she'd had Officer Joe Fitzer scrub down the cells because one Roger Pasley had vomited there on Saturday night. She couldn't imagine how someone as meticulous about his laundry as Rod would've reacted to the stench. He didn't seem too happy as it was, especially when the door clanged shut behind him.

"You have one call. Would you like to use it?" she asked as she removed his handcuffs and handed him the red shirt through the bars.

He cocked an eyebrow at her. "Who do you think I'd be able to reach at this hour?"

"I guess it can wait till morning, then." Planning to work in her office for an hour before heading out on patrol, so she'd have some time to collect herself, she started toward the front. She hadn't made it to the door when Rod spoke behind her.

"Leonard Taylor has your picture in his bedroom with the words *Die, Bitch!* written across your face. Did you know that?"

She didn't. She'd been out to Leonard's place, had tried to talk to him about the murders, but he'd ordered her off his property. And because she didn't have a search warrant and couldn't get one without physical evidence linking him to the crime, she'd had no choice but to respect his wishes. She'd been hoping to come up with the necessary evidence ever since—was still hopeful, especially now that she'd found those shell casings—but the judge who issued search warrants was Leonard's uncle, so she needed a compelling reason.

She rubbed her face. Judging by the black on her fingertips, she'd smeared her mascara. "That doesn't surprise me." What *did* surprise her was that Roderick knew it. He'd been in town for one day and had already visited Leonard's place? He worked fast….

"I guess you aren't as popular as you were in high school," he said, dropping onto his cot.

"I'm not running for class president." She tried to laugh it off, but he wasn't finished.

"Too bad Daddy's money won't be able to fix this."

He thought he knew her and her situation. But he had no clue. He was judging her based on facts and impressions that were fourteen years old.

"Your opinion of me is pretty smug, isn't it?" she asked.

"You're saying I'm wrong?"

"I'm saying if you believe you're the only one who's ever suffered, you need to take a look around."

"Meaning I should take a look at *you?* The pretty little rich girl who's always had everything?"

"*Rich* girl? Obviously, you haven't bothered to keep up. My father's dead, Rod. He lost his business the year after you left, became an alcoholic and moved to Phoenix. He was basically homeless—until he was struck by a car while crossing the freeway. My mother couldn't tolerate the loss of status that went along with the bankruptcy, so she'd already divorced him—which is part of the reason he never recovered—and immediately remarried some guy she met online. Her new guy had money, still does. Gary O'Conner bought the feed store and moved to town the same winter. He put a roof over my head and food on the table, but…"

She stopped talking. She'd never told anyone this. Except her mother. And Starkey.

"But…" he prompted.

Somehow it was more important to humble Rod than it was to guard her secret. "He felt I owed him a few liberties for his generosity."

"What kind of liberties?"

He sounded much less confident. She'd succeeded in surprising him. And although part of her balked at stating what she'd kept to herself for so long—what felt dirty and shameful and better off forgotten—another part was dying to pour it all out and put him in his place.

"Let's just say I had to make sure I was never alone with him. I was so scared he'd come into my room late at night that I couldn't sleep. When I started losing weight, ten pounds and then twenty, my mother said I was becoming anorexic in my attempt to compete with the other girls at school." She laughed, still incredulous that her mother could live in such denial. "I'd tried to tell her what was happening, but she wouldn't believe me. She'd salvaged her image and found another meal ticket. She wasn't about to let go of Gary and end up with nothing."

His expression was inscrutable. "So what'd you do?"

She curled her fingernails into her palms, hoping the physical pain would diminish the crushing sensation in her chest. "What you did. I moved out."

He propped his head on his arms, but he was far from relaxed. "That's when you moved in with Starkey?"

"That's when. But, as it turned out, his place wasn't such a safe haven."

"He's a member of the Hells Angels. Was then, too. You didn't know that?"

"I knew it. His reputation and his contacts were what protected me from Gary."

"And once you no longer needed his protection?"

"I didn't use him, if that's what you're implying. At the time I thought I was in love with him, enough to give up a regular law-abiding life. But once I learned the kind of sacrifices that would require, I realized it was impossible for me and struck out on my own. So forgive me if I'm not willing to offer you the pity you think you deserve," she said and walked out.

Pity? That was the *last* thing Rod wanted. But he could see how Sophia might've misinterpreted his words and actions. He'd been pretty hard on her since he'd come back. Maybe *too* hard.

Muttering a curse, he sat up. He was usually better at remaining objective, at looking beyond preconceived notions in order to evaluate a situation. But he'd been too prejudiced against Sophia to do that. His body language, maybe even his tone of voice, had conveyed that he didn't like or respect her. So how could he have expected her to react any more positively than she had?

Given their history, he probably would've rejected his help, too.

Remembering her embarrassment as she tried to get him into his boxers, he felt the sudden urge to laugh. She'd busted into his room with her cop tools, feeling she finally had the advantage—and got a little more than she'd bargained for.

Burying his face in his hands, he stopped laughing and sighed. Why had he wasted his time behaving in such a counterproductive manner?

Because he'd been attempting to assuage his pride, which was what he'd accused *her* of doing, although the damage to her pride had been a lot more recent.

They were stupid to fight each other. That only aided and abetted whoever was behind the murders—and Sophia's political enemies—which could be one and the same. He didn't want to side with Leonard, a man who'd used the threat of deportation to force a woman to have sex with him, did he? And if that wasn't enough, Sophia's picture on the back of his bedroom door proved conclusively that Leonard was a prick.

He stood. "Hey! Sophia!"

Had she left? Since he hadn't seen another officer, he figured she was working all night, but maybe she'd gone out.

She hadn't. Not yet, anyway. She appeared a few seconds later, holding a cup of coffee. "What do you need?"

"Why are you still here?"

"I traded Grant for graveyard this week, just in case there are any more shootings. Why are *you* still here?"

When he gave her a dirty look, she smiled sweetly. "Oh, I forgot. You interfered with my investigation. Then you refused to turn over the evidence. And now you're under arrest."

He studied her for a few seconds. "You did this because I embarrassed you."

"I did it because you gave me no other choice."

Leaning a shoulder against the bars, he tried to look as innocent as possible. "Do you really want to keep fighting me instead of your enemies?"

"I thought you *were* one of my enemies." She took a sip of coffee. "I don't have many friends whose life mission is to get me fired."

"You'd just shocked me with a Taser when I said that."

Her eyebrows went up. "You're telling me you didn't mean it?"

Noting her skepticism, he scratched his arm. "Not entirely."

"How does that improve our situation?"

"I'm wondering why we can't be professional allies. You need some help. I'm here to provide it."

"But I'm not interested in having you involved. I thought I made that clear. The FBI is forming a task force. I think we can handle it."

He tried to conceal his annoyance. "Why turn any help away? You're being stubborn and illogical."

She took another sip of coffee. "Sticks and stones."

"Give me one good reason we can't work together."

"Just *one?*"

"That's all I ask."

A slight smile curved her lips. "Well…it could get uncomfortable."

"How?

"I've seen you naked, remember?"

Was she flirting with him? If this had come from any other woman, he would've taken that for granted. But not Sophia.

What was she up to now? He had no idea, but he was intrigued enough to find out. "We could always even the score."

"Meaning…"

Damn, she had pretty eyes. He didn't trust the sultry note in her voice, but he felt a flicker of excitement all the same. "You could take off your clothes—give me the same opportunity."

She made a show of considering it. "And this would benefit me how?"

"I wouldn't want you to be the only one who's embarrassed when we run into each other."

"So you'd be doing me a favor."

He pretended to think about it and eventually nodded. "Basically."

"Thoughtful of you." Her mouth quirked, drawing his attention to lips that looked even softer than they had in high school.

"Contrary to what you probably believe, I'm a nice guy," he said.

She ran her thumb over the handle of her coffee cup. "Nice enough to talk me out of my clothes."

"Nice enough to make you *glad* you lost them." He was teasing, but she definitely had his attention. "Want me to prove it?"

"Why not? We could do it right there." She pointed

at the cot in his cell. "Fulfill all my captor-captive fantasies."

He let his gaze sweep over her. "You want to get your handcuffs?"

"We're alone. Who'd know?"

"*I'd* certainly never tell." He produced the crooked smile that seemed to work so well with women.

"Of course you wouldn't. At least, not until morning, when you'd use my, shall we say, poor judgment to get me fired." She straightened triumphantly, as if she'd called his bluff.

Bringing a hand to his chest, he scowled. "You have so little faith in me. We're old friends, remember?"

She laughed. "Hardly! You scared the hell out of me back then."

"I scare you now, too."

"No, you don't."

But she was nervous; he could sense it. "If you prefer, *I'll* be the one in handcuffs."

"You're such a gentleman. But if you think I'll make it that easy for you to get revenge, you're crazy."

When he'd jumped into this conversation, he'd merely been curious. And playful. But he wasn't feeling so playful anymore. As much as he didn't want to admit it, he was starting to feel aroused. Apparently, things in Bordertown hadn't changed as much as he wished. He still thought Sophia was beautiful. And, more than ever, he wanted her to want him. Maybe he believed that would make up for the brutal rejection he'd suffered at her hands fourteen years ago.

"You're assuming I'd hurt you if you gave me the chance."

"You would. And you'd enjoy doing it."

And yet she was the one who'd changed the tone of their conversation, their relationship, from what it had been moments before. "You're tempted."

Her chest rose as she took a deep breath. It was as if he could see the weight she usually carried settling back on her shoulders. "Not really."

That was a lie. She was as intrigued by the idea as he was or she wouldn't have continued flirting with him.

"There's no reason for us to be at each other's throats," he said. "There are bigger battles to fight."

"That's true."

"So…"

She set her coffee cup on a table that stood in the corner. "I'll make you a deal."

"I'm listening."

"I'll let you go, if…"

"If…" he repeated.

"You leave town tomorrow. For good."

Gripping the bars above his head, he leaned close. "That's not exactly the kind of deal I was hoping for."

She stepped up to him, her breasts just inches from his chest. "What if I agree to the handcuffs?"

As their eyes met, a powerful surge of sexual current arced between them, almost as strong as the shock Rod had felt from her Taser. It nearly knocked the wind out of him and, if the look on Sophia's face was any indication, it affected her the same way. "At this point, just imagining your body against mine would probably be enough motivation to get me to do anything you want."

Her tongue darted out to wet her lips. "So you'll leave town afterward?"

Was this real? An hour ago, she'd shot him, twice, with her Taser, and he'd wanted to wring her neck for it.

Now he had something far less violent in mind. "You're serious...."

Catching her bottom lip between her teeth, she worried it as if she was having difficulty deciding.

"Sophia?" His grip tightened on the bars. "What, exactly, are you offering me?"

Stepping out of reach, she pressed her fingers to her forehead. "Nothing. I...I don't know what I was thinking."

"It's not that hard to guess. You want to escape the pressure you've been under and forget all the terrible things that've happened—the controversy around your appointment, Leonard Taylor's anger, the murders. But you don't want it to come with any repercussions. That's why you want me to leave afterward."

"Maybe. But an escape like that always comes with repercussions."

"You don't trust me."

"I don't trust anyone."

Thinking of what she'd told him about her stepfather, he pictured the frightened girl she must've become. No wonder she'd reacted the way she had when he'd appeared at the crime scene. He'd plunged into an already tense situation as if he had every right to force her hand and, not unreasonably, she'd lashed out.

"How long has it been since you had a good night's sleep?" he asked.

She rubbed her eyes again. "I'm fine. It's just...late, and I'm getting punchy."

"Let me out of here so I can take you home."

"You don't have a car."

"We can use your car."

He didn't know if she would've gone for it or not. There

was no question that she wanted to check out of regular life for a while, ignore her responsibilities. She'd admitted as much. And since he was only in Bordertown temporarily, he thought he was the perfect candidate to become her partner in escape.

But she never got the chance to answer. At that moment, someone called out to her from the front.

"Sophia? Hello? Hey, where are you?"

The door separating the jail from the station swung open and Stuart Dunlap stuck his head through the gap.

11

Sophia felt her face flush hot. She hadn't done anything wrong, not yet, but she'd wanted to. She'd considered allowing Rod to deliver on his promises, imagined it. And that was bad enough.

Stuart glanced between them. "What's going on?"

"Nothing. I was just having a few words with my inmate." She retrieved her coffee cup and stepped toward the door. "What are you doing here?"

He didn't answer. Neither did he move. He was too busy glaring at Rod.

"Stuart?" she said.

He pulled his gaze away. But only briefly. "I ran into Half-pint Harris at the pool hall a few minutes ago. He told me he was driving by the motel earlier and saw you load a man into your backseat. I came by to make sure you were okay."

She saw no need to thank him; he wasn't really concerned about her welfare. He'd stopped by to see if that "man" was his hated half brother. But he couldn't gloat over Rod's incarceration as he'd probably planned, because he sensed that something was going on between them, and Stuart was nothing if not possessive, even though he didn't have any right to be.

"Don't worry about me," she said. "I can take care of myself."

He jerked his head toward Rod. "What'd he do to land himself in the cage?"

"That's none of your damn business." Rod stalked to the back of his cell and once again stretched out on his cot.

Sophia wished she hadn't gone to the trouble of arresting Rod. She'd been well within her rights. But doing it had required energy she didn't really possess. They'd both let what had happened in the past tempt them into creating a problem that didn't need to exist in the present.

"I caught him jaywalking," she said.

Stuart didn't seem amused by her flip remark. "Half-pint said he wasn't wearing a shirt."

"That's a crime around here?" Rod said.

"It is if you're messing with my girl," Stuart snapped.

Rod sat up. "Your *girl?*"

"I'm not his girl," Sophia said. "We're not having this conversation. Come on, Stuart. Let's get you out of here."

She tried to grab his arm, but he jerked free and approached the bars. "What are you doing in town, Rod? No one cares about you. You know that, don't you? You're not wanted here today any more than when you were born."

Rod sounded bored when he replied but Sophia knew his reaction hid a deep reservoir of feeling. "You can take that up with your father, *Stu*. He's the one who asked me to come."

"And you rushed back to town, hoping he'd finally accept you."

"Stuart, stop," Sophia said.

"He invited me to stay at the ranch. Did you know

that?" Rod covered a yawn. "Maybe I'll have to take him up on that offer, *brother*."

"Over my dead body!"

Rocking forward, Rod came to a sitting position. "I'd be more than happy to accommodate you."

"Are you threatening my life?" Stuart glanced at Sophia. "Did you hear that?"

Releasing a sigh filled with disgust, she pushed him toward the door. "It's time for you to leave."

He pulled out of her grasp. "The old man seems to think you might've turned into something."

Rod shrugged. "Considering the disappointment you've become, I don't blame him for hoping I'd make a better showing."

"You filthy spic!"

"That's enough!" Sophia attempted to step around Stuart, but he shoved her out of the way, knocking her cup to the floor, where it shattered.

Rod was on his feet and at the bars in a second. "I suggest you get out of here before you really piss me off."

"Or what?" Stuart taunted. "What's the big Navy SEAL going to do from in there?"

Removing the key to Rod's cell from her pocket, Sophia dangled it in front of Stuart's nose. "If you don't leave, I'll unlock the cage and we'll find out."

The surprise on Stuart's face told Sophia he hadn't expected her to take such a hard line. But this was *her* jail, and she wouldn't put up with him heckling a prisoner. Especially since Rod had had enough of that kind of abuse while growing up.

"What the hell, Sophia? You're taking *his* side?" Stuart complained.

She didn't care if he liked it or not. It was about time

someone in Bordertown took Rod's side. "He didn't start this. You did."

"This is screwed up, that's what it is," he said, and stomped out.

In the silence that followed, Rod didn't speak. He returned to his cot and glared at her as if he suddenly resented her as much as he had before. "I don't need you to stick up for me."

"You've made it abundantly clear that you don't need anyone." She unlocked the cell. "But since you've already sent my evidence to a lab, there's nothing to be gained by keeping you in here. I hope you've learned your lesson. Let's go."

His eyes shifted to the door. "Where?"

"I'm driving you back to the motel."

No response.

"Are you coming or not?" she asked.

"Will you be staying there with me?"

The shift from anger to lust knocked her off balance again. "No. Whatever insanity possessed me before is gone."

He came toward her with the restrained energy of someone who used only a fraction of his true strength. "Have you ever slept with my half brother?"

She scowled. She hadn't even been tempted, but she wasn't about to reveal that and create a challenge he couldn't resist. "Every weekend."

"You're lying."

"Either way, it's none of your business. I'm not getting involved in the family feud."

"We both want you. That means you're already involved."

We both want you. Those words made her heart pound

until she could feel every beat in her fingertips. On a very primal level, she wanted him, too. Somehow, the uncomfortable feeling he'd given her fourteen years ago had transformed into a powerful attraction.

"You don't want *me*," she clarified. "You want to punish Stuart and anyone else you blame for how miserable your life was when you lived here."

"And you're the weapon. Is that what you think?"

"That's what I think."

As he gazed down at her, she had to acknowledge that he was even more attractive up close.

"Poor beautiful Sophia," he murmured, and when she didn't pull away, he lowered his lips to hers.

Sophia told herself to stop him. This kiss wasn't motivated by anything as tender as his "beautiful" compliment sounded. Deeply angry, he was trying to see if he could get more than she'd give Stuart. And once she accommodated him, he'd no longer be interested. Chances were he'd brag about the conquest tomorrow.

She wouldn't allow him to make her look like a desperate idiot. She'd rather survive the rest of this difficult year without that kind of humiliation. But daring to kiss a wildly handsome man who was, in some ways, a stranger, made the experience all the more alluring.

"What, are you hoping Stuart will walk back in and see this?" she muttered against his warm lips.

"Hell, no. Then I'd have *no* chance of rounding first base."

He was teasing her; she could hear the humor in his voice, but there was enough underlying tension to let her know he was at least half-serious.

"You have no chance *now*," she said, but she didn't balk when he drew her up against him. She slid the fingers of the hand not holding the keys into his thick hair and closed her eyes as he parted her lips.

When he touched her tongue with his, she felt her knees go weak. This was a dangerous indulgence, but one that was too welcome to refuse. When was the last time she'd been kissed? It'd been more than a year—before she'd found out about Dick's underage lover. It seemed even longer because Dick's kiss couldn't compare to Rod's. The strength Rod held in check, the contours of his firm body, even the way he moved his lips, threatened to drown her in bone-melting desire….

Only when she accidentally dropped the keys and they clattered on the floor did she realize she was getting too carried away. Summoning what resistance she had left, she let go of him and, under the guise of reclaiming the keys, stepped back. "I'll take you back to your motel."

The pupils of his eyes had nearly swallowed the colored irises—and he'd lost the teasing quality of a moment earlier. "As long as you bring your handcuffs."

He shouldn't have touched her. He'd thought getting her to assent to his kiss would finally douse the hunger that'd been burning in his gut since he was fifteen. Instead, feeling Sophia's lips yield beneath his had whetted his appetite for deeper intimacy. He knew now that he wouldn't be satisfied until he'd made love to her. Maybe that was because he wanted to best his white half brothers, as she said, but she was also the culmination of his boyhood fantasies, the prize he'd been denied. And he was pretty sure if he could have her just once, he'd be able to close that terrible chapter of his life.

That alone was worth the trip to Bordertown. Worth facing Bruce, Patrick, even Stuart. Especially Stuart. If

Rod had his guess, Stuart hadn't been able to get anywhere with Sophia. Her reaction to him would've been very different if they'd been intimate.

"So will you let me help with the investigation?" he asked as she drove.

"Will I really hear from the governor if I don't?"

"It's a distinct possibility."

Her radio crackled; she turned down the volume. "So even if I say no, you won't leave."

"Nope."

"Great."

He pretended to be insulted. "That's harsh."

"You're surprised I'm not happy about it?"

"Confused. Now that we've made nice, I can't see why you'd be so eager to get rid of me. You seemed to like me well enough a few minutes ago. After the Taser part, of course. I liked you better after that part, too."

They entered the western section of town, which was Rod's favorite, even as a boy. "I like your body," she admitted. "I don't know about the rest of you."

She was trying to offend him, to put him off, so he merely smiled. "I can accept that."

"You're kidding," she said with a laugh. "Only a guy would be willing to settle for so little."

"I admire your honesty. Besides, I'm not asking for a commitment."

She stopped at a traffic light. "One night is enough to get me in trouble. I've made too many mistakes in my life already. I don't need you to be another one."

"You're looking at this too seriously. Starkey was a mistake. I'd be a…temporary fling. You wouldn't even have to take me home to meet your parents."

His words strengthened rather than lessened her resolve.

Before this moment, she hadn't actually thought it out, hadn't decided that she was searching for the love of her life. But his offer made her realize that she was tired of all the Mr. Wrongs and, as much as she longed for an all-consuming escape, she wasn't really interested in a cheap fling. She wanted to find someone she *could* bring home to her parents—if she had the type of relationship with her parents where that would be expected, of course. "Thanks for the offer, but…I'm not sleeping with you."

"We'll see," he said with a shrug.

"*That's* your response?" she asked, incredulous.

He conjured up an innocent expression. "You don't like it?"

"You don't find it a bit cocky?"

"We're being honest, remember?" He motioned toward the light. "It's green."

"Got it," she grumbled, and accelerated.

"Living in a small town can make you a little sex-starved," he said.

She turned the radio down even further. "How do you know I'm sex-starved?"

"Process of elimination. You're not married. And you don't have a boyfriend. What's a girl like you supposed to do?"

"Just because I don't have a husband or boyfriend, doesn't mean I'm sex-starved."

"It's not as if you can take care of that kind of craving via a casual encounter. The chief of police has to protect her reputation."

She smiled. "*Now* you're starting to get it."

"No one would have to know about me. Provided we can get the door you broke to stay closed, that is," he added.

"The door's fixed. I called Leland after I booked you, told him what happened. I didn't want to be responsible if your stuff got stolen. So he took the lock off the laundry room door."

"Leland's the manager?"

"You never knew him?"

"No, but it's nice of him to accommodate us. That means we'll have all the privacy we could want."

"Until tomorrow, when you tell everyone what we did." He began to interrupt, but she wouldn't let him. "I can't imagine you'd really keep your mouth shut—not when you have such good reasons for wanting others, like Stuart, to find out."

He wouldn't do that in a million years, but she didn't know, did she? "That really wounds me."

"Yeah, well, even if you don't tell, there's no such thing as privacy in Bordertown. You, of all people, should understand that." She turned into the Mother Lode and stopped in front of his unit. "Besides, we have a killer to track down, which means we can't afford any personal involvement. Getting the bad guy has to come first."

"Can't you wait until tomorrow to make me a coworker?"

"Nope. You wanted in, right?"

"Is this where you start talking about ethics?"

"I'm pretty sure we've been talking about ethics all along but, just to clarify, we can't get involved."

"Damn it! And here I was, hoping to make a sex tape."

She rolled her eyes. "You really know how to break down a girl's defenses."

"I try."

"Indiscriminately?"

"Sometimes."

Letting the engine idle, she gave him a wry smile. "Forgetting sex for a moment, what lab has that cigarette butt?"

"One in San Diego. They're reputable. If there's any DNA, they'll find it."

"And you'll share the profile with me as soon as you have it."

"Of course. I already told you I would."

"Wonderful. It's been interesting. Have a good night."

He didn't get out. He'd finished teasing her about going inside with him, but he had other questions. "What does your gut say?" he asked. "Is it Leonard? Is he killing people in an attempt to get back at the woman who told on him for forcing her to have sex?"

"That's my best guess. I suppose it could be a rogue border patrol agent or a disgruntled rancher—Charlie Sumpter comes to mind. But I've found no proof of either."

"I've never met Leonard, but...his trailer looked like shit and didn't smell much better. Seems he's had a lot in his life go bad lately. That could cause the mildest of men to snap."

"Exactly. Although, to be fair, his marriage was on the rocks before I ever learned about Rosita Flores. It was just a matter of time."

"That's the Mexican woman's name? Rosita?"

"Yes."

"How old was she?"

"Barely eighteen."

He remembered his father telling him about Sophia's

former boyfriend. "That must've sounded a bit too familiar."

She sobered instantly. "What are you talking about?"

"I'm saying he was in a position of authority, and he took advantage of that with a teenager, like the preacher who used to be your boyfriend."

"Who told you about Dick?"

"Bruce."

"You mean your father."

"Bruce," he repeated.

"Yeah, well, next time I see him I'll have to thank him for airing my dirty laundry."

"He likes you. He's hoping you'll marry Stuart."

This evoked an incredulous laugh. "There's *no* chance of that."

"You're sure? He'll be a wealthy man someday."

She glared at him, obviously upset by the implication that she could be that shallow. "Get out."

"One more question. What did the preacher have to attract you that Stuart doesn't?"

At first, he figured she wasn't going to answer, but she surprised him. "I thought he had a conscience, for one," she said. "He was religious, the opposite of Starkey. I suppose I thought the grass would be greener on the other side, as the saying goes."

"But he cheated on you and broke your heart."

"That pretty much sums it up. Thanks for the recap."

"I guess what I really want to know is if you're over it."

She didn't regret losing Dick, didn't want him back. But that experience had certainly left its mark. "I'm getting there."

"You're dating again?"

"I've gone out a few times. Why?"

"Just curious."

"About my love life?"

"I've been wondering if that kiss in the cell was your first since the preacher."

"Does it matter?"

"If the answer is yes, you've been keeping yourself on a pretty tight leash."

"It's a small town. I don't have a lot of options, as you've mentioned."

"Not a lot of *discreet* options," he clarified. "But there's one."

"I'll keep that in mind," she said with a laugh.

He opened the door. "Tell me something."

She tucked her hair behind her ears. "What?"

"Did your stepfather ever get away with…you know… anything?" The color drained from her face, which made Rod's muscles tense. "Because if he did, I'm going to break his jaw."

She frowned. "Let me save you the trouble. He didn't get away with anything. I wouldn't let him."

Was it true? Or was it another defense mechanism— like the one that kicked in whenever someone asked him about the Dunlaps? *I don't care about them…. I hope I never see my father again…. I don't have a father….*

"Can I break his jaw for trying?"

He expected her to tell him no, for her mother's sake if not for any other reason. But when he saw tears in her eyes, he realized just how alone she must've felt in those days. And just how tired and battle weary she was right now.

Clearing her throat, she glanced away. "That's enough catching up for one night. I've got to go."

He nearly reached over to squeeze her hand. But he didn't want her to think he pitied her. He knew from experience that pity was worse than contempt or anything else. So he got out and let her leave.

12

Sophia wasn't sure why she'd told Rod about her step-father. Except for Starkey and her mother, *no one* knew. Even her brother, Tyler, who would only feel too guilty for not being there to protect her. And it wasn't as if she could go to her real father. After the divorce, he'd been on the verge of a complete meltdown; she couldn't break his heart with something like this.

So why had she exposed the truth to *Rod Guerrero?* And why did the past seem to be so present tonight? She'd mostly forgotten that terrible year and a half, hadn't she? Of course she had. She and her stepfather were now on speaking terms. When she attended holiday gatherings at her mother's place, they were polite to each other. They'd never be close, but she had no business dredging up the past when they'd all moved on. The fact that she felt the need to do so didn't make sense.

But her reaction to Rod didn't make sense, either. So what if he was good-looking? She'd known other good-looking men who didn't affect her in the same way. Was she drawn to him because he could so easily identify with her pain? Because they were both struggling to overcome an earlier period in their lives that dealt with this town and its people? Or because she hoped for his understanding, maybe even his forgiveness, for standing him up at such a vulnerable age, when he'd already been going through so much?

Maybe it was a mixture…

Wrapped up in her thoughts and the lingering memory of Rod's kiss, she almost didn't notice the pickup parked behind the Mexican restaurant across the street. Even after she spotted it, she didn't think much about it until the headlights came on. Then she realized that someone was inside, and got the strangest feeling that whoever it was had been watching her. She also got the impression he—or they—didn't mind if she knew it.

Pulling a U-turn, she swung around to see if it was Stuart. It hadn't looked like his truck, but she'd just caught a glimpse of the front grille before turning. And watching her like that was something he might do, especially if he was still angry at her for siding with Rod at the jail.

Once, when she'd gone over to Starkey's to pick up Rafe, she'd come out to find Rod's half brother sitting in his vehicle as if he'd followed her there. When she stopped to ask what he was doing, he'd said he was in the area to see a friend who lived nearby. But the only person Stuart knew who lived that close to Starkey was Ellen Broomsfield—someone else they'd gone to high school with. Sophia had never known Stuart to hang out with Ellen, or even be kind to her. Ellen weighed at least three hundred and fifty pounds and was virtually a recluse. A friend like that would be an embarrassment to Stuart. Sophia couldn't imagine him visiting her.

Still, that incident hadn't really alarmed her. Not the way this one did. The earlier one had happened in the light of day and before she'd known they had a killer in their midst. There was also the fact that she hadn't been tempted to stay and take off her clothes for Starkey, so it hadn't felt like such an invasion of privacy.

What if she'd decided to spend a few hours at the motel? She wouldn't have wanted Stuart or anyone else to know about it. Although she didn't plan on getting intimate with Rod, she wanted to feel as if she *could* make that decision without someone creeping around behind her, taking notes—whether she was on duty or not. Because she was always on duty. There was so much responsibility involved in being chief of police, her private and professional lives had merged. There wasn't any other way to live if you were a small-town cop.

Red taillights up ahead told her she was closing in on the vehicle she'd spotted. But if the driver knew she was behind him, he didn't seem concerned. He appeared to be going too fast, and she was pretty sure he'd just run a red light.

Hoping this was merely a random DUI, she flipped on her flashers and checked for oncoming traffic before charging through the same intersection.

Whoever it was, it wasn't Stuart. The truck was too old and dented. The Dunlaps prided themselves on having money and made a point of showing it. And the person behind the wheel was wearing a cowboy hat. If Stuart ever wore a hat, it was a baseball cap.

Thanks to the driver's speed, she didn't catch up with him until the town's buildings had fallen away to desert. Even then, he didn't pull over.

Once she drew close enough to see the license plate, she put the number in her computer to get the DMV information and found that the truck was registered to a Dwight Smith.

It wasn't a name she recognized....

In case Dwight was too drunk to notice the red and blue lights behind him, she turned on her siren and came right up on his bumper.

Finally the driver slowed and pulled onto the shoulder.

They were so far from Bordertown, Sophia couldn't see anything that wasn't in the direct beam of her headlights, which made her uneasy. But she had a job to do. Grabbing her flashlight with her left hand, she kept her right on the handle of her gun as she cautiously approached the truck.

"Step out of the car and put your hands up," she called out.

"Somethin' wrong, *Chief?*"

Sophia had yet to see the driver's face, but she knew that voice. This wasn't Dwight Smith. It was Leonard Taylor. He'd lowered his window, but he wasn't getting out, as she'd asked.

"I said to step out of the vehicle."

The door still didn't open. "Have I done somethin' wrong?"

"Get out!"

Making sure she heard his exaggerated sigh, he opened a door rusty enough to squeal on its hinges. "Is this really necessary?"

She ignored his irritation—and his question. "Where'd you get this truck?"

The salt-and-pepper goatee he'd grown since quitting the force strengthened his resemblance to Kenny Rogers. They had the same build, were probably about the same size and had similar blue eyes and tanned faces. Leonard wasn't unattractive; it was what he harbored inside that Sophia didn't like.

"This is a company vehicle, provided by my employer. Name's Dwight Smith. But you already know that, don't you? You had plenty of time to look it up. Standard procedure and all."

"He doesn't mind if you drive it for personal use?"

"He knows I don't have a choice. Lorna took the car when she left."

The accusation in those words suggested he blamed her for his wife's actions. But that came as no surprise. Sophia already knew he blamed her for everything.

"You abused your power and cheated on your wife, Leonard." Which, rumor had it, wasn't the first time he'd stepped out. He liked the attention the uniform brought him. He'd even hit on her once or twice when they'd started working together. "Why not do the right thing and take responsibility for your actions?"

"That's easy for you to say. It's not as if you'd ever be tempted to have sex with anyone. You're the ice queen." He lowered his voice. "You're probably so frigid you wouldn't know what to do with a cock if—"

"That's enough," she snapped. But he didn't back off. He moved closer.

"No, it's not. It's not nearly enough. You think you're such a ballbuster. That you don't have to worry about your own secrets getting out. But I'm here to tell you that no one's secrets are safe in Bordertown, not even yours."

"What are you talking about?"

"I'm talking about the reason you hate men."

"You know nothing about me!"

"I know your stepdaddy spent more time diddling you than he did your mother. That's something, isn't it?"

Sophia opened her mouth to deny it but nothing came out. It felt as if he'd been doing more than following her and watching her; it felt as if he'd been listening to every word she said.

"Your mother came to me once," he explained with a victorious smile. "Crying."

So Anne *had* heard when Sophia tried to tell her what was happening. And, on some level, she'd believed it. But if that was the case, why hadn't she done anything?

Her mother's refusal to protect her hurt more than the memory of the instances, before Sophia had turned to Starkey, when her stepfather had pressed her to let him touch her. She'd always resisted, but his attempt alone made her feel dirty.

"You expect me to believe my mother sought *you* out?" she said.

"It's true."

But if Leonard was as sure of that as he pretended, he wouldn't be telling her. He'd be spreading it all over town, twisting key parts of the story to make it appear that *she'd* seduced Gary, or at least actively participated in an inappropriate relationship. If he was following her around, heckling her, he suspected but didn't *know*. Which meant that whatever her mother had told him left room for doubt.

Acting as indifferent as she could, she slipped her gun back in its holster. "That's crazy. Even if my mother believed I was sleeping with her husband, she'd never turn to *you*."

"She actually came to talk to Chief Bernstein, but I happened to be the only one at the station. And she was in desperate need of advice. She wanted me to tell her, given my extensive background in police work, whether I'd ever encountered a situation where a teenage girl had falsely accused a stepfather of molestation. She thought you might be lying to get attention or to get rid of Gary." He lowered his voice almost to a whisper. "But you weren't lying, were you?"

How could her mother have betrayed her in this way as well as all the others? How could she have been that selfish?

It would be foolish to react to the throbbing ache inside her. At least, right now. Straightening her spine, she poured every ounce of energy into a performance she hoped would put an end to this.

"If she really said that, she was just being paranoid. There was a period when she didn't feel she was getting enough of Gary's attention. But there was *nothing* going on between us. Nothing at all."

For the most part, that statement was true, despite her stepfather's advances. And she suspected her mother knew the truth on some level and had been jealous, which was why she hadn't fought to keep Sophia at home when Sophia moved out.

But this explanation didn't seem to sway Leonard. He remained as smug as ever.

"Maybe I'd believe you if not for what your stepfather carries in his wallet."

Sophia had the terrible feeling that this encounter was about to go from bad to worse. "How do you know what my stepfather carries in his wallet?"

"Gus happened to be at the Firelight tonight."

Gus was one of the men who worked at her stepfather's feed store. He ran tractor rentals.

"And what does Gus know?"

"Just what he's seen with his own eyes."

"Which is…"

"Your stepfather carries your picture."

She could hardly breathe. "A lot of people carry pictures of their children."

"In this one—" he smiled, relishing the moment "—you're *naked*."

Sophia wished she could rally with a quick denial. But he'd succeeded in leveling her. When, if ever, could her stepfather have taken that picture? She'd never undressed for him. He used to come into her room after her mother was asleep and sit on the edge of her bed. He'd talk to her about life, school, her father—always her father, as if he was trying to differentiate between himself and her real dad. And sometimes he'd touch her in ways that would, at first, seem harmless. He'd smooth the hair off her forehead or tuck her in, actions designed to win her trust. Then he'd "accidentally" brush her breasts or even try to lie down with her.

But, to her knowledge, he'd never seen her naked. She'd made sure of it. She'd become ultramodest, wouldn't even shower unless he was out of the house.

"That can't be true," she said decisively.

"Gus swore on a stack of Bibles. Said you have the most amazing tits he's ever seen."

Of course Leonard would have to add that. He couldn't miss an opportunity to embarrass her. But she didn't react to the "tits" comment. The past—the divorce, the new marriage, her brother's absence at college, Starkey, her real father's decline and subsequent death when she was only twenty-five—it all came rushing back. She'd felt so vulnerable in those days. She'd promised herself she'd never be that vulnerable again.

Yet here she was, feeling completely exposed. Not that she'd let him know it. Whether or not she could defuse the situation depended on this very moment. "I'm afraid I'm going to need you to take a Breathalyzer test, Leonard."

"What?" He seemed shocked that he hadn't set her back the way he'd intended.

"You're not making sense. My stepfather couldn't have any such picture, because I've never been naked in front of him. You must be drunk."

"I'm not drunk!"

"Then you shouldn't mind proving it."

His eyes glittered in the darkness. "God, I hate you. You are *such* a bitch!"

"Hating me doesn't change anything."

"Leave me the hell alone." He turned to get in his truck, but she grabbed his door when he tried to close it and drew her gun.

"If you won't submit to a Breathalyzer, I'll arrest you," she said. "I can't let you back on the road until I know the rest of us are safe."

He laughed loud and long at that. "Fine, I'll prove I'm not drunk. But don't think you'll *ever* be safe."

"Are you threatening me?" she murmured.

"Just making sure you know not to count me among your friends."

"I'd never make that mistake." She went to the car to retrieve the Breathalyzer.

She'd almost cost him *this* job, too. Leonard couldn't believe it. For a few minutes last night, he'd had the upper hand. He'd enjoyed wielding some power. And then Sophia had nearly hauled him off to jail. If he hadn't passed the Breathalyzer, she would've locked him up and impounded his car. As it was, she'd given him two tickets he couldn't afford, one for running a red light and one for speeding.

Although things could've been worse—if she'd impounded his truck and found the receiver he used to eavesdrop on her—he'd been so angry by the time he got home he couldn't sleep. It wasn't until dawn that he'd finally dozed off, and then he'd overslept.

He'd called ahead to tell Dwight he'd be late, said it was because he woke up feeling ill. He couldn't admit to getting pulled over in the middle of the night for breaking traffic laws while driving his employer's truck. But it was obvious that Dwight wasn't happy to hear another excuse. Since Leonard had returned to animal husbandry, which was what he'd done before his uncle had encouraged him to try his hand at law enforcement, he'd had one problem after another. He couldn't seem to climb out of the mire he'd fallen into the day Sophia had heard about the Mexican girl who'd ratted him out to her loser brother.

Frowning, Leonard watched a tumbleweed roll across the flat desert landscape. He felt just as dead, just as disconnected, as that wind-tossed weed. And it stemmed from one mistake. That was all it took to destroy his life— one mistake and a vengeful, power-hungry fellow officer who'd never liked him to begin with.

"¿Qué quieres que hagamos?"

Saul, one of the migrant workers who helped out at the ranch, approached him.

Lowering the brim of his hat to protect his skin from the broiling sun, Leonard replied in Spanish because none of the men who worked with him could understand English. "Move all the birds from house number one to house number two," he told him. "It's time to rake out the droppings." Which they would sell to a fertilizer company, but the laborers didn't need to know that. They just needed to do the raking and leave anything that required a brain to him.

Saul passed the word to two other migrant workers who waited nearby, wearing their usual sweat-stained baseball caps and filthy work clothes. Then they all walked to house number one.

At least they were obedient. And they worked hard. Their women were well trained, too. The ones he'd met could really cook and clean. They knew how to take care of a man….

Dwight would be along shortly to see how the transfer was progressing, so Leonard needed to join the crew. But he couldn't dredge up the energy to overcome his resistance to such lowly work. Not after his latest indignity at the hands of Sophia "the Bitch of All Bitches" St. Claire. And what was all that business his bug had picked up about Rod being in his trailer? What right did Bruce's bastard have entering anyone's place of residence without permission?

Lingering under the spray mister near the corrugated metal shack where two women—one Mexican, one white—made sure the eggs produced on the ranch were clean and contained no dark spots or blood, he gazed off into the distance. Here he was, overseeing the removal of chicken shit instead of driving around Bordertown in an air-conditioned cruiser, enjoying the envy of the men and the respect and admiration of the women. Lorna, his wife, was gone. His girls were gone, too. For the most part, they refused to talk to him. Lorna said it was because he couldn't say anything nice. She claimed the children were suffering enough, that they didn't need him making them feel guilty every time he called. But they couldn't be hurting as badly as he was. And it wasn't as if he was asking for the moon. He just wanted them to convince their mother to forgive him and come home so they could go back to life as it was before.

Lorna said she wanted to give their separation a while before she filed for divorce, as if there was a chance she might reconsider, but there were moments he feared those happier times were gone for good. Every day seemed harder than the one before. Staring at the trailer they'd once shared, with its missing furniture and the dog and cat the family had left with him because their new place didn't allow pets, had changed him, hardened him.

He thought about the guns he had at the trailer. Lately, his mind returned to them constantly. Until the past six months, he'd never understood those guys who felt compelled to shoot up their workplace or school. But he understood now. He wanted to walk into Bordertown and kill Sophia, the council members who'd supported her and Bruce Dunlap, the worst of all hypocrites. Bruce had pulled his support the minute he'd learned about the Mexican girl, and then he'd coaxed his bastard half-breed home to help solve a crime Sophia couldn't solve on her own. They even had a cigarette butt from which they were hoping to get a DNA profile. That could mess up everything.

But as much as Leonard dreamed of taking everyone out in a hail of bullets, he told himself he wouldn't let Sophia or anyone else tempt him into acting rash. That was no way to win. If he shot up the town, he'd die, too, or he'd go to prison, and that wouldn't fix anything.

No, he'd take her apart piece by piece, beginning with what she'd stolen from him first—her job. And he'd do it without anyone being able to prove it was him. He finally had the tools he needed to insure success. Over the past few weeks, he'd managed to bug her house, her car, even the station.

She wouldn't make any progress on the UDA murders because he'd know everything she did and he'd stay one step ahead of her.

What he'd learned about her relationship with her stepfather while listening to her conversation with Roderick was simply a bonus....

13

It was midafternoon by the time Sophia woke up. Because of the pressure she'd been under, she hadn't been able to sleep for several days, so she'd taken a sleeping pill, and it had definitely done its job. She'd been unconscious for eight solid hours. But the first thing she thought of when she opened her eyes was what she'd been thinking about when she fell asleep—her conversation with Leonard Taylor.

Was what he'd told her true? Did her stepfather have a nude picture of her in his wallet?

She couldn't imagine how that could be the case. For one thing, she had no idea how or when he would've gotten it. For another, he couldn't risk having her mother come across it. Anne preferred to live in denial, but that kind of proof would be too obvious to ignore, even for her.

And that wasn't the only part of Leonard's story that seemed suspect. He said Anne had gone to the police station and asked for his advice. But Anne had never particularly liked him. He'd dared to come on to her once, when they were both young and unmarried, and Anne was appalled that he thought he was good enough. Some of his cousins had money, but he didn't. Plus, Anne's pride meant everything to her. She'd never be able to hold her head up in Bordertown if people thought she couldn't keep her husband's sexual interest away from her own daughter.

So…where would Leonard have come up with that if it wasn't true? And how ironic that he'd mention it right after she'd divulged the truth to Rod. During the past decade, she'd heard no allusion to her stepfather's inappropriate behavior, had made no allusion to it herself. Yet the subject had come up twice in the same evening only minutes apart.

Definitely odd….

A knock at the door told her she wouldn't be able to go back to sleep even if she could forget about the sickening possibility that her stepfather might have such a revealing photograph in his wallet.

You have the most amazing tits. How many people had seen that picture? If it existed…

"Hey, you home?"

It was Rod, calling to her from outside her front door. She recognized his voice, but wasn't sure she wanted to see him. She'd kissed him last night and had considered doing even more. Which seemed crazy in the light of day. They barely knew each other. Besides, she felt a little superstitious about what she'd told him, as if that moment of weakness might bring the world as she knew it tumbling down around her. She'd been too tired and, when it came to Rod, too influenced by guilt and attraction to maintain her usual defenses.

Still, there wasn't much point in leaving him standing outside, banging on the door. He'd be able to get hold of her later, if not now. Why procrastinate?

Dragging herself out of bed, she pulled on a pair of cutoffs and one of the T-shirts she generally wore around the house and answered the door.

* * *

Sophia's tattoo sleeve took Rod by surprise. When he'd known her, she'd been a cheerleader, a good student. Such a classic symbol of rebellion seemed incongruous with all that. But, as he'd discovered, she'd changed quite a bit after he left Bordertown....

"That's a lot of ink," he said dryly.

She glanced down. "A remnant of my Starkey days."

"Ever thought of having it removed?"

"You don't like it?"

"I'm not sure yet," he admitted. But he liked the rest of what he saw—the braless chest, the shapely legs. She was far more appealing out of uniform. Which did nothing to bolster the decision he'd made after she'd gone home last night. He wasn't going to let himself get physically involved with her. As much as he was tempted to coax her to submit, as much as he believed that would bring him the closure he'd craved for years, he knew a "love 'em and leave 'em" experience wouldn't be best for her. She'd been through enough.

"Then I'm glad I don't care," she said. "What's up?"

He ignored her tart response about the tattoo. He'd asked for it, after all. "I just spoke to Milt."

"Who's Milt?"

"My boss."

She shoved her sleep-tousled hair out of those bottle-green eyes. "Is he planning to have the governor call me?"

"I told him it wasn't necessary. He was pleased to learn that you like me now."

Her eyes met his. "Who said I like you?"

He smiled. "I can tell."

"How?"

"You don't have your Taser out anymore, for one. I figure that's a step in the right direction."

"Why bother with a Taser? Even electrocution won't get rid of you."

He lowered his voice. "And then there was that kiss."

"A peck."

"You melted like butter. That had to mean something."

She grimaced. "It means I'm hard up, remember? You were the one who pointed that out last night."

"I didn't say you were hard up. I said you don't have a lot of discreet options."

"And you offered me a one-night stand."

"An offer that has since been rescinded, by the way. You missed your opportunity."

She folded her arms beneath her breasts and, although it wasn't intentional, the action drew his attention to the cleavage showing above the top of her wide-necked T-shirt. "You're saying you don't want me anymore?"

Want had nothing to do with it. "Nope. Not now that I've seen you without makeup."

She slugged him. "Thanks for the ego boost!"

"About time I returned the favor," he said as he laughed. "After all, you're the girl who destroyed *my* ego fifteen years ago."

He'd meant that last part as a joke, but she sobered immediately.

"I'm sorry about that, Rod. At fifteen, I was nothing but a…a spoiled brat. I can't tell you how bad I've felt about that incident ever since. When Starkey told me you were back in town, I was hoping I wouldn't even have to see you, I was still so embarrassed."

He hadn't expected such an honest and heartfelt apology.

It made the grudge he'd been carrying seem childish. But he wasn't noble enough to completely relinquish the power her contrition gave him—not without having some fun with it first. "So what are you going to do to make it up to me?"

"What do you want?" She sounded suspicious, but she was smiling.

He stepped inside, crowding her.

She moved back to make room for him. "I'd like to see if you have any more tattoos."

"I don't."

The door closed with a click. "Prove it."

Her throat worked as she swallowed. "How?"

"Lose the shirt."

"Here? *Now?*"

"Quit stalling. You've already seen everything I've got. Now you owe me."

"I thought we were even."

"Not by a long shot."

She took another step back. "I let you out of jail last night."

"You shouldn't have arrested me in the first place."

"That's not strictly true."

"Excuses. What, are you too chicken to give as good as you got?"

Her chest rose as she drew in a deep breath. "Still getting up my nerve."

She was going to do it? "Should I help?"

"Absolutely not."

He raised his eyebrows. "Then why don't you start?"

Slowly, she began to bare her midriff.

"That's it," he murmured as more and more of her came into view. He spotted a pretty little beauty mark below her rib cage, noticed how smooth and creamy her skin looked. But once she exposed her breasts, all his blood headed to his groin, and he could hardly breathe, let alone think.

When he didn't react, confusion and uncertainty entered her eyes. She assumed his silence meant he didn't like what he saw and was lowering her shirt.

He needed to say something. But he was too busy wrestling with himself. Part of him wanted to seduce her, to slip his hand up under that shirt and cup her breast. He was pretty sure she'd let him. She was lonely, hungry for physical fulfillment, as vulnerable as he'd been fourteen years ago. The tables had turned just as he'd always dreamed. But he couldn't allow himself to take advantage of her. He refused to be that selfish, that callous.

Swallowing hard, he lifted his shoulders in a shrug of indifference. "Not bad."

Such a bland response was almost a slap in the face, but it worked. His lack of appreciation stung her enough to make her defensive, unwilling to trust him again.

She crossed her arms over her chest, even though her shirt was back in place. "Well, whether you enjoyed the show or not, I did what you asked. So…you forgive me, right?"

"For what?" He was so busy battling the effects of the testosterone flooding his body that he couldn't even remember what they'd been talking about.

"Standing you up for Homecoming."

"Of course. You made the right decision. Whoever you chose over me probably took you out for steak and lobster. I barely had enough money for pizza."

He'd just been referring to the practical benefits of going out with someone who had more money than he'd had at the time, trying to divorce feeling from action so they could forget what had happened and move on. But his words only made the strain between them worse.

"That wasn't why I did it," she said softly.

Suddenly angry at himself for using her apology as leverage to get her to flash him, he scowled. "Yeah, well, forget it. I was joking earlier. You were never that important to me."

She blinked several times. "You can be an insensitive jerk, you know that?"

But an insensitive jerk was better than what he'd be if he carried her into the bedroom and convinced her to give him what she wouldn't give anyone else. "Better you learn that now."

"Or?"

"Or it might be a harder lesson later."

Her laugh was more of a scoff. "Don't flatter yourself."

Those words offered a fresh challenge, a new temptation, but he didn't let himself react the way he wished he could. "Milt called to tell me the FBI has formed the task force you've been waiting for and they're going to jump all over this UDA case," he said, turning the conversation to business, where it should've been from the beginning.

She avoided his gaze but made an effort to speak more stridently than she had a moment earlier. "Took them long enough."

"They had to replace two senior agents. They won't say why, but they made some transfers and are now ready to come on board. The special agent in charge wants to meet us in an hour."

"Us?"

He knew she must want to be rid of him now more than ever. He'd coaxed her to let go, to be daring, and then he'd made her regret it. But once she'd actually lifted her shirt, he didn't see that he'd had any other alternative. "Us," he repeated.

"They called *you* to set it up, even though I'm the chief of police."

Thanks to him, she was having a very bad afternoon, and he knew it. "I told you I have friends in high places." He was joking, but she didn't crack a smile, and he wasn't feeling very happy, either.

He waved at her general dishevelment. "Why don't you jump in the shower while I make breakfast?"

She shook her head. "There's no need for you to wait here while I get ready. I'll meet you. Where do I go?"

He'd been hoping to make up for what he'd just done. He liked to cook, liked taking care of people. But she wasn't about to let him. She was slipping back into tough-cop mode.

"The meeting's at the Sierra Vista Resident Agency," he said. "There's no point in both of us driving that far."

"Except that I have a lot of errands to run on my way home."

"You've got to eat."

"I can manage on my own."

It wasn't going to be easy to work with her. They couldn't seem to find any middle ground. They were either too busy hating each other or wanting to make love.

Figuring it might help to give her more space, he nodded. "Fine. I'll see you in an hour."

She waited politely until he went out. She even waved as if he hadn't embarrassed her. Then she closed the door and when he heard the dead bolt slide home behind him, he understood she was barring him from more than the house.

* * *

Damn, she was an idiot. What had she been *thinking?*

Sophia slid down the wall to the hardwood floor. She'd just flashed Roderick Guerrero, and he'd looked at her as if he wasn't the least bit interested or impressed. She couldn't imagine anything more humiliating, couldn't imagine feeling more self-conscious than she had in those few seconds when he went silent and still. She usually avoided situations that made her emotionally vulnerable. So why had she taken such a risk? What had she hoped to achieve?

Forgiveness. She'd been sincere about that. And, regardless of the fact that she'd had the law on her side, she regretted bursting into his motel room without even allowing him time to dress.

But still… She'd been crazy to set herself up for his revenge. He'd exacted it so quickly and easily, with a mere look. Or maybe it was the lack of a look. His face had gone completely blank.

Obviously, she wasn't her usual self. Not only was she fighting a deep-seated fear that she wouldn't be able to solve the UDA case, she was terrified that there'd be other victims. She didn't want to feel responsible for their deaths. Roderick was handsome and exciting and he'd created a distraction from the endless worry and doubt. Then there was the drive to prove herself desirable enough to appeal to a man like that. Dick's behavior—cheating on her with a seventeen-year-old girl—must've taken more of a toll on her self-esteem than she'd realized.

So she'd made a mistake. It wasn't catastrophic. She'd pretend it had never happened and go on. Roderick had wanted to get even, and she'd let him. Done. Over. She had too much going on to worry about the fact that he hadn't been the slightest bit tempted by what he'd seen. He lived in Southern California, for crying out loud. Hard for natural breasts to compete with all the surgery-enhanced beach bodies in L.A.

Determined to get moving, she scrambled to her feet and called Lindstrom to tell her about the meeting. Then she headed for the shower. But the phone rang before she could turn on the water, and caller ID showed her a number she couldn't resist. It was a number she'd called again and again and again—the one she'd found in José's sock.

14

"Hello?"

The man on the other end of the line had the same strong accent Sophia had heard on his voice-mail recording. "You left me a message?"

"Yes. My name is Sophia St. Claire. I'm the chief of police here in Bordertown, Arizona. Who are you?"

"I'd rather not say."

He didn't have papers. He was afraid she'd turn him in and he'd be deported. She was astonished he'd even called.

"You were trying to contact me about José Sanchez," he said.

"Yes."

"What about him? Has he done anything wrong?"

This man hadn't heard about the shootings. Which meant he hadn't been in recent contact with José's or Benita's families. Surely the Mexican consulate had notified them by now. "I'm afraid I have some very bad news."

"They're dead?"

"Yes."

"*That's* why I haven't heard from him." The fatalistic note in his voice said he'd expected something terrible like this. "How did it happen? Did they get lost? Run out of water?"

"They were shot and killed early Sunday morning."

"By the border patrol?"

"No. It was a random act of violence. We're still looking for the perpetrator."

"I promised him it would be okay," he muttered, almost to himself.

"You encouraged him to cross?" she asked.

"He was already set on it. He wanted to bring his wife here. I told him I'd help him get a start."

"So he was planning on meeting up with you?"

"He and his wife were going to live with me until he could get a job and they could move out on their own."

She eyed the clock. The minutes were ticking by, but she couldn't risk asking if she could call this man back for fear he'd change his mind about talking to her. "Can you tell me anything that might help me track down the people they met along the way?"

"I recommended a good coyote. And I told them about a safe house in Bordertown."

She'd found their coyote, so she focused on the other part of that statement. "I'd like to talk to the people who run that safe house. Can you tell me how to find it?"

"No. I don't dare."

"I have no interest in shutting it down." That wasn't her job. "I can't promise it won't happen, but I only want to find José and Benita's killer. I need your help in order to do that. I'm guessing you're a friend or a relative of some sort, right? So you want to see justice done. The person who killed your friends has killed before—ten other Mexican nationals. We have to stop him before he acts again."

"*Pero*…I could get in trouble if I say too much. There are people who will be angry if I give out this information."

"You're talking about the owners of the safe house?"

"*Sí*. I think it might be the Mexican Mafia. That's what they act like. Anyway, whoever owns it won't be happy that you know about it."

She got the impression he'd done some work for the Mafia, maybe as a mule for drugs. Otherwise, he wouldn't have assumed they were affiliated with the safe house. "I'll say I found the address on José's body. They can't do anything to him now."

He blew out a sigh. "You're asking me to be disloyal, to help the *policía*."

"I'm not your adversary. I'm trying to solve José's and Benita's murders."

Nothing.

"Do it for José," she prodded.

Finally he responded. "It's at Wildflower and Dugan Drive—2944 Dugan Drive."

"Thank you. Thank you for doing the right thing."

"I hope you find the person who killed them. And I hope he goes to prison for the rest of his life." A click sounded in her ear and he was gone.

First, Lindstrom. Now the Feds. Until the UDA shootings, Sophia had never joined forces with another police entity. This was only her second murder investigation. The first one had involved a jealous husband and a cheating wife. The evidence had been overwhelming and the husband had been apprehended shortly after leaving the scene.

Unfortunately, this case wasn't as easy. It was going

nowhere fast and becoming a political hot potato. On her way out of town, Sophia had spotted two different news vans, one at Bailey's Breakfast Dive and the other at the hardware store. Although she hadn't turned on her television set in more than a week, she was guessing that the national media had picked up on what had been reported in the local papers. They'd broken the story on a much bigger scale and were now swooping in to monitor developments. From here on out, they'd be attempting to scoop each other, and she'd be hounded constantly for more detail and commentary. Unlike some of the bigger police departments, she had no media-relations personnel. The buck stopped with her in every respect. And she felt the weight of it from the minute she arrived at the meeting and was introduced to the FBI agents.

"Chief St. Claire?"

Sophia blinked and refocused on Special Agent Charles Van Dormer, who sat across a large oak desk from her, Roderick, Lindstrom, Sean Carver and Glen Billerbeck, the other two FBI agents assigned to the task force. She'd already briefed them on everything she knew about the murders. Everything except the information she'd just received on the safe house. She wasn't quite sure she wanted to share that in mixed company, so to speak. Her desire to trust the FBI warred with her *dis*trust of Lindstrom, who was also part of the conversation. "Yes?"

"When you submitted the cigarette butt found at the last scene, did the state crime lab give you any indication of how long it would take to process?"

She shot a glance at Rod. When she'd entered the room, she'd purposely taken the seat farthest from him. Still, he'd been kind enough not to reveal that he'd found the butt *after* she'd finished processing the scene. She hadn't lied about its discovery; she'd merely presented the information in a general way, talked about *what* was found instead of how and when. And he hadn't added any further detail.

"It's not at the state crime lab," she said.

"Where is it?"

Rod cut in. "I recommended a lab I've worked with before, in San Diego."

Van Dormer leaned back in his chair. "Who cleared that?"

Again, Rod answered. "No one. But it's a reputable lab. And they'll be much quicker."

"If you didn't get clearance, it might be hard to get the state to pick up the tab."

"I'll pay the tab," he said.

"Suit yourself." Van Dormer shrugged; then he began to discuss the various ways in which he wanted to support the investigation. He talked about canvassing gun shops and pawn shops and, for that, Sophia was grateful. Going from location to location would take a lot of man-hours she didn't have.

"We won't leave a single stone unturned. We'll find the bastard who's doing this, and we'll make him pay," Van Dormer said.

One of the other agents brought up the ranchers again, which they'd already discussed.

"It could easily be a rancher," Van Dormer agreed. "Which is why I want every landowner between Bordertown and Mexico interviewed, too."

As the meeting progressed, Sophia pretended not to notice the hostility of Lindstrom's icy glare. But while the others were busy getting out an assessor's map, Lindstrom scooted closer.

"Cigarette butt? You told me you found spent shell

casings," she muttered. "You never mentioned a cigarette butt."

Because *she* hadn't found it; Rod had. And her knowledge of its existence had occurred after she'd last spoken with Lindstrom. But she couldn't admit that without revealing that she'd missed an important piece of evidence, something she wasn't eager to volunteer, especially to Lindstrom, who was keeping a running log of her shortcomings and missteps. "I wasn't sure it would tell us anything," she said. "I'm still not."

"You're *unreal*. You know that?"

There was no time to respond. Van Dormer had the map spread out on his desk. If she continued to talk she'd only call attention to their little side conversation.

"Who owns this parcel?" he asked, pointing.

Sophia immediately recognized the property. She'd used a similar map, pored over it so many times that she knew the information by heart. On her map, she'd marked the locations of the murders, and she'd measured the distance between them in an attempt to do some rudimentary geographic profiling. She didn't have any training in that area, but she'd thought seeing one crime scene in relation to another might tell her *something*.

Unfortunately, it hadn't. Except that the killer was keeping his work inside the city limits. And each kill was about three miles from the one before. The triangle formed when she connected the dots encompassed most of the town. She'd already guessed the perpetrator lived close by.

"That piece belongs to Kevin and Alma Simpson," she volunteered. "They're cattle ranchers. They have a son, James, who lives with them. I went out there a few days ago."

"And? What did they have to say?" Van Dormer asked.

Sophia actually liked the SAC. Thanks partly to the way FBI agents were often portrayed on TV, she'd expected someone who was bland and homogenous, if not arrogant and stuffy. But Van Dormer wasn't any of those things. Maybe ten years older than she was, he had gray hair at his temples, nice hazel eyes and a strong jaw and chin. Not only was he handsome, he seemed capable, professional and easy to work with.

But *anyone* would be an improvement over Lindstrom.

The other FBI agents weren't so attractive. Sean had considerably more gray hair, a paunch that wasn't hidden by his suit and short, stubby legs. Glen was tall and skinny with a dated tie, a bad haircut and acne scars. They all wore wedding rings.

"The Simpsons hate UDAs," Sophia said. "And they make no secret of it. They even have a blog to try and impact public opinion on the issue of tougher immigration enforcement. I can give you the URL, in case you'd like to take a look at it."

He shoved a piece of paper toward her so she could write it down. "Do you think they hate illegals enough to start killing them?"

"It's possible. Or maybe one member of the family's snapped and decided to do something drastic to protect the other two from the threats they perceive."

"If you had to pick one, who would it be?"

This surprised Sophia. He wasn't asking her for hard evidence. He knew if she had any, she would've presented it already. He was asking for her opinion—as if he valued it despite her lack of experience working big cases like this one.

Remembering Kevin Simpson's callous responses when she'd mentioned the victims, Sophia had no trouble deciding on her answer. "The father. He's grown tired of the situation and has no empathy for the illegal immigrants. He acts like they're not even human."

"Good to know. Instinct counts for a lot in police work." He pointed to another spot on the map. "What about this parcel?"

"That's Charlie Sumpter's place," she said. "I've been trying to reach him but can't get a response."

"I know Charlie," Roderick put in. "He was a friend of my father's, used to come by the ranch quite a bit."

Sophia could tell the word *father* left a bitter taste in Rod's mouth, but he'd used it for ease of explanation.

"He's probably in Wyoming." Rod went on. "From the bits and pieces I overheard as a child, he used to go there for several weeks every summer."

"Not anymore." Sophia's gaze had automatically moved to Rod, since he was the one speaking, but the sight of him with his legs stretched out and crossed at the ankles and one elbow slung over the back of his chair reminded her of what'd happened at her house an hour and a half earlier. So she directed her attention to Van Dormer instead.

"He's gotten too old for that," she continued. "I'm guessing he's with his daughter and her family in Yuma. When I bumped into him at the café not too long ago, he mentioned planning to see her over the summer. He said he can't handle Wyoming anymore but felt he could manage driving someplace that's only a few hours away. I didn't get the impression that he'd be gone for an extended visit, so he should be back soon."

"Any idea how he feels about UDAs?"

"Ever since that rancher near Portal was killed—apparently by an illegal alien—he's been pretty vocal about his hatred." Sophia had heard him spouting off plenty of times, but it had seemed harmless enough, a reaction to the loss of a friend. "He and the victim were close. They went to the same school when they were young, at least for a few years, and became lifelong friends."

"Then he's someone to watch," Van Dormer said.

The SAC pointed out several more parcels, and Sophia gave him the owner information. She'd talked to almost all the ranchers in the past six weeks, including Charlie, but now that there were new victims, they needed to be interviewed again.

"Are you considering calling someone in to do behavioral profiling?" she asked when he'd split up the workload by geographic area and given them their assignments.

"I'm not a strong believer in that," he admitted. "Unless you know quite a bit about a killer or he has a very unique signature, it can mislead as much as it can help. But—" he rubbed his chin as if deep in thought "—maybe. Let's get what's out there already and meet again day after tomorrow."

They arranged a time. Then everyone stood. Sophia had her assignment and was about to leave without mentioning the safe house. She didn't want Lindstrom leaking word of it to Leonard, or at least not before she could visit there. She preferred to call Van Dormer about the house and its location. Except then she'd have to explain why she hadn't shared it with the group, and telling him that Lindstrom might have a conflict of interest could make her look paranoid, petty or both.

No, she had to risk speaking to everyone. She just hoped

the FBI's involvement would keep Lindstrom honest. "One last thing," she said.

All eyes turned her way.

"I received a call from someone at that number I found on the body of José Sanchez."

Van Dormer stopped folding the map he'd been trying to wrangle into submission.

"He wouldn't reveal his identity," she added. "But he told me about a safe house in Bordertown where José and Benita were supposed to spend the night."

"And you didn't bring this up until *now?*" Lindstrom snapped. "I mean, having you part of this isn't going to work if you keep holding out on everybody." She looked at Van Dormer. "She does this with everything. She didn't even tell me about the cigarette butt, and we've been working together for a month."

Van Dormer frowned at Lindstrom, revealing that he wasn't too impressed with her waspish reaction. So Sophia figured less was better and didn't respond to the accusation. "It might be owned by the Mexican Mafia."

"What makes you think so?" Van Dormer asked.

"That's what my informant believes."

"Have you pulled up the deed?"

"I did. The owner of the house is listed as a limited partnership—Cochise Partners—but it could be backed by the Mafia."

Paper crinkled again as he finished with the map. "You know your town better than anyone else, Chief St. Claire. What do you suggest we do?"

"I'd like to go there tonight. See what I can learn. Someone was expecting José and Benita, knew when they were due to arrive. I'd like to find out where that person was at the time of the killings. There's even the possibility that

certain details or suspicions about the murderer are circu-
lating underground. If we could tap into what's being said
on the Mexican side, we might come up with additional
details."

"I agree," he said. "But…you plan to do this alone?"

"I think that would be the least threatening and most
effective approach. I—"

Rod interrupted. "No way."

Glancing up to see him towering over her, Sophia
placed her hands on her hips. "Excuse me?"

"You are far too white and far too female for that
job."

"You think it should fall to you."

"In short, yes."

Van Dormer didn't get involved. His eyes shifted to her
as if awaiting her answer. "But I came up with this lead,"
she said.

"I don't care," Rod responded. "Do you have any idea
how dangerous it might be?"

"I'll have my Glock."

"The possession of which could get you killed quicker
than anything else. They won't let you through the front
door with it."

"Then I'll stand on the porch."

He indicated the tattoo extending several inches below
the short sleeve of her uniform shirt. "What, you think
you're going to flash that tattoo and they'll believe you're
tough?"

"This has nothing to do with size or gender or—or
toughness."

"Sure it does! They won't respect you, won't be willing
to give you the information you need, because they won't
fear you. If you think American culture can be sexist, you

haven't seen anything until you've experienced Mexican machismo."

"I know. I'm experiencing it now," she said. "But it's not as if you look all that Mexican. There are white people with tans as dark as you."

"So what? At least I speak Spanish. Do you?"

Divulging the truth would put her at even more of a disadvantage, so she began to hedge. "Enough to handle what needs to get done."

"That's a no." He turned to Van Dormer. "Obviously, I'm the right candidate for this assignment. Not only am I fluent and more capable of blending in, I'm better prepared to defend myself with or without a weapon."

Sophia stepped forward. "As a man, you'll be perceived as more of a threat."

Van Dormer pinched his lips as he decided between them. "Let him do it," he said at length.

Sophia glanced from the SAC to Rod. These men didn't understand. She didn't want to hide behind them. Her experience in Naco had empowered her, made her feel she could hold her own in any situation. And she *wanted* to prove it. Maybe then her detractors would shut up and quit waiting for her to blow it so they could take her job.

"She won't go along with it," Lindstrom interjected. "She invites danger. She went into Naco *alone* a few nights ago."

Sophia had finally had enough of Lindstrom. "And I got the information I went after. Information you were too scared to pursue. What's wrong with that?"

Lindstrom's nostrils flared as if she had a quick retort on the tip of her tongue, but Van Dormer held up his hands. "I don't care if you two like each other or not.

Make this easy on the rest of us and figure out a way to get along, huh?"

"What if I go with *Mr.* Guerrero?" Sophia emphasized his title to convey that he actually had no rank, no business being involved in the first place.

"There's no need for both of you to take that risk," he said and turned away.

Rod tried to catch Sophia before she left. He knew Lindstrom's type, knew she'd been difficult to work with and didn't want Sophia to assume he'd be the same. It was just that he felt strongly about keeping her away from the safe house, especially if there was any chance it was owned by members of the Mexican Mafia, who had no compunction about killing whenever and wherever they wanted.

But she'd turned on her heel and stalked out, and Van Dormer had stopped him to ask a few questions about his background and experience. By the time he'd been free to jog out of the building, she was already on her motorcycle with the engine running.

"Hey, where's your helmet?" he called. Sounding like a bossy parent wasn't the best way to convince her he wasn't a pain in the ass, but he was afraid that was all he'd get in before she took off. He'd heard of too many accidents to feel comfortable having her on the road without that protection. One of his good friends had died in a motorcycle accident. And he knew she owned a helmet. He'd seen it on the seat of her motorcycle earlier, when he'd visited her house, which suggested she normally used it. The fact that she wasn't wearing it today told him she'd been upset before she'd even left the house.

"Are you talking to *me?*" she shouted, then revved the engine, drowning out his response.

He'd never known a person her size who could handle such a big motorcycle, but she seemed skilled enough. "Why are you mad? You know I'm the better candidate to visit that safe house," he yelled, trying to make himself heard.

With a shake of her head, she put on her sunglasses and raised the kickstand. "Sorry, I can't hear you," she said, and drove off.

Rod considered jumping in his car and going after her. She had no reason to be so angry. Maybe he'd embarrassed her earlier when he'd pushed the shirt incident too far, but it wasn't as if she hadn't done worse to him. He'd stood in front of her with his hands cuffed behind his back.

So why did he feel so frustrated, so intent on trying to improve her opinion of him?

He pulled out his keys, but didn't move toward his car. The detective from the sheriff's office had just appeared.

"Too bad she's on the case," Lindstrom grumbled. "She's trouble."

If not for the uniform, she'd *look* like trouble riding that Harley with her shades and tattoo sleeve. "You don't approve of her?"

"She bristles too easily. Won't let anyone get close to her."

Sophia was sensitive and high-strung. But Rod sort of liked her mercurial nature. He couldn't always guess what she was thinking, or what she might do next. Who would've thought she'd actually lift her shirt for him?

"She seems to have an aversion to you, too," he mused.

"I don't understand why. I've done everything I possibly can to get along with her. *I* can't help it if she's not cut out for police work."

Rod bristled a little himself. "How do you know she's not cut out for it?"

"You heard her. She thinks she should be able to waltz into that safe house and get her own answers."

"She's got guts. You have to give her that."

"No, I don't. She's *crazy*. This case would already be solved if we were dealing with someone like Leonard Taylor instead of her."

If she thought that, she had no clue how long an investigation like this could take. But he didn't react to her inane statement. He was too busy remembering the newspaper article on the back of Leonard Taylor's door. "You're a friend of Leonard's?"

"I grew up hanging out with his sister. It's a shame what the powers that be allowed her to do to him."

"And what, exactly, was that?"

"You haven't heard? She manufactured some testimony to discredit him, then took his job."

"His sister told you that?"

"Everyone knows it," she said.

"Everyone except Rosita Flores."

She shaded her eyes against the glare of the sun and looked up at him. "Who?"

"The Mexican woman he threatened to hand over to the border patrol if she didn't let him take advantage of her."

Lindstrom frowned. "Have you ever met this woman?"

The question took him by surprise. "No."

"I didn't think so," she said with a superior smile, and pressed the button that would unlock her car.

15

Her stepfather was still at the feed store, but so was one of his workers. It wasn't Gus; it was Tony, a kid of nineteen.

Having changed into a white tank top and a pair of jeans now that her meeting with the FBI was over, Sophia sat at the back of the parking lot on her motorcycle, feeling the sun bake the skin on her bare arms. She was waiting for Tony to leave. She knew her stepfather always closed, since he didn't trust anyone else to handle the day's receipts.

He'd be by himself soon. But would she have the nerve to confront him? She preferred to forget what had happened, to sweep it into the dark corners of her mind, as she'd been doing for fourteen years.

But if he had a nude picture of her in his possession, she had to make sure it got destroyed.

Wally Deloit, the only customer left, judging by the lack of cars in the lot, spotted her as he came out the back of the store. "Hey, Chief," he said with a wave. "What's going on?"

"Not a lot, Wally. How are you?"

"Hot. I'm about ready to become one of them snowbirds who just live in Arizona for the winter."

The screen on the door slammed shut. Tony had come out with hay hooks so he could load a bale of hay into the back of Wally's pickup. He waved, too, but didn't stop to talk. Gary wouldn't let him socialize while he was on the clock. Despite her stepfather's other weaknesses, he was good at business. He'd turned a feed store that was barely getting by into a solid success. The local paper had done a big write-up on him not long ago.

"You won't like leaving for months at a time," she told Wally. "This place is in your blood."

"You're probably right." He pulled a handkerchief from one of his pockets and mopped the back of his neck. "Any news on those murders?"

"Not yet. But I'm working on it."

"You seen all them news trucks around town? Leland Jennings and his mother over at the Mother Lode are loving it. The motel's filled up. First time they've had the No-Vacancy sign on in ages. But I can't say I like having to wait for a table at the café when I've never had to wait before."

So far, Sophia had managed to duck the news crews. Several had stopped by the station. Joe Fitzer, the officer on duty until her shift started at eight, had called to alert her. But they hadn't tracked her down yet. They were just figuring out the characters in this drama and, out of uniform, she hardly looked like the chief of police, especially when she was riding her Harley.

"I'm planning to solve it as quickly as possible so they can all go home," she said as Tony finished loading the hay and went inside.

Wally grinned at her. "I believe you'll do that, Chief. Yes, I do. You'll show this town what you're made of."

She flashed him a smile of gratitude for his support as

he got in his truck and left. Then she was alone near the row of tractors and backhoes her stepfather rented out in conjunction with his feed-store business.

Seeking relief from the heat, she climbed off her bike and went to stand beneath the overhang, where there was a strip of shade.

Fifteen minutes later, Tony came out with a spring in his step that signaled he was off work. Her bike was still in the lot, parked not far from his truck, but he didn't seem to notice it or her. He was preoccupied with placing a call on his cell phone. She was preoccupied herself, too stressed to take on the burden of being polite, so she said nothing.

After he drove off, she fidgeted for another few minutes, trying to gather her nerve. Then she went into the store.

Her stepfather was busy counting out the till. He turned when he heard footsteps behind him and smiled, but wariness entered his eyes, and his posture revealed surprise. She never came by after hours. If she visited at all it was by order of her mother—to pick up some hay for Anne's horse or drop off a sack lunch. Even those visits were rare.

"Afternoon." His voice was casual but his smile seemed a little forced.

Stopping a few feet away, she jumped into her purpose in coming. "I have a question to ask you."

He looked down at the money in his hands, then put it back in the till. Her tone indicated this would not be an easy question to answer; she could see him mentally preparing.

"No problem. I can take care of this later." He closed the drawer. "What's on your mind?"

"I'd like to see your wallet."

He blinked. "My *what?*"

"Your wallet. Will you hand it over?"

"Is this a holdup?" he joked, but she didn't crack a smile. The butterflies in her stomach made her feel nauseated. She was so afraid she'd see a picture of herself in his possession—a picture of her at sixteen or seventeen without any clothes—that she was having a difficult time keeping her voice from shaking.

"I'm serious."

His eyebrows came together. His reaction seemed genuine, but he was *such* a good liar. She couldn't trust his protestations of innocence. He'd lied to her face before— told Anne he'd never been in her bedroom, let alone tried to touch her.

"Something wrong?" he asked.

"Yes. And I think you know what it is."

He hesitated, obviously searching for answers he couldn't find. Finally he shook his head. "I'm afraid I don't."

"Gus told Leonard you have a picture of me in your wallet."

The confusion didn't clear entirely, but he seemed somewhat relieved. "I do. It's getting a bit tattered after so many years, but it's of all three of us." He pulled out his wallet and showed her. "It's from Christmas that last year you were living at home, remember?"

Even though he was holding it out to her, she barely glanced at it. "That's not the one I'm talking about."

He dropped his hand. "I don't have any others, Sophia. I don't know how Gus could say what I carry in my wallet, anyway. It's not something I leave lying around."

She wasn't sure how Gus knew, but she had to see if

Leonard was right. "I—I need to look through it myself. *Please.*"

Surprisingly, he passed it to her.

She went through every compartment, even searched for secret nooks and crannies but found nothing. Her stepfather had some cash, a few receipts, several credit cards—what most men carried in their billfolds. But the only picture she could find was the one he'd already shown her.

Sophia would've been relieved, except there had to be *some* reason Leonard had said what he did. Had there been a picture that had since been removed? Or was Leonard trying to stir up trouble between her and her mother, between her and her stepfather, and between her and the people who'd been in her corner since the scandal involving Rosita broke?

"What's going on?" Gary asked as she returned his wallet.

She bent over so the blood would reach her head.

"Sophia?"

"Like I told you," she mumbled, staring at the floor, "Gus claims he's seen a picture of me in your wallet."

"It was probably this one—"

She didn't look up. She didn't want to see his expression when she told him why she was so upset. "No, in this photo I'm naked."

"*What?* That doesn't make sense."

It would to anyone who understood his true nature. But his wife had protected him from exposure, had stood by him at the expense of her relationship with her daughter. How—and why—was Leonard coming up with this all of a sudden?

Gary shoved his billfold back in his pocket. "When did Gus tell you this?"

"He didn't tell me. He told Leonard Taylor at the Firelight last night."

"Wait—that can't be true. Maybe Gus hangs out at the bar, but he wasn't there last night. He's in Flagstaff, attending a real-estate seminar. He thinks he's going to open his own office someday. I've been shorthanded for the past three days because of it."

She straightened. "What did you say?"

"I said Gus is out of town. He couldn't have been at the Firelight yesterday."

She felt her fingernails curve into her palms. "So where the hell is Leonard getting his information?"

"No idea. I've never had a picture like that. Where would I even get one?"

Cursing under her breath, she pivoted and started out, but he stopped her.

"Sophia?"

She paused, one hand on the screen door.

"I'm sorry that we remember what happened when you were living at home so differently."

She knew better than to take the conversation any further, knew better than to ask. But she couldn't help herself. "How do *you* remember it, Gary?" she asked, whirling around to face him.

"As being what it should be," he said. "Maybe not *idyllic.* But I was a good provider and—"

"What happened between us has nothing to do with *providing,* and you know it."

"But I never meant you any harm! I was just trying to love you, to be demonstrative. It wasn't as if you were getting any hugs or…or affection from your father." He spread out his hands. "And this is what I get for it?"

His feigned innocence conjured up instant rage. Had he admitted to what he'd done and taken responsibility for it, even privately, she might've been able to forgive him. But he was attempting to rewrite history, to erase his actions altogether. And he was doing it by making *her* the liar, which invalidated all the pain, the fear and the insecurity he'd caused her.

"You didn't do anything because I wouldn't let you get away with it," she said. "But don't think I'll ever forget how hard you tried." She slammed the screen door as she went out.

"Sophia, come on." He stood by the door and held it open. "This grudge of yours—it's killing your mother."

She faced him again. "So now what happened is *my* fault?"

"I'm not saying that." He switched to a conciliatory tone. "I'm just saying…let it go, okay? I'm tired of you trying to make me look bad. It wasn't that big a deal."

How dare he try to minimize what he'd done or make himself out to be the victim! "I believed you were carrying around a picture of me *naked*. That's how big a deal it was," she said, and got on her bike.

Needing some time alone, some time to deal with the emotions pouring through her and the memories the confrontation had called up, she started her motorcycle and tore out of the lot, hoping for a few minutes of quiet solitude at home.

But as soon as she hit Center Street, a news van began to tail her.

Driving downtown, Rod tried to put Sophia out of his mind. He was officially on the case, under the vague title of "consultant." And Special Agent Van Dormer had, for the most part, taken charge, so Rod didn't need Sophia's acceptance and cooperation as much as he'd needed it before.

Yet he was still thinking about her.

When he saw her in the parking lot of Denny's surrounded by reporters, he nearly stopped his car. With the dust and the heat, that ring of vans reminded him of a rodeo. She was the calf in the center, being hog-tied. Sophia had been expecting the pressure; they'd discussed it at the meeting—what to say and what not to say should one of them be cornered by a reporter—but she didn't seem comfortable despite being prepped. She kept edging away from them, trying to return to her bike.

Tempted to rescue her, he let his Hummer idle at the next light so long the vehicle behind him honked.

She's fine. He drove on. Considering the dynamics of their relationship, he should keep out of it. She'd been hell on his ego once before. Why ask for a second helping? Besides, she was part and parcel of this town, a town he was as determined to leave behind now as he'd been fourteen years ago.

Because Van Dormer had asked them to tape their interviews, he pulled into the drugstore lot, parked and went in to see if they had any voice recorders—and nearly bumped into Edna, who was just coming out.

"Excuse me." He held the door open, as he would for any woman, but averted his gaze so he wouldn't have to look at his father's wife, a woman who wore vast amounts of makeup and owned an extensive wardrobe.

Much to his chagrin, she didn't simply accept his polite gesture and go on her way. "That's all you've got to say to me?"

He clenched his jaw. Apparently, the Dunlaps weren't as willing to ignore him as he was them. "What else do you want?"

"Bruce says you'll be staying with us next week. I would think you could at least *greet* me."

What was his father doing? He had no plans to stay at the ranch, and he'd made that very clear. He figured this had more to do with a power play between the two of them than whether or not he was ever going to become a houseguest.

Rod hated to weaken his father's position; Edna didn't deserve the relief the truth would bring her. But he wasn't about to get drawn into their games. "Fortunately, your husband's wrong. I won't be staying with you. Ever. Why would I want to?"

The relief he'd expected didn't appear. "How long will you be in town?"

Physically, Patrick took after Bruce, but Stuart resembled his mother. They had the same broad, determined forehead and fathomless gray eyes. Edna had been pretty enough once. She still tanned herself and spent plenty of time doing all the things women liked to do—having her hair and nails done and whatever else. But she was already becoming a mere shadow—or maybe a caricature—of what she'd been in her glory days. Her cheeks drooped like jowls, and her chin seemed to disappear into her neck.

"If I keep my distance, what does it matter?" he asked.

"Can you really be that uncaring? You must understand how difficult it is for me and my children to have my…my husband's…well, you know what you are, showing up all over town, inviting speculation and gossip. Ever since you arrived, I've had to hear about it from just about everyone I know."

"Forgive me for not being more sensitive to your discomfort, but I'm here until I leave." Since she didn't have the sense to pass through the door he held open for her, he let it swing shut and walked inside. But instead of going out, she marched after him.

"He already has two sons," she cried. "He doesn't need you!"

Turning, Rod forced her, with a steely look, to back up. "You're right. And I don't need him. Or you."

Quickly recovering her nerve, she poked a finger into his chest. "How I wish you'd never been born."

She'd lowered her voice, no doubt to avoid being overheard, but Rod caught every venomous word. "You've made that clear from the beginning."

"He was *married,*" she said, scrambling to justify herself.

"So? It's not my fault you couldn't keep your husband satisfied."

At this, she nearly choked. She hadn't expected him to go on the offensive. As a child, he'd been cautious whenever he encountered her. He hadn't wanted to incite her anger for fear she'd have his mother kicked off the farm. Or that she might do something even worse to Carolina. She'd been the only Dunlap who truly frightened him, the only one who was more mean than stupid. But she didn't frighten him anymore. His mother was gone. There was no way Edna could hurt Carolina now.

"You think you've climbed so far above the lettuce patch that you're too good for *us?*"

"Anyone with a heart or a conscience would fit that description."

Her eyes nearly bulged out of her head. "I don't care what you've become. You'll always be a dirty *Mexican* to me and anyone else who matters!"

"It's not my *Mexican* blood I'm ashamed of." Leaving her standing where she was, he strode off in search of the recorder he'd come to buy. He wished the fact that he'd let loose and said what he wanted made him feel better, but it didn't. He'd long since learned that he could find no peace where the Dunlaps were concerned. He could cover the wound, hide it from the curious, but it would always fester….

By the time he left the store, Edna was gone and so was Sophia. He spent the rest of the late afternoon and evening visiting the farmers, ranchers and homeowners who lived in the area he'd been assigned. All the while, he tried to put his encounter with Edna out of his mind. It required some effort, but he was determined not to let the Dunlaps get under his skin the way they had when he was growing up.

His last interview ended at close to ten, but he'd finished what he'd hoped to do and headed back to the motel, eager to check his e-mail and get some sleep, since he couldn't visit that safe house for a number of hours yet. But there was no longer a parking space available. After circling the lot twice, he eventually wedged the Hummer into a corner spot next to a van with ABC News on the side and walked to his room from clear over by the ice machines.

Since he was still analyzing his interviews, he didn't notice anything amiss until he drew close. Then he could see that his door, the one the manager had fixed after Sophia had taken a battering ram to it, was standing open.

Problem was, he'd closed and locked it when he left.

16

It was Leland Jennings, the motel manager, who called Sophia shortly after she reported for work. She wasn't sure Rod would've bothered. When she arrived, Leland stood in the doorway while Rod sat on one of the beds, arms and legs spread wide as he leaned back on his hands, frowning at the destruction around him. Someone had emptied his clothes out of his duffel bag and cut them up, presumably with the knife sticking out of his pillow. Even the bag had been slashed. Writing covered the walls and the place smelled like gasoline. But if the person who'd broken in had meant to torch the room, something had stopped him.

"Wild night?" she said as Leland moved to admit her.

Rod glanced up. "Someone had fun. But it wasn't me."

"He's a trouble magnet," Leland complained with a shake of his head. "I just replaced the lock on this door last night. You remember. I took it from the laundry room. And look, it's broken again."

"Good thing the city's going to replace it for you, right?"

He gestured for her to follow him into the bathroom. "And that's not all the damage."

A giant penis had been spray-painted on the mirror. Below that, Sophia read the words, *Go home, Mexican cocksucker.*

"Anyone see who did this?" She withdrew a notepad from the breast pocket of her uniform as they returned to the room.

Rod nudged his laptop with his foot. It had been thrown to the floor and lay there broken. "No. I roused the ABC camera crew, a few of whom are staying on either side of me, but they said they didn't notice anyone coming or going."

"They didn't hear anything, either?" she asked in surprise.

"In one room the TV was on so loud the two people staying there could barely hear me pounding on their door. It's just one woman on the other side, but I woke her out of a dead sleep. I figure I'll have to wait till morning to canvass the rest."

"I don't know what to do," Leland said. "My mom's not going to like this. It'll really upset her. She had a cow when Hillary Hawthorne set up shop in room six and pasted a nine behind it." He added, as an aside to himself, "Something I actually found sort of titillating."

Sophia held up a hand. "Keep your sexual fantasies to yourself, Leland."

"What?" he said in a desultory tone. "You guys are in your sexual prime, right? I'm a single man in my forties who lives with my widowed mother. Knowing Hillary was putting out a few doors down was the highlight of my whole year. If my love life doesn't improve soon, it might be the highlight of my whole decade. But that isn't what I'm trying to tell you."

"Then you'd better get to the point," she said.

"I don't have another room for you. I never did make it over to the hardware store today so I can't steal the lock from the laundry like I did before. I'm afraid Mr. Guerrero will have to find another place until I can get this room repaired."

Leland made it sound as though he wouldn't mind if Rod stayed away indefinitely. What with the damage that seemed to follow him, his brand of trouble wasn't nearly as "titillating" as Hillary Hawthorne's.

A V formed between Rod's eyebrows. "So where do you suggest I go?"

Choosing to stare at the carpet rather than brave Rod's displeasure, Leland rocked back and forth, and Sophia understood why. Rod could be intimidating when he was angry. She knew that from when she'd used her Taser on him. His expression then, and now, brought new meaning to the saying, "If looks could kill."

"There's the Sundowner on the other side of town…" Leland said.

Rod glared at him for several seconds more, then finally responded. "Which has, what, *eight* rooms?"

"That's about right." He nodded. "Yeah. Eight. I'm sure of it."

"You don't think that, owing to the recent influx of reporters, they'll be full over there, too?"

Leland shrank back a step or two, out of the doorway. "You could try getting a room in Douglas or Sierra Vista…."

"I'm not leaving town."

Sophia decided this might be a good place to break in. "Any of your stuff missing?" she asked Rod.

"No."

"You've checked?"

"I've checked."

"So…whoever did this just meant to send you a message."

"Whoever did this hates my guts and wanted me to know it."

"Who do you think it was?"

His beard rasped as he rubbed a hand over his face. "The same person you think it was."

"Stuart."

"Who else?"

It had to be his half brother. One of them, anyway. As far as Sophia knew, no one else in Bordertown felt strongly enough about Rod to do something like *this*.

She unclipped her radio from her belt. "I'll call my officer, have him dust for prints."

After getting off the bed, Rod grabbed the keys he'd tossed on the dresser. "You don't want to do that yourself?"

"And let you confront Stuart on your own? No way," she said. "I've had to see the M.E. enough for one summer." She didn't specify which man she believed would be left standing but, in her opinion, there was no contest. Maybe Stuart could hold his own against a regular guy.

But Rod was no regular guy.

"This has been a really shitty day, you know that?"

Rod had insisted on driving his Hummer. They'd already been to the Dunlap ranch but were unable to rouse anyone at Stuart's place, so they'd gone next door, where

Patrick had answered as soon as they knocked. Once he got over his initial surprise at finding Rod on his doorstep, he said he didn't know a thing about the trashed motel room. He also claimed he hadn't seen his brother since they got off work at dinnertime.

Sophia believed him. Rod must've believed him, too, because he'd stalked back to the Hummer without taking Patrick up on his offer to have his wife come to the door and vouch for his presence at home.

They'd left the ranch without stopping at the main house. All the windows had been dark, suggesting that the older Dunlaps were already in bed. Now they were on their way to the Firelight, Stuart's favorite bar.

Rod's bad mood translated into a lead foot, but Sophia let his speeding slide. It was late, there wasn't much traffic on the road and she could understand why he might be a little eager to get ahold of Stuart.

"I can't say today's been too stellar for me, either," she said. After leaving her father's feed store, and fending off reporters who'd tried every possible tactic to get her to say more than she should about the UDA killings, she'd holed up in her house. She'd been trying to get some rest before working graveyard. Tonight, she planned to patrol the ranches, see if she could spot anything that might help solve the UDA murders or at least discourage a fourth incident. But her attempt at sleep had been a wasted effort. Instead, she'd lain on her bed, wide-awake, pondering whether or not to approach her mother with Leonard Taylor's story.

If Anne had gone to the police, it meant her mother had believed her and yet had done nothing to protect her. And if she hadn't, Sophia would've dragged their most horrifying skeleton out of the closet for nothing. They'd struggled so hard to get beyond what Gary had done....

Sophia didn't want to have that awkward conversation. She preferred to let her mother keep pretending, so they could have *some* semblance of a relationship. As contemptible as Sophia found Anne's actions regarding Gary's behavior, Anne was trying to make up for her shortcomings in other ways. She brought over produce from her garden, had just quilted Sophia a blanket, saved magazines and news clippings she thought Sophia might find of interest. As imperfect as Anne was, she was really the only family member Sophia had left. Her brother visited occasionally but work demands kept him on the East Coast, where he was busy raising a family.

In any case, Gary didn't have a nude photograph of her, at least not in his wallet, so it was reasonable to assume that Leonard had been lying about Anne, too.

But if he *was* lying, how had he guessed that there was any impropriety in her relationship with her stepfather?

"Sophia, you still with me?"

Bringing her mind back to the present, she shifted her eyes away from the steady beam of their headlights on the asphalt in front of them. "What?"

"I said, what was so rotten about your day?"

Where did she start? With the call she'd received from Councilman Fedorko informing her that her time was running out? With the embarrassment of flashing Rod, only to have him immediately withdraw? With the outright hostility she'd faced from Detective Lindstrom during their meeting with the FBI? Or the confrontation she'd had with her stepfather, in which he'd basically denied everything she knew to be true?

Choosing not to go into any of it, she shrugged and kept her answer vague. "A lot of things."

"Like…"

Apparently, he wouldn't let it go, so she decided to tell him a portion of the truth. "After I left your motel last night, I caught Leonard Taylor speeding."

"And you pulled him over."

"That's right."

Rod startled her by cursing.

"What?"

"You couldn't have turned a blind eye for once? Shit, Sophia, are you *trying* to get yourself killed? He could be responsible for twelve murders!"

"What are you talking about? I'm the chief of police around here—at least, for now," she added under her breath. "It's my job to enforce the traffic laws."

"Your safety comes before the damn traffic laws!"

She straightened in her seat. "Slow down."

He didn't change his speed but he seemed to realize he was out of line and stopped harassing her for doing her job. "What did Leonard have to say?"

She didn't really want to continue the conversation. His flare of temper didn't sit well.

"Are you going to tell me or not?" he prodded.

"He didn't say much."

Draping an arm over the steering wheel, he took a moment to study her. "You brought it up for a reason."

She took a deep breath. "I just wanted to tell you that he was openly belligerent, threatened me, that sort of thing." She'd also wanted to tell Rod what Leonard had said about her stepfather having a nude picture of her, but she'd already told him too much about her personal life. He was only in town for a short while. She wasn't sure why she felt this urge to lean on him, why she was curious to hear what he'd have to say about Leonard and where Leonard could've gotten his information.

Maybe she was latching onto the first person to come along because she didn't feel she could count on anyone else. Which was pathetic. She had to stand on her own two feet.

"If you see him in town again, leave him alone," he said.

"Even if he's breaking the law?" she snapped.

"Unless someone's life is at stake, you can wait until you have help."

She folded her arms. "You don't think I can do this job any more than anyone else does."

Scowling, he hesitated, then blew out a sigh. "I didn't mean it that way. I just… Some men, men like Leonard, don't seem to care how they deal with people. It's not necessary to put your life at risk to give out a speeding ticket, that's all."

She didn't have the opportunity to respond. They'd reached the Firelight, and he was already getting out.

Rod was looking for a fight. He didn't kid himself that he wasn't. He supposed he'd been hoping Stuart or Patrick would provoke him enough to justify a reaction like that ever since he'd returned to Bordertown.

The damage done to his belongings at the motel certainly gave him the excuse he'd been looking for. But he couldn't find Stuart.

He and Sophia walked through the Firelight, asking the men huddled on stools or sitting around tables if anyone had seen him, but every response was the same—he hadn't been in tonight.

"Where could the little prick have gone?" Rod muttered.

Sophia stood with him at the back of the bar, surveying the scene. "I don't know. It's nearly midnight on a week-night, and he works early in the morning. Everything else in town is closed up. He should be here if he's not at home. Unless…" She nibbled at her bottom lip as she considered whatever had occurred to her.

He leaned close to compensate for the loud, thumping music coming from an old-fashioned jukebox. "Unless what?"

"Unless he's with a prostitute or someone else for the night. I suspect Trudy Dilspeth does a bit more than cut hair for quite a few guys."

That meant they might not find him till morning. It wasn't what Rod wanted to hear, but…he couldn't think of any other place to look. "If that's the case, we're wast-ing our time."

"We could drive by Trudy's house, see if we spot his truck."

"And what, wait for him to come out? Drag him from her bed? We'll go about our business and take care of this later." Rod hated to delay his gratification. But he still needed to visit the safe house Sophia had mentioned in their meeting with the FBI. By this time of night there should be some activity.

"You're willing to do that?" she asked.

He managed a shrug despite the anger knotting his muscles. "Murder is worse than a few slashed clothes."

"He destroyed your laptop, too."

"Thanks for reminding me."

Her grin told him she was being a smart-ass on purpose.

"Anyway, the laptop and the clothes can be replaced. I'm ready to head over to the safe house."

"Then let's go."

He was about to tell her that he planned to drop her off at her car. There was no point in taking her to the safe house. In his view, that was another example of unnecessary risk. But just as he opened his mouth to say she wasn't going with him, a tall thin man with sandy-blond hair approached, his gaze fixed on Sophia.

"Hey, long time no see."

Even in the dim atmosphere Rod could tell that this man's skin was about as white as any he'd ever seen. That meant he wasn't a rancher or a farmer or anyone else who worked outside....

"Dick," Sophia responded with a bit too much emphasis on his name, and Rod realized this was the pastor she'd once dated. The one who'd impregnated a teenager. He must've been in the restroom or something when they first came through because Rod hadn't seen him.

Smiling, the pastor took her by the elbow and dropped his voice to an intimate level. "How is everything?"

It was pretty obvious Sophia didn't want him to touch her. She tried to break contact, only to bump up against Rod. That made her step backward to avoid them both. "Fine. And you?"

"I'm hanging in there. I've tried to reach you a couple of times, but...I'm not sure you're getting my messages. You never call back."

"I've been busy." It was a throwaway statement, spoken with little concern. "Was there anything in particular you wanted?"

He moved in close again. "No. I haven't seen you at church in a while, that's all."

"That's why you called? To see why I wasn't at church?"

"I wanted to make sure there aren't any—" he glanced at Rod and lowered his voice even more "—hard feelings between us that would keep you from worshipping with me on Sundays."

"I have no interest in worshipping with you, Dick," she said flatly.

A pained expression yanked his eyebrows together. "Why not? I've apologized, Sophia. I don't know what more I can do."

"You could quit calling and leave her alone," Rod said. "That'd be a good start." He shouldn't be getting involved in this, but he had no other outlet for the aggression churning inside him. And Rod didn't like what the pastor's body language conveyed. Wife or no wife, he'd cheat with Sophia if given half a chance. The mere thought of him sniffing after her bothered Rod. He didn't want someone like Dick, the married pastor, trying to climb into her bed.

"Excuse me?" Dick said.

Rod rested his hands loosely on his hips. "You heard me."

Sophia stepped between them. "But, of course, he didn't mean it. Since what happens in my life is *none of his business*."

Emboldened by Sophia's pointed response, Dick lifted his chin. "I don't believe we've met."

"Name's Rod. Rod Guerrero."

"I've heard of you. You're Bruce Dunlap's—"

Rod broke in before Dick could grapple too long for the right euphemism. "Bastard. Yes. But you know what they say. You can't choose your family."

That left nowhere for Dick to go as far as subtle put-downs went, so he turned his attention back to Sophia. "Are you two...*together?*"

"No," she said. "At the moment, I'm even beginning to rethink our friendship."

Sliding his arm around her shoulders, Rod offered Dick a conspirator's smile. "Don't listen to her. She's got a terrible crush on me. She just doesn't like to admit it."

"If only I'd brought my Taser," she said dryly.

He gave her a visible squeeze. "The handcuffs will be enough for tonight, honey."

Dick's confusion grew more apparent. "Aren't you new in town?"

"I got here a couple days ago."

"That's what I thought."

"And he'll be leaving as soon as we solve the UDA murders," Sophia chimed in. "Which reminds me... You haven't seen Stuart Dunlap, have you?"

"I saw him earlier, pulling out of the Mother Lode Motel," Dick said. "Why?"

Rod dropped the arm he'd slung around Sophia. "What time was that?"

Dick checked his watch. "Musta been about...two hours ago, around eight-thirty."

Not too long before Rod had returned from his interviews.

"I know, because I was on my way here and remember thinking I had about an hour and a half to enjoy myself before I had to get home," Dick added with a weak laugh.

Rod pressed the time display on his phone. "I hate to break it to you, but your curfew's come and gone."

"I made it home by ten, but...married life isn't always

easy, you know? Tonight was one of those nights." He whistled. "So what if my wife's young. She's a handful." He chuckled but there was no real humor in it, and if he was hoping to incite Sophia's sympathy, it didn't work.

"Was Stuart alone when you saw him?" she asked.

"Alone and driving like a bat out of hell. He just about crashed into me. And when I honked to let him know I was there, he ignored me. He didn't seem to care that he could've killed us both."

Because he knew that having Pastor Dick honk at him was the least of his worries if Rod got back to that motel room before he made his getaway.

17

They had fingerprints. Officer Noyes had called to let Sophia know he'd picked up several from the door handle and Rod's computer. She needed to have those prints analyzed to see who they belonged to, but deep down she wasn't particularly optimistic that they'd prove it was Stuart who'd trashed Rod's room. She couldn't imagine he'd do something like that without wearing gloves. He wasn't the smartest man she'd ever met, but he wasn't stupid, either. If she had her guess, the prints belonged to a combination of Rod, Leland and the maid who tidied up during the day.

But she'd gathered what evidence she could, just in case. And they had Dick's sighting to corroborate their suspicion that it'd been Stuart. In the morning, she'd ask Grant to search for more witnesses and work from there. Not that they'd be able to spend much time on a vandalism case. She had bigger things to worry about. Like the fact that Rod had gone into the safe house fifteen minutes ago and hadn't come out yet. After he'd dropped her at her car, she'd waited long enough to make sure he wouldn't realize she planned to follow him and had arrived just in time to see him go in. She'd expected him to come out almost right away, but he hadn't. And each passing minute wound her nerves a little tighter.

She turned her police radio down so low she could hardly hear it. She was in a poor neighborhood filled with aging tract houses, cracked sidewalks and weed-infested yards. Most of the folks who lived here had their own secrets to hide, so she'd rather they not know there was a cruiser parked on the street. Besides, the radio's crackling made her even more apprehensive than she already was. Rod hadn't wanted any backup. He'd claimed he wasn't used to it and that undercover didn't usually work that way, which was true. But that didn't mean he was bulletproof.

As far as she was concerned, he should've been out of that house by now. How much longer should she sit and wait?

"Damn it," she muttered when it grew even later and there was no sign of him.

She had to get closer, see what was going on. Maybe something had gone wrong and he'd been shot or overwhelmed by a number of men. Maybe, if she didn't go in and help, he wouldn't make it out….

Hoping Grant was still awake after collecting those fingerprints, she gave him a call.

"'Lo?"

His sleepy answer told her he was already in bed. "Grant?"

"What's up, Chief?"

"Sorry to bother you again. I just… I'm investigating a safe house and wanted to let someone know where I'm at. That's all."

"A safe house?"

"Right. It might be owned by the Mexican Mafia. The address is 2944 Dugan Drive."

"Okay."

"You got that?"

"Oh, you want me to write it down?"

Would she have been so specific otherwise? Of course not, but Grant was new and young and he needed everything spelled out, so she did her best to keep the irritation from her voice. "That would be a good idea."

"Is this in connection with the vandalism earlier?" He sounded confused, but more alert, as if he'd sat up.

"No, I'm working the UDA murders."

"Do you need me to come over and back you up?"

"I don't think so." He wasn't very experienced; if he came she'd only have to worry about him, too, and that wasn't the kind of help she needed. "I'm actually backing up a consultant we have on the case. I wanted you to know where I was in the event that…in the event there's a problem."

"Okay. I get it. How about this? If I don't hear from you in fifteen minutes, I'll drive over."

"Perfect," she said, and hung up.

There still was no sign of Rod.

Checking for movement or activity in the other houses, Sophia got out of the car and closed her door quietly, then locked it. She couldn't bring her rifle without looking antagonistic, but she wasn't going to make it easy for someone else to get hold of it, either. Bad enough to get shot. Even worse to be shot with her own gun.

The windows of 2944 Dugan Drive had been blacked out. At first glance, it appeared as dark inside as all the other houses on the street. But there were three cars out front, not counting Rod's Hummer. And there'd been some activity. Rod's body had been silhouetted in light for a brief moment when he was admitted. The question was—what were they doing?

For all she knew, they had a meth lab in the bathroom or kitchen. The scent of harsh chemicals hung heavy on the warm air, like the smell of an overripe peach, suggesting *someone* in the area was cooking dope. She knew how unstable those compounds were, how easily a meth lab could explode. That alone made it dangerous to approach. And sometimes guys on crack didn't feel pain. It could be very difficult to bring one down. Even for a Navy SEAL.

As she reached the yard, she was tempted to draw her gun and circle the house before knocking. She wanted to make note of the number of exits, the number of windows and the condition of the dilapidated cinder-block fence that partially enclosed the backyard. But if the people living in this house were really involved in smuggling—humans or drugs or both—or if they were cooking meth on a large scale, they'd likely have some surveillance equipment to protect the operation. Because of the heavy shadows, she couldn't see any cameras, but she was willing to bet they were there, under the eaves.

Rather than risk being spotted by a surveillance system sneaking around in uniform and with her gun at the ready, which would certainly signal trouble, she decided to approach from the front and to do it boldly, as if this was a routine call.

She just wished she knew how many people were inside. Was Rod armed? After what he'd said to her at the meeting, she doubted it. Whether that decision turned out to be a good one or not depended on how this went down.

The front door loomed a few feet ahead of her, looking

more daunting by the second. As she drew close, she recalled the murder Starkey had told her about not long after
the split up. Hick, a fellow gang member she'd met once,
had been assassinated by a Mexican drug lord, who'd cut
off his head and mounted it on a spike along the border
fence. Using that gruesome incident as proof of the rapid
rise of violence in Mexico, the newspapers had made a
huge deal of it, convincing Sophia, and probably many
others, that something had to be done to stop the bloodshed. That drug lord was one reason she'd gone into law
enforcement, that and the fact that she could make a decent
living while helping her community. And she could carry
a gun and knew how to defend herself. But the cruelty of
his crime also gave her a clear idea of the type of men
she could be dealing with here—men who were capable
of calculated, merciless killing.

Refusing to let fear undermine her confidence, she
managed a neutral expression in case someone was watching her from inside…and knocked.

No one answered.

After waiting two or three minutes, she knocked
again.

Finally the porch light snapped on. A stout Mexican
man, wearing a Paradise Taqueria T-shirt and a tattered
pair of jeans, answered the door. Tattoos covered his arms
and neck, diamond studs glittered from both ears and his
shaved head gleamed with a sheen of sweat. "Can I help
you?" he said.

His English was pretty good. Sophia was glad of that.
At least she'd be able to communicate. "Yes. I'm looking
for the driver of the white Hummer that's parked right
over there." She pointed to Rod's vehicle, which sat at the
curb behind an old Mustang.

"What do you want with him?"

"He's a suspect in a crime."

"I don't know who drives the Hummer. He doesn't live here."

She stepped back, pretending to search for the house numbers. "This is 2944 Dugan Drive, isn't it?"

"Yes."

"That's the address I was given. Someone called in, said he saw the driver of that vehicle go inside this house."

The man stared malevolently at Sophia—as if he wanted to choke her to death and toss her body aside. She was an inconvenience, and he obviously wasn't sure what to do with her. But she wasn't leaving here without Rod. If she had to pull her gun, she would.

He seemed to come to a decision. "Um, my brother's got a friend over. Let me see if that Hummer belongs to him."

"Thank you."

The door closed and Sophia was left sweating on the doorstep, wondering whether she'd just made a huge mistake—or saved Rod's life. Maybe she'd done neither. If Rod was already dead, she wouldn't have much chance of walking away, either. Whoever killed him couldn't let her leave knowing 2944 Dugan Drive was the last place he'd been seen alive. And there was another possibility. If Rod was actually making inroads toward getting the information they needed, her interruption might cut that short….

But she could only act on instinct, and her instincts told her Rod had been inside too long.

After an extended wait, she worked up her nerve and knocked again. Twice. The same man answered, but this time when he opened the door, she also caught sight of

Rod. What lighting there was came from a back room. It was too dim to see much, but when Rod stepped closer, the glare of the porch light revealed marks on his face that hadn't been there before.

"You wanted to talk to me?" He acted sullen, belligerent, like a complete stranger.

Sophia played along. "Yes."

"What for?"

Drawing her gun, she assumed a defensive stance. "I need you to come with me. You're under arrest."

"What'd I do?"

He should've been an actor. He was that convincing. Sophia only hoped she could hold up her end. "You were seen fleeing the scene of a robbery. With a weapon."

She wasn't sure the man sporting all the tattoos would let them walk off, but once she flicked the barrel of the gun toward the cruiser, indicating that Rod should precede her, he made no move to intercede.

"What about my Hummer?" Rod asked as he stalked past her.

"The towing company will pick it up within the hour."

Sophia was afraid to turn away for fear the man at the door would pull out a pistol and shoot them both, or rush them from behind. But she had no alternative. If she didn't keep up the charade, they'd have no chance of getting out of here.

Training her Glock on Rod as if he might make a break for it, she followed him to the cruiser, where she slapped him in handcuffs and helped him into the backseat. As far as she knew, the man in the doorway didn't move. She imagined his eyes boring holes in her back as she loaded her "prisoner." But once she got behind the wheel and glanced at the house, she could see that the door was already shut.

"You okay?" she breathed.

"I'll live," Rod said. "But, God, am I glad to see you."

Resting his head on the back of the seat, Rod closed his eyes and listened as Sophia called Grant, the officer who'd dusted for prints at the motel earlier, to say she was fine and he could go back to bed. His jaw ached, he had a wicked cut on the inside of his cheek, and he'd been kicked in the stomach so hard he couldn't draw a breath without pain. But if Sophia hadn't interrupted when she did, he would've sustained a lot more injuries—maybe even a fatal one.

"What happened in there?" Sophia asked as she pulled out of the neighborhood.

He didn't answer. He was too busy trying to recover.

"Rod?"

Opening his eyes, he met her concerned gaze in the rearview mirror. "Those guys weren't happy to have a stranger show up."

"What guys?"

"The six who beat the shit out of me."

The car lurched as she punched the gas pedal. "Why were there so many? And what were they doing when you got there? Cooking meth?"

"No. I smelled that, too, but it must've come from a different house. There was no evidence of drugs I could see."

"That doesn't surprise me. It's not the best neighborhood in town."

"The guys in 2944 were feeding a group of illegals who'd just arrived."

He couldn't see her face—only her eyes—but he could hear a frown in her voice. "Why'd they start hitting you?"

"The man in charge decided that I needed some incentive to give them the answers they wanted."

"What were the questions?"

He explored the depth of the cut in his mouth with his tongue before responding. "Mostly they wanted to know how I learned about the safe house."

"Why didn't you say you heard about it from a friend of José and Benita Sanchez? What could that hurt?"

"I tried. But they didn't seem to know José and Benita, so that didn't help."

"You didn't tell them you're a cop?"

"Are you kidding? I'd already represented myself as a two-bit hood hoping to get a piece of their action. Suddenly changing my profession would've gotten me killed for sure." He stretched his jaw to check that it still worked. "I shouldn't have shown up without an introduction or a sponsor of some sort. In the interests of time, I tried to take a shortcut, thought I could lie my way around it, and that turned out to be a mistake." He'd been so successful in past operations that he'd gotten cocky, hadn't taken this one seriously enough.

"A *mistake?*" she repeated. "You could've *died* back there."

There were several minutes when he'd thought that was exactly what the outcome would be. "It was a distinct possibility."

"Aren't you supposed to be good at your job?"

He cocked an eyebrow at her. "I'm going to have to get

you back for that one. When my head stops feeling like it might explode."

"I almost didn't follow you, almost didn't go to the door," she said. "What if I'd listened to you and stayed away?"

Her nerves were causing her to revisit the same thought over and over again.

"Like I said, I'm glad you didn't. I owe you. If you have to say 'I told you so,' do it and get it over with."

"I'm not saying 'I told you so.'"

"Then what are you saying? That you should've gone instead of me? Do you really wish you had?"

"No. Of course not. It's just… I don't know. I'm upset that you're hurt, and it makes me want to yell or hit something, even though that isn't logical."

"We're both freaked out." He'd done a dozen undercover jobs in which he could've been killed at any moment. Yet he'd survived them all relatively unscathed only to come close to goodbye forever doing pro bono work in Bordertown? What were the chances?

Jonah, who also worked for Department 6, had been shot in the back a year ago. He survived, but while Rod was with him in the E.R. he said something that seemed pretty damn apropos: It's always the jobs where you think you can skate by, the ones you don't expect to get you.

"So how will we get my Hummer back?" he asked.

"*We* won't. We'll drop off the keys and let the towing company grab it. You're done for tonight. If I'd shown up any later they would've killed you."

Here we go again. "But they didn't," he pointed out. "You arrived in time, and I'm okay. So we can both relax. What could've happened doesn't matter anymore."

"Maybe we should've gone in *together*," she murmured

as if better planning might have changed the situation. But taking her in there wouldn't have been an improvement. He shuddered to think of what they would've done to her.

"Then we'd both be planted in the backyard." He braced against the sway of the car as she turned. "By the way, how long are you going to drive before you pull over and let me out of these handcuffs?"

"Oh, right." The car slowed and the tires crunched on the rocky shoulder as she came to a stop. Seconds later, she opened the door and prodded him to lean forward.

Given the kick to his gut, it wasn't a comfortable position, but he didn't feel like getting out of the car, either. He swallowed a groan while she released him. Then he fell back, rubbing his wrists. "That was a close one."

"*Too* close." She turned his face to take advantage of the cabin light and clicked her tongue. "*Look* at you."

Hoping to put her at ease, he attempted a playful grin. "Do I look tough?"

The worry didn't leave her eyes. "No, more like you've been hit by a bus."

"Do you feel sorry enough for me to take me in?"

"*Take you in?*" she echoed, letting go of him.

"I don't have a motel room anymore, remember? I don't even have a change of clothes." He grimaced to make himself appear more pathetic. "And I really need to lie down."

She bit her lip. "We haven't checked the other motel. Maybe they have a room."

"You'd leave me there like this?"

He saw her soften a little. "Good point. Maybe you should see a doctor."

Now she was going too far. "I don't need a doctor.

Those boys were barely getting started. I just need some rest."

"But I only have one bed."

"I'll take the couch."

She pushed his hair to one side to examine some injury he couldn't feel, thanks to all the others. "You don't suppose you have a concussion, do you?"

"Why? Am I not making sense?"

"You're making sense, but…"

He gave up the games. "I'm fine, Sophia. I need sleep. That's all."

Letting her breath go, she straightened. "Okay, I'll take you home. But if I wasn't so relieved you made it out of there alive, I'd never go for it."

"I should've told you how beautiful you are," he muttered.

"Excuse me?"

"When you lifted up your shirt earlier." He allowed his eyes to slide shut. "It's all I can think about."

18

In the end, Sophia didn't have the heart to make Rod sleep on the couch. He was too banged up. She helped him clean off the blood, put some antiseptic on his cuts, then guided him to her room, where he peeled off everything except his boxers and fell into bed. Less than fifteen minutes after they'd arrived at her place, she had a trail of clothing across her floor and he was taking up most of her bed.

"I'm *such* a sucker," she mumbled. But she was on duty until four, which meant she had to go back to the station for a couple of hours. If she wasn't going to be home, anyway, she couldn't see putting someone who was injured on her uncomfortable leather couch, especially someone as tall as Rod. She'd figure out where she was going to sleep later.

She'd just opened her front door to let herself out of the house when a shadow loomed over her. Startled, she grabbed her gun before realizing it was Starkey.

"Whoa!" He raised his hands, eyes on the barrel. "What's with the quick draw, Tex?"

Embarrassed, Sophia put it away. She was used to hearing Starkey's motorcycle when he came by, but he'd wrecked it a few weeks ago and been borrowing vehicles from friends and other gang members ever since. An old Camaro sat across the street, engine idling. She thought there was someone behind the wheel, but she couldn't make out who it was.

"Sorry. I normally hear you coming. And I guess I'm a little jittery tonight."

"Is it those killings you've been investigating? They startin' to get to ya?"

Starting? They'd been "getting to her" from the beginning. "Among other things." Instead of inviting him in, she stepped out of the house and closed the door behind her. She preferred not to let him know that Rod was staying at her place. She wasn't sure why. It was none of his business, yet she knew it would make him jealous. He hadn't been willing to change his lifestyle to keep her but openly admitted he'd been a fool to lose her. She had the feeling that as he aged, he'd begun to wish for a more stable life and regretted that he hadn't done more for Rafe.

"What other things?" He accompanied her as she walked toward her car, which she'd parked in the driveway.

"Roderick Guerrero's motel room was vandalized tonight. You don't know anything about it, do you?"

"Hell, no. Why would *I* know anything about it?"

Because if anyone had his ear to the ground and could tell her what was happening in the seedy underbelly of this seemingly tranquil town, it was Starkey and his Hells Angels buddies. He was generally tight-lipped, didn't want to undermine his badass image by narking to the cops, but every once in a while she pried a few details out of him that came in handy. "The company you keep." She jerked her head toward whoever was waiting in the Camaro.

"Johnny Greer don't know nothin'. He's part of the

Prescott chapter. He's thinkin' about relocatin' so he came down to check out the scene."

She'd reached her car, but paused to finish the conversation. "I was hoping someone out there might be bragging about it."

"Someone like Stuart?"

She felt her eyebrows jerk up. "That was fast."

"You ask twenty different people in Bordertown and you'll get the same answer. It's no secret that Stuart hates Rod. Always has."

True and yet...Starkey had spoken with such certainty. "Maybe so, but you've heard something, haven't you?"

"I've heard Stuart talking trash around town ever since Rod came back. That's it."

"You're positive."

He stepped close enough that she could smell the alcohol on his breath. "Would I lie to you?"

"If it served your purposes, yeah."

He laughed. "Come back to me, and I'll never lie to you again. I'll change, get a real job, become respectable."

Maybe he would. If he didn't get himself killed first. He *wanted* to change, but the partying had too firm a grip. His taste for drugs and alcohol always drew him back. "What am I supposed to say to that?"

"You could say yes."

"That wouldn't work, and you know it. I can't imagine you really want to be with me. We've been apart for nine years. We're not even the same people anymore."

"All I know is that I can't get over you."

She backed away when he tried to touch her. "Starkey, please. It's been a hell of a night."

Breaking eye contact, he sucked in a hissing breath as if her words had stung. "Yeah, right."

"Is that why you came by? So we can go through this again?"

"No, I don't know what I'm doing. Sometimes I see you and I realize what I could've had, how the past decade could've been different for Rafe."

"You can change your life without me. You know that, right?"

"Yeah, maybe." He didn't sound too convinced. "If I wanted to spend the rest of my life going to AA meetings. Anyway, I came to tell you I've got a bead on a guy who's selling silencers out of his garage."

At last, a possible break. "Who is it?"

"Name's Jackson Riollo. Lives in Sierra Vista."

"Has he sold one to anybody in Bordertown in the past six months or so?"

"Don't know yet. Got an appointment with him. Told him I'm in the market. Figure I'll see if he'll tell me anything about his clientele once I get there."

"When's the appointment?"

"Tomorrow night."

"Good. Tell me how it goes." Planning to drive out to the Simpson ranch to see if Kevin, Alma or James was monitoring UDA activity tonight, she opened her car door. She also wanted to go over to Charlie Sumpter's. Since she had to perform her usual duties and had fallen behind, the SAC had given her a light assignment—get hold of Charlie to see if there was anything backing up his blistering diatribes against illegal aliens. That was it. But she'd placed two more calls without success.

She'd have to look up his daughter, see if she could reach him that way. Until then, she figured it wouldn't hurt to drive out and take a look at his place, see if it appeared to be shut up for an extended period. If he'd left his dog behind to be cared for by the neighbors, he'd probably be coming back fairly soon.

But Starkey made no move to leave.

"Is there something else?" she asked when he caught her door so she couldn't shut it.

"I have a question." He hunched over so he could see her face.

She didn't bother inserting the key into the ignition. "What is it?" Surely he wasn't going to come up with more nonsense about getting back together….

Leaning close, he lowered his voice. "Is it true?"

She searched for clues in his face but couldn't see where he was going with this. "Is *what* true?"

"What I heard at the Firelight?"

His mention of the bar put her on edge. The Firelight had come up a lot lately…. "What did you hear?"

"That you and your…er…stepfather are…you know…having an affair."

"What? When did you hear this? I was there earlier, and nothing like that was being said. I didn't even *see* Leonard."

"It was right before closing." He tapped the side of her car. "So…are you going to tell me?"

She couldn't believe he'd need to ask. He knew what had happened in the past, how abhorrent she'd found Gary's advances. "Starkey, I'd never have an affair with my mother's husband. He didn't get away with anything even when I was a teenager. That's why I moved out, remember?"

He seemed to breathe more easily as he straightened. "Okay. Good. I wanted to be sure. Leonard was flashing around that picture and, well, it made me wonder."

Leonard?

Sophia gripped the keys so tightly the jagged edges cut into her palm. "What picture? Did you see it?"

He nodded. "You're naked."

"What?" Leonard had said *Gary* had the picture. Was it the same one? If so, how'd he end up with it? "You're sure it was me?"

"Positive. Had your tattoo sleeve and everything."

A hard knot formed in her stomach. "But…where was it taken? How long ago?" She hadn't gotten her tattoos until after she'd left home. There was no way her mother would've allowed it when they were living together. Anne would've kicked her out even before Sophia chose to leave. To this day, she hated Sophia's sleeve.

"Hard to tell. Looked like it was taken in a bedroom, maybe, somewhere in the past couple years."

Sophia shook her head. "That makes no sense. Where could Leonard have gotten hold of such a thing?"

"He said he got it from someone who works at the feed store. Wouldn't say who. Claimed he didn't want to get the guy in trouble."

"That makes me sick! I can't even imagine…" Her mind reeled, but she couldn't come up with a plausible explanation for what Starkey had just told her. "You're *sure* it was me," she said again.

"No question. And…"

That *and* didn't sound like good news. Was there more? "What is it?" she asked.

"Liz Torres was at the bar tonight."

Liz was a member of city council. "What was she doing there? She doesn't even drink."

"She was with friends from out of town."

"No way." Liz never went to the bar, especially so late. "Don't tell me *she* heard what was going on."

"She saw the picture. The way everyone was talking and showing it around, I don't see how she could've missed it. And she didn't seem pleased."

Of course she wouldn't be pleased. Sophia was in the middle of the biggest murder case ever to hit Bordertown. If she was having an affair with her mother's husband—or anyone else—that would create a scandal, and it would look as though she wasn't concerned enough, as if she wasn't doing her job.

"I've never slept with Gary, or undressed for him, or *anything*," she said.

After seeing that picture, even Starkey seemed unsure. "For your sake, I hope not. Because I'm gettin' the feeling this town's about to lynch someone…."

And he didn't have to say who'd be the victim of that lynching.

Instead of visiting the ranches, Sophia headed straight to Leonard's place. She had to get ahold of that picture. The thought of the whole town seeing her naked and hearing the shocking story of an affair with Gary made her ill even without considering the rest of the implications. What if the city council let her go without so much as a recommendation? What would she do? How would she find work? And what if her mother believed the gossip? Surely, deep down, Anne *had* to know she'd never have an affair with Gary. Sophia had never liked him. But the gossip would embarrass them all. And Anne's insecurities and jealousies would once again come to the forefront, where they could easily blind her. This could break up her mother's marriage or, worse, Anne might blame Sophia for the whole thing and take Gary's side, as she'd done before.

Once she arrived, she sat at the edge of the property, staring at Leonard's dark trailer. She knew Rod would be angry at her for coming out here by herself. He'd say it was too dangerous. But she'd taken other risks that'd paid off, like going to Naco and the safe house. Besides, what choice did she have? She had to defend her job, her fragile relationship with her mother, her reputation.

Taking a deep breath, she turned off the engine and got out. A slight breeze sent a chill down her spine as she approached the front door. Until that moment, she hadn't realized she was sweating, but she wasn't surprised. It'd been so hot lately—at least one hundred and ten degrees during the day. With temperatures over ninety at night, there was no reprieve.

The cicadas weren't out tonight. The desert stretched silent and still in all directions—until she came closer to the house and Leonard's rottweiler started barking. Sophia flinched as he jumped against the fence and bared his teeth but she continued to the front stoop.

She could barely hear the sound of her hand hitting the wooden door above the ruckus of the dog. But she wasn't worried about being heard; the dog was loud enough to bring Leonard to the door even if her knock wasn't.

Fingering the butt of her gun, she backed up a couple of steps and moved to the side to wait. Nothing happened.

"Leonard?" she called, and pounded on the door again. "It's Chief St. Claire. I need to speak to you. Open up."

The trailer remained dark, with only the dog making noise.

Sophia checked her watch. Nearly three. The Firelight

closed at two, which was why she'd come out to his trailer
without checking the bar first.

"Leonard?" she called again, then tried the door. It was
unlocked.

Leonard couldn't believe he'd found her. He'd been
searching all over town, and here she was at his own
trailer. He could see her patrol car sitting right out front.

A trickle of excitement ran through him, the first he'd
felt in ages. This was a lucky turn of events. If he caught
her inside, he could shoot her. He'd say she woke him out
of a dead sleep, that he thought it was a burglar or maybe
the UDA killer, which was plausible since he lived so far
out of town, and claim he acted in self-defense.

But he had to get into his trailer, and he had to do it
while she was still rummaging around.

Parking his boss's truck at a distance so the sound of
the engine wouldn't tip her off, Leonard took his gun from
the seat beside him and got out. Then, planning to go in
through the back door, he circled wide. It wasn't as if he
had to worry about setting off the dog. Caesar knew him.
There'd be nothing to alert her to his return.

You're gonna get what you deserve. This wasn't exactly
what he'd had in mind these past few months. He'd first
wanted to strip her of everything she held dear and watch
her topple from her lofty perch.

But some opportunities were too good to pass up.

This one was absolutely *golden*. The light in the bedroom told him where she was. He imagined her sorting
through his belongings, searching for that picture he'd
shown around the bar. Maybe she was even hoping to
find some evidence to link him to the UDA murders. But

the only thing she'd find was the newspaper clipping of herself on the back of his bedroom door.

Would it frighten her to read what he'd written across her face? Or would it simply anger her?

The door creaked as it swung open. He paused to listen for footsteps, but couldn't hear a sound from inside, especially when Caesar barked once, twice. He wanted to kick the damn dog, would've had him put down a long time ago if not for the hope that his family would come back. Caesar belonged to Millie, his oldest daughter. He didn't dare get rid of him. It was going to be bad enough if she found out he didn't allow the dog inside anymore because he was tired of the hair, the smell and the bother of letting him out every few hours.

Gun in hand, he stepped into the tiny laundry room his wife had once kept so tidy and edged into the hallway. Sophia wouldn't be expecting him. He hadn't even driven past the trailer. He'd turned onto the road, spotted her cruiser and stopped before coming close enough for his headlights or anything else to give him away.

Taking a moment to calm his nerves, he went through the logistics of what he hoped to achieve. If he shot her while entering his bedroom, he'd have to say he'd fallen asleep in Kayla and Millie's room, or the forensic evidence wouldn't match. Their room was where he stored his guns, anyway, so that would make sense.

It would all be over with the squeeze of a trigger.

After she was dead, the city council would probably reinstate him. He could convince his wife that Sophia had been lying all along, that this was proof she'd been after him from the beginning. And he'd be able to get his former life back.

He could hardly wait to quit that dusty egg ranch, to tell Dwight to take his job and shove it….

His heart raced as he poked his head into the room. He didn't see Sophia, but the light in the master bath was also on.

Come out, come out, wherever you are, he chanted silently and slipped through the open doorway. The floor squeaked ever so slightly with each step, but he wasn't worried about the noise. He'd seen her shadow in the bathroom. She was trapped.

Keeping his finger on the trigger, he led with his gun. But that shadow didn't belong to Sophia or anyone else. It was merely the reflection of the dark blue towel he'd hung on a nail that had once held a picture his wife had taken when she left him.

Frustrated to think he didn't know his own home anymore, he was about to swing toward the bedroom when Sophia came up behind him and pressed a cold, hard object into the base of his skull—an object he recognized even before she spoke.

"Drop the gun, or I'll blow your head off."

19

Leonard froze but didn't lower his weapon. He couldn't believe Sophia would fire. She didn't have the nerve. That was partially why he was so upset that the town had been stupid enough to give her his job. The mayor, the council members, they were all pretending she had the balls, but she couldn't compete with him, not when it came to the rough stuff. And police work was full of rough stuff.

Political correctness disgusted him. But Sophia's supporters would pay a high price. He was watching that happen, was *showing* them their mistake. "You fire, and you'll go to prison. Is that really what you want?" he asked.

"I won't go to prison. I called my cell phone from your number fifteen minutes ago."

She didn't have to explain why. He knew. She'd say that call came from him. That once she arrived, he attacked her. And it wouldn't be a hard lie to sell. He'd made it very clear how he felt about her—to just about everyone in town. He couldn't imagine there'd be many people who'd have difficulty believing that scenario. To make matters worse, he'd left his cell at home so no one could use it to place him in a particular area if he was ever caught doing what he was doing.

"How'd you know when I got here?" He'd been so damn careful, so sure he had the upper hand. "Did you hear me coming down the hall?"

"I heard everything from the moment you opened the door. I was waiting, listening. I figured you had to come home sooner or later." She jammed the gun into his head. "Drop your weapon."

Maybe she *would* fire. She didn't like him any more than he liked her. She certainly hadn't hesitated to destroy his marriage, his reputation or his career.

Whether she'd act on her threat or not, this situation had grown too risky. There was no need to get into a shoot-out with her. His original plan was working; all he had to do was stick to it.

Slowly, he bent to put his gun on the floor, and she kicked it into the bathroom, out of reach.

"Where've you been tonight, Leonard?"

If only she knew what he'd been doing for the past twenty-four hours. Too bad the listening devices he'd planted in her car, home and office only worked if he was close by. Eager to catch up since he'd last "tuned in," he'd tried to find her after he left the bar, but he hadn't succeeded. She'd deviated from her usual home, station and patrol routines; she'd been in his trailer.

"None of your damn business," he said.

"It will become my business if you've been out in the desert shooting illegal immigrants."

He laughed softly. "Sorry, Sophia. I'm not the one who's killing wetbacks. But if you want my opinion, I think the guy who's doing it deserves a medal."

"Then you're as twisted as he is," she said. "But that doesn't surprise me."

"You're so sure it's me that you're missing the obvious."

"Which is…"

"Oh, no." He shook his head. "You'll have to work that one out for yourself. I'm the *last* person who'd ever help you."

She lowered the gun so it wasn't pointing directly at him, but she didn't put it away. "I don't need your help, Leonard. That's not why I'm here."

Easing himself onto the bed, he stretched out his legs. "No?"

"I'm here for the picture."

He smiled. "Oh, that. Of course."

"Where is it?"

Eager to witness her reaction, he shifted to one side so he could pull it from his back pocket. Then he turned it face out but held it far enough away that he could snatch it back if she grabbed for it. News of her having an affair with her stepfather would be all over town by tomorrow. The picture had already served its purpose, but he couldn't relinquish it to her or anyone else. He'd had to do a lot of work in Photoshop to get that picture to look as real as it did. The image seemed authentic in the dim light of a bar, even here in the bedroom if viewed from a distance, but he had no illusions that it could withstand a close inspection, especially by the subject herself.

To his gratification, the sight of what he'd created made the color drain from Sophia's face. "Where did you get that?"

"Where do you think?"

"Not from Gary. There's no way he could've taken that photo. For one, it's recent."

When he hadn't been able to find any pictures of Sophia

except those snapped at Lake Powell during a trip they'd taken at the invitation of the former chief of police, Leonard had had to adjust his story. But gossip about a current affair would do more damage to Sophia, anyway. Councilwoman Torres definitely hadn't liked what she'd seen. She'd stiffened the moment she took hold of the picture and recognized who it was. Then she'd assumed an air of superiority that told him exactly what she thought of Sophia St. Claire. And she'd been one of Sophia's most ardent supporters!

"I guess I misunderstood," he said. "I was sure Gus was talking about an old affair, but when he brought this to the bar tonight I realized it was taken within the past couple of years."

"Gus didn't bring that to the bar," she said. "Gus isn't even in town. He's in Flagstaff."

Leonard hadn't been aware of that when he'd used Gus's name. Other than running into him at the Firelight occasionally, they had little or no contact. But it didn't matter. Leonard was only trying to torment Sophia; making her scramble to suppress the rumors he'd started would certainly do that. Especially because those rumors were founded on a kernel of truth—a kernel that was already painful for her.

"Then someone else must've given it to me."

"Or it isn't me at all," she said. "What'd you do? Doctor one of the pictures we took at Powell?"

She'd caught on quickly, even though he'd done an excellent job of changing the background. But knowing what he'd done wouldn't improve her situation. She wouldn't be able to counteract the damage to her reputation. Too many people had seen the photograph. Regardless of how much she denied that anything had happened, they'd secretly wonder what had gone on between her and Gary. Particularly since there'd been rumors when she'd left home before graduating from high school.

"I guess you'll never know, huh?" Laughing, he pulled out his lighter. The breasts he'd superimposed over her bikini top were gorgeous—for all he knew they were nicer than the real thing. He'd been careful to choose someone about her size and shape. But as fond as he was of his work, the time had come to destroy it.

Realizing what he was about to do, she lifted her gun again. "Oh, no, you don't."

"Go ahead and shoot," he said, and lit the edge of the photograph.

With a curse, Sophia tossed her gun aside and lunged to stop him. He blocked her with one arm, but he was sitting on the bed, which put him at a disadvantage. He had to drop the picture in order to keep her away from it. Fortunately, it continued to burn where it landed on the floor. He just had to hold her down until it was too late.

"There goes your proof," he whispered in her ear. "Proof that I got those tits off a porn site on the Internet. At least I made you look good, huh? I could've used a picture of some tits that'd been butchered by an implant operation gone wrong. *That* would cause a stir with all the guys who like to dream about getting in your pants."

If she could've reached her gun at that moment, she might've shot him. He'd never seen her fight so hard or become so incensed, but she was no match for his size and strength. The picture was completely destroyed by the time he let go of her and got up to put out the fire that was beginning to lick at the carpet.

Sophia's chest heaved as she scrambled off the bed and watched him stamp out the ashes. She looked utterly distraught. And that made Leonard happier than he'd been in more than a year.

Victory. At last. He could hardly wait till she saw what he had in store for her next.

When Sophia arrived home, she was wiped out, physically and emotionally. She now knew, beyond the shadow of a doubt, that Leonard was out to destroy her. It was as personal as it could get. But knowing didn't help. Her life was unraveling so fast Sophia didn't seem able to stop it. She kept searching for the quickest, surest way of breaking her fall, but she couldn't grasp so much as a handhold.

Part of her wished she'd shot him. The way he'd taunted her, he'd asked for it. But she was a cop. That meant something to her. It meant she couldn't abuse her right to carry a firearm, couldn't abuse her power in any way, or she'd be no better than he was.

She told herself that what he'd done wasn't the end of the world. That picture was a fake, the type of prank some stupid boy might play in high school. She'd simply deny any wrongdoing, do what she could to silence the rumors and weather the embarrassment. What other option did she have? But none of this would be easy. Everyone she met would wonder if it was true. Her mother would freak out and blame her, maybe quit speaking to her. And it could affect her job. Elizabeth Torres had seen that photo, which might legitimize the gossip, take it beyond the realm of a few guys talking dirty over beer.

Covering a yawn, she shuffled up the walk, her feet feeling like lead. She needed a chance to regroup and recover. But one question made it impossible to put the picture fiasco out of her head: How did Leonard find out about Gary? She doubted her mother had told him. Gary must've said something to someone recently, intimated that she'd been receptive to his advances. And Leonard had heard about it, probably at the Firelight, where so much of Bordertown's gossip got started. That was the only reasonable explanation....

She walked into her bedroom before remembering that she'd let Rod stay the night. Until this second, she'd been too upset to think of anything but Leonard and what he was doing to antagonize her. Now she realized she didn't even have a bed to fall into.

While she stood in the middle of the room, trying to decide whether she should make Rod move to the couch or sleep there herself, he leaned up on one elbow.

"Hey," he murmured sleepily and slid over. "'Bout time you got home. You coming to bed?"

He said it as if there was no reason they couldn't share her bed, and suddenly Sophia couldn't name one, either. Although his injuries were more visible, she was hurt, too. What would it matter if they curled up together?

"Why not," she said, and took a pair of boxers and a T-shirt into the bathroom to change. After hanging her uniform over the door, she crossed the room and climbed into the spot he'd vacated for her.

The residual heat from his body was a welcome contrast to the cool air pumping into the room, courtesy of her hard-working air conditioner. But he didn't move, didn't touch her. She was so sure he'd gone back to sleep, she inched closer to his body, searching for the comfort she couldn't seem to find anywhere else. Somehow it helped just to hear him breathe.

He must've felt her move, must've sensed that she wanted to be near him, because he rolled over and scooped her up against his side as if they'd been sleeping together for years.

Once she noticed he was partially awake, she thought he might try to kiss her or touch her. She'd certainly made herself accessible, had even slipped one of her legs over one of his.

But he didn't. "You okay?" he asked.

"I'm fine," she lied. "What about you?"

"Better now," he said with what sounded like a smile, and drifted off to sleep.

It felt good to be held, so good Sophia didn't want to fall asleep despite the fatigue that had been dragging at her only minutes before. She lay awake for a long time, her head on his shoulder, her arm on his bare chest.

And then she began to crave something far less platonic.

Rod felt Sophia touch him while he was still half-asleep. Her hand traveled across his chest and hesitated briefly on his pectoral muscle before skimming lightly over his nipple. He told himself she was just shifting, trying to get comfortable. He thought maybe she was asleep and didn't realize that her movements were so sensual. But a second later, he felt her press her lips to the indentation above his collarbone and knew she was doing more than merely seeking a new position in which to sleep.

Should he accept the invitation she was extending?

Should was a difficult word. The answer was probably not. Maybe *definitely* not. He'd made that decision, hadn't he? But he'd fantasized about Sophia so many times when he was younger that he knew it would take a stronger man than he was to refuse her. He was already rock hard, already thinking about the moment he'd feel her hips lift to meet his.

Determined to take it slow and savor every second, for old times' sake if for no other reason, he moved his hand up the back of her shirt to massage the muscles on either side of her spine.

"I thought your offer had been rescinded," she whispered.

He grinned at the slight taunt in her voice. "And I thought you had to protect your reputation."

"I don't seem to have much to lose anymore."

This sounded more serious than he'd expected. "Something happen tonight?"

"Nothing I want to talk about."

Should he force the issue? Not now. He had the one person he'd always dreamed about in his arms and she was finally receptive to him. There'd be time to talk later. In the morning. Right now, he preferred to communicate with his hands.

Her breathing grew shallow when he cupped her breast. "You sure you're not sex-starved?" he teased. "Because it feels that way to me."

"If I wasn't, I am now."

He chuckled at the honesty of her response. Her flesh was so supple, so smooth. But before he took this any further, he wanted her to know she could trust him to keep his mouth shut. "I won't tell anyone about this, Sophia. This is between you and me, and no one else. I promise."

"Okay."

"You believe me?"

Her response was barely audible but sounded sincere. "I do."

"That's my girl."

He wasn't sure where that last remark had come from. It was a little too possessive; she wasn't *his* "girl." But it'd slipped out, and he chose not to draw attention to it. Instead, he pushed up her shirt and rocked back to see her.

With the blinds drawn it was too dark to admire what she'd shown him earlier. But he didn't really mind. There was something incredibly erotic about having to rely on his other senses. He could get lost in making love to her without worrying about what his own expression revealed, wouldn't have to guard himself. That freedom seemed vitally important with Sophia, even though he'd never thought of it with anyone else. Maybe it was because of who she was and what she meant to his past.

Kneeling over her, he bent his head to run his lips across her stomach. He could smell some sort of fruity lotion and liked the scent. When her fingers delved into his hair, he took her hands and held them above her head as he slowly made his way up her abdomen to the tantalizing swell of one breast.

When his mouth closed over her, she shivered and he felt himself letting go, getting caught up in the moment. Suddenly, all that mattered was the way her hands moved to his head when he released them, the taste of her, and the fact that she wanted him.

The girl who'd stood him up for the big dance fifteen years ago, who'd turned up her nose at the half-breed bastard, was now trembling at his touch.

20

The rhythmic pull of Rod's mouth made heat pool in Sophia's belly. She liked the way he moved, but the reverence with which he handled her body surprised her. He didn't treat her as if this was cheap and easy, the means toward an ultimately selfish end. He acted as though every touch, every gasp, meant something.

The problems that had threatened to overwhelm Sophia—the murders, Leonard's desire for revenge, the fake picture he'd shown at the Firelight—seemed to break up and disperse, float away from her along with all her smaller concerns. Or maybe her problems weren't going anywhere. Maybe *she* was. Rod was carrying her to some far distant place, where there were no worries. Only physical sensation. *Exquisite* sensation.

She caught her breath as his deft fingers slipped beneath the elastic of her boxers. He wasn't someone who'd be able to give her what she wanted in the long term. She'd known that from the beginning. But he seemed to have exactly what she needed right now.

"You're perfect," he said.

She jerked as he touched the most sensitive part of her, and he chuckled softly. "Look what I've found."

"But do you know what to do with it?" she teased.

"I'll see if I can figure it out. Hmm…"

Darts of pleasure shot through Sophia and she writhed against his hand.

"That seems to work," he said. "Yeah, you like that."

She was breathing too hard to speak.

"You'll let me know when you're looking for something a little larger, right?"

The way her legs began to shake answered for her—and triggered a powerful response in him. She could sense it.

"You're so warm. So…wet," he said, but he wasn't teasing anymore. The ragged edge to his voice told her he was being swept away, just as she was. He'd started their lovemaking slow and lazy, as if he planned to take hours. But she could already sense his mounting tension, his struggle to retain control of the desperate urge to reach completion. And his arousal excited her more than anything else.

Picturing his handsome face, because she couldn't actually see it, she arched upward, and he shoved her boxers down over her hips. A moment later, she lost them entirely. Her T-shirt, too. Soon they were both naked, kissing deeply, rubbing and tasting and straining….

"We'll do it again." His words sounded more like an apology for being unable to wait. But she wouldn't have changed anything. She couldn't resist the compulsion that propelled her forward, either.

Wrapping her legs around his lean hips, she urged him to deliver what he'd promised almost since the day she'd first seen him, at Debbie's trailer. And he was more than willing to accommodate her. But he tried to do it gently. Supporting the bulk of his weight on his hands, he started to ease into her. But she craved force, *wanted* to be overpowered.

"Take me now, hard and fast," she whispered, and that was all the encouragement he needed. Throwing his head back, he drove into her as powerfully as she'd asked him to, again and again, stretching, filling, satisfying.

"That's it—ah, that's it," she gasped, and let the natural rhythm of their lovemaking take it from there. She was on a runaway train speeding into the night, and it had never been a more thrilling ride.

The bug he'd planted was too far away to pick up everything. But Leonard didn't have to hear each moan to know what was going on inside the house. Muted or not, those noises were pretty obvious. The chief of police was getting busy with someone, and it didn't require much effort to guess who.

With a smile, Leonard started his truck. They were making this almost too easy for him.

It was morning. When Rod lifted his head, he could see the glimmer of sunlight around the blinds. But Sophia was still sleeping.

Shifting carefully so he wouldn't wake her, he studied her sleeping face and bare breasts in what little light filtered into the room and chuckled as he thought about how freely she'd encouraged him to let go of all restraint. Their lovemaking had been fulfilling. Satisfying. The best. Because she made love as passionately and fearlessly as she did everything else—driving her Harley, wielding that battering ram, showing up at the safe house even though he'd told her not to.

He remembered her chasing him through town the day he'd arrived, lights flashing, siren screaming and blare horn held out the window with one hand. *Pull to the side of the road!*

"What's so funny?" she muttered sleepily, but moved the arm she'd flung over her head, covering her chest as if his close perusal made her self-conscious.

He hadn't realized she was awake. Knowing she wouldn't find their chase as funny as he did, he wiped the smile from his face and came up with a scowl to replace it. "Nothing. I'm just mad that you didn't let me get any sleep last night, that's all."

She arched her eyebrows at him. "You wanted to make love three times in two hours, and you're blaming *me?*"

Running a finger down the length of her tattoo sleeve, he grinned. He hadn't liked all that ink when he'd first seen it. But he did now. Somehow it suited her. "The room was dark, so I pretended you were someone else."

She wasn't buying it. "You knew exactly who I was," she said, rolling her eyes.

That was the point. She'd been different from every other woman. Better. But he wasn't about to admit it.

"You were probably pretending we were back in high school and doing it in the cab of some pickup after the Homecoming Dance. Maybe you were even dreaming that Stuart stumbled upon us. Vindicated at last, right?"

Because she'd hit somewhere fairly close to the truth— he hadn't needed to pretend they were in high school, but it had been particularly satisfying to get what he'd wanted for so long—he laughed. "Not yet, but it's not too late." Rising up on one elbow, he nuzzled her neck. "How 'bout you put on your old cheerleader uniform?"

"I was wondering when we were going to get to that," she said dryly.

"Without the little panties," he added.

She hid a yawn. "You have cheerleader fantasies?"

Only when it came to her. "I could put on a cowboy hat and play the wealthy rancher, pretend to be someone you'd consider good enough."

She winced as though he'd slapped her, and he instantly regretted the barbed reminder. He wasn't even sure why he'd said it.

"I have to get up," she mumbled, and moved away from him, taking the bedding with her.

"I didn't mean anything by that," he said.

"Yes, you did. You still resent me, still want to punish me for how I treated you in the past. To you, I'm no different from Bruce or Stuart or any of the other Dunlaps."

"Sophia—"

"Don't worry about it. You wanted me, and I rejected you. And now you've come back to town and nailed the girl who turned you down. Your job is done. Except for rubbing Stuart's nose in the fact that you got what he wanted, of course. There's still that to enjoy."

He sat up. "I said I wouldn't tell anyone, and I meant it."

"Go ahead. Like I said last night, I don't have much more to lose."

"What were you talking about?" he asked, but he never got an answer. The doorbell interrupted them.

Her gaze darted to the clock—7:10. "It's too early for visitors," she murmured, and dropped the bedding so she could pull on some clothes.

She didn't need to say it. He knew what she was thinking: More murders.

Bruce Dunlap was waiting on Sophia's doorstep, dressed in his usual—jeans and a golf shirt with cowboy boots. Only today he was also wearing a worried expression. He was about the last person she'd expected to see. He'd never visited her at home. She'd thought it was Officer Fitzer coming by to break some news that was too catastrophic to be shared over the phone.

So what was this? What could Bruce Dunlap possibly want from her?

Self-consciously smoothing down her hair, she glanced at the bedroom door, which she'd closed as she came out. Rod was behind that door. She shouldn't have let him stay with her, shouldn't have let herself get intimately involved. She'd known that. He'd come back to Bordertown to prove he was better than everyone who'd once shut him out or looked down on him. And that included her. But she wasn't going to let him laugh victoriously while breaking her heart.

Good thing her heart had nothing to do with it. She'd wanted what he had to offer last night. It was that simple. She wasn't willing to torture herself with regret, wouldn't make it more than it was. As long as she didn't care about him any more deeply than he cared about her, she'd be fine.

Wondering what Bruce wanted, she opened the door, but because she had his illegitimate son hidden away in her bedroom, she stood in the doorway rather than invite him in. "Bruce. What can I do for you?"

He adjusted his baseball cap. "Sorry to bother you, Sophia, but I stopped by the station to see Officer Fitzer and he suggested I talk to you."

She couldn't imagine Joe had meant he should drag her out of bed, but she didn't mention that. Bruce was obviously upset. "About what?"

"He said you were working graveyard last night."

"That's true…"

Drawing a deep breath, he scratched his neck. "You didn't run into Stuart in town, did you?"

She thought of the vandalized motel room and wondered if Bruce had heard about that but didn't bring it up in case he hadn't. She wanted to see where this conversation was going first. "No, I didn't." Even after they'd started actively looking for him. "Why?"

"He hasn't shown up for work today. We're doing a lot of soil prep, getting ready to plant. He was supposed to drive the tractor."

"What time?"

"Six. We'd planned to meet in the clearing, but he wasn't there. He's never done that before."

"You've checked his house, of course."

"Of course. From the looks of it, he never came home last night."

"Is that unusual?"

"Extremely."

"Maybe he had too much to drink and passed out somewhere."

"Where? I've spent the past thirty minutes driving through town, hoping to see some sign of him or his truck. But he just…disappeared."

"Could he be with a woman?"

"You're the only one he talks about."

"I didn't necessarily mean someone he was interested in dating."

He shifted his feet. "You're talking about a call girl or a hooker?"

"Maybe someone from Douglas or Sierra Vista," she said. Or Trudy. Sophia knew Stuart visited her on occasion.

"If so, it'd be the first time he's pulled this. I can't even get him on his cell."

"It's still early."

"Listen, Patrick told me something that has his mother a little...concerned."

Bruce seemed concerned, too. "What's that?"

"He said that Roderick came by last night, looking for Stuart. According to Pat, Rod wouldn't say what he wanted, but he seemed angry, upset."

"You're not suggesting Rod had anything to do with Stuart's disappearance."

There was a moment of silence as he stared at the ground. Then he said, "No, I can't believe that. I wouldn't have asked Rod to come back here if I thought something like that could ever happen. Except...except I know there's never been any love lost between them. And Edna..." He blew out a sigh.

"Edna?" she repeated, prompting him to finish.

He rubbed his face. "She's sure Rod's the devil incarnate. She won't give him a chance, never has. I hoped bringing him back to Bordertown might...I don't know... allow us to do things...better. He's never really had a family. I feel guilty about that. But maybe I was stupid to think our relationship would be different now that so much time has passed. Edna is as bitter as she ever was. Maybe more so. What happened thirty years ago is a thorn in her side that still festers."

That was a lot for Bruce to reveal. He'd certainly never taken Sophia into his confidence before. She knew he wouldn't be doing it now if he wasn't so upset. And although he stopped short of saying Edna had become impossible to live with, she got the impression they'd just had a big argument. The push-pull of his obligations to his legitimate family and the guilt he felt for neglecting his illegitimate son obviously ate at him and had been eating at him as long as that thorn had been festering in his wife's side. Sophia actually felt sorry for him.

"If it'll help, I know why Rod was looking for Stuart," she said.

He'd been nervously jingling the change in his pocket, but at this, he went still. "You do?"

"Someone trashed his motel room last night. He wanted to ask Stuart about it."

"Why would Stuart do that?"

Her cell phone vibrated. She could hear it shaking against the counter, where she'd plugged it in to charge after coming home last night. But she made no move to answer. She'd call whoever it was back after she'd finished speaking to Bruce. "I think you already know."

"But are you sure it wasn't an attempted burglary or—"

"Nothing was stolen, Bruce. Someone cut up Rod's clothes, wrote obscenities on the wall, broke his computer, that sort of thing."

"I'm sorry to hear that. I wanted him to feel welcome, accepted. So he's not staying at the Mother Lode anymore?"

"He couldn't. His room had to be cleaned and repaired. Even the door was broken."

"The door seemed fine a few minutes ago. His Hummer wasn't in the lot, but I knocked to be sure he wasn't there."

Apparently, Leland had managed to get the door fixed. He'd probably known all along that it wouldn't take much, but he preferred to rent to someone who didn't attract trouble. No doubt he also realized that he could now demand a higher price, given the sudden shortage of lodging. "It was broken when I was there after ten."

"So where's Rod?"

Sophia had been in law enforcement long enough that she hated a liar and didn't want to be one. She tried to sidestep the question rather than answer it directly. "Have you tried his cell?"

"At least a dozen times. He's not answering."

"I'm pretty sure he never found Stuart, if that's what you want to ask him. We were at a safe house that might be connected to the UDA murders until pretty late."

"But someone has to know where Stuart is. And if Rod was out searching for him, maybe he found him…."

Her home phone began to ring. Sophia glanced at it. This interruption was harder to ignore because she wasn't the only one to hear it. Excusing herself for a minute, she went to answer.

Because she'd left the door open, he stepped into her living room. Knowing Rod was so close, she felt a jolt of alarm, but Bruce stayed by the door as she lifted the receiver. "Hello?"

"Chief?"

Her alarm grew but for a different reason. It was Joe, and his tone was somber. "Yes?"

"We've got another murder on our hands."

Closing her eyes, she dropped her head in her free hand, bracing for the worst. "Just one?"

"Just one."

"Another UDA?"

"Not this time."

She snapped up straight and eyed Bruce, who was watching her curiously. "Who, then?"

"Stuart Dunlap. Someone shot him in the head."

21

Rod had no idea how to react. He dropped the sheet he'd been holding around his waist while listening at the door, and simply stood there, waiting for the reality of what Sophia had told his father to sink in. The wail Bruce had emitted when he learned his youngest son—youngest with Edna, anyway—was dead set Rod's teeth on edge. It was a wail of torment, of pain.

All the time he was growing up, Rod had told himself he hated the Dunlaps. At times, he'd grown so bitter he'd wished them dead. But he wasn't glad to hear of Stuart's murder.

The door opened and almost hit him before he could make himself move. Once he'd stepped aside, Sophia came in, but she was so busy staring at his face she didn't seem to notice he'd dropped his only covering. He didn't care, *couldn't* care, about modesty or propriety. He couldn't feel anything at all, except guilt. He wasn't sure why. He'd had nothing to do with his half brother's death. Was it just because he'd always hated Stuart? There were times when the depth of his hate made him feel capable of almost anything. Or maybe his return to Bordertown had in some way contributed....

He closed his eyes as the truth—the truth he'd refused

to face—became clearer. He didn't really hate Stuart. His feelings about Stuart were strong but they had more to do with jealousy than hate.

"You heard?" she murmured.

"Yeah." He bent to reclaim the sheet. He had to get out of here. He didn't want her to see how deeply this affected him. He'd acted so tough where Stuart and Patrick and his father were concerned. And now, somehow, he didn't feel tough at all. He felt raw and vulnerable and as exposed emotionally as he was physically….

"Hey." She put a hand on his bare back. Her fingers were cool, delicate. He could remember her threading them through his as he made love to her, remembered thinking that Stuart would give anything to be in *his* place for once.

God, he was screwed up. Was that why he'd stayed with her—to punish his half brother? "I gotta go."

"Where?" she said.

He wasn't sure. He wanted to leave town and pretend he'd never returned, wanted to ignore that Stuart's death had ever happened, as if it didn't relate to him in any way. His life in California was so far removed. He felt compelled to get back to it right away, to force down all the emotions that'd been dredged up since he drove into town, including his attraction to Sophia, which suddenly seemed as threatening as everything else.

But his father's wail would stay with him forever. He knew that. Just as he knew Bruce had to be wondering if he'd killed Stuart. "I've gotta get some toiletries so I can at least brush my teeth and replace the clothes that were ruined in my motel room. Then I'll get to work on the UDA murders."

Folding her arms, she leaned against the wall as she watched him dress. "This could be related."

"You can brief me on any similarities you find later."

He had his shorts on and was reaching for his T-shirt when she came over and held it away from him. "Of course he thinks it's you, Rod." She didn't have to say who "he" was. "As far as he knows, Stuart doesn't have any other enemies. You come back to town, your motel room gets trashed, you go on the warpath searching for the person who was most likely responsible and that person winds up dead. It doesn't look good, but it's all circumstantial. So why don't we go to the crime scene and find some evidence that proves otherwise?"

He didn't want to see Stuart's body, didn't want to witness any more of Bruce's heartbreak.

"Someone could be setting you up," she went on. "You realize that."

He hadn't thought about it until this moment. He'd been dealing with the sudden panic.

"Why let them get away with it?" she pressed.

"I shouldn't have come back here." He grabbed his shirt from her.

She released it but didn't back off. "Yet you did. And this happened. And now you have to make sure the right person gets punished."

He didn't know how to describe to her how it would feel to have his father blame him. Stuart's murder would destroy the few ounces of pride Bruce was finally exhibiting in his bastard son, would make Bruce regret the overtures he'd made in recent years. And although Rod had told himself all along that he didn't care whether his father was proud of him or not, that Bruce was wasting his time hoping for forgiveness, he knew now it wasn't true. Maybe he'd rejected his father's advances, but only because he was afraid to trust them. More than anything, he wanted to avoid feeling the way he'd felt as a child—worthless, unloved, less than his white half brothers.

"If I show up there, things could get ugly. I don't want to wind up making this worse by hurting Bruce or Patrick."

"They don't even know where his body is yet. They may get word somehow and show up, but if that happens, you'll just have to control yourself. Because if you take off, they'll have one more reason to think you did it."

She had a point. Now that he'd stopped reacting and started thinking, he knew he *had* to go to wherever Stuart had been shot. He *wanted* to go, wasn't sure why he'd initially thought the opposite. He didn't care about the Dunlaps. How could he have forgotten? Not caring was the only way to survive.

Setting his jaw, he found his flip-flops where she'd placed them neatly in her closet and put them on. "Fine. Let's go."

Sophia drove in silence. Rod sat in the passenger seat. He wouldn't have a vehicle until they could get over to the tow yard to pick up the Hummer, but now wasn't the time to worry about that. It was just something to fixate on instead of thinking about the fact that Stuart Dunlap, a man she'd known her whole life, had been murdered. It was difficult enough to confront a crime scene involving complete strangers. Sophia had no idea how she was going to hold up while viewing Stuart—who'd been very much alive when she'd last seen him at the jail—gazing sightlessly up at her.

Despite the early hour, it was ninety degrees outside.

She unfastened the top button of her uniform, then turned on the air-conditioning and stole a glance at Rod. He sat rigidly, staring straight ahead. A bruise blossomed on his left cheek, more purple than red now that some time had passed since the injury occurred. And there was a cut on his lip, which was still a little swollen. But those injuries hadn't slowed him down last night, and she knew they weren't bothering him now. He was dealing with something deeper.

Not that he'd be willing to share what was going on in his head. He'd completely withdrawn. As open and gentle, even funny, as he'd been last night, he connected her with his past, and when he couldn't bear the pain associated with those years, he shut her out. She was a reminder of who he'd been, part of the town and everything he'd worked so hard to escape since he was sixteen.

Sophia understood, but it was difficult not to try and comfort him. Knowing she'd be rebuffed was all that stopped her. "You okay?" she asked, in spite of herself.

His manner remained aloof, his eyes flat when they shifted to her face, nothing like the eyes he'd turned on her yesterday. And that stony look was the only response he gave her.

"Okay," she said. "Good to know."

Another mile passed before he spoke. "Who would do this? You've been here your whole life. What enemies did Stuart have?"

She couldn't name any. He was popular among single men because he was a frequent visitor at the Firelight and bought them a lot of drinks. He had a Harley and occasionally rode with Starkey and his friends, so he blended with a variety of groups, even the Hells Angels. He was just as popular among single women because he was considered a "catch." Even married couples and families seemed to like him, mostly because of Bruce's and Edna's standing in the community, but that borrowed respectability hadn't been difficult for him to maintain. He wasn't a nuisance to anyone except her. He used to call and ask her out much more often than she wanted to hear from him, and it became awkward to keep refusing him. But...

She couldn't imagine anyone wanting him *dead*.

"It might not have been an enemy. Maybe he was killed because he saw something he shouldn't have," she said.

"You think he witnessed the UDA killer?"

"The shell casings, if they're there, or the bullet, if it's recoverable, should tell us more. But it's entirely possible that there's a connection between the two. He died the same way as the illegals, right? By gunshot. His body was discovered on the Simpsons' ranch, out in the desert—a similar setting to where the UDAs were killed. And if he's the one who trashed your motel room, he was okay midevening, which means he died after that. Murder in the middle of the night is also typical of the UDA killer's work." She glanced at him again. "Besides, Bordertown has only had one other murder in the past ten years, and even that was a domestic dispute. Nothing like this, ever. How many killers do you think we have running around here?"

"But we haven't heard of any other murders occurring last night," he said. "What could Stuart have seen?"

"Maybe the UDA killer shot some Mexicans first and their bodies haven't been discovered. Or he interrupted a murder attempt and the illegals got away."

There was a call on her radio—Officer Fitzer.

She removed the handset and pressed the button. "What do you have for me, Joe?"

"Just wanted to let you know that the ballistics report you've been waiting for came in."

Sophia could feel Rod's interest spike along with her own. "What does it say?"

"The casings you found at the Sanchez murders match the bullet lodged in the spine of victim number three, the unidentified male at the very first crime scene."

That was good. That tied the murders together forensically—important if it ever came to prosecuting a defendant. But it didn't bring her any closer to naming a suspect.

"Any word on the type of gun?"

"Yeah. Pretty specific, actually. Hang on, I'll read you part of the report."

She heard some paper shuffling as Joe searched for what he wanted to share with her. "'Bulge in the web area…very distinctive…have seen this one before…'" He cleared his throat. "Here we go." He began to read. "'This type of deformity most often occurs in .40/10 mm and .45-caliber Glock pistols with higher than normal pressure ammunition, poor quality brass, or both.'"

"So the killer's using a .45 Glock pistol and some cheap ammo."

"Says here the ammo might've been reloaded or remanufactured."

Sophia wasn't convinced that really meant anything. *Could* be. *Might've* been. Maybe it was just a bad box of ammo. "Have we heard anything from the coroner's office about when the Sanchez autopsies will be done?" Among other things, she needed to know if they'd be able to recover any bullets from the bodies.

"Not yet. Vonnegut's had the flu, at least that's what my mother told me. She's good friends with his wife."

"Will you call over there and find out? The flu doesn't usually last for days."

"Will do."

"Thanks, Joe."

She was about to hang up when he spoke again. "One more thing, Chief."

"What is it?"

"Detective Lindstrom stopped by a few minutes ago."

Sophia recalled Lindstrom's anger at the FBI meeting yesterday. The detective wasn't even making an effort to be civil anymore. Learning about that cigarette butt, and believing Sophia had purposely withheld the information regarding it, had proven to be the point where subtle signs of dislike and resentment transformed into outright hostility. "Did you tell her about Stuart Dunlap?"

"I didn't. I wasn't sure if you wanted her to know."

At least her staff was loyal. At this point, they felt like the only ones who were willing to stick by her. "Thanks. I'll give her a call."

"She said something that struck me as odd," he said.

"What?"

"It wasn't to me. She got a call on her cell phone while I was making her a copy of the ballistics report. I have no idea who she was talking to, but she said, 'I'm meeting Stuart for breakfast at Bailey's. I'll let you know what I find out after we're through.'"

"Stuart," she repeated.

"That's right. Since I'd received the call about Stuart Dunlap's death only a few minutes before she walked in, the name jumped out at me. You don't suppose she meant *him,* do you?"

"It's possible she knows some other Stuart." But Bailey's

was a local restaurant. Sophia doubted there was another eating establishment with the same name in all of southern Arizona. And Stuart Dunlap was the only Stuart in Bordertown. "She say anything else?"

"Nope. She started to whisper as if she was afraid I was listening in, then said she had to go. That's it. It may be nothing, but…I don't know. It felt funny."

Sophia could see why. As far as she was aware, Stuart and Lindstrom didn't know each other. Lindstrom was at least six years older than he was, so even when she'd lived in Bordertown and attended Bordertown High they wouldn't have gone to school together. What business could she and Stuart have had together? How had their paths crossed? "This *just* happened, Joe?"

"She walked out the door less than five minutes ago."

They'd passed Bailey's a mile or so back. Sophia was in a hurry to reach the crime scene, but this made her curious enough to turn the car around. It might be in some way related to Stuart's death, or provide information that could help with the coming investigation.

Lindstrom was at Bailey's, all right. Sophia spotted her car in the parking lot. And when she and Rod went inside, they found the detective sitting in a corner booth, wearing an orange sheath dress with her red hair pulled back in her typical tight fashion. She was alone and had her nose in a menu, but a second menu lay near the place setting across from her. She was obviously expecting another person.

"You waiting for someone?" Sophia asked as soon as Lindstrom noticed them.

A scowl creased her forehead as she glanced from

Sophia to Rod and back again. "I'm having breakfast with a friend. What does that matter to the two of you?"

"It doesn't," Rod said. "Unless that friend happens to be Stuart Dunlap."

Her eyes narrowed. "That's none of your business."

Sophia blinked innocently. "You don't want to tell us?"

"No."

"Then you can continue to wait, and we'll leave you in peace." With a shrug, she turned to Rod and they began to walk out. But Lindstrom seemed to catch on that it might be in her best interest to find out why they'd asked.

"What if I *am* meeting Stuart? What would you say then?" she called after them.

Sophia pivoted, returned to the table and lowered her voice so she wouldn't be making the shocking announcement to the whole restaurant. "I'd say that you might as well go ahead and eat without him. Stuart Dunlap is dead."

22

Kevin, the older Simpson, had found Stuart. He was waiting for them when James drove her, Rod and Detective Lindstrom to the site via ATVs. Sophia rode behind James, Lindstrom behind Rod. Although Fitzer confirmed that Dr. Vonnegut had been called—and that he was fully recovered—he hadn't arrived. It was just the five of them. Bruce would've been there and probably Edna, too, except that Sophia had refused to tell them where their son had died or even who had discovered him. She couldn't risk having him get involved this early. She needed time to process the scene and gather any evidence she could. She'd told Bruce to go home and break the news to the rest of the family before they heard it from someone else and promised she'd be in touch as soon as she had some answers.

But, so far, she knew very little. According to what James had told her when she met him at the house, Kevin had gotten up early to drive the perimeter of the property and had come upon Stuart's truck in a washed-out gulley. One tire was flat, suggesting it'd been driven over quite a bit of rough terrain. The truck would've *had* to traverse a lot of rough terrain to get where it was. They weren't anywhere close to a road.

"This is exactly how you found him?" Lindstrom asked when Rod came to a stop and she was able to get off the ATV.

Sophia thought it was obvious that the body hadn't been disturbed but didn't say so. The last thing she needed was an argument with Lindstrom. She climbed off the all-terrain vehicle she'd been riding, and walked to within three feet of the cab door, which stood open.

Kevin spat on the ground before answering. "I opened the door, but that's it."

Sophia's arms and legs felt rubbery as she caught her first glimpse of Stuart. James cursed; apparently, this was his first glimpse, too. And Rod stood close by but said nothing. He revealed no outward sign of distress, yet she could sense the negative emotions churning inside him.

Stuart sat slumped over the steering wheel. Blood ran down the door and brain matter speckled the window. Thanks to the recent heat wave, relentless even at night, his corpse was giving off a pungent odor that turned Sophia's weakened stomach. Blowflies crawled over the corpse, attracted to the moist areas of the eyes, mouth and nose, where they liked to lay their eggs. Sophia was afraid to look too closely for fear she'd already find maggots. According to what she'd learned about entomology, the eggs could hatch within hours, especially in warm conditions like this.

"So you didn't touch him, try to revive him?" Lindstrom was doing her best to appear unaffected and professional, but the strain in her voice was unmistakable.

"Hell, no," Kevin said. "One look at him, and I knew he was dead."

Sophia told herself it was fortunate that Kevin hadn't disturbed the body. They'd have a better chance of reconstructing the crime, and any evidence the killer had left behind wouldn't be compromised. Sophia had heard Locard's Exchange Principle a million times. "Wherever he steps, whatever he touches, whatever he leaves, even unconsciously, will serve as a silent witness against him." But that principle only seemed to apply on TV.

"Whoever did this took him by surprise," Rod said.

"He didn't see it coming, didn't attempt to get out," Sophia agreed. "But what brought him here in the first place? Why would anyone drive for several miles over rock, cactus, even a few broken bottles, to reach such a remote location? To do that kind of damage, he had to be driving fast."

"Maybe he was meeting someone," James said.

Lindstrom shook her head. "There're no other tracks."

"It's hard to see tracks in this kind of soil."

Sophia gestured to the plants around them. "There *is* smashed vegetation."

"But, with the illegals constantly tramping through here, there's always smashed vegetation," Kevin said. "That's part of my complaint against what's going on. It's ruining my property."

"I think he was drunk and patrolling for illegal aliens to harass, and he ran afoul of a drug deal," James said. "This feels almost like an execution."

Or it could be the retaliation they'd all feared—the Mexicans striking back—but Sophia didn't say it.

Rod shoved his hands in his pockets. "He could've been participating in a drug deal."

Sophia thought of Jamie Skotto, a white girl who was raped in Douglas. At first, Jamie had claimed the culprit was a Mexican national, which incited the whole area.

White men from all over Cochise County headed into the desert to avenge her attack on whatever UDAs they could find. When she admitted that she'd actually been beaten and raped by her own uncle, the vigilantes slunk back to their regular lives, but the rise in racism never really receded. Falling back on the recent murder of the rancher near Portal, some people still came out here to harass UDAs. Although they tried to put a patriotic slant on it—"Those sons of bitches have no right to come into our country!"—it often boiled down to basic cruelty. "As much as I don't want to believe this, he could even be the UDA killer. Until we know more, we can't rule out any possibility."

"We can rule that out," Lindstrom said.

Sophia eyed her thoughtfully. "Why were you meeting him this morning?"

"He called me last night around eleven," she said. "Told me he had some information on the murders. If he was guilty, I doubt he'd do that."

Why hadn't he called *her?* Sophia wondered. Because he was angry? Because he hadn't been able to find her? That would've been while she was looking out for Rod over at the safe house. But she'd had her phone with her. No call had come in…. "Did he give you any idea what he had?"

"No. None. He was acting a little paranoid. Said he didn't want to go into it over the phone."

"And then he was killed."

"From what I'm seeing."

Kevin spat again, hitting the dirt not far from his boot. "He wasn't out here just for kicks. Tormenting UDAs isn't something he'd do alone, not unless he was seriously planning to hurt someone, which I highly doubt. And if he was with friends, we would've heard from them by now. You don't see your buddy get shot and not say anything."

"Was the car running when you found it?" Lindstrom asked.

Kevin's hand scraped over his beard growth. "No. And there was no other vehicle in the area."

Rod stepped closer to the body. "How'd you spot him?"

"I caught a glimpse of red from the ridge up there—" he pointed to his left "—just as the sun was coming up. I used my binoculars, so I wouldn't walk into anything dangerous. Maybe this is my land, but I know not to interrupt the wrong people out here," he explained. "And this is what I saw." He took the walkie-talkie from his belt. "Since there are no cell phone towers out here, we use these around the ranch. First thing I did was notify my wife that we had a problem."

A problem. Sophia already had a problem. This made it worse. "I hope the Feds will come in on this one, too," she muttered to Rod. To start with, they needed someone who knew more about blood spatter analysis than she did. A blood-spray expert would be able to determine the angle of fire and how far the gun had been from Stuart's head when it went off. It appeared that the shooter pulled the trigger from inside the truck, which meant they might be able to glean some of his DNA—if the Locard principle held true.

Edging closer, she peered into the cab. A piece of flesh hung from an exit wound above Stuart's left ear. Sophia didn't want to fixate on that morbid detail, didn't want to acknowledge that she was seeing someone she'd dated a few times in a state like this. And yet she couldn't tear her eyes away.

Suddenly, her vision dimmed. Afraid she might pass out, she closed her eyes and took some deep breaths, and when she opened them again, she tried to convince herself that none of this was real. It was merely a puzzle that needed to be solved, and *she* needed to do the solving. But in the past several weeks, she'd seen everything from skeletalized remains to this. It didn't matter. Death was something she could never get used to.

"Look at his eyes," she said.

"What about them?" Rod leaned around her. "Are you talking about the bruising?"

"Yeah. You think he got in a fight before he came here?"

His face more masklike than ever, Rod shook his head. Sophia guessed he, too, was struggling to distance himself from the fact that he'd known this person. It had to be even harder for him. Stuart was—had been—his half brother. Maybe they'd never been close but in some ways the animosity between them only complicated matters. Now they'd never have the chance to put their differences aside. "Raccoon eyes are typical with a gunshot wound to the head," he said. "I've seen it before."

"What are you talking about?" Lindstrom tried to squeeze between them.

Careful not to touch the truck, Sophia stepped out of her way. She found it difficult enough to hold herself together without having to tolerate Lindstrom. "I didn't notice it on Benita Sanchez," she murmured to Rod.

His gaze remained fixed on the bruising. "Doesn't happen every time. Depends on the damage. Besides, it wouldn't have shown up so clearly against darker skin."

"So something's wrong with his eyes?" Lindstrom asked.

Rod also stepped back. "The bruising. It's normal for this type of death."

He seemed to know a fair amount about murder. How many other cases had Rod worked? Sophia wondered. What had they been like? He'd become so distant this morning she could hardly believe he was the same man she'd slept with last night.

"What's your guess on time of death?" Sophia asked.

A muscle twitched in his cheek, the only outward sign—besides his general reticence—that this was difficult for him. "Without an M.E. here to get a body temp, it's hard to say. But…I'd guess maybe three hours."

Lindstrom inserted herself into their conversation once again. "Why not longer?"

He gestured toward Stuart's corpse. "Rigor's just setting in."

Sophia knew rigor mortis was caused by a chemical reaction involving the loss of adenosine triphosphate, which made the muscles contract and hold rigid. She also knew that it typically started with the small muscles in the face, neck and hands and that it set in about two hours after death. She'd read a lot of forensics books since the UDA murders had begun, hoping for insights. But she'd never actually seen rigor before. In her first murder case—the domestic dispute that had ended so badly—she'd been called to the scene immediately. And all the illegal immigrants who'd been killed since then had been discovered either before or after the thirty-six-hour period when rigor became a factor.

"Provided your estimate is accurate, he died around four." Lindstrom stated the obvious.

Wondering where Vonnegut could be, Sophia turned to James. Maybe the M.E. felt no sense of urgency to respond quickly to the deaths of illegal aliens, but now they were dealing with the murder of a prominent citizen. "Have you heard from Dr. Vonnegut?"

He checked his watch. "After Dad called Mom and I reported this, Officer Fitzer contacted us to say he'd notified you and Dr. Vonnegut. I guess he's been sick. A day he'd spend golfing in Tucson with some old college buddies."

"I hope we caught him before he could leave," Lindstrom cut in.

"I was told he was going to turn around," James said. "He's on his way. I'm sure it won't take much longer. My mother will call me on the radio once he arrives, and I'll go back for him."

"How will we get the body out?" Lindstrom asked.

"That won't be as hard as you might think," Kevin told her. "We can hook a trailer to one of these ATVs. That's how we deliver food to the cattle."

"Makes sense." Sophia pulled her digital camera from the case hanging around her neck. Now that she'd had a few minutes to deal with the shock and the upset, she needed to get down to business. She had to photograph and take a video of the scene before she could touch it. And then she planned to search for any scrap of evidence. She wasn't going to miss a cigarette butt this time. She wasn't going to miss anything ever again. She didn't expect to find the murder weapon, but hoped she'd at least recover a shell casing.

And if that shell casing had the familiar bulge she'd seen in the casings from the Sanchez murders, this was the work of the same person.

If that bulge wasn't there… She didn't even want to think about that.

Sophia had just snapped her first picture when Rod spoke up. "What's that?"

"What's what?" She turned to face him.

He was standing behind her, keeping out of the way so she could do her job. He pointed. "That silver thing in the ashtray."

How had he even seen that?

Careful not to brush against anything, she leaned in. "It's a memory stick."

"Can you read the logo?"

"Looks like…Department 6." Recognizing the significance of that, she gaped at him.

"With my computer broken in pieces on the floor, I didn't even think to check for it," he said. "But why would he take something like that?"

"I don't know. Maybe because it was the only personal thing you brought with you." Or it had been planted by the killer.…

"What would he want with my work files?"

"I doubt it was the work files that interested him. It was the possibility of more personal stuff. Which goes to show you that he was as curious about you as he was frightened."

That evening Rod sat in a booth at the Rockin' Rooster Drive-in. He had the bag of toiletries and clothing he'd just purchased on the seat beside him, and his Hummer was parked where he could see it through the window. But he didn't have a room yet. The Sundowner had been full, as he'd expected. Before Stuart's death, he'd hoped the news crews would leave soon, that they'd do a story on the UDA killings, maybe shoot some footage of the border fence with the patrol officers at work, then go on their way—at least until a break in the case or some new development brought them back. It wasn't cheap to keep these people on location, and there had to be bigger news breaking someplace else. But that all changed when Stuart was killed. Now the whole town was buzzing like a hornet's nest, and the newspeople wouldn't leave. They'd stay for another day or two, make the most of the drama involved in other people's pain.

Taking a deep breath, he pushed back the tray that'd held his double cheeseburger and stretched out his legs. A few reporters had even shown up at the Simpsons' as the boys from the morgue were loading Stuart's body. Fortunately, the ranch was a big place, the crime scene remote. They hadn't been able to pinpoint its exact location any earlier from what they'd heard on the police radio.

Rod was glad he and Sophia had left about then. Any later, and he would've bumped into Bruce, who'd figured out where his boy had been killed and come out to defend whatever he felt was there to defend. Rod had heard Sophia talking on the phone with him the whole time they were driving to the towing company to get the Hummer. Bruce was furious that she hadn't checked in with him sooner. He seemed to think he was entitled to know what was happening every step of the way. But she'd told him in no uncertain terms that he had no right to interrupt her when she needed to focus, that she'd been doing her job, and if he wanted his son's killer caught, he had to respect that.

Already full, Rod picked at the remaining fries and finished his shake. He wasn't in any hurry to leave the drive-in. This little spot was more popular for lunch than dinner, and today it seemed to be overlooked completely, which gave him time to adjust to what had happened and what it might mean.

The two teenage girls working the counter giggled, momentarily drawing his attention. But they were only talking to each other, so he lapsed back into his own thoughts.

Stuart had been shot twice in the head. One bullet had penetrated his temple and exited on the other side, where it had struck the window, without shattering it, oddly enough, and fallen to the floor. The other had gone in through his jaw. There didn't seem to be an exit wound for that one. Both entrance wounds were round, about four-sixteenths of an inch in diameter, and there wasn't any soot or stippling to suggest the gun had been fired right up against the skin.

The killer must have been a few feet away, which led Rod to believe he might not have been sitting in the cab, as Detective Lindstrom had initially surmised. If the killer had ridden with Stuart, he'd gotten out before turning and shooting him. And he'd collected his shell casings, just like the perpetrator of the UDA murders when he'd shot his first ten victims.

That wasn't how he and Sophia had wanted it. A couple of shell casings could've tied Stuart's case to the UDA murders quite neatly, but at least they had the bullet found on the floor of the truck and should have the one in Stuart's jaw. An X-ray would locate it and enable Vonnegut to extract it during the autopsy—

Rod glanced up when the door opened. Then he froze. Edna and Patrick had walked in. And it didn't look as if they'd come to order a burger.

23

"Did you do it?" Edna's eyes, red-rimmed and bloodshot, were riveted on him as she shuffled closer. She appeared ten years older than when he'd seen her at the drugstore—old and shrunken and weak, as if she couldn't manage without the help of her oldest son.

Patrick allowed his mother to lean on his arm but avoided Rod's gaze. He, too, seemed like a shadow of his former self. The shock of his brother's death had apparently leeched all the fight out of him.

Rod sat up straight. "What are you asking me?"

Tilting her head, she glared down her nose at him. "You know what I'm asking you!" Her voice shook, but not with the threat of tears.

Mesmerized by the scene unfolding before them, the drive-in employees had fallen silent as soon as she spoke. Everyone in Bordertown knew Edna. Normally, she was dressed to the nines, smiling and waving like some sort of prom queen riding on a float. Tonight, however, she looked as if she'd been dragged off the street after being hit by a car. But there was no question that the girls who'd made his burger recognized Bordertown's first lady.

"I have no clue." Rod refused to be the first to mention murder in connection with his own name. He figured he'd be smarter to make *her* spell it out, and she instantly accommodated him.

"Did you *kill* him? Did you kill my son?"

A muscle began to tick in Rod's cheek; he could feel it jump. He'd known that if he stayed, things would go this way. But leaving hadn't really been an option. It still wasn't. He had to face this down or it would only follow him. "Of course not. You don't know what you're talking about."

"You were jealous of him."

The venom in those words made Rod uneasy, but he couldn't deny it. He *had* been jealous of Stuart—and Patrick—from the day he was born. They'd had it all and had taken great pleasure in flaunting it in front of him. "Go home to your husband, Edna, and let the police do their job," he said wearily.

"The police?" she echoed. "You mean *Sophia?*"

"She *is* the chief."

"As if she'd ever look at *you* as a suspect."

He didn't like the sound of that. Sliding out of the booth, he stood. "Calm down. There's no need to drag other people into this."

"Calm down?" she shrieked. "My boy is dead! Someone killed him. Everyone's up in arms, ready to blame the Mexicans, but I think that someone was you. And I'll never get justice as long as the chief of police is so eager to warm your bed."

Rod caught his breath. How did she know he'd been intimate with Sophia? They'd been seen around town quite a bit since he arrived, but they hadn't touched in any way that would make it obvious. Not in public. "What I do in my private life is none of your business."

"It is now," she snapped. "Stuart told me himself. He

said you were here to take the girl he wanted, just to show him you could."

Was that what he'd done? He hoped not, but the way he was feeling today—out of touch with everything he thought he'd become—he couldn't be sure. "I've only been in town a few days," he said, instead of giving her an absolute denial. "Sophia and I have barely become reacquainted."

"Doesn't matter."

"You're right," he agreed. "It doesn't matter. What matters is that I didn't kill Stuart." He'd promised Sophia discretion. And she'd trusted him. The last thing he wanted was to leave her worse off than she'd been before he came.

"That's what *you* say. But I'm going to prove otherwise. You wait and see if I don't." Edna gave Patrick's arm an emphatic jerk. "Tell him. Tell him what you told me."

Patrick shoved his free hand through his hair, making it stand up, which added to his look of harried bewilderment. While his mother had aged since hearing the news about Stuart, he seemed to have regressed into boyhood. "I told her you came by searching for Stuart last night."

Rod scowled. "So what if I did? He wasn't there and I left. Did you tell her that?"

Edna didn't let Patrick respond. "What did you want from him?"

"Someone trashed my motel room. Cut up my clothes, wrote obscenities on the wall, broke my computer. I wanted to know if it was him."

Her lips pursed as she shook her head. "He would never do anything like that. My boy was a good man, an upstanding citizen. He wouldn't waste his time with such… such petty actions."

Rod knew it was just the opposite, but what was the point of arguing with her? The family was going through enough. So he simply stuck with the facts. "Dick, the pastor, saw him leaving the Mother Lode not long before I came home. That's why I dropped by to talk with him. Do you know of any other reason he'd have to visit the motel?"

She didn't seem capable of taking it all in, but refused to be forced on to the defensive. "Where did you go after you left Patrick's?" she demanded without answering.

"To the Firelight. But Stuart wasn't there, either. I never did find him."

"You expect me to believe that? You chased him into the desert, and you shot him!"

He glanced at the two girls who were standing behind the counter, their eyes round as silver dollars. "No, I didn't."

"Then where did you go after you left the Firelight? Where were you last night?"

He'd been at the safe house and then Sophia's. *She* was his alibi. But he couldn't say so or it would cost Sophia her job. Edna would settle for no less. Not if she learned they'd been together, as she already suspected. "I was asleep."

"Where?"

He stretched his neck. "Look, you're wrong, okay? It wasn't me."

"Where were you last night?"

"It wasn't me."

She stepped up as if she'd strike him, but Patrick pulled her away. "Mom, let's go. He's not worth it."

"The police will handle it," Rod said. "I'll be questioned and the investigation will go from there."

"You think you're so smart!" she ground out.

When he didn't respond, her eyes shifted to the bruises on his cheek and the cut on his lip. "Where'd you get those injuries to your face?"

"I ran into a brick wall."

"Sure you did. You were up to something last night. You attacked my boy."

He refused to flinch as she glared at him.

"I hate you," she breathed.

They were just words and yet their malevolence settled over him as oppressively as a thick fog. He'd sensed her animosity from the very beginning, experienced it almost as a tangible force. But, until now, she'd never actually expressed it, at least to him.

"I know you do," he said. "You always have."

Patrick began trying to drag her out. "Come on, Mom. Let's go. If he killed Stuart, we'll hire whoever we have to hire to get the evidence and prove it. But we're not going to solve this right now."

"I want him to know," she said. "I want him to know that I won't rest until I see him six feet under, like my boy."

Patrick straightened his shirt, obviously uncomfortable. "Don't talk like that."

"I want him to know," she repeated, and allowed her son to lead her out.

The girls behind the counter didn't move even after she left. They continued to gape at Rod as if they believed the accusations she'd flung and were afraid he'd hurt them next.

Muttering a curse for letting his father talk him into returning to Bordertown in the first place, he piled his trash on the plastic tray. But before he could reach the garbage can, the bell jingled over the door again.

This time it was Sophia. No longer in uniform, she wore a pretty blouse, a skirt and some sandals. But her eyes were wide with worry and her face was pale as bleached bone.

"What is it?" he asked.

Sophia held the paper she'd found on her nightstand tightly in her right hand. She had no idea who'd written the numbers on it if not Rod. *She* certainly hadn't.

"Did you write this?" Pulling him outside, where they couldn't be overheard, she uncurled her fingers. The crumpled sheet of paper she'd ripped from the notepad by her phone rested in her palm.

Lines creased his forehead as he took it and smoothed it out. "Yes. Last night. I didn't want to forget it." He glanced up as if he couldn't believe this was any kind of problem. "Why?"

"What business do you have with my stepfather?"

"Your what?"

"My *stepfather*. Why do you have his number?"

Confusion clouded his expression. "I don't— Wait a second. You're telling me *this* number belongs to your stepfather? I don't see how that can be."

"Why not? You didn't get it from him?"

"No. I've never even met him."

"Then how—"

"I saw it on a wipe board attached to the fridge at the safe house," he broke in. "There was no name, but the way it was written gave me the impression that it was significant to the people inside. There was no area code, either, so I assumed it was local. I memorized it just in case it turned into a lead of some sort."

Sophia struggled to make the connection. Could her stepfather be involved with the people who'd beaten Rod? Involved in smuggling illegal aliens? He was the absolute *last* person she'd ever suspect of such a thing. There had to be another answer. But she couldn't think of one single reason his number would be inside that safe house. "My stepfather has never stated an opinion on the immigration issue one way or another."

"People who get involved in human trafficking don't do it for political purposes," Rod said. "They do it for the money, Sophia. You know that."

Of course she did. But…her stepfather? Where would he have made the contacts? Why would he take the risk?

An image of the mansion in which her mother lived appeared in Sophia's mind. Then she thought about the feed store and the article in the paper praising Gary O'Conner for his business prowess. Did he really earn such a great living from selling hay and other animal supplies and renting farm equipment? Or was that merely a front for a much more lucrative business?

"Oh, God."

"You've thought of something?"

"Just growing suspicious. But we can't tip him off. I need to talk to my mom, see what I can get out of her before they realize he might be at risk and clam up." She knew instinctively that Anne would protect Gary. Anne would refuse to believe he could be involved in human smuggling just as she'd refused to believe he could be slipping into her teenage daughter's bedroom at night. Anything short of complete denial threatened life as Anne knew it.

"I won't say a word to anyone," Rod said.

Taking the paper, she turned to head to her cruiser, but Rod caught her by the elbow.

"I don't have anywhere to stay tonight."

She blinked up at him. "And you think that's *my* problem? That I'll let you stay with me again?" He'd made it clear that last night hadn't meant anything to him. Why would she be so foolish as to welcome him back?

His gaze dropped to the sidewalk before lifting again. He studied her, looking extremely unhappy, but he didn't speak. She sensed that he wanted her to understand what was in his head but couldn't sort out his own feelings enough to explain them.

"Are you going to answer?"

"I'm sorry. That's all I can say."

"Sorry doesn't change anything, Rod."

Nodding, he drew a deep breath. "I had no right to even ask. It's just… I thought once would do the trick, that once would be enough, you know?"

"For what?" she asked.

"To get you out of my system," he said, then walked away.

Anne's house was like a mausoleum. Expansive. Sterile. Filled with art and sculpture. The only thing that moved, except the ceiling fans in the glass extension overlooking the backyard, was Dolly, the poodle.

Tail quivering with excitement, Dolly sat on her perfectly groomed behind and begged for a morsel of Sophia's food.

"You've already had yours, baby." After sliding the plate she'd prepared for Sophia away from the edge of the table, Anne scooped the dog into her lap. "Let Sophie enjoy her dinner. It's rare enough that I get to see her."

Sophia didn't miss the chastisement in her mother's words. She knew Anne wished she'd come out more often. Her mother always had some new trinket or painting or antique to show off. And the tennis courts were done now, as Anne had pointed out twice in the time it took to warm up a few leftovers. Her mother insisted there was so much to do at Casa Nueva.

That she'd actually named her estate was a bit too arrogant for Sophia's tastes, but it certainly wasn't the most pretentious thing her mother had ever done.

"Isn't it beautiful?" Anne asked before Sophia could once again point out how busy she was with her job.

Sophia gazed over the garden where her mother spent the majority of each morning. The tranquility of it should've drawn her out here more often. Except that every time she came, she saw herself as a teenager hiding in the pool house or skulking around the backyard to delay her entry into the house if her stepfather happened to be home.

"It's lovely," she said. "As always."

"I have a new kind of dahlia." She smiled proudly while petting Dolly. "An import from Denmark. I'll have to show it to you after you finish eating."

"I'd like to see it."

Adjusting her Dolce & Gabbana sunglasses, Anne sat back, looking cool and comfortable in white linen pants, a peach blouse and leather sandals that were peach and turquoise. A scarf around her neck tied all three colors together. She also wore a white headband to keep her shoulder-length blond hair from her face. Sophia suspected she'd had a facelift last year, but even if she asked, Anne would never admit it. She wanted everyone to believe she was vanquishing the years without help. Either way, with her fingernails and toenails polished the same shade of peach as her blouse, she was a class act, still very attractive at fifty-five.

"How's work?" she asked.

"Fine." Sophia didn't want to get caught up in a discussion of the UDA murders. That could waste an hour or more, and she knew her stepfather would be coming home in forty-five minutes, assuming he kept to the same routine as usual. She didn't want him to interrupt them, didn't want her mother censoring what she said to make it more pleasing to Gary's ears.

"Gary called a little while ago to tell me about Stuart Dunlap," Anne murmured, lowering her voice. "I'm so sorry. I know he was a friend of yours."

Not as close a friend as her mother would've liked. "I feel terrible for the family."

"So do I. Those two boys are everything to Edna. I have no idea how she'll get through this."

"It won't be easy."

"Do you know who did it?"

"Not yet. But I'm working on it."

"What about those other murders?"

"I'm working on those, too."

"Are you getting any sleep?" The dog jumped down as Anne leaned forward to smooth the hair out of Sophia's face, like she used to do when Sophia was a girl. Sophia didn't bother stopping her. She knew her mother would take it as a subtle form of rejection if she did.

"Enough. There's been a lot going on lately."

"No kidding. But please tell me you're taking time for yourself."

Obviously, Anne had no clue what a murder investigation involved. "When I can."

"How's your love life?" She gave Sophia a conspirator's grin. "I hear there's a new man in town. And that he's gorgeous!"

Sophia rolled her eyes. "Don't get your hopes up, Mom."

"I hear you two have been spending a lot of time together."

The singsong quality of her voice made Sophia scowl. "He doesn't like me. Not since I shot him with my Taser."

"You…what?"

"I shocked him. You know, like with a stun gun?"

Her mother rocked back. "No!"

"Yes."

"Why?"

"He broke the law and resisted arrest."

Resting her chin in her hand, Anne sighed. "I'm afraid you'll never get married."

"He broke the law!"

"So? I've told you and told you—men don't like women who carry guns and have tattoos and ride motorcycles. That's intimidating. They prefer soft, frail females who make them feel powerful."

Like her. Anne fit that stereotype perfectly. "Yeah, well, I'm not pretending to be feeble in order to build some guy's ego, especially *this* guy's. It's big enough already."

"Is it?"

Sophia wanted to say yes, but because her mother's eyes had lit up as if she was eager to hear—and spread—the inside scoop, she couldn't do it. Rod could be cocky, but she'd figured out that his cockiness was a defense mechanism to cover his vulnerability. If he felt he'd meet with rejection or hostility, he added a swagger to polish up that outer shell, so folks would assume he didn't really care. But he did care. And when he opened up, he was kind and gentle and funny and sexy and...so many things she liked. "I can't really say," she hedged. "I don't know him that well. I didn't even when he used to live here."

Playing dumb seemed the safest route, the easiest way to hide her feelings, but Anne wasn't about to let the subject go. "He had a rough childhood, Sophia."

"I know. I lived here, too, Mom. But..." She groped for the right words. But what? The Dunlaps had hurt him deeply. They would've destroyed a lesser heart. And yet Rod's beat strong and true. Or was that only what she wanted to believe?

"And I hear he's got money now." She slipped that in before Sophia could go on. And there it was. The reason for her mother's sudden interest in the Dunlap bastard.

"Maybe that's true. Maybe it's not," she said. "It's none of my business. Anyway, I don't want to talk about Rod Guerrero, okay?" She was having a hard enough time putting him out of her head. He'd wanted to stay the night again. And, heaven help her, she was tempted to call him up and let him do it.

"Are you dating anyone else?" her mother asked.

"Not right now." Finished with the food she'd eaten only to make Anne feel she was doing a good job of being a mother, Sophia pushed her plate away. "Hey, I saw that article in the paper about Gary. That was pretty nice, huh?"

Her mother seemed surprised by her choice of topic but was pleased enough not to question it. "Very nice."

"So his store's doing well?"

"Better than ever."

"Who would've thought there'd be so much money in feed?"

"The rentals help, too."

"Still, the guy before him couldn't make it," she mused.

"The guy before him wasn't as smart as he is."

"Right." Sophia took a sip of the iced tea she'd brought out with her food. "He must be putting in a lot of long hours, though, huh?"

"Too many," her mother agreed.

"But he spends his evenings with you, doesn't he?"

Anne waved a dismissive hand. "Sometimes. But even then he's up till all hours."

"Doing what?" Sophia settled back in her seat to make the conversation seem more casual.

"Who knows? He's always on his laptop. He started trading stocks a few years ago and has gotten more and more involved in it. I'm sure that's what he's doing a lot of the time."

Sophia wasn't nearly as convinced. "Do his cell phone bills come here to the house? Or do they go to the store?"

"To the store, I guess. I never see them. Why?"

"I was just wondering if you balanced the bank statements, that kind of stuff. I remember you used to do it when I was younger."

"Only when I was married to your dad. Gary's so much better about money. He takes care of all that. And he does it at the store. I haven't seen a bank statement in ages."

Sophia knew she could be wrong, but she had a hard time giving Gary any credit for that. From her perspective, he did what he did to keep her mother completely insulated and oblivious to his actions.

He was good at that. She'd seen him act in a similar manner with what he'd tried on her. "How do you get money?" she asked.

"He gives me an allowance." Anne smiled meaningfully. "A generous allowance."

Sophia returned the smile as if a rich husband was as important as Anne believed. "It's amazing that he's been able to turn the feed store around. Why do you think the guy who owned it before couldn't make it?"

"He was an idiot."

"The article in the paper said that Gary attributes part of his success to his ability to deal with Mexican Americans, to speak their language."

"That's probably true. A lot of farm laborers come in. Knowing Spanish helps him communicate. Gary taught himself," she added proudly.

"I remember." The tapes he'd purchased to learn it had blared through the house for hours.

Anne scooted her chair closer. "You know…I'm glad to see a little interest on your part toward Gary. You've always been so…resistant to accepting him."

You mean in my bed? The words went through Sophia's mind, but she didn't speak them. She didn't have much time to accomplish what she'd come for. "Yeah, well, maybe I'm growing up," she said vaguely, and glanced at her watch. Six-thirty. The store closed at six. What time did Gary usually get home? It'd been too long since she'd lived with her mother to have any sure way of knowing. It could be soon.

"Can you excuse me for a minute?" she asked. "I need to use the restroom."

"Of course." Her mother picked up her plate and followed her inside but veered off toward the kitchen.

Sophia walked to the entrance of the guest bathroom, paused to be make certain her mother was busy washing up and wasn't paying attention, then crept across the marble entry and beneath the curving staircase to her stepfather's office.

French doors opened into a luxurious denlike room with white paneling, white carpet and floor-to-ceiling windows overlooking grass so green and so carefully trimmed it could've been used as a golf course. At Casa Nueva, there were no reminders of the heat outside—no desert landscape, no Southwestern art, none of the beige stucco that was so popular this close to the border. Her mother considered all of that to be "common" and "vulgar."

The thick padding beneath the carpet made it easy to walk without sound. Sophia crossed to the desk and jiggled Gary's mouse to dissolve his screensaver. She wanted to check his browser history, see where he'd been on the Internet. But the first thing that came up was a page requiring a password.

"So that's how you keep Mom out of your business," she murmured, and started to search the files and drawers instead.

In one drawer she found quite a bit of cash. Marveling that he hadn't bothered to put it somewhere safe, she thumbed through the stack of hundred-dollar bills and counted nearly five thousand dollars. Five grand was a lot to have on hand, the type of cash smugglers often carried. But cash wasn't incriminating in and of itself.

She tried another drawer. Office supplies.

Another drawer. Checkbooks. A few photographs—none of her, thank God.

The last drawer. Paper for the printer on the credenza behind her.

Hoping to discover something solid to explain the reason his phone number had been written on that wipe board, she moved to the filing cabinet. And found a handgun.

It was a Glock. She recognized that right away. But was it the same caliber as the one used in the UDA killings? She was just lifting it out of the drawer when a noise at the doorway made her turn.

Gary was standing there.

24

"What are you doing?"

Sophia raced through a series of excuses, searching for one he'd believe.

"What are you looking for?" he demanded before she could answer, and came into the room.

Although she'd been caught red-handed, Sophia couldn't reveal the truth. If she was lucky, finding Gary's number in that safe house might finally make it possible to unravel the mystery behind the UDA murders. And even if it didn't, even if it was completely unrelated, she had to keep that information to herself long enough to figure out what it meant.

After dropping the gun back in the drawer, she pressed a finger to her lips to indicate that he should keep his voice down and jutted out her chin. "What do you *think* I'm looking for?"

To Sophia's relief, the emotions registering on his face changed from shock and suspicion to irritation. "Don't tell me. You're hoping to find that picture you think I have of you."

She silently released the breath she'd been holding. "What else?"

"That's crazy, Sophia. I let you search my wallet at the

store. Now you're here, going through my office? What gives you the right?"

"The lies that Leonard is spreading, for one!" she said with a dark scowl.

It was his turn to act as if he was concerned that Anne would hear. "Keep your voice down."

"He's ruining my reputation!" she snapped.

"But I don't have any such picture!"

"Then how does he know that anything inappropriate went on? And how is he extrapolating some unwelcome groping when I was sixteen and seventeen to mean I'm having an affair with you now?"

The hardness that entered Gary's eyes told her he didn't like how consistently she held him to the truth of his actions. "I have no idea. He hates you."

She got the impression Gary did, too. She knew he'd deny it if she accused him. Her mother was still hoping they'd achieve peace as a family. But she'd been a problem for him, in one way or another, ever since he'd married her mother, and as long as she refused to let him escape responsibility for what he'd done, that wouldn't change.

"Maybe Leonard's doing whatever he can to make your life miserable," he was saying. "But he's lying about me. I don't have any naked pictures of you. And I can't understand why you won't believe me. I'm not even attracted to you!"

That comment, more than any other, told her he was no different than he'd been years ago. He sounded like a high school boy, not a stepfather. "I wish you never had been." At least, not in that way. She'd needed a stabilizing force, someone or something to shore up her crumbling world. Instead, she'd gotten a sexual predator, which had made her world fall apart even faster.

"You misunderstood what I was trying to do. You misunderstood everything," he said.

"Oh, quit playing the martyr."

He moved toward her as if to strike her. Instinctively, she raised her arms to protect her face, but he caught himself, and said only, "I wish you'd stop saying that."

Sophia bit back the many angry responses that vied for expression. Arguing about the same old thing wouldn't change the past. She had to focus on the reason she'd come here today. "How long have you owned a gun?" she asked.

His eyes cut to the filing cabinet she'd just closed. "For years, why?"

"You've never mentioned it."

"I haven't mentioned a lot of things. You and I don't talk, remember?"

"Where'd you get it?"

He was in a full sulk now. "That's none of your business."

"Gary? Is that you?" Her mother's voice carried in from the living room. She was coming toward the office.

"I don't want to deal with that old...*issue* again," he said. "Ever. This is your last warning."

Warning? Sophia stepped closer. "Or what?"

He didn't answer, but the pressure of his lips against his teeth expunged all color from them and told her he had plenty to say. "You make me so—" he put some distance between them as he threw up his hands "—crazy."

"There's my sweetheart." As Anne came to stand in the doorway, she realized Sophia was here rather than in the bathroom and looked curiously between them. "What's going on?"

The mask Gary always wore with Anne fell neatly into

place. Sophia felt chilled to see him slip into character so effortlessly.

"Nothing." He smiled. "I was just giving Sophia a sneak peek at your birthday present."

Blushing with pleasure, Anne came farther into the room. "What is it?"

He slid his arm around her. "I'll never tell. Not until the big day."

Anne appealed to Sophia. "*You'll* tell me. Won't you?"

"Not me. You've got to wait." Her voice was a little too flat to make her "birthday" enthusiasm believable, but her mother was a pro at twisting any situation into what she wanted it to be.

"Isn't he a wonderful husband?" she gushed.

Sophia struggled against her gag reflex. "He's a keeper."

Gary kissed Anne, a bit too passionately for having an audience. Apparently, he had trouble understanding what was appropriate, even now. But he succeeded in distracting Anne, which was probably his intent. "It's too bad, what happened to Stuart, don't you think?" he said as he pressed his forehead to hers.

"It's terrible!" Anne agreed.

Sophia toyed with a paperweight from Gary's desk, momentarily tempted to throw it. "You don't know anyone who'd want him dead, do you?"

Gary frowned as he considered the question. "We've got two possibilities. Either the Mexicans are retaliating, or…"

"Or?"

"It's Roderick Guerrero."

She shook her head. "No."

"According to the sheriff, he's the one."

"The *sheriff?*" she echoed.

Anne piped up. "Sheriff Cooper is a cousin of Edna's, you know."

Around here, everyone seemed to be related or have some type of connection. When it came to investigating criminal proceedings, that wasn't a good thing. "So?"

"Rumor has it Stuart trashed Rod's motel room only hours before he was killed," Gary replied. "That's what set him off. But he's always had it in for Stuart. Everyone knows that."

"It *is* pretty coincidental that Stuart would wind up dead less than a week after his half brother came back to town," Anne said, as if that was as incriminating as finding Rod's DNA at the crime scene.

Sophia had thought the Dunlaps might point a finger at the bastard child they'd rejected. The sheriff was probably going along with it to avoid a panic and to curb the chances of a backlash against undocumented aliens. But there wasn't any hard evidence to tie Rod to the murder, so she hadn't been too worried. "We don't prosecute people on coincidence," she said.

"Folks at the Firelight are saying he stopped by looking for Stuart just before the murder," Gary pointed out.

"That's circumstantial, too. It wasn't Rod. I was with him at the Firelight, helping him look."

"But what did he do *after* he left you?" Gary said. "That's the question. He won't tell anyone where he went."

They couldn't talk about the safe house and he had enough honor not to drag her down with him by mentioning that he'd ultimately gone to her place.

Sophia had hoped to keep her sex life out of public

scrutiny, especially when there was already talk of an affair between her and her stepfather. Especially because, for a certain period of time, he'd been at her place alone. But this gave her no choice. She had to provide as much of an alibi as she could.

"I'm telling you he didn't do it," she said. "Thanks to whoever damaged his motel room, he needed a place to stay. So I let him stay with me."

This revelation apparently wasn't clear or specific enough to change her mother's mind. But Sophia couldn't blame her for not catching on sooner. She'd denied having much contact with Rod only twenty minutes earlier. "That doesn't necessarily mean anything," Anne said. "Maybe he slipped out while you were asleep."

"He was there alone for a while, but he was hurt and had no transportation. And once I got back, which was close to the time we believe Stuart was killed, he didn't go anywhere." Sophia sent her mother a significant look, but it did no good.

"You're sure?"

"Yes. I would've known about it."

"Not if—" she began, but Gary nudged her and realization finally dawned. "You mean…he wasn't on the couch?"

Sophia sighed. "That's exactly what I mean."

Detective Lindstrom had picked Rod up for questioning at the Boot and Spur Dude Ranch five miles west of town. Because the rooms came as part of an expensive vacation package that included an entire week's stay, chuck wagon dinners, hoedowns and trail rides, and very few people wanted to spend a week riding horses in one hundred and ten degree weather, they'd closed for a few weeks to do some remodeling. But the manager was nice enough to rent Rod a room, anyway. Fortunately, they didn't have to worry about the newspeople bugging them to do the same. The crews weren't interested in sequestering themselves outside of town; they didn't want to miss any of the action.

Although he'd been sitting in an interrogation room for the past fifteen minutes, trying to tell Sheriff Cooper and his sidekick, Detective Lindstrom, that he'd had nothing to do with Stuart's murder, they weren't listening. Just as they really started grilling him, a deputy with hair even redder than Lindstrom's poked his head into the room.

"Sheriff, I got a call for you."

"Take a message." Intent on his purpose, Cooper scooted his chair closer to Rod. "It'll be a lot easier on everybody if you tell us the truth, son."

The country charm was no doubt calculated to make Cooper seem like a trustworthy parent figure. He'd probably been taught that in Successful Interrogation 101. But the only parent figure Rod could trust had died a long time ago and he wasn't likely to forget it. "I'm not your son," he pointed out. "And I have nothing to say. Either charge me with a crime or let me go."

"Don't ask for more trouble than you're already in. I don't have to explain to you—"

"Sheriff?"

Irritation etched deep grooves in Cooper's weathered face as he realized the deputy who'd interrupted him was still there. "What now, Phil?"

"It's that phone call, sir."

"What about it?"

"Chief St. Claire says she needs to talk to you right

away. She claims she has information pertaining to the murder of Stuart Dunlap."

This gave him pause. "Did she say what it was?"

"No, sir."

Muttering a few words that sounded like, "This better be good," he hefted his considerable weight onto his feet and left.

Meanwhile, Lindstrom folded her arms, crossed her legs and sat back. "Did you do it?"

Rod didn't bother answering. This was a load of crap, a waste of time. They had nothing on him. He was more concerned with what was happening *outside* the room. He didn't want Sophia to do what he figured she was doing. He could handle this on his own.

Lindstrom spoke up again. "The D.A. will go easier on you if you tell the truth."

He shot her a dirty look. If she thought she could take over for Cooper and do a better job, she was more clueless than he'd supposed, which was saying something. "Easier for whom? You?"

"You know how these things work."

"Exactly." And even if he *had* killed someone, it would take smarter interrogators than Tweedledum and Tweedledee to make him crack.

She tried to talk to him again, but he leaned his elbows on his knees and stared at the floor without responding, and she finally understood that she wasn't going to get anywhere. She fell silent, leaving Rod to wonder what was being said on the phone. Was Sophia telling the sheriff that they'd been together almost all night?

He hoped not. He didn't want to give them *anything.*

Maybe she'd come up with a piece of hard evidence, something that pointed to someone else....

A few minutes later, the door opened, and Sheriff Cooper stood there looking as disappointed as a kid who'd just had his Halloween candy stolen by the neighborhood bully. "That's it for today. You can go."

"Excuse me?" Rod said.

"You heard me," Cooper replied. "This doesn't mean I won't bring you back in, if necessary, but we've talked enough for now. Lindstrom, drop him off at his motel."

Lindstrom came to her feet. "But...what's changed?"

"Coroner says Stuart was killed at about four-thirty. I called him as soon as I hung up with Chief St. Claire."

"And?"

"Rod here has an alibi from four on."

Her eyebrows arched. "Where was he?"

Cooper gave her a look that said this was going to be good. "Having sex with the chief of police."

Her mouth dropped open but she quickly recovered. And then she grew angry. "So that's why you took her side at the FBI meeting," she snapped. "She was putting out for you!"

Damn it. Sophia shouldn't have confessed. Her enemies, including Lindstrom, would use this against her, try to sway public opinion, make her look irresponsible and morally compromised all because she'd lowered her defenses and let him stay the night.... "That had nothing to do with it."

"What else could it be?" she said with a smirk.

Determined to shut Lindstrom up, at least for the moment, he offered her a taunting grin. "You mean other than the fact that she's worth two of you under *any* circumstances."

The call came much sooner than Sophia had expected. She wished she'd ignored it, let it go to voice mail and saved herself the humiliation of facing Mayor Schilling and the other four council members when she already felt so beleaguered. But she wasn't sure she'd feel any stronger tomorrow. Her days seemed to be getting steadily worse, no matter what she did. So she'd taken the call and received her summons and here she was, hurrying so she wouldn't be late. Pride wouldn't allow her to skulk off and hide just because the powers that be had obviously heard the rumors about her. She hadn't had an affair with her stepfather. Despite Leonard and his attempts to damage her reputation, there'd been no impropriety on her part at all. And maybe she'd slept with Rod, which probably wasn't the best decision, but she didn't think one night's escape affected her ability to do her job. If she was never really off duty, they had to give her enough leeway to live a little while she was *on* duty, didn't they? Besides, technically she'd been off.

But it wouldn't matter. Not to most of the council. Bordertown was nothing if not conservative; it was surprising they'd promoted her to chief of police in the first place. And, whether her private life was any of their business or not, she had to answer to them. So she'd hold her head high and fulfill that responsibility along with all the rest.

As she stood in the back of the room, Paul Fedorko glanced up and nudged Liz Torres, who was sitting next to him. Schilling was in the middle of a tirade about budget overages on the city park being built on Hampton Street, but everyone on the council was soon murmuring and fidgeting, and Sophia knew they were distracted by her presence. Their preoccupation became so noticeable that the short, stout mayor, who'd always reminded her of the man behind the mirrors in *The Wizard of Oz,* finally turned to see what was going on and gave up trying to make his point.

"Chief St. Claire, thank you for responding to our invitation," he said. "Please, come up and join us."

Taking a deep breath, she forced her legs to carry her to the conference table, where she sat in one of a handful of empty seats. Despite the mayor's polite address, there was a frostiness in his manner that had never been there before. That, combined with the reluctance of certain people to look her in the eye, spelled trouble. She was going to be given another warning, probably a harsh one. They'd tell her that her behavior as a public servant was under constant scrutiny and that they expected her to comport herself as a true professional at all times. Then they'd make it clear, once again, that they required a quick resolution to the illegal immigrant murders. And she'd tell them about everything she'd been doing, hoping to convince them that she was, indeed, fulfilling the requirements of the job.

She had no idea what they might have to say about Stuart's death, however. Some of them had known him as well as she had. They were all grieving, which made the situation even worse and meant they'd want answers she didn't have. Rod was the only person she knew with any kind of significant grudge against Stuart. She couldn't guess why anyone else would want him dead, unless his murder was what they'd feared might happen all along, an act motivated by revenge against Americans. They wouldn't want to hear that. But she wasn't about to let Edna and her friends and relatives villainize Rod. Maybe he'd had issues with Stuart, but he didn't kill him.

Hoping she'd be able to convey that with sensitivity and clarity, she waited as Wayne Schilling turned the floor over to Liz Torres. Councilwoman Torres shuffled the papers in front of her, formed them into a neat stack and got to her feet. Instead of avoiding Sophia's gaze the way she had a moment before, she nearly leveled her with an angry, piercing glare.

"Chief St. Claire," she said tightly. "It is with the *utmost* regret that I must make you aware of the terrible disappointment you have become to the city and, in particular, those members of this council who lobbied so hard to have you instated as chief of police. It was a first for the women of this town and I was especially pleased. I felt you'd do a good job, that you'd be honest and forthright—"

"I've been both of those things!" Sophia interrupted, taking exception to the councilwoman's tone.

"Nevertheless, there has been substantial evidence of conduct unbecoming a public official."

Sophia also got to her feet. "If you're referring to the picture you were shown at the—"

Councilwoman Torres lifted her hand. "Please, allow me to finish."

Stifling all the protests that clogged her throat, Sophia kept still.

"We have deliberated long and hard on what should be done about your behavior," she continued. "Most of the afternoon, in fact. And it is with great sadness and reluctance that I must inform you we need to make a change."

This didn't sound anything like her previous warnings. No one else was chiming in, redirecting the conversation, disagreeing, adding details. Everyone, except Torres, who Sophia now understood to be her "executioner," sat still.

"What are you saying?" Sophia asked. "Are you firing me?"

"We're giving you thirty days' notice, Chief St. Claire.

We'll be interviewing other candidates for the position of chief at our earliest convenience."

Heart pounding, Sophia straightened her shoulders. She had so much to say. And yet there was one question that seemed more important than all the rest. "And do those candidates include Leonard Taylor?"

Liz bent her head. "If Mr. Taylor cares to apply, we'll consider his application as well as everyone else's."

"He raped a woman!"

"A nasty accusation to be sure, but one that's never been proven. For all we know, his accuser was lying to get back at him for some slight. Or...you were."

"You've got to be kidding me!"

"I don't want to believe that. But we can't ignore that you had sufficient motivation."

"This is unreal!"

"That's it for now. We will address our specific complaints in a formal letter."

Sophia swept her arm around the room. "Why not do it now? When we're all sitting here face-to-face?"

Richard Lantus coughed into his hand. Deep down he knew, and so did one or two of the others, that they were using gossip as an excuse to get rid of her. Her age and gender were the real reasons behind this, just as they'd been the issues that had caused problems with her appointment. She was fine when policing the city consisted of passing out a few parking tickets and hauling in drunks, but give her a murder case and even Paul Fedorko pulled his support. Now that the situation had turned dicey, they were too afraid to go out on a limb. And although Liz claimed to be big on women's rights, she cared more about punishing Sophia for the sin of fornication than she did advancing the cause of women. She'd recently become a very devout follower of her faith and seemed compelled to push her religion onto others.

"Fine," she said. "If you must know, we have taken testimony from Detective Lindstrom—"

"Who's a good friend of Leonard Taylor's!" Sophia broke in. "Don't you get it? This is the same fight we had before. Except now, those of you who were brave enough to take a stand against Leonard's misuse of power are willing to embrace it again as long as it relieves the difficult situation we've found ourselves in. You don't believe I'm capable of solving the UDA murders. But how do you know the next person will be any better? These are random slayings, the hardest to deal with."

"Leonard Taylor says he could've solved them by now." This came from Paul Fedorko, which only proved her theory about his defection.

"If he knows something about these murders and he's not coming forward, he deserves to be punished right along with the perpetrator," she said.

"It's not just the UDA murders," Torres responded with that same disapproving tone. "We talked to Dr. Vonnegut, too. *Everyone* has issues with you. And now, one of our own is dead—God rest his soul."

"You're blaming *me* for that?"

"Of course not. But we can't help wondering if we'd had someone who was taking the job more seriously—"

The ferocity with which Sophia shoved aside the empty chair between them surprised Liz into silence. "More seriously than working day and night?" she cried.

"You were hardly working last night, now were you, Chief?" The speaker was Neil Munoz, who'd stood by Leonard Taylor from the beginning. His smug smile told

Sophia he'd been looking forward to this moment as much as Leonard.

"Unless Mr. Guerrero made some form of payment we're not aware of…" he added as an aside to Schilling, who snickered.

"I had consensual sex with a man my own age and in the privacy of my own home," she said. "I don't see how that affects my job."

Liz jumped back into the fray. "It doesn't look good. You're the chief of police, for crying out loud. Show some restraint. I mean, we've got naked pictures of you floating around, and…and rumors that you're having a sexual relationship with your stepfather, and—"

"None of that is true! I slept with Rod. That's it."

Her expression remained pinched with distaste. "Still…"

"Still?" Sophia burst out. "None of us are perfect, Councilwoman Torres. Weren't you kicked out of your church once upon a time for getting pregnant out of wedlock?"

Liz's eyes nearly popped out of her head. Her shock and embarrassment were gratifying enough to make Sophia want to go around the room, naming something that would embarrass them all. But what was the point? These people held a great deal of power in Bordertown, and they felt it gave them the right to be judgmental and self-righteous whenever it suited their purposes. Obviously, the political winds had changed, and she was caught in the cross draft.

"How dare you!" Liz sputtered when no one else came to her defense.

"No, how dare *you*," Sophia responded.

"Does that mean you quit?" Neil sang out, and it was

then that Sophia realized she was destroying all hope for a career in law enforcement by letting her anger take control. She was also paving the way for Leonard to get what he wanted. She had to rein in her temper, get ahold of herself.

With as much dignity and calm as she could muster, she turned to confront Neil. "No, I won't quit," she said. "I owe it to the people of this community to protect them as best I can during the coming transition. Maybe you've forgotten what's happening here, but I haven't. We've got at least one killer on the loose. And, as far as I'm concerned, that killer could be Leonard Taylor. You might keep that in mind when you interview him for the position of chief of police, because he's playing you. He's playing us all."

Pivoting once again, she stomped out and slammed the door.

25

Rod was waiting for Sophia when she returned home.
Sitting in his Hummer with the seat back, he had his feet
up on the dash and was reading the paper. It was getting
fairly late—eight-fifteen, according to the clock in her
cruiser—but the sun hadn't yet gone down.

Sophia didn't know how long he'd been parked in front
of her house, but he was the last person she wanted to
see. Twisting the rearview mirror toward her, she quickly
checked her makeup. Would he be able to tell she'd been
crying? *Yes...* Of course he would. Swollen eyes stared
back at her from a splotchy face. Even her nose was red
from the number of times she'd blown it since leaving that
council meeting.

He opened her door while she took her time collecting
her purse and other belongings. "I dropped by the station,"
he said. "I thought you'd be starting at eight, as usual. But
the place was locked up. What's going on?"

Briefly protected by the curtain of her hair as it fell
forward, she slipped her car keys in her purse. "The sheriff's office is covering for me tonight."

"Why?"

She found a pair of sunglasses and put them on before
looking up. "We contract with them to patrol whenever

we need the extra help. Unless someone dials the station's direct line, all emergency calls go through their dispatchers anyway."

"So you have the night off."

"Basically."

"But…what's going on?" He hesitated. "Are you okay?"

"I'm fine."

"You haven't been answering your cell."

"I turned it off."

"What if there'd been a break in the case?"

"Which case?" They seemed to be piling up. Maybe the council had been right to fire her….

"Either case."

"That would take luck. Something I don't seem to have at the moment." She attempted a laugh, but it didn't sound very convincing.

"This isn't over yet," he said. "We're going to find the son of a bitch who's killing illegal aliens. And we're going to figure out who shot Stuart. You can't expect too much too soon. These things take time."

That was the one commodity she didn't have. Not anymore. In just four weeks someone else would take over. Where would she go then? What would she do? Until those poor victims in the desert had forced her to question her investigative abilities, she'd thought she'd found her niche in life. "We'll see."

Hoping to step around him and into the house before he could get a good look at her, she got out of the car. But he blocked her path and caught her chin, tilting it up so he could see her face. "What happened?"

"Nothing."

He removed her sunglasses. "Sophia—"

Grabbing the glasses, she pulled out of his grasp. "What does it matter to you? You'll either solve these murders or you won't. And then you'll leave and go back to your other life, in which Bordertown will cease to exist for you. You'll be able to go on, completely unaffected by events here and you won't have to live with the aftermath."

"You think I'll be able to forget that Stuart was *murdered?* That my father suspects *I* did it?" He strode after her.

"You don't care about your father's opinion, remember?" she replied, tossing the words over her shoulder.

"Maybe I'm not quite as indifferent as I'd like to believe. Have you ever considered that?"

"No." She was safer *not* to consider it. Because then she'd start hoping that he did care. *About her.*

He followed her into the house, pausing to shut the door with his foot. "What went wrong today? I mean, besides the obvious."

She hurried into the kitchen without stopping. "They fired me, okay? I have thirty days while they interview possible replacements."

He nearly missed a step. "You're kidding."

"That wouldn't be my idea of a joke. Although *this* should be funny—I bet it'll be Leonard Taylor who replaces me."

A frown tugged at his lips as he shoved his hands in his pockets and leaned against the doorway. "Come on, they couldn't be *that* stupid."

"Wanna bet? He's been talking big, telling everyone that he could've solved these murders weeks ago. That Stuart never would've been killed if he'd been chief of police."

"That's easy to say when you don't have to prove it."

"Doesn't matter that it's all talk. It's what they want to hear. Think about it. The council's so desperate they're searching for a savior, and he's setting himself up as just that."

"Which has given his supporters a chance to gain power again and reverse everything that happened when you were hired."

"Exactly. But it's all good for you, right?"

His eyes narrowed. "What do you mean by that?"

"Your revenge is complete. Not only did you bag the girl who stood you up for Homecoming, you stuck around long enough to see it ruin her career."

His frown darkened into a scowl. "That's not what I wanted. Besides, *I* didn't tell anyone, *you* did."

She slumped into a chair. "I know," she said miserably.

"Why'd you do it?"

"Isn't it obvious? I couldn't let them continue investigating you when I knew you weren't involved."

"Yes, you could have. They wouldn't have been able to pin Stuart's murder on me."

Pressing a finger and thumb against her closed eyelids, she shook her head. "Innocent people go to prison all the time, Rod. Why take the chance?"

The difficult-to-read front he sometimes maintained slipped, giving her a glimpse into the far more accessible, maybe even vulnerable, man she'd made love with last night. "Because, contrary to what you might think, I don't want to be responsible for this," he said.

She dropped her hand so she could look at him—and recognized that, even now, after her whole world had collapsed, she wanted to touch him. And she wanted it more than last night.

"How ironic," she muttered.

His eyebrows came together. "What's ironic?"

"Nothing," she said, but she found *all* of it ironic. For years, she hadn't been able to summon much passion for the men she dated, hadn't even realized it was passion that was missing. Not until Rod had walked back into her life had she felt so compelled to be with someone.

She was finally tempted to love—the one person most likely to hurt her.

"Why are you here?" she asked. "What do you want from me?"

He crossed the room and squatted in front of her. "I'm sorry."

Sophia wasn't sure why he was apologizing. For the resentment he felt toward her? For giving her mixed signals, treating her as if he couldn't keep his hands off her one minute and snubbing her the next? For being part of the reason she'd lost her job?

Maybe that "I'm sorry" was meant to cover it all.

She told herself to accept his apology and let it go at that. If she was careful, maybe she could finish out her month without making her situation any worse. It was even possible they'd solve the UDA murders or Stuart's murder or both, as he'd said. Then she could probably get a recommendation and find a job somewhere else.

But she didn't speak. She couldn't come up with the right words. Instead, she raised her hand and ran her fingers down the side of his face, feeling the rugged contours, the prickly beard growth and, eventually, the softness of his mouth.

His eyes drifted closed as she touched him.

"You're so handsome," she said.

Parting his lips, he flicked his tongue against the pad

of her thumb, and that was all it took for desire to swallow Sophia's other, far more conflicting emotions.

"*And* you're dangerous," she added.

His hand went behind her neck, bringing her mouth to his for the lightest, sweetest kiss she'd ever had. "I'm harmless," he whispered. Then his tongue met hers and five minutes later he had her naked on the living room floor.

Rod didn't want to think about what he was doing, didn't want to examine the consequences. He knew he shouldn't be forming any ties to Bordertown. His goal, from the beginning, had been to break free. He'd only come back to do his duty by his mother's people—to stop a killer—and, at the same time, celebrate the fact that he'd escaped so cleanly.

Instead, he was celebrating the feel of the girl he'd always wanted clinging to him with her bare skin against his. Why couldn't he resist her? It wasn't, as he'd thought before, that he had something to prove to Stuart. Stuart was gone for good. Rod couldn't even claim he was acting to satisfy the promise of a dream long denied. He'd fulfilled that promise last night.

So what the hell was he doing? Sophia belonged to his past, and yet, when he made love to her, he forgot all the reasons he wanted to turn his back on her. The rise and fall of her chest, her hands clutching his hair, her mouth moving greedily on his—these were the only things that seemed important.

Outside, the sun was beginning to set, but enough light filtered in that he could see her, and of that he was glad. Last night he'd welcomed the darkness. It had allowed him to hide what he wasn't ready to reveal. This time, he didn't have that same need. He wasn't sure what Sophia meant to him, but she meant *something,* and he wasn't afraid to let her know. Whatever they had, for however long it lasted, he wanted it to be honest.

"You make me forget," he murmured against her neck.

She angled her chin. "Forget what?"

Smiling at her breathless response, he pinned her hands above her head and pulled back to admire her. "Everything."

As she gazed up at him with her hair fanning out on the floor, her body glistening with a damp layer of sweat and her pupils so dilated that her eyes looked black, he thought she had to be the most striking woman he'd ever seen. He even liked her tattoo sleeve because it was so much a part of who she'd come to be.

A crease in her forehead told him she wasn't quite sure how to take his words. But she didn't question him. "You make me remember," she said.

He wondered where she was going with this. "Remember what?"

A faint smile curved her lips. "Everything."

He didn't ask her to explain. Whatever they felt, it was too new to define. It was there. They'd acknowledged it. That was enough.

"Good. Then remember this," he said, and bent to kiss her again.

It had grown completely dark outside, but Sophia was still on the living room floor with Rod. She was too exhausted to move, even to the bedroom. She'd known she was under a lot of pressure, but she hadn't realized just how heavy the burden of her job had been until that burden was removed. The UDA murders would become someone else's problem soon. The fight was over. She'd lost—but at least it was over, right?

Maybe she'd move out of state, she decided. Sell everything she couldn't fit on her Harley and go wherever the road took her....

"What are you thinking?" Rod murmured. He'd dozed for the past half hour or so while she'd been absently running her fingers through his hair and staring at the shadows cast by the rising moon.

"Montana."

He lifted his head from her shoulder. *"Montana?"*

"I'm wondering if I'd like it up there."

"You're planning to move?"

"After everything that's happened, I don't think I want to stick around here." Her heart nearly broke when she thought about Rafe. He'd be homesick for her by the time he returned from camp. And where would she be? Packing, with only a few weeks left in town?

No, more than a few weeks. She'd need to sell her house. She couldn't move right away. But she'd have to make a change fairly soon. Without substantial savings, she wouldn't have enough money to last long....

Hoping to put off difficult decisions, she squeezed her eyes shut. But there was no avoiding the truth. She couldn't leave Bordertown without feeling she'd abandoned Rafe, which she'd promised herself she'd never do. She knew what it felt like to be abandoned, emotionally if not physically. And yet she couldn't be happy living among the people who'd let her down so terribly....

"It's a lot colder in Montana," Rod pointed out. "You don't want to go there."

"Everywhere's colder than here. Except...I don't know...maybe Africa."

"You wouldn't mind leaving your mother?"

She wanted to mention Rafe, but wasn't positive he'd understand. And why bother? She doubted he'd be around long enough for her bond with Rafe to become an issue. "Our relationship is...complicated. Sort of like your relationship with Bruce."

"Bruce and I don't have a relationship."

"But you're not quite as indifferent as you'd like to believe, remember?"

"I wasn't referring to *him*."

Smiling at the implication, she continued to thread her fingers through his thick hair. "I can tell you one thing—I wouldn't mind leaving my stepfather."

"Did you ask him why his number was in that safe house?"

"No. First, I want to go through his office at the feed store." She told Rod about her aborted efforts at her mother's place, and finished by saying, "All his bank statements and business documents are at the store. If there's anything that's going to reveal his connection to the safe house, I'm guessing it'll be there."

"What about the gun you found?"

"What about it?"

"We should test it."

"You think *Gary* could be the UDA killer?"

"After what you told me about him, I wouldn't put it past him."

"Sexually unscrupulous doesn't automatically equate with murder."

"It proves a lack of integrity. And we did find his number at the safe house. Besides, the murder weapon is the same make, model and caliber as his. That's a bit coincidental right there. Why not have a ballistics expert take a look?"

"He's not racist enough to have killed those immigrants."

"How do you know?"

"He likes Mexico. The people. The culture. He taught himself the language, and he always wants to vacation there. He's already talking about going to Rocky Point for Christmas."

"I still think we should do some testing."

She pursed her lips, considering it. "I suppose we could ask him to turn the gun over to us voluntarily. But I doubt he will. He'll use it as yet another example to show my mother that I'm out to get him."

Rod's breath fanned her cheek as he placed tiny kisses along her jawline. "We might be able to get a warrant."

"Owning a Glock isn't illegal, not if he has a permit. And it's not as though the judge is remotely sympathetic to our cause."

"If Special Agent Van Dormer will step in, we could go federal. That might help."

She didn't respond. She was battling a fresh wave of frustration and disappointment. Just when she thought she'd given in and succumbed to her fate, planned her motorcycle escape into the wild blue yonder, she realized she wasn't willing to let her days in Bordertown end so negatively. She was too much of a fighter. Besides, she couldn't really bring herself to leave Rafe behind. What'd happened to her had left too deep a scar to do the same to him.

Rod rolled up on his elbows. "Sophie, you still with me?"

"Sophie?" Only her mother and Rafe ever called her that.

"It's an endearment. You don't like endearments?"

"I don't mind them if you don't, Roddy."

Laughing, he stole one of her throw pillows, then blocked the punch she tried to land to his ribs. "Whoa! So much hostility."

"You deserve it. You cost me my job." She knew that wasn't strictly true. News of her and Rod had only been the proverbial "last straw," but it felt better to blame someone. Maybe it would shore up some of her crumbling defenses where he was concerned.

He tweaked her nipple. "No, the fact that you couldn't resist me cost you your job."

"What are you talking about? I can resist you." She feared it was a lie, but it was a lie she wished he'd believe.

"If I remember correctly, you made the first move."

"After you strategically placed yourself in my bed!"

"Strategically?" He feigned shock. "I was injured."

She rolled her eyes. "Tell the truth. You weren't that injured. You were hoping to get laid."

"True, but I had no idea that plan would work so well," he said with a chuckle. "Anyway, don't worry. I'm going to help you get your job back."

"How, exactly, do you plan to do that?"

"We'll solve the case within the next thirty days. Then, even if they boot you out, you can feel good about what we accomplished. What do you say?"

She nudged his hand away from her breast. He drove her crazy, but he made her happy, too—odd, since she should be in the depths of despair after losing her job. And yet when she was with Rod, all she could think about was the way he made her feel and how much she enjoyed his company. "I say you're dreaming."

"Not necessarily."

"Not necessarily? What have we got so far? Disgruntled ranchers who are irate over the loss of one of their own, as well as having their property damaged. Border patrol agents who are tired of rounding up UDAs only to see them attempt another crossing the very next night. Racists who'd sooner shoot a Mexican than look at one. Political enemies who'd love nothing more than to run me out of town." She considered her list. "We haven't even begun to narrow it down. Which group should we focus on first?"

He bit her earlobe before his tongue traced the sensitive rim. "I know which one *you'd* choose."

Suppressing a shiver, she batted him away. "Leonard should already be in jail," she grumbled. "Instead, he's dusting off his résumé in hopes of taking my job."

"He doesn't have your job *yet*. So stay focused. We know that whoever's killing illegal immigrants is free to move around at night. He probably lives in town or close to it. He might smoke. He hates Mexicans. And he uses a .45 with a silencer."

"That could be half the town. And we don't know if the perpetrator is a 'he,'" she said, but Rod's reference to the silencer reminded Sophia that Starkey had a lead on a man who was selling silencers out of his garage. She mentioned it and added, "He's supposed to meet with him tonight."

"Will he call us afterward?"

"I think so."

"Starkey seems like a pretty loyal friend."

She wasn't sure if he was trying to get her to explain her

relationship with Starkey, or if he was merely making an observation. "He's not a bad guy—for a Hells Angel."

Rod moved onto his back. "Van Dormer left me a message. Probably left you one, too, but since you turned off your phone you might not have gotten it."

"Not yet."

"The autopsies are scheduled for tomorrow."

Now that Rod was no longer touching her, she felt as if he'd taken away the warmth and relief she'd been feeling. God, she was in trouble where he was concerned. She was in trouble all the way around. "The Sanchezes or…"

"Stuart, too. You're not the only one feeling the pressure. Vonnegut's catching grief, too, for not getting to them sooner."

"It doesn't help that he's been sick. On top of that, he's about to retire. All he cares about is golf." The air conditioner came on so she used it as an excuse to curl up against him. "Stuart was the last one killed, but I bet he's first when it comes to the autopsies."

Rod put his arm around her, making it more comfortable for her to lie on him. "Of course. My father's a friend of Mayor Schilling."

"You mean the Wizard of Oz?"

"The what?"

"Nothing." She used her foot to drag the throw blanket down from the couch. "What do you think they'll find?"

"That Stuart's heart shriveled up and turned black long ago."

"Seriously," she said, sharing her blanket.

"That he drank too much. That he should've done more to stay in shape. And that he was killed by a gunshot wound to the head."

Sophia bit her lip as she considered the possibilities. "His stomach contents might help establish the time of death."

"It might even tell us who he was with."

She raised her head. "How so?"

"If it's…say…a teriyaki burger with pineapple on it, he probably bought it at Big Ed's Burgers. Big Ed's is famous for that, right?"

"Oh, right. So if we know he ate there before he died, we can interview the employees on duty and find out roughly when he was there and whether or not he was with someone."

"Careful," Rod warned. "You're starting to sound hopeful again."

"*Cautiously* hopeful," she said. "I don't see how the UDA killer can be responsible for Stuart's death, too. Stuart doesn't fit the profile of the other victims. And the way he was killed doesn't feel like a reprisal. Maybe I could believe that if it was one of the ranchers who'd been shot, but what I saw makes me think he was lured out there."

"And yet the killings are somehow related," he said. "The timing would be too much of a coincidence otherwise."

Sophia agreed. But *how* were they related? And what about that distracting business with her stepfather's telephone number on the refrigerator of the safe house? "What we know is too sketchy and random. It won't come together."

"Be patient. There's an answer. There's *always* an answer."

"But will we find it before I lose my paycheck and head to Montana?"

"You won't like Montana."

She'd already realized she couldn't leave Bordertown, not until Rafe was older. But it was alluring to think she could break away if she really wanted to. "You don't know that."

"Maybe not. But I do know you'll have a better chance of keeping your job if we get back to work." He rolled over and got up, then extended his hand to her. "Come on. Let's get dressed so we can visit your father's feed store."

"Now?"

"Why not? It's dark and I happen to know that none of the local police are on duty. Perfect time for a break-in."

As she let him pull her to her feet, she said, "We don't have to break in."

"We don't?"

"No." After closing the curtains and turning on the lights, she retrieved her purse. Then she fished out the key she'd dropped in her coin pouch earlier and held it up. "I've got this."

"That's for the feed store?"

"According to the neat little label that was above it, yes. Fortunately, my stepfather's very particular about his things. His spare keys are neatly organized and readily available, provided you have access to his house, of course." She smiled broadly. "It was right there, hanging inside a cupboard in my mother's kitchen, exactly where it used to be when I was living at home. I grabbed it while she was heating up my dinner, and she never had a clue."

Rod gave her bottom a pat. "Way to go, champ. See? This isn't over yet."

26

Leonard's hand shook with eagerness and anxiety as he sat in his truck and dialed Gary O'Conner's cell phone. He knew Gary couldn't be happy with him. In his determination to ruin Sophia, he'd gotten impatient and possibly a little overzealous and flung some mud at Gary in the process, but this was the perfect way to repair their relationship.

The phone rang several times before transferring to voice mail. Was Gary already asleep? He had to get up at five every morning to open the store at six. The ranchers depended on those early hours; that was when they rented most of the farm equipment, which meant Gary went to bed early....

Hanging up without leaving a message, Leonard checked the clock on the dashboard. It was ten-thirty. Did he dare call Gary's house? He had to tell him that Sophia was on her way to the feed store.

A car came down the street and turned into the tiny brown house on the corner, but Leonard wasn't worried about being seen. The moment he'd realized that Sophia and Rod would be leaving, he'd driven several blocks away, winding deeper into her neighborhood rather than risking a chance encounter on her street or the main roads. He didn't need to keep Sophia and Rod in view to know where they were going. He'd heard them make their plans.

He tried Gary's cell phone a second time, got his voice mail again and decided to try his house. Hoping Anne wouldn't answer—he knew how touchy Gary was about anything that might arouse her curiosity—he waited through three rings. He was about to give up when he finally heard a man's voice.

"Hello?"

"Gary?"

"Yeah?"

"It's me, Leonard."

"Uh, hello, Mac. Hang on a sec, will ya?"

Mac was Gary's brother who lived somewhere in Texas. Leonard had never met him, but he'd heard Gary talk about him on occasion.

There was some rustling and talking in the background. When Gary spoke again, his voice was low but filled with annoyance. "What do you want? Why are you calling me here?"

Leonard turned off the listening device that'd enabled him to hear Rod and Sophia's conversation—and the grunting and groaning that had gone on before. Who would've guessed Bordertown's straitlaced chief of police could be so hot, he thought with a pang of jealousy. "I tried your cell. You didn't pick up."

"Because it's nearly eleven o'clock. We were in bed. Did you ever think of that?"

"Sorry, this can't wait."

"Sure it can wait, because we're not speaking to each other anymore," he said. "What the hell do you think you were doing, flashing that naked picture of Sophia around and telling everyone it was mine? She's been all over me like flies on shit ever since. And if my wife gets wind of the rumors, so help me—"

"I had to do it," he interrupted. "I had to get Sophia riled up, make her look bad."

"Make *her* look bad? Idiot! You're making me look bad, too!"

"No, I'm making you look like the luckiest man in the world. There isn't a guy in town who doesn't want a piece of that."

"What about my *wife?*"

"Calm down. You're making too big a deal out of it. Anne won't believe those rumors, anyway. She loves you. Trusts you. Besides, it worked. Neil called tonight. Sophia was just given thirty days' notice."

There was a brief pause. "She's being fired?"

"Sure as the sunrise. And if you give me the support I need to get her job, I promise your life will get a lot easier."

Gary was too tempted by the money he could make with Sophia out of the equation to hold a grudge over the picture, and Leonard knew it. "That's something," he mumbled.

"Exactly what we've been hoping for, buddy."

"So that's it? That's why you called? To let me know?"

"No, that could've waited until morning."

"Then what's going on?"

"Sophia's on her way to the feed store. Somehow Rod visited the safe house and saw your phone number. They're trying to figure out why it was there."

"Oh, God. That's what she was looking for."

"When?"

"Earlier, here at the house. I caught her in my office."

"I heard her say something about that, too. She found your gun. So if it's any danger to you, you might want to make it disappear while you still can."

"I already knew she found my gun, but where did you get the information? How did you 'hear' it?"

"That's none of your business. I'm doing what you pay me to do. That's all you need to know."

"And now you're telling me she's on her way to the feed store."

"That's right. She's trying to uncover your link to the safe house, like I said. Bruce's bastard is with her."

"Son of a bitch! What now?"

"What do you mean, 'what now'? Isn't it clear? You have to stop her."

"How? If she already knows I'm connected to the safe house, keeping her from searching the store won't solve the problem."

"It'll keep her from getting the proof she needs."

"She won't give up. I know her."

"Then maybe you should do something…permanent."

Gary's voice was a harsh whisper. "What kind of man do you think I am?"

"One who'll spend the rest of his life in prison if he doesn't act quickly."

Several tense seconds passed. "I hate that woman," he complained. "She's been the bane of my existence from the beginning."

"Then have the balls to take care of it! Get rid of her."

"Oh, you'd like that, wouldn't you? I'd be doing you a huge favor. You hate her even more than I do."

"At least I'm man enough do what needs to be done."

"You think *you* could put a bullet in her head?"

For months, Leonard had dreamed of little else. "Without a second's hesitation. Is that what you want? Because it'll cost you a pretty penny, since I'd have to do Rod at the same time."

"You're so cavalier," he said bitterly. "Did you kill Stuart? Did you shoot him in the head the way you're talking about shooting Sophia?"

Leonard's hand tightened on his cell phone. "No, I didn't. Why do you have to bring that up?"

"Because I believe you did kill him. And he was your friend."

"I'm telling you I didn't. But this isn't about friends. This is about business."

There was another silence, one that told Leonard Gary was in turmoil.

"We don't have all day," he reminded him.

"We're talking about my stepdaughter. That's a lot to consider."

"It's you or her. Consider *that*."

"Are you sure you can do it without getting caught? If my wife ever found out that I—"

"Relax. I'm going to be the chief of police, remember? It's not as if I won't be able to cover up whatever I want."

"But if you turn that feed store into a crime scene, the police will cart everything away and go through it with a fine-tooth comb. I can't risk that."

"What's there?"

"Everything! I'm running a business. That means there's paperwork."

"Fine. I can call you when I'm done, give you a chance to collect what you need. I've got to do it there. We may not have another opportunity."

"You expect me to go down there and…what…step over two bodies to get to my files?"

"Do you have a better idea?"

He sighed heavily. "Can't you just…take them out in the desert and shoot them?"

"There are two of them, and one happens to be an ex-SEAL. I think surprise is my best option. Don't you?"

Gary didn't react to the heavy dose of sarcasm. "I don't want a bloody mess."

"A bloody mess is better than a life sentence. Maybe the next time you have to worry about blood, it'll be your own. Those yard fights can get pretty brutal, from what I hear."

Still, he wouldn't commit.

"Come on, man. Make a decision. She's linked you to the safe house. That makes her a threat to the whole operation."

When Gary finally spoke, his voice sounded strangled, but there was no mistaking the sudden resolve in his words. "Fine. Do it," he said, and disconnected.

Rod felt more pressure than ever to solve the UDA murders. He'd come here to help, had big plans for making a difference and for finally proving, to himself if no one else, that he was better than anyone here had given him credit for being. Instead, he'd gone straight for the one thing he should've left alone. And now, thanks to his involvement, Sophia was in more trouble than she'd been in before his arrival.

So much for improving the situation...

He had to fix the damage he'd done so he could leave without regrets. At this point, that was the only way to clear his conscience. He just hoped that whatever they were about to find in Gary O'Conner's feed store would make a difference.

"You got it?" He was hunched beside Sophia at the back door. They'd driven his Hummer but parked it down the street, at the Firelight, so it wouldn't be sitting in the lot.

"Yeah." The key seemed to fit smoothly. A second later, the door swung wide, but a beep warned that they had about sixty seconds to turn off the alarm system.

"Did you know he had security?" Rod asked.

"No. Why would anyone worry about someone breaking into *this* place? It's not as if he leaves any money here overnight. I can't imagine it would be easy to fence a tractor."

Rod switched on one of the two flashlights they'd brought with them and pointed it in various directions. "People will steal anything. Just tell me you have the code to shut the damn thing off before we get busted." The feed store looked completely innocuous, exactly as he would've expected. But that intermittent beeping was a problem. He might be able to protect Sophia against a physical threat, but not criminal prosecution.

"I don't have the code! I didn't realize we'd run into this."

"Maybe I can stop it."

"How?"

"Help me find the pad for the key code."

The beams of both flashlights bounced as they jogged to the front.

"I've dealt with a few systems," he said. "If this one's typical, it'll be somewhere logical—and handy."

"But what good is the key pad if we don't know the code?"

The beeping ground on his nerves. "The guts of the system will most likely be close by."

"Here." Holding up her flashlight, she motioned to a shelf below the sales counter.

Rod cut the wires seconds after the alarm began to make a racket. Then they stood in the sudden silence, listening to see if there'd be any response from outside.

When nothing happened, Sophia sagged in relief. "You think you killed it before it could signal the monitoring company?"

"I doubt it. I just stopped the bell so it wouldn't attract any attention from the street. But—" he examined the complexity of the system "—this looks new and expensive, far more expensive than you'd expect to find in Bordertown."

The phone rang.

"That's the alarm company." Grabbing her hand, he started guiding her to the back door. "Let's get out of here."

She pulled out of his grasp. "There's got to be a reason he'd go to the trouble and the expense of installing security," she said. "We have to look around. There's something here he doesn't want anyone to see."

"We'll go to jail for breaking and entering if we don't make a run for it *now*."

The phone had already rung three times.

"Let's go!" he insisted, but she dashed in the opposite direction.

"What are you doing?"

Sophia held up her hand for silence and did exactly what he was afraid she'd do—she picked up the handset. "Hello?...Yes. No, it's nothing.... Mmm-hmm....Sophia St. Claire. I'm chief of police here in Bordertown....I received a call that someone with a flashlight was lurking around the building. My stepfather owns it, so I've got a key....Place looks fine....I don't know the code, but there's no need to wake him. Just take down my badge number and verify my identity through county dispatch. Sure, no problem...." She laughed, then gave her badge number. "Lucky for everyone, I happened to be just around the corner. That's it....Mmm-hmm....Thanks."

Because of the dark interior, Rod couldn't make out her expression. "Did they buy it?"

She released her breath in an audible sigh. "I think so. The woman on the phone didn't balk when I told her to check me out through dispatch. If I sold it right, she won't even bother to do that much."

The beam of her flashlight preceded her as she headed into the office, which was located between the actual shop and the storage area in back.

"What if she does?" he asked, following.

"It'd probably go fine—a simple 'Yep, that badge number matches Chief St. Claire's.'"

"And if she contacts Gary instead? I mean, he *is* the one paying for the service."

She closed the door before switching on the light. "I'll stick to my story, say I received a call that there was a man with a flashlight and I came to check it out."

Rod set his flashlight aside. "Babe, you're not even on duty tonight."

"I'm still a police officer. I'd protect a Border-town business day or night, even if I had to do it in my underwear."

He'd started toward the file cabinets, but paused long enough to let his gaze range over the soft curves he'd enjoyed earlier. "Don't distract me by talking dirty."

She sat at the main desk and began digging through drawers. "I *could* distract you? At a time like this?"

She had *no* idea. "I'd like to think I could keep my pants up if I wanted to."

Sensing the power she held, she grinned as she dug through another drawer. "That wasn't a firm declaration."

"You've cost me a little confidence," he said, thumbing through a stack of employee records and pay stubs. "So what are you going to say when they ask who told you about the flashlight?"

She had her head bent, which made it difficult to hear her. "I'll say it was you. And you'll stand behind me, right?"

"Will you still be in your underwear?"

"Forget I ever mentioned underwear. It was an exaggeration, okay?" She laughed despite the mad rush to cover as much territory as possible in the shortest amount of time. "And I need you to be able to think clearly."

"I can think clearly," he said, but it was a lie. He hadn't been able to think clearly since he first saw her marching toward him at the crime scene and felt like the fifteen-year-old boy he'd once been. The one who'd had to keep his chin from hitting the ground every time she walked by.

* * *

Leonard turned off his headlights before slowly driving down the narrow alleyway behind the feed store. He parked his truck to one side of Trudy Dilspeth's cubby of a house, which was situated above her two-bit hair salon. A single mother, Trudy did whatever she could to survive. She had four small children, by a variety of fathers, none of whom had hung around for long.

With a brood like that, she'd be in bed by now, and her darkened windows seemed to confirm it. Even if she wasn't asleep, she was someone he could trust. She'd entertained him for years, once a month at fifty bucks a visit. He'd stop by and have his hair trimmed. Then they'd disappear into the room she kept for her massage clients and she'd wax his back before spending an extra fifteen minutes performing any other service he wanted.

She flirted with him constantly, trying to get him to come in more often. Being married, he'd tried to keep it to a minimum, but he'd sent her quite a few other clients over the years. So she wasn't likely to get involved in a situation—like the one tonight—that didn't concern her. That'd only deprive her children of what she was able to provide. She made far less cutting hair than doing what she did in the massage room—that was for damn sure. Besides, she had reason to be jealous of Sophia. She'd had her eye on Stuart Dunlap ever since she came to town. Once, she'd even hinted that she was pregnant by him. But nothing ever came of that. Leonard didn't know if she'd miscarried or if Stuart had insisted she get an abortion. Probably the latter. No one as rich as Stuart wanted the town whore to be pregnant with his child.

The country-western station he'd been listening to as he drove went silent as soon as he killed the engine, but he sat in the quiet for a few more minutes, taking a moment to appreciate the peaceful evening. He loved hot summer nights. They carried him back to better times, when his wife was happy being married to him and his kids were running around the place barefoot and screaming like banshees.

He'd expected so much more from life, so much more than he'd gotten.

But it wasn't too late. The fact that Sophia was being fired meant his luck was finally changing. And he was all set up for it to keep changing. He already had two council members who were eager to see him take the helm. With Gary and some of the ranchers behind him, too, he'd make a comeback.

Taking his rifle from behind the seat, where he'd hidden several guns, he jammed his cowboy hat on his head, pulling it low to conceal as much of his face as possible, and lit a cigarette. He didn't usually smoke. Only when he wanted to feel like a Clint Eastwood type. And only when he needed the calming effect of the nicotine.

After a couple of drags, he let the cigarette dangle between his lips and stalked toward the back of the feed store.

He decided to wait in the parking lot. He could hide among the tractors and backhoes and pick Sophia and Rod off as they came out the back door. They wouldn't be stupid enough to exit through the front, where anyone on Bordertown Boulevard could see them.

Yeah, that's it. Two bodies in the parking lot would be better than two bodies in the store. The cleanup would be easier, which would make Gary happy, he could maintain a safe distance from Rod, who looked as if he could row a boat from California to China on manpower alone, and there'd be far less chance of anyone being able to find trace evidence or DNA.

Of course, once he became chief of police, he could make what happened here appear to be anything he wanted, so trace evidence wouldn't matter a whole lot in the end. But he preferred to play it safe. Once the FBI solved the UDA killings, Leonard believed he'd have it made.

He'd definitely need that to happen fast, however. He'd made too many promises he couldn't keep when he'd said all that stuff about being able to solve the case. He'd been bluffing, taunting Sophia and all those who'd opposed him with the pretense that he could've done a better job. But he wasn't too worried. Time was on his side. According to what he'd read in this morning's paper, the FBI was now on board, and they knew their shit. They'd find the bastard. And if they didn't do it quickly enough, he could always pretend they were getting in his way.

He smiled as he envisioned what the next year would hold. Sophia would be punished for everything she'd done to him, and that would restore his pride. His wife and kids would return to him. He'd move closer to town and buy them a big, fancy-ass house. Hell, maybe he'd start socializing with the Dunlaps and Fedorkos. They'd always acted as if they were out of his realm but they'd be kissing his ass once he gained new respect in the community. At that point, even Mayor Schilling wouldn't be too much of a stretch.

Soon. Once Sophia was dead and he was in charge of law enforcement in Bordertown, there wouldn't be anyone standing in his way. Business would be booming—for him and all who supported him.

27

Sophia found what she was looking for in a file cabinet she'd managed to unlock simply because she knew her stepfather's habits. A stickler for organization, he had to clearly identify every key he owned, and that didn't change just because this was his business instead of his house. She went through his drawers until she came across the plastic container that held all the keys to the farm equipment and drew out the only one that wasn't marked.

Rod glanced up; he'd obviously noticed that she'd stopped moving. "What? You find something?" he asked. "Because there's nothing over here."

Numb, she sank into her stepfather's chair.

"Sophia?"

"He's involved with the safe house, all right," she said dully.

Rod left the drawer he'd been searching and strode over to have a look. It was logical that Gary's smuggling business would be kept separate from his regular business, which explained the lock on the file cabinet she'd chosen. But there was still a part of her that'd been hoping she wouldn't have to deal with this, that her antagonistic stance toward her stepfather could remain in the past.

"*How* involved?"

"It's not the Mexican Mafia that owns it." She handed him the limited partnership agreement that provided the link they'd been searching for.

"Oh, hell," he said with disgust. "Gary O'Conner is the general partner."

Sophia stared at the document he was perusing. "That means it's largely his operation, right?"

"Probably."

"Why would he risk including so many people?"

"Capital. It's expensive to run a business. Maybe he wanted to go big, didn't have the start-up money and this is how he raised it."

"Question is…do his partners know they've invested in a company that's breaking the law?"

Rod flipped through the agreement until he found a list of the limited partners. "Looks like Neil Munoz is involved, too."

She got up. "You're kidding me! He's on the city council."

"And Charlie Sumpter."

"Then the partners *don't* know. Charlie hates illegal aliens. He wouldn't do anything to bring them into the country."

Rod spoke slowly, skimming pages at the same time. "Maybe he's tired of fighting the problem. Maybe he decided to turn the situation to his advantage."

Sophia couldn't imagine it. Charlie, more than anyone, lamented that other rancher's death and blamed the immigrants for it. She'd planned to drive over to Charlie's tonight. She didn't care how late it was. Even if he wasn't home, she needed to take a look around. She'd left a message for his daughter but hadn't heard back. Where could he be? "Who else is on the list?" she asked, peering over Rod's shoulder.

"Joel Lawson, Newt Woods and—"

When he stopped, she read the name herself. "Carmelita Dunlap."

"Don't tell me that's Patrick's wife."

"It is. She owns—"

"The nail salon. I know."

"Joel and Newt are business-owners, too. Joel owns the burger joint at the north end of town. Newt owns the tire store."

Rod rubbed his chin as if trying to make sense of the information. "Are their businesses as thriving as your stepfather's?"

"I'm not sure, but they seem to be surviving despite the tough economy."

"Maybe this is why. Maybe it's the downturn that drove them to break the law."

It was a possibility. Sophia couldn't escape that. "No wonder Gary's been making so much money," she said.

He waved around them. "My guess is this is a front and always has been. He probably makes five times as much through his illegal activities as he does renting farm equipment and selling feed. At six to eight hundred a head, he'd have to be."

"Boy, is the reporter who wrote that story on his 'amazing success' going to be surprised," she grumbled.

Rod pointed to the date on the deed. "He's owned the safe house for a little over three years."

"That doesn't mean he wasn't involved earlier."

"No, but it confirms that the house isn't a recent purchase, that he's been in business for a while."

"I've never heard him talk about buying a rental. I'll bet my mother hasn't, either."

"He doesn't want anyone to know. Hence the obscure name of the limited partnership—Cochise Partners. I'm guessing that holds no special significance for anyone."

"Look at this." She flipped through another document. "They're supposed to be importing coffee from Mexico."

"So maybe some or even all of these people *don't* know the truth."

"You're saying he could be a con man along with everything else."

"That's what I'm saying."

Sophia imagined Anne prancing around her elegant house totally oblivious—and dropped her head in her hands. "My mother is going to be publicly humiliated."

Paper crackled as Rod dug deeper into the file. "Don't you mean brokenhearted? If this stuff means what we think it does, her husband will be carted off to jail."

"It was embarrassing enough for her when my father lost his business and her first marriage ended in divorce. But having her second husband thrown in prison? Yikes. Anyway, I suspect her image means more to her than he does. At least, it's always meant more to her than I have."

Rod put a hand on her shoulder as if he understood and sympathized with how her mother made her feel. Considering what he'd been through, he probably did. But he didn't comment on it; he was too cognizant of the ticking clock. "I'll make a copy of this," he said. "You put the office back together so we can get out of here. We've pushed our luck too far already."

Her stepfather was so fastidious, so particular, he'd

know someone had been in his office if the slightest article was out of place. She had to leave it precisely as they'd found it. But as she straightened up, she couldn't help wondering how she'd break the news of their discovery to Anne.

What would she say?

Nothing yet, she realized. She couldn't. Simply owning the safe house and possessing an agreement that suggested he was in the coffee business didn't make Gary guilty of anything. She had to keep this quiet until they could stake out Dugan Drive and note what went on there. They had to get testimony from some of the illegals who paid for lodging, speak to any neighbors who'd talk and figure out the identity of the men who ran it and had beaten Rod, so they could *prove* Gary was breaking the law. Then Anne would have to believe her.

Or maybe not. Few criminal cases were solid enough to eradicate all question of guilt and, as long as a shred of hope remained, her mother would cling to it and insist Sophia had been out to get Gary from the start. Their relationship was about to get a lot rockier than it'd been in years....

"This sucks," she said as she arranged the papers on Gary's desk. "And how crazy is it that we stumbled across this safe-house business right in the middle of the UDA murders? If not for what happened to José and Benita, I would never have spoken to the man who told me about the safe house, and you would never have gone there and seen Gary's number on the fridge."

Rod was too busy to answer. He'd finished at the copier and was trying to see out by peering through the blinds at the only window.

"I mean, I wanted to leave with a bang, but putting my

stepfather away for twenty years wasn't exactly what I had in mind," she said.

Rod tuned in again. "The fact that we came across this while we were investigating several murders makes me more than a little nervous."

"What do you mean?"

"It might be too coincidental. But we'll talk about that later. Hurry up."

"Anything out there?" she asked as she righted a trophy Gary had received for coaching Little League. He had a dozen trophies. What a pillar of the community.

"Nothing on the side. I need to check the front but the lights have to be off for that. You ready?"

"Just a sec." Sophia slid the file with the partnership document and the deed for the house back into the drawer. She was about to close and lock it when she spotted a small brown binder behind the separator. What was that?

It looked like an account ledger….

"I think I may have found something else." She had to wiggle the binder back and forth to get it out, but once she'd flipped through the pages, she was glad she'd gone to the extra trouble. "Rod?"

"What?" He was still standing at the side window, gazing out at the neighboring building, the side parking lot and a section of Bordertown Boulevard.

"Get over here."

When he didn't move, she glanced up again and this time she noticed that he seemed to be on high alert. "What's wrong? Is everything okay?"

"I'm not sure." He changed his angle of vision. "What does your stepfather drive?"

"A pearl-colored Escalade. Why?"

"A vehicle matching that description has driven past here twice and seems to slow down when it goes by."

Sophia's heart began to pound with a renewed sense of urgency. "That's not good," she said. "It's late. And he's no night owl. Anyway, everything except the bar is closed up at this time of night. What do you think he's doing?"

"I get the feeling he knows something's going on in here."

"Then why doesn't he come and check?"

"That's what I can't figure out. It's almost as if he's waiting for someone...."

Swallowing hard, she closed the ledger book. "Maybe he's expecting a sheriff's deputy to show up."

Rod remained flattened against the wall, watching. "No. He has too much to hide. He wouldn't call the sheriff."

"So who would he call?"

The look he shot her scared the hell out of her.

"You're not saying you think he's called the safe house and some thug is coming to take care of us, are you? Gary might be a smuggler and a con man but he's not a murderer."

"You sure about that?" Rod responded. "We're already aware of two murders that are connected to that safe house. How do we know he's not behind them?"

"Because a smuggler would have no reason to kill illegal immigrants. If those people don't make it safely across the border, he doesn't get paid."

"Well, he has plenty of motivation to kill *us*. He knows what's here, what's at stake if we find it."

A chill rolled down Sophia's spine. She'd never liked her stepfather, never respected him, but...could he really be a *killer?* She couldn't see it. "No..." she murmured.

But Rod was right about the level of Gary's motivation.

Everything he had, everything he purported to be, was at stake.

She chewed her lip as she waited to see what would happen next. "Any sign of the Escalade?"

"Not since it came by the last time."

"How do you suggest we get out of here?"

"Very carefully." He got his flashlight and motioned for her to do the same. Then he pulled his handgun from his waistband.

She stopped him before he could turn off the lights. "I have to make a copy of this before we go."

"What is it?"

"A ledger of some kind. Maybe answers, evidence."

The fact that he didn't press her for details told her how anxious he was. "Doesn't matter. It's not worth your life."

"It'll just take a minute."

She thought he might argue with her, but he didn't. While the copier whirred, he slipped out on his own. She thought she heard him heading to the back room. What he was doing there she had no idea. The area was mainly for storage, so he had no way of seeing outside.

When she finished, she returned the ledger to the file drawer, turned off the lights and joined him with her own flashlight. He'd cracked open the back door and was waiting, listening.

"I got it," she whispered. "We're good to go."

He held up a hand to stop her.

"Don't tell me my stepfather's Escalade is in the lot."

"No." Closing his eyes, he breathed in. "Don't you smell it?"

"Smell what?"

"Cigarette smoke."

The minute he said it, she caught the scent, too. It was just a wisp but it was enough to bring back the memory of Rod finding that cigarette butt at the scene of Benita's and José's murder. Her knees went weak.

Closing the door very softly, Rod took her by the arm and propelled her to the front.

"What are we doing?" she asked.

"We're going out the main entrance."

"But that opens onto the street! And my stepfather has already driven by *twice*. What if he sees us?"

"I'd rather face him than what might be waiting in the alley."

Because of that scent of cigarette smoke, Sophia agreed. What they'd learned, and what they might be perceived as knowing, put them in a very dangerous position, especially if all the partners were as involved as her stepfather seemed to be. According to the payoffs listed in that ledger, even Mayor Schilling was on the take. Apparently, the corruption in Bordertown extended much further than Leonard Taylor extorting sex from a Mexican national.

When they reached the front window, Rod shielded her with his body, keeping her out of gunshot range. But she was a police officer, not some frightened civilian. Determined to pull her own weight, she slipped around him and moved to the other window.

"Looks clear," she said. "I say we go for it."

"I shouldn't have let you come with me," he muttered.

"Stop it. We can get out. And—" she checked the street again, saw no one "—this is our chance."

He nodded and turned the bolt. "Ready? Remember. Stay behind me."

Sophia focused on the comforting weight of the gun

strapped to her calf. She wanted to draw it, but there was still a chance they were merely spooked and overly cautious. She didn't want to scare some random citizen she might bump into on the street. "Ready?" She began to go out first, but he grabbed her by the shirt.

"*I* go first," he said. "Once we're out, cross the street immediately and head down the other side toward the Hummer."

"Got it."

"And if anything happens to me, whatever you do, *keep running.*"

The vision of Stuart slumped over his steering wheel appeared in Sophia's mind and suddenly she couldn't make her feet move. Especially when her imagination created a slow-motion scene of Rod being shot in the street and crumpling to the pavement.

He made a move to duck out, but this time she stopped him. When he turned to see why, she slipped her arms around his neck and hugged him fiercely. She didn't care what he thought, whether or not it revealed her true feelings. Stuart certainly hadn't expected to die.

"Don't let anything happen to you," she said. "Because I *will* stop. I won't go on without you."

Tenderness softened his expression as he touched her cheek. "I shouldn't have brought you," he said again.

"You didn't have any choice," she told him and, despite her earlier reluctance to brandish a weapon, drew her gun as she followed him outside.

28

They didn't go down in a hail of bullets as Rod half expected. No one chased them, fired a single shot or yelled for them to stop. They didn't even see Gary's Escalade. They walked swiftly, keeping to the shadows of the storefronts until they reached the Firelight's parking lot. Then, just as Rod popped the Hummer's locks and was coming around to the driver's side, Bruce got out of a vehicle parked close by and approached him.

Rod couldn't tell if his father was drunk, but he was leery of this meeting all the same. Bruce had obviously been waiting. For him.

"There you are," he said.

"What are you doing here?" Rod asked.

"When I couldn't find you inside I didn't know where else to look, but I assumed you couldn't be too far if your car was here. I was just about to give up." His eyes flicked toward Sophia. "I thought maybe you'd gone home with someone else...."

"What do you want?"

"Can I have a word with you?"

Conscious of the photocopies tucked under Sophia's shirt and what they signified—she'd mentioned the mayor and a city council member, both of whom were receiving payments from Gary—Rod was tempted to refuse. They were onto something, and it was big. But Bruce's daughter-in-law was a limited partner in the safe house they were investigating, which meant the Dunlaps could have more bad news coming. For whatever reason, Rod felt bad about that. And, as much as he disliked Edna, he wanted his father to know he hadn't harmed Stuart or anything else Bruce loved. Under the circumstances, that was probably stupid, but there it was. Whatever connection he had to his father could not be destroyed, no matter how hard Rod tried. Perhaps because there were aspects of Bruce's personality that he'd always secretly admired.

"I didn't shoot Stuart," he said. "I know what Edna has to say. She and Patrick already told me to my face at the Rockin' Rooster. But…it's not true. None of it."

"I know. I—I'm not here about that. Well, I guess it *is* about that, but only because I've found something I think you should see."

This threw Rod. What could his father be talking about? Judging by his manner, this wasn't an errand he relished. With his hands shoved in his pockets and his shoulders rounded in a sort of sick resignation, he looked miserable.

"What is it?" Rod asked.

Bruce glanced around them. "I don't want to talk about it here, out in the open." His gaze shifted to Sophia, who was sitting in the Hummer. Turning his back to her, he lowered his voice. "Right now I can only talk to someone I trust."

Rod never would've guessed his father trusted *him*. Didn't Bruce believe what Edna believed? "And that's *me?*"

"That's you. Regardless of the past, you're my son. My

blood. Will you be there for me when it really counts? I know I don't have the right to ask, but...I need you. I need you to—" his voice cracked "—to help me get through this."

The pain Bruce felt showed in the lines of his face and the muscle that twitched in his cheek. Such evidence of suffering was to be expected from a man who'd just lost his son. But he seemed to be talking about something else. What more could there be? Had he discovered Carmelita's involvement in the smuggling ring? Did he suspect Stuart had been a participant, as well?

Or was this an attempt to exact retribution for an act Rod didn't commit? *I won't rest until I see him six feet under, like my boy....* That was what Edna had said at the Rockin' Rooster. Had she convinced Bruce to try and undo the mistake he'd made thirty years ago?

Rod knew she'd like nothing more. "What is it you want me to do?"

"Will you come with me?"

"Now?"

"Please."

As much as Rod had always wanted his father to love him, even a fraction as much as his half brothers, Bruce had never been capable of it. Rod owed him nothing. Leaving with him wasn't smart. But if Bruce was sincere, maybe some good could emerge from the tragedy of Stuart's death. Maybe they could finally make peace with the past and establish at least a cordial relationship. That had to be better than continuing to grapple with the resentment he'd felt for most of his life, didn't it?

The problem was, in order to form a more positive bond, they had to put some trust and faith in each other. His father seemed ready to do that, had seemed ready for a while. But it wasn't until now, until Stuart's death had torn away the shield of bravado Rod had erected, that he'd become open to the idea.

"Sure," he said. "Just give me a second to talk to Sophia."

Rod watched Bruce walk back to his truck; then he opened the door of the Hummer and leaned in.

"What's going on?" In the cabin light Sophia's eyes gleamed with curiosity.

"Will you be okay on your own for a while?" Since no one had accosted them as they were leaving the store, it was easy to believe he'd overreacted to seeing that pearl-colored Escalade. Maybe Gary and Anne had an argument and Gary had gone out for a drive to cool off. Or maybe that hadn't been his Escalade at all. Thanks to the UDA killings and all the press they'd generated, there were more strangers in town than usual.

"Of course," she said. "Why? Where are you going?"

"Bruce has something he wants to show me."

"What is it?"

"He wouldn't say. But I'll call you as soon as I have some idea."

She nodded, then reached for his hand. "Be careful."

"You, too." He gave her the keys and started toward Bruce's truck but turned back at the last second, catching her as she got out of the Hummer to switch seats.

"What's wrong?" she asked.

"Nothing really." He was just hesitant to leave her. She was the chief of police, she had a gun and she'd managed on her own for all the years he'd been gone. But what they'd discovered at the feed store was dangerous, and with all the killings… "I was hoping you'd do me a favor."

She studied him for a second. "What kind of favor?"

"Will you stay at the Boot and Spur until I get back?"

"You mean the dude ranch west of town?"

"That's it. I rented a room there earlier, but no one except the manager knows it. I doubt anyone would look for you in such a remote location, especially since it's closed for repairs."

"You think it's too dangerous for me to go home?"

"It could be dangerous to go anywhere you normally go."

He knew she had to agree. There was a risk. "What's your room number?" she asked.

He pulled the key from his back pocket. "Thirteen."

"All right. First I'm going to swing by Charlie Sumpter's ranch. I'll meet you there after, okay?"

He didn't want her anywhere besides the Boot and Spur, but with Charlie out of town, no one would expect her to go to his place, either. And if Charlie's house was locked up, Rod was sure she wouldn't stay long. Not at this time of night. "Okay," he said, and rested his hands on her shoulders as he dropped a kiss onto her mouth.

She blinked up at him as if the action surprised her, and he could understand why. It'd surprised him, too. He hadn't planned on making his affection for her a matter of public record. That kiss had been spontaneous.

But somehow he didn't mind.

"See you soon," he said, and heard her start the engine as he walked away.

"Where are you?" Gary wanted to know.

"In the parking lot behind the feed store." Leonard held his cell phone to his ear with his shoulder as he squashed his fifth cigarette into the dirt. Since he wasn't used to smoking, the nicotine no longer had a positive effect. It wasn't calming; it was sickening. But he was so angry he didn't know what else to do. At least smoking kept his hands busy.

"So...did you do it?"

"No."

There was a drawn-out silence. "You can't be serious."

Tilting his head back, Leonard let his breath seep out as he stared at the sky.

"You *are* serious," Gary said when he didn't respond. "What happened?"

Leonard massaged his temples to ease the headache that was beginning to pound behind his eyes. He was too obsessed with getting his old life back to slow down and sleep, and his body wasn't happy with the situation. He couldn't keep up this pace, couldn't work all day in the hot sun and stay up all night following Sophia. But he'd been so sure it was almost over. "I waited, but they never came out."

"They're still there, then! It's not too late!"

"No. They're gone."

"How do you know?"

"I checked. The place is locked up and empty."

The string of curses that came out of Gary's mouth surprised Leonard. Gary wasn't typically foulmouthed. But then, there'd never been so much at stake.

"You said you'd take care of it! You said I could rely on you!"

Straightening, Leonard began to pace. "It's not my fault. They didn't come out the back. Something must've tipped them off. That's all I can imagine. Why else would they go out front onto the main street when there's a nice quiet alley in back?"

"This can't be happening," Gary muttered.

"Rod's a former Navy SEAL. I expected stealth."

Gary didn't seem to hear him. "I'm dead. She's got me this time. There's no avoiding it. Do you know what's in my office? Everything." He seemed to grow more lucid. "But if I go down, you're going down with me. I promise you that."

"It's not over yet. Maybe—" Leonard pivoted and headed toward the backhoe he'd used as cover while waiting for Rod and Sophia to leave the building "—maybe they never even came here."

"They were there, all right. I called the company that monitors my alarm. They said the system was tripped at eleven-fourteen by my stepdaughter."

Leonard's boots crunched on the gravel as he made another pass. "How do they know it was your step-daughter?"

"Because they called the store to verify whether it was a false alarm, and she answered. She identified herself as my stepdaughter *and* as the chief of police. That's why they didn't call me at home when it happened. Can you believe it?"

"She's got balls, that's for sure."

"I tried to let you know, but you wouldn't pick up your damn phone."

Leonard resented the accusation in his tone. "Because I had it turned off. I didn't want it to ring when I was trying to sneak up on two people with a rifle, if you know what I mean."

"Keep your voice down!"

There wasn't a soul around, but Gary was right. He was

overreacting. He had to reel in his emotions, figure out the best way out of this before everything went to hell. "Look, they might've found some evidence to back up their suspicions, but they won't be able to use it against you."

"Why not?"

"They didn't get it with a warrant. They have a lot of work to do before they can act on what they found. That buys us some time."

"They can talk, make other people suspicious."

"They won't talk because they won't want to tip you off. Why give you the chance to prepare a defense before they're ready to spring their trap?"

"You never know what they'll do. We have to stop them both right away. Tonight."

Leonard agreed. They could still contain this thing if they acted quickly. But what should he do next? He'd bugged Sophia's house, her office and her cruiser, but he hadn't had access to Rod's Hummer. And that was what they'd driven to the feed store. Sophia's cruiser was still sitting in her driveway.

"Maybe they've gone back to her place," he said. "I'll check and tell you what I find out."

"I'll be at the store. I already drove by a couple of times, but if they were in my office they must've closed the door because I couldn't see any light from the street and I didn't dare get any closer."

"You're not at home? What about Anne?"

"I told her the alarm went off at the store, that it was probably vandals but I had to go check that it was secure."

Leonard was walking to his truck. "Fine. Wait at the store—do anything you want. I'll call you when I've taken care of the problem."

"You're sure you *can* take care of it?"

Leonard wasn't sure at all. Now that Sophia was with Rod, she wasn't half as vulnerable, and her actions were much less predictable. It was a crapshoot. But they couldn't be far. He had that going for him. Bordertown wasn't big. "I got it."

"The quicker you handle it, the better."

"What happened to wrestling with your conscience?" Leonard asked dryly.

"I just want it to be over. For good."

The pressure was getting to Gary. But this kind of thing was never over. Killing became a lifelong secret and wasn't an easy one to keep.

Too bad Sophia had boxed them into a corner.

As Sophia drove away from the Firelight, she wasn't thinking about murder. She was grinning like a silly schoolgirl with her first crush. That brief kiss of Rod's had absolutely no sexual intent behind it, but that was precisely why it made her so happy. The slightly possessive way he'd gripped her shoulders and his concern for her safety made her believe he cared about her as much as she was beginning to care about him.

Was she crazy to go with it? To take such a chance with her heart? She'd always managed to recover from past breakups. But she knew instinctively that greater heights meant harder falls. And there were more practical issues to consider. Even if Rod could somehow disassociate her with the pain of his past, there was no way they could stay together. He wouldn't move to Bordertown. He hated it here. His life, his job, was in L.A. And she couldn't leave Arizona, not as long as Rafe needed her.

Her goofy smile began to falter, so she backed away

from confronting those harsh realities. She could worry about that later, couldn't she? Would it be so terrible to forget caution for a change and accept whatever came to pass?

She didn't realize the light had turned green until a honk behind her said she was holding someone up. Embarrassed, she accelerated, heading south on Bordertown Boulevard toward Charlie's place. It was late, and she was tired. What she really wanted to do was go to the Boot and Spur and simply wait for Rod. She'd had enough upsetting revelations for one night. She preferred to cling to the euphoria of falling in love as long as possible.

But, for another month, she was still the chief of police. And while she was in law enforcement, she wouldn't let Gary get away with breaking the law. His incarceration would be her parting gift to the town.

She was about to turn onto Roadrunner Way when her cell phone vibrated in her pocket. She'd set it to silent when they'd entered the feed store.

Assuming it would be Rod, she answered without checking caller ID. "Hello?"

"Sophie?"

Rafe. She recognized his voice immediately, even though he sounded too dejected to be the kid she knew and loved. "What's up, buddy? You back from camp?"

"Yeah. Got back today."

"What's the matter? You seem upset." She glanced at the clock on the dash and silently cursed Starkey for letting Rafe stay up so late. It was after one.

"I'm not upset. I'm fine."

He didn't sound "fine." She was about to question him further but he spoke before she could frame the question in a way that he might actually answer it.

"Where are you? I stopped by the station, but it was locked up. You're not at home, either."

Slowing, she pulled onto the shoulder. There wasn't another car as far as the eye could see, but she didn't want to continue to Charlie's ranch if Rafe needed her. "How do you know that, Rafe? Where are you?"

"In your front room."

She'd shown him where she kept the hide-a-key, told him he could use it whenever he needed. She'd wanted him to understand that he always had a safe place to go. "Where's your father?"

The answer, when it came, was as sulky as any she'd ever heard. "At a stupid *party*."

"Does he know you're at my house?"

"No."

"You didn't tell him?"

"He doesn't care, anyway. I was gone for a week, and now he can't even stay home for one freakin' night. All he cares about is getting high or drunk and acting like an idiot."

Sophia could've chastised him for speaking so disrespectfully about his father. She almost did. But it seemed pointless. Starkey deserved the criticism. "So...you got home and he took you with him to a party?"

"Yeah."

"Where they were serving alcohol and doing drugs?"

"What else? He acts like that's all there is in life."

"Is that why you decided to leave?"

"No. Shoot, every party has that stuff."

Sophia hated the thought of what he'd witnessed in his young life. "So what happened?"

No answer.

"Rafe?"

"I don't want to talk about it."

Starkey had done something worse than usual.

"He just… He doesn't love me," Rafe confided at last.

Wincing at the heartbreak in those words, Sophia remembered when she'd first started losing Starkey. They hadn't been together long before the lure of belonging to "the brotherhood" overcame his love for her, for Rafe, even his own self-preservation. The Angels provided a forum in which he could be accepted, admired. And for years that had meant more to him than anything, despite his occasional twinges of conscience. Now she knew it was alcoholism and habit that kept him bouncing between his conscience and his friends. She wasn't sure he'd ever win the tug-of-war, not until bad health or something else forced a change. It was one thing to want a better life and another to make the sacrifices necessary to obtain it.

Grateful to be out of the situation, Sophia wished she could get Rafe out, too. "That's not true, babe," she said. "I think he does care about you."

"No, he doesn't. And he doesn't love you, either. He says he does. He talks like he wishes we could all be a family. But…" When his words fell away, Sophia suspected he was fighting back tears.

Resting her forehead on the steering wheel, she let her breath go in a long exhalation. For the past few years, she'd been contemplating trying to effect a change where Rafe was concerned. But was this the best time? She was losing her job….

Regardless, she'd had enough. Suddenly, she seemed willing to take a lot of risks she'd avoided in the past. "Do you think your father would ever let you come and live with me?" she asked.

"You'd want me to?"

The excitement in his voice made her regret not offering sooner. She would have. But she'd never really believed Starkey would give Rafe up. Now...she wasn't so sure. There was a chance he would, if she made it clear that he could visit whenever he wanted. Why *not* let her take care of Rafe? He had to know she'd do a better job, and he certainly didn't want the responsibility. True, she wouldn't be happy with Starkey intruding on her life as often as he would if Rafe lived with her; that was part of the reason she'd always hesitated before. But she had to do it. For Rafe. "I'd like that very much."

"Then it doesn't matter what he says. If I told half the shit—"

"Stuff," she inserted.

"—stuff that I've seen, I'd be put in foster care, anyway."

"But would you really want to sacrifice your entire relationship with your dad, Rafe?"

This question met with silence. As she'd thought, Rafe was upset but he didn't want to lose his father completely.

"I love him. It's just...I don't know what to do. If he doesn't quit, he'll end up in prison someday. Or dead."

"What's he doing?"

"I can't tell you. But...it's not right."

She had enough to worry about tonight without pressing Rafe to list the laws Starkey had broken most recently, so she moved on. "I'll talk to him. See what we can work out."

"All I know is that I don't want to go back," he said.

That was a huge admission. Rafe had never arrived at this point before. "What's changed?"

"I want a different life. I want to be normal, like Chase."

Apparently, Chase wasn't as bad an influence as she'd feared. "We'll see what your father says," she promised.

"Where are you?"

Putting the gearshift in Drive, she pulled a U-turn and headed back. "I'm coming home."

"Will you bring me something to eat? I haven't had dinner. Unless you count the pretzels they had at the party. They never buy food. They only care about beer."

"Nothing's open. But there's plenty of food in the fridge. Make yourself a sandwich. I'll be there in a few minutes."

There was a slight pause. "Am I stopping you from working or…seeing someone? Because I can wait until you're done."

She glanced at the documents in Rod's passenger seat. She had work to do, but she couldn't leave Rafe at her place. With everything that'd been happening lately, she wasn't sure it was safe. "I have to take care of a few things. But I'm coming to pick you up first."

"Why don't I crash on the couch and see you in the morning? It's okay, you know. I'm used to staying alone. I don't want you to think I'll be a pain in the ass to live with or anything."

She didn't bother pointing out his bad language. If Starkey allowed Rafe to move in with her, she'd have plenty of time to work with him on that—and on going to school, keeping up with his homework and getting home safely at night. "No, I'd rather bring you with me. I've missed you. Besides, we'll be staying somewhere else tonight."

"We will? Where?"

"The Boot and Spur."

"What's the Boot and Spur?"

"A dude ranch."

"You mean with horses?"

"That's it. But I don't think we'll be able to ride. It's closed for renovations."

He seemed to be calming down. Later, with any luck, he might even tell her what had set him off in the first place. "Lock the doors until I get there," she said.

"You're the chief of police. Who's going to be stupid enough to break into your house?"

"You've heard about the shootings."

"But I'm not an illegal alien."

Obviously, he wasn't aware of Stuart Dunlap's murder, and she didn't want to discuss it right now. "Shootings can happen anywhere. Just do as I say. Lock the doors and don't open them for anyone."

"Okay." He said it as if she was acting crazy. His father never locked their house, and he ran around town unchaperoned half the time. But Rafe was willing to indulge her. "I'm doing it now."

"Good. I'll be there soon."

Sophia tossed her phone on the passenger seat and waited through two stoplights before reaching her own neighborhood. She was going right where Rod had told her not to go. But she couldn't leave Rafe at the house alone. What if whoever had killed Stuart was involved in the smuggling operation with her stepfather? If he thought she was on to him, or would soon be onto him, he might be coming after her.

And there was a chance he'd break in and shoot before realizing that she wasn't the one standing in the kitchen making a sandwich.

29

Leonard couldn't believe his luck. Just as he was turning into Sophia's neighborhood, he'd spotted Rafe Robinson riding a bike a few feet ahead and had known instantly that they were headed to the same place. He'd followed him to her house, even sat at the curb visiting with him. He'd insisted Rafe go inside so he wouldn't have to "worry about you being out and about so late at night." Then he'd driven around the block and parked where he could hear what went on inside. At that point, he'd known it was just a matter of time before Sophia and Rod returned. The Hummer was the only car that was missing, and they wouldn't leave Rafe by himself for long.

Minutes later, he'd heard part of a telephone conversation that confirmed it. They were on their way.

A rush of adrenaline prompted him to text Gary, to let him know what was going on, and check his guns. He'd chosen the rifle at the feed store. Now he selected one of the two handguns he'd also brought. Sophia and Rod wouldn't live to see the sunrise, at her place *or* the Boot and Spur. But it wasn't going to be as easy to get away with killing them at the house as it would've been at the store.

The boy was another obstacle....

So what was his plan? Should he wait for them to get home and go to bed before sneaking inside? No. They'd mentioned staying elsewhere, at the dude ranch west of town. They probably wouldn't hang out at the house for very long before going there. But dealing with three people could get messy very quickly.

He should let himself in now, get rid of the boy and be waiting for Sophia and Rod when they came home, he decided. They wouldn't be expecting an ambush.

And it was always better to go with the unexpected….

According to the clock on Rod's phone, Bruce had left him sitting in the truck outside the Dunlap ranch house for nearly fifteen minutes. Since he didn't even have a vehicle to drive back into town, he was about to head inside to see what the hell was going on, when his father finally emerged, looking even more drawn and worried than he had in the parking lot of the Firelight.

"Sorry that took so long," he mumbled as he got behind the wheel again.

"Is everything okay?"

He shook his head. "It's Edna. She…well, she's being Edna. I didn't want her to know you were here so I couldn't ask you in. Not today, anyway. That'd be too much for her after…" He didn't finish. "Anyway, I had to calm her down. She's worked herself into quite a state." He sighed heavily. "She's taking this very hard, of course."

So was Bruce. Only his was an inner battle, one that raged beneath a far more placid exterior. Rod could tell he was fragile by how gingerly and cautiously he moved and spoke. Every word, every step or gesture, struck him as deliberate, as if he'd shatter without perfect control.

Rod knew it'd be healthier for him to vent his anger and pain. And yet he understood why Bruce couldn't, or wouldn't. Edna was going to pieces. He had to be the strong one.

"Sorry," his father said again, and started driving toward the central clearing, where all the farm equipment waited for a sunrise that would be anything but ordinary, when only two Dunlap men awoke on the farm.

Rod had never seen Bruce like this. His father certainly didn't seem like the austere figure he'd regarded with as much awe as contempt ever since he was a little boy. "Don't worry about it."

"I finally got her to take a sedative. I think it'll help her get through the night." He spoke as though this was a major victory, or at least information Rod would want to know. But he obviously didn't expect a response. It was just more of the pep talk he'd been giving himself all along: *We'll pull through it together. Sure we will. We'll cope... We're not the only family to have suffered a loss....*

He didn't really feel he *could* cope. That was clear.

"Why'd we stop at the house?" Rod asked.

Bruce glanced over at him. "I needed to get the keys."

"Keys to what?"

"Stuart's place."

They were going to his dead brother's house? "Where's Patrick?"

"At home with his wife, I guess. I haven't talked to him in the past couple of hours. I'm hoping they're all in bed. They need the sleep."

Bruce probably needed sleep more than anyone else. If he'd kept to his regular habits, he'd been up since five this morning—for twenty-one hours. "Does Patrick know what you're going to show me?"

"No. I didn't tell him. I don't think I will."

"Why not?"

"You'll see."

Rod was almost afraid to guess what this might be about. Bruce seemed disillusioned in some way, which meant it wouldn't be good. "Does this have anything to do with what Patrick and Edna had to say to me at the Rockin' Rooster?"

They passed the farm equipment and took the side road along the fence in the opposite direction from the laborers' shacks. "No. I'm sorry about that, too. At first glance, you seem like the person to blame, I guess. And Edna's looking for a target. Anger is so much easier than grief."

"What about Patrick? He's just angry, too?"

"He's defensive of his mother. As the oldest, he tries to look out for her. Feels it would be disloyal to see you as anything other than an interloper. Crazy thing is, the whole situation's my fault, as you've tried to point out. I'm not sure why they've always blamed you and not me, but I've often wondered."

"They love you," Rod said simply.

There was a faint smile on Bruce's lips. "I guess. Edna used to, anyway. Now…I think we're destroying each other." He'd attempted to turn it into a casual statement, but Rod sensed that the breakdown of Bruce's marriage was hurting him almost as badly as the loss of his son.

Rod had always believed he'd be happy to see the Dunlaps' "perfect" world crumble. But he didn't feel that way at all. Fourteen years seemed like an awfully long time to carry a grudge. These people were as human and fallible as he was. They'd been so frightened of him, so frightened by what he might become to Bruce, that they'd reacted viciously to protect their own.

"Have you considered marriage counseling?" he asked.

"No. Do you think that might help?"

"It's worth a shot, right?" That was the *last* thing Rod had ever expected to say to his father. And yet...he meant it. What good would it do him to see Bruce and Edna break up? Especially at this late date?

Suddenly, he wanted the Dunlaps to go back to being perfect. Not only did he want Stuart to be alive, he wanted Edna to be confident of her superiority and Bruce to be doing his level best to keep them all happy, even if it meant ignoring the bastard child he'd accidentally sired. Because *he* was that bastard child, and he could take it. His past had made him strong. He wasn't sure he could say the same for them, wasn't sure they could withstand the opposite, the change. It just took seeing them up close to realize how he truly felt.

"There's something you need to know." Rod figured now was the time to say it. They might never be alone again, never have another opportunity.

Swerving to avoid a pothole in a road he must have navigated a million times, Bruce adjusted the air-conditioning, but the way he tensed made it clear he was preparing for more of the biting criticism Rod had thrown at him in recent years. "What's that?"

"I forgive you. And that forgiveness is free. It doesn't cost you anything. Not the sacrifice of your marriage. Or the relationship you have with Patrick. Or the positive memories of Stuart. Or a cent of your money. Or an acre of the farm. It's completely free."

Bruce stopped the truck. "You'll get an equal share. I've already decided it. And nothing Edna says will ever change my mind. You're in the will."

"I believe you'd like to do that for me," Rod said and, as he spoke, he knew it was true. He did believe his father's remorse was real. "But you can take me out. I don't need it. I'm okay just as I am. Except for one thing."

Bruce seemed to be having difficulty accepting that Rod meant what he'd said. "What's that?"

"I want you to forgive yourself, too."

Tears began to streak down his cheeks. Embarrassed by his display of emotion, he averted his face and tried to wipe them away, but now that the veneer had cracked they wouldn't stop coming. "Ah, I'm a mess," he muttered into his hand.

"You've lost a son. I think you're entitled."

For the first time in Rod's life, his father squeezed his shoulder with affection. "God, I'm proud of you," he said.

Because Sophia was in a hurry, she didn't get out of the Hummer. She pulled to the curb and called Rafe to tell him to come outside.

The phone rang four times. Then her voice mail picked up. *Hello. This is Chief St. Claire....*

She didn't bother leaving a message.

The light was on in the living room. She could see it through the closed curtains. And she'd talked to Rafe less than five minutes ago. So where was he? Why wasn't he answering?

Maybe he was using the bathroom.

She waited a couple of minutes and dialed a second time.

Again, there was no answer. If he was in the bathroom, he was taking a long time. Or did he think the call might be from his father? Was he trying to avoid a confrontation with Starkey?

Shoving the gearshift into Park, she turned off the engine, got out and locked the vehicle to protect the evidence she'd collected at the feed store. She was halfway to the house when she decided not to leave that information in the Hummer and went back to retrieve it. Where she was going to stash it, she didn't know. Anyone who came looking for it would probably search her house. But it would be safer with her than left unattended in a car, even for a few minutes.

The locks made a thunking sound as she pressed the button on Rod's key ring. She was about to open the passenger door when a car turned at the corner. From what she could see thanks to the streetlights, it appeared to be an old souped-up Ford Ranchero. She didn't know whose it was, and the tinted windows made it impossible to see inside.

Afraid it might be a gunman, Sophia dropped to her knees so she could use the Hummer as a shield. She definitely didn't want to run for the house and draw the danger toward Rafe or be shot while she was crossing the yard. But there were no shots. The Ranchero stopped across the street, a door opened and closed, and the heavy step of a man approached.

Taking her gun from its holster, Sophia held it ready as she peered around the front bumper of the Hummer. Then she breathed a huge sigh of relief. It wasn't a gunman. It was Starkey. She would've recognized his shape and walk anywhere. Where he'd gotten that Ranchero, she didn't know, but since he'd wrecked his motorcycle it seemed he was always driving something different.

Sagging against the tire, she lowered her gun and breathed deeply to counteract the adrenaline pumping through her system. With Starkey's arrival, she knew she and Rafe had a fight on their hands. He wouldn't be happy with Rafe's defection. But at least this was a familiar fight. Not a life-threatening one.

He hadn't spotted her. He walked straight past her and up to the door with the determination of someone who was angry and felt he had every right to be.

Not in any rush to get into an argument with him, Sophia returned her gun to its holster. She still had to get the ledger evidence from the car. She figured she'd do that first, hide it in her garage, then go inside to support Rafe.

She was just getting to her feet when she heard two blasts from inside.

Starkey broke into a run and threw open the door. Sophia barely had a chance to wonder why it was unlocked when a third shot echoed through the otherwise silent night.

For a moment, she felt as if she was watching the scene from much farther away. Probably because she couldn't get to Starkey fast enough. It felt as though she was living one of those dreams where she ran and ran and ran but couldn't move. She wasn't even sure if she'd yelled his name. Maybe she'd only screamed it in her head. Everything froze for three or four heartbeats, just long enough for her to grasp what had happened, then jolted into fast-forward.

Starkey had been shot. She'd heard him cry out and hit the door as the bullet knocked him back. She'd grabbed her gun and started across the lawn before realizing that it wouldn't do him or Rafe any good if she walked into a bullet. Instead of continuing to the doorway, she returned to the Hummer and ducked behind it to collect her fractured thoughts.

Was Starkey dead? What about Rafe? She'd heard two shots before the one that'd hit Starkey….

Oh, God! Someone had come after her. Whoever it was had beaten her home and encountered Rafe instead of her, exactly as she'd feared.

Blinking to clear the tears that automatically welled up, blurring her vision, she called 911 on her cell phone. She asked county dispatch to send her some backup and an ambulance, then climbed into the driver's seat and pulled the Hummer into the driveway, where she wouldn't be visible from any of the windows when she got out.

After hiding the photocopies she'd made at the feed store beneath the seat, she locked up and dashed over to the side door of her garage. She had no idea what she'd encounter when she went inside. For all she knew the person who'd just shot Starkey could be coming out the same door. Or, if he'd stuck around long enough to see that he'd shot the wrong person, he could be waiting for her….

There was no way to tell. But whether the gunman was in the house or not, she had to enter. She couldn't call the police and stand safely on the sidelines, because she *was* the police. And the last she knew, Rafe had been inside. If he lay bleeding on the floor like Starkey, she had to get to him before it was too late.

The hope that she might be able to reach them both in time gave her the courage she needed. *I'm coming,* she promised silently, and cracked open the garage door.

Nothing happened.

She listened for any sound of movement, but there was only silence.

Prepared for the worst, she slipped into the garage and weaved through the boxes of Christmas decorations and extra clothing she'd put into storage during spring cleaning. As far as she could tell, she was alone. But she hadn't entered the house yet.

The door was locked. Fortunately, she had her keys in her pocket.

As she unlocked the door, she listened carefully—and thought she heard a strange noise. Crying? Her name being called?

Was it Rafe? Or Starkey, begging for help?

She couldn't decide. When she listened again, she could no longer hear it.

Please, God, let Rafe be okay. Starkey, too.

The click of the tumbler sounded abnormally loud. She was afraid it might give away her approach, but using the wooden panel of the door as a shield, she pushed it open and braced for attack.

If there was someone inside, waiting for her, the noise hadn't drawn him out.

Now! she told herself and stuck her head inside, once again waiting, listening….

To silence.

Eyes wide and heart pounding, she led with her gun as she crept into the kitchen.

Pale streamers of moonlight filtered through the window over the sink. From what Sophia could see, Rafe had never had the chance to make himself a sandwich. The kitchen was just as she and Rod had left it.

Cringing to think of what might've stopped him, she walked toward the living room.

From where the kitchen met the living room, Sophia could see the couch, the TV and her favorite painting hanging on the opposite wall. And she already knew what she'd find if she came far enough into the room to face the front door—Starkey. It was what might be lurking near the slider leading onto her back porch that worried her. Judging by what had happened, the gunman had either been waiting in the alcove near the bookshelves or he'd been coming out of her bedroom. He couldn't have fired from the kitchen because the front door would've blocked his vision when it first started to open. The bedroom didn't seem viable, either, since there was no exit. Sophia couldn't imagine that the shooter would place himself in a situation he couldn't escape.

Was the culprit still around? Or had he fled after the shooting?

Part of her hoped he'd taken off. That would allow her to focus on saving Starkey and finding Rafe. The other part craved justice for even the *chance* that one or both of them might die.

Crouching so her antique secretary would obstruct the path of any bullets, she came out of the kitchen and leaned around the furniture, pointing her gun in the direction of the slider.

It stood open, the space around it shadowy but empty. Either the gunman was gone... Or he wanted her to believe he was.

She glanced over her shoulder toward the front door, which was also standing open. It couldn't shut, not with Starkey slumped in the entry. She didn't think he was dead. Fortunately. Eyes closed and hands pressed to his chest as if he could stop the blood from pouring onto his leather cut, he seemed to be concentrating on surviving. She wanted to go to him, or at least offer some words of comfort to let him know that help wouldn't be long in coming, but she couldn't give herself away. First, she had to find Rafe.

Where was the damn ambulance? Why couldn't she hear it?

Because it'd only been a few minutes since she'd called and it had to come from Douglas. *Shit!*

A slight breeze stirred the drapes at the slider and sent the wind chimes on her porch tinkling. Under the cover of that sound, Sophia crept farther into the room to confirm that it was, indeed, empty. Feeling much safer, she double-checked that shadowy alcove—the only place a full-grown person could hide in the living room besides the coat closet, which she also checked—and headed for the bedroom.

Her room was just as empty. But the bathroom door was closed. And there were two bullet holes in it.

Unable to stop herself any longer, she called out. "Rafe? Are you in there? Are you here?"

"Sophie?"

She almost couldn't believe it when he answered. He was in the bathroom. "It's me," she said. "Come on out. I'm here now. Everything's going to be okay."

The lock clicked and, a second later, the door opened very slowly. Only after Rafe actually saw her did he forget all caution and hurry toward her. "Someone tried to break in!" he said.

She set her gun on the bed so she could hold him. "Who was it? Do you know?"

"Leonard Taylor."

"You're sure?"

Rafe nodded. "He came by earlier, too. He was talking to me as if he and my dad are friends. But they're really not. And then he came back. This time, he didn't say a word. Not at first. Just kept messing with the door, trying to unlock it."

"Where'd he get the key?"

"I think he saw me put it back under the frog earlier. But the lock was sticking. He had to wiggle it."

"And you heard him."

"Yes. I locked myself in the bathroom, but after he got in he started banging on the door, telling me you'd been in an accident and asked him to come and get me. But if that was true, why didn't he say so when he was trying to unlock the front door?"

Rafe took a deep breath. "He said you were going to die. I was so afraid it was true I was gonna come out. But I guess I wasn't fast enough 'cause he screamed that he was in a GD hurry and I'd better open the door or he'd kill me. He tried to break the door down. When that didn't work, he started shooting."

At last Sophia heard sirens. *Thank God!* "How was it that he didn't hit you?" she asked, hugging him closer.

"I was lying in the tub."

"Good for you. You're so smart, bud!" He'd already been living by his wits for a long time; she supposed that helped. He was a tough kid. But should she let him see his father? Starkey might die. It would be gruesome for a fourteen-year-old to see that, especially as a result of violence. But he had the right to say goodbye, didn't he?

Sophia had just decided to break the news to him when a telltale creak and the glimpse of a dark shape in her mirror made the hair stand up on the back of her neck.

Rafe screamed as she turned. But the horror on his face had already told her what was happening. There, in the doorway, stood Leonard. He must've been out in the backyard. Must've heard her call out to Rafe and come inside to finish the job. Perhaps he was so determined to put an end to her that even self-preservation couldn't overcome the impulse.

"Leonard, listen." Hoping for a way to get hold of her gun on the bed, she pushed Rafe behind her. "Don't be stupid. Can't you hear the sirens? A sheriff's deputy will be here any minute. You kill us and you'll get the death penalty."

"I'm going to get your job. That's what I'm going to get. That's what I should've gotten six months ago." He lifted his gun, aimed. Looking at the intent expression on his face, Sophia expected to be hit by a bullet any second. But there was another noise, this one from directly behind him.

Flinching, Leonard whirled around, giving Sophia just enough time to dive for her gun. Then everything went into slow motion. Leonard put a second bullet in Starkey, who was coming after him with one last surge of effort, growling like a bear. And she fired right afterward, hitting Leonard once, twice, three times.

No way would he get up and come after them again, she told herself.

And he didn't.

30

The inside of Stuart's house resembled something out of the old TV Western *Bonanza*. Even the wallpaper that ran from the chair railing to the burgundy-colored carpet appeared to be made of leather, or simulated leather, and had big brass decorative thumbtacks holding it to the wall. The wood-framed paintings, hung against a green background, were all of horses and cowboy scenes. And the few pieces of art that sat on various accent tables were brass sculptures—bucking broncos and the like.

Although Rod didn't care for most of it, he admired the furniture, which was constructed of rough-hewn logs and Navajo-blanket-covered cushions. The antler lighting fixtures weren't bad, either. Had Stuart stuck with rustic instead of veering into 1960s Western chic he might've been onto something. Regardless, it was quite obvious that he'd spent a lot of money on his place and was proud of it. No matter what their relationship had been like in life, Rod felt the tragedy in the sheer permanence of his half brother's death. Stuart would never walk into his house again.

Bruce emerged from somewhere in the back. After he'd shown Rod inside, he'd gone to retrieve whatever it was he wanted to show him. What he brought back looked like a box full of keepsakes for a scrapbook, or maybe the contents of someone's files or desk. "What's all this?" he asked.

"I found it in the closet of Stuart's office."

"When?"

"Just a few hours ago."

"Why were you going through his office? I heard Sophia tell you not to come in here. That the police would have a better chance of solving his murder if you left this place alone until the FBI's forensic techs could go through it."

His father put the box on the couch. "I was scared," he admitted.

"Of what?"

"Of what they might find."

Rod felt his eyebrows shoot up. "Like what?"

"He'd been acting strange lately. Secretive. And he'd been staying out late, after the bar was closed. I couldn't even guess where he was going. At first I thought he had a girlfriend or maybe he was visiting a prostitute. I tried to tell myself it was none of my business. He was a grown man, after all. But he hated Mexicans so much that…"

His words trailed off as if he'd only belatedly realized who he was talking to. Stuart had hated Mexicans because of Rod and his mother and what their presence in his life had meant, and Rod knew it. Stuart probably got a lot of his resentment from Edna, but the superiority he felt wasn't unusual among farm owners.

"You thought he might be the UDA killer," Rod said.

Bruce sighed. "I'm sad to say it, but the suspicion was there. Especially when…when I heard where they found Stu's body. I kept imagining him heading out into the desert, going hunting, if you will, and coming upon a group of illegals whose guide was prepared for him. There wasn't any weapon in the truck with his body, but I figured it could've been stolen. Why leave it behind? Anyway, I wanted to see if his guns were here, that sort of thing." He shook his head. "But mostly I didn't want his mother to suffer, knowing her son had murdered twelve people. That's not the kind of grief and shame that will ever go away. And if he was dead, he couldn't hurt anyone, anyway. I decided I could get rid of the evidence and at least save her that much pain."

"So you came here and looked around."

"That's right. His guns are here and accounted for. But I also found this box of stuff. And now I don't believe it was him at all. I believe he figured out who the real killer was, and that's why he's dead." Bruce pointed to the bits of paper, envelopes, even photographs, in the box. "Take a look."

Rod sat on the couch and pulled out an envelope filled with pictures.

"See that white Ford?" Bruce asked as soon as Rod had had a chance to study the first one.

Rod nodded.

"That belongs to Charlie Sumpter."

"How can you tell? This picture was taken from too far away."

"It says so on the back."

Rod flipped it over. Sure enough, someone had written *Charlie Sumpter* and *1:23 a.m.* "That's Stuart's writing?"

"Without a doubt. Stuart even had that picture magnified so you can see a closer view of the vehicle. It should be next."

It wasn't. The other photos were various shots of Charlie's house from the front, side and back.

"Where'd it go?" Bruce muttered, rooting around in the box until he came up with a photo that had fallen out. "Here it is. See this? This shows part of the license plate. CFF432. That's Charlie's, all right."

"But what does this picture prove? That Charlie was out in the desert somewhere on—" Rod glanced at the date stamp "—June 21?"

"It proves his truck wasn't at his house the night the Sanchez couple was killed."

"That doesn't mean Charlie killed them."

"It means he could have. Look at the other pictures."

Rod went back to the shots of Charlie's house. They had the same date stamp but showed no truck anywhere on the premises. And they also had times written on the backs—times that were within seconds of each other but twenty minutes after the picture of the truck in the desert.

It was hardly a smoking gun, but…it did raise some questions. "So Stuart was watching Charlie's place and following him?"

"That's right."

"You think he was following Charlie last night?"

"I do. I think Charlie somehow guessed that Stuart was onto him and shot him."

Rod wasn't so sure. "Charlie's been out of town. We haven't even been able to reach him."

"Not according to this."

Bruce took out another picture of Charlie's vehicle. This one showed it turning out of his drive. The surprising part was the date. It had been taken the night before last, when Charlie was supposedly gone. "Interesting."

"That picture suggests he's been home," Bruce said.

Stuart's research was amateurish and haphazard—circumstantial, at best. But he'd obviously believed in his suspicions enough to have done a lot of surveillance. Had he been hoping to impress Sophia by solving the puzzle of the UDA murders? Had to be. Either that or he'd wanted to come off as a hero to the whole town, because he sure as hell didn't give a damn about the poor murdered UDAs.

Still, the fact that he'd wound up dead while trying to keep an eye on Charlie was unnerving, especially since Rod knew Sophia was out at Charlie's place right now.

Suddenly in a much bigger hurry to get back to her, he stood. "I'll look into this. Let's keep it between us until we have concrete evidence."

"No problem." Bruce met his gaze. "Just…catch the son of a bitch who shot Stu, okay?"

"I'll do that," Rod promised.

His father stared at him for a long second. "I wish things could've been different between you and me."

"You're not supposed to worry about that anymore, remember?"

"I'm only saying."

"There's still the future. So how am I getting back to town? You taking me?"

"No. Edna needs me tonight. I'll drive you to the house and give you the keys to one of the farm trucks. I can send a worker to retrieve it in the morning. Where are you staying?"

"The Boot and Spur." Rod started for the door, then thought of something else. "By the way, does Charlie smoke?"

"Like a chimney," he said. "Always has."

Starkey's widowed mother met them at the hospital in Douglas, where Starkey had been taken by ambulance. The doctors weren't making any promises as to his chances of survival. They hadn't said much at all. But they were doing their best to save him. At least, that was the message conveyed by the middle-aged nurse who'd just poked her head into the room to give them an update.

"Do you think he'll live?" Rafe asked Sophia, his face pale and somber.

Sophia didn't know what to say. The situation didn't look good. Starkey had taken two bullets, one that had barely missed his heart and one that had punctured a kidney. That had been part of the nurse's update. Fortunately, neither of those injuries had proved instantly fatal, but he'd lost a lot of blood. Maybe too much.

"I'm praying he does," she responded. He'd saved their lives. How he'd found the strength to interfere when he did, she had no idea. He'd been so weak when she'd seen him slumped in the doorway. The only thing she could figure was that he'd heard her call for Rafe and realized his son was still alive but would die if he didn't do something. "He's always been tough," she added, and that, together with a smile, seemed to have the most positive effect on Rafe.

"I'm praying, too." Careful not to come too close to his grandma, who sat on his other side, he settled back in his chair.

Starkey's mother, her face pinched with worry, glanced at him, but she didn't speak—to him or to Sophia. She'd been silent almost since they'd arrived. But Sophia hadn't expected her to be friendly. Somehow she blamed Sophia for Starkey's inability to straighten up and live a law-abiding life. She'd once claimed that he'd be a different person if Sophia had married him.

Sophia knew he wouldn't have changed. But she wasn't going to argue with the woman. Grandma Starkey had lived a hard life. She'd worked in a two-bit diner for the past two decades and didn't have a lot of reserves—mentally, physically or financially. She would've taken Rafe from Starkey years ago if she'd been in a better position to raise him.

"The guy who shot him is dead, though, right?" Rafe piped up. He was still trying to process everything that had occurred.

Sophia nodded. She'd shot him. Then she'd left him lying on the floor of her living room. The sheriff's department had come while the paramedics were loading Starkey into the ambulance. Because Sophia had fired her weapon, she couldn't also work the police end, couldn't get involved in it at all. The sheriff would handle that, and possibly the FBI. On her way out she'd passed Cooper, who'd indicated he was going to call Van Dormer.

What conclusions were they drawing from the evidence? She couldn't even make a call to see what was going on. Cell phone use wasn't permitted in the hospital. She didn't want to interrupt them in the middle of their work, anyway.

Planning to step outside so she could notify Rod of her whereabouts, she stood up, but Rafe grabbed her arm.

"Where're you going?" he asked. "You're not leaving, are you?"

He didn't particularly like his bony grandmother, who looked eighty instead of sixty and often muttered aloud but rarely made sense. Reading the panic on his face at the prospect of being left alone with her, Sophia didn't have the heart to abandon him, even for a few minutes. "You can come with me, if you want. I'll just be a minute."

He shook his head. "No. What if the nurse comes?"

Judging by the determination on his face, he wouldn't budge. She decided to wait until they heard about his father. But in the rush to get Starkey the help he needed, Sophia hadn't been able to check in with Rod. She'd tried once, in the ambulance, got his voice mail and hadn't left a message because she'd planned to call back right away. What with all the chaos and people coming at her with questions, she hadn't had a second chance, not until everything had slowed to a crawl right here in the waiting room. And then she couldn't use her cell.

She glanced at the clock on the wall. Almost two. Surely Rod would've started looking for her by now. He must've already stopped by her house and talked with Van Dormer or the sheriff, so he'd know where she was and why. Or maybe when she didn't show up at the dude ranch, he'd called the sheriff's department to see if they'd heard anything. Those were his two most logical options and, either way, he would've been given the same information.

Putting her phone back in her purse, she slipped her arm around Rafe. She needed to relax and concentrate on getting him through this. Rod was probably waiting for her at the Boot and Spur.

The ranch truck rattled and chugged as Rod pushed it to go faster on the drive to Charlie Sumpter's ranch. He'd received a call from Sophia earlier, but had somehow missed it. He wasn't sure how; he'd never heard it ring. And now it kept transferring to voice mail on the first ring, as if she'd shut it off. Considering what he'd learned from Bruce, he was terrified Sophia had come out here and gotten herself killed. She didn't believe Charlie was dangerous—not really. Of all the names listed on that limited partnership agreement, his was the one she'd been most skeptical of. She obviously had some affection for him. So Rod was afraid she hadn't been as cautious as she should've been. The UDA killer could be almost anyone.

He couldn't be sure Charlie was dangerous, but he was going straight to the place she'd said she'd be, just in case she needed him. He couldn't imagine where else she could've gone. She hadn't shown up at the Boot and Spur. He'd called the ranch four times. He'd even had the manager check the lot for his Hummer and go down and bang on the door of his cabin.

Once he hit the long straight section of road heading toward the ranches near the border, he pushed the needle on the speedometer higher and called Sophia again.

It was no use. She didn't answer.

What the hell was going on? Why wasn't she picking up? He'd left her at least six messages, all of which had gone unanswered.

Had her stepfather caught up with her? Waylaid her somehow? Hurt her? That thought was almost as frightening as thinking of her face-to-face with the UDA killer. For all he knew, Gary was just as dangerous. But his best guess was that she'd be at Charlie's, because that was where she'd been heading when he left her.

Charlie's place came up on the right. Rod remembered it from when he was a kid. Jorge used to bring him out here to help load the pickup with wrapped meat from a butchered cow for the Family. The Dunlaps purchased one each fall.

Slowing so abruptly the truck shuddered, he turned into the narrow, dirt drive. His tires spun rock and gravel and his back end fishtailed, but he got the truck under control. Then he rolled down his window and crept along, taking in everything he could see in the darkness, everything he could hear on the quiet night air.

When he emerged from the trees that had initially blocked his view of the house, he saw that the Hummer wasn't parked in the clearing. But, oddly enough, Charlie's white pickup wasn't there, either. Which made no sense. How could his pickup have been photographed a few days earlier if Charlie had taken it to visit his daughter in Yuma? Either he'd left it behind or he hadn't, and this made it appear that he hadn't.

Shoving his gun into his waistband, Rod stepped out. Moonlight fell gently on the front lawn, which smelled of freshly mowed grass. Someone was keeping up with the watering, too. And yet, even with the cicadas humming, the place had a lonely, shut-up feeling….

What was going on? Had Sophia been here? If so, where was she now? There was no sign of her.

Rod strode to the front door and rang the bell. He didn't give a damn how late it was. If Charlie was home, he wanted to talk to him, to see if he'd heard from Sophia and to ask why he hadn't been returning her calls, which was the reason she'd come out here in the first place.

His summons brought no response. "You're not here," he muttered. "I can tell you're gone, and you've been gone for a while."

He tried the door, found it locked and went around to the back. Everything was locked up tight. Short of breaking a window, there was no way to get in, no way to see if anything strange was going on. Except…

Rod looked more carefully. There was a small cut in the screen of the porch. Was it merely a coincidence that it was so close to the door handle?

He didn't believe in coincidence. Sliding his hand

inside, he flipped the lever that would let him in, and found the back door slightly ajar, as if whoever had gone out the last time hadn't bothered to latch it. Was that person Sophia? If not, Rod thought the open door was almost as strange as the missing truck. What if whoever had been here wasn't Charlie *or* Sophia?

The pent-up heat inside the house hit Rod like the blast from an oven. In this part of the country, homes that were closed up during the summer, without a few open windows to allow for an exchange of air, could be sweltering. This one certainly was—further evidence that Charlie was out of town for an extended period. No one could tolerate living in a place this hot.

Standing in the mudroom, Rod listened to the settling noises of the old house. A toilet was running in back, but that was about it. No wind buffeted the trees. No animals scurried about, padded around, meowed or barked. A kibble bowl and a neatly folded towel suggested that Charlie owned a pet, probably a dog, but he must've taken the animal with him.

Confident that he was as alone as he'd assumed when he entered, Rod stepped into a pitch-black room. All the blinds had been drawn to keep out the sun. Flipping the closest switch, he found himself in a clean but dated kitchen. The cupboards, the table and chairs, the clock and pictures, were simple, like their aging owner, but had most likely been purchased by Charlie's wife. She'd died when Rod was only ten or thereabouts, so the old guy had been on his own for quite a while. He didn't appear to have improved the place since then, but he was clearly keeping up with indoor as well as outdoor maintenance.

Spotting a calendar hanging above a small built-in desk next to the fridge, Rod walked over. The month was current, but a line had been drawn through the past week and extended for three more days. Above that line, a shaky hand had written Sumpter Family Reunion.

At least Rod now understood why Charlie hadn't responded to the message Sophia had left for him at his daughter's house. The daughter wasn't at home, either. They were probably off camping somewhere, or boating at Lake Powell.

Rod checked his phone to make sure he hadn't missed another call from Sophia, saw that he hadn't and moved on to the living room. But, once again, it was too dark to see. He'd just begun searching for a lamp when headlights hit the front window and the sound of a motor told him he had company.

Hoping Sophia had finally shown up, he peeked out. But it wasn't the Hummer. Someone was driving the white truck he'd seen in the photos.

31

The ambulance that screamed through town gave Gary hope. Planning to move his records for the smuggling enterprise to a new location, a more secure location, he'd been hastily packing all the files and ledgers into boxes. Now he stopped. That siren signaled good news. It had to be on its way to pick up Sophia and Rod, didn't it? With any luck, they were both dead. But if Leonard had taken care of them as promised, why hadn't he called?

Cursing Taylor for leaving him on tenterhooks, Gary paced in the front of his store, where he could see the street. Maybe Leonard was watching the action, making sure it all went as it should. Or maybe he was having difficulty getting to a place where he felt comfortable talking. Either scenario was possible, but Gary was more inclined to believe Taylor was relishing the fact that he had him at a disadvantage.

"Bastard." Unable to wait any longer, he called Leonard's cell. It rang several times before transferring to voice mail. What was going on? What was happening? He *hated* not knowing.

More agitated by the second, he was about to try again, when Leonard called him. "Finally," he muttered, and punched the talk button. "Did you do it? Is it done?"

Whoever answered wasn't Leonard. At first, Gary couldn't place him. He was talking too low. But then he realized it was Sheriff Cooper. "Leonard's dead."

"*What?* What about Sophia? And Rod?"

"Sophia shot Leonard. Scene's a mess. I don't know where Rod is."

"Where can I find them?" Leonard didn't matter, except that he hadn't done his job. All Gary cared about was making sure Sophia and Rod couldn't ruin him and the business he'd worked so hard to build.

"I can't talk. I'm going to do you a favor and destroy this phone. And if the phone records are requested in an investigation, I'll do my best to switch them out. That'll sever any obvious tie you have to Leonard, make it look as if he's the only one to blame for what happened here. If you have any records of any amounts you've ever paid me, destroy them immediately," he said, and hung up.

Gary's left arm began to tingle and the pressure he'd been feeling in his chest grew worse, until it felt as if he had an elephant sitting on him. Afraid he might be having a heart attack, he gingerly lowered himself to the floor and stretched out on his back. *Take it easy. You're gonna be okay. Deep breaths. That's it. It's not over. You'll find them. You'll save this thing yet.*

And he would. As he played back what Sheriff Cooper had just told him—the bit about destroying Leonard's cell phone so no one would see the calls between them tonight—he remembered that Leonard had also sent him a series of texts. The pain began to ease. Pushing himself into a sitting position, he reread them.

Taylor: No worries. They're coming back here.

Gary: How do you know?

Taylor: I've got big ears.

Gary: You've bugged her place.

Taylor: Office and car, too. Info's dependable. Trust me.

Gary: We need both people.

Taylor: I know. I'm on it. If I miss them here, I know where they're staying.

Gary: Where?

Taylor: At the Boot and Spur.

Gary had asked if Leonard meant the Boot and Spur Dude Ranch about five miles out of town because he was pretty sure that was closed at the height of the summer. He'd never received an answer. But it didn't matter. He'd been given enough information to find them.

The truck parked in front of his neighbor's house wasn't one James Simpson recognized, but he knew it couldn't be Charlie's. They'd spoken just this morning. James had assured him that he'd irrigated the fields, and Charlie had said he wouldn't be home for another three days.

So who was this? Patrick Dunlap? That would be his guess. Prior to his death, Stuart had opened his big mouth to his older brother and talked about his suspicions. Now Patrick was here to find his brother's killer.

"Shit. Why can't everyone mind their own business?" James checked the .45-caliber Glock he'd purchased in Phoenix several years ago. The gun had no serial number and was supposedly untraceable. Which was a good thing. Because it was about to be used in another crime. So was the silencer he'd purchased at the same time.

The door squealed as James opened it, and he reluctantly got out. It wasn't as if he wanted to kill Patrick. Hell, he hadn't *wanted* to kill Stuart. He'd had no choice. Stu wouldn't quit snooping. He kept trolling the ranch, night

after fucking night, making James's job more difficult.
James couldn't allow that. If Stuart kept at it, he'd eventually see or hear something he shouldn't and, as much
as Kevin talked about hating illegal aliens, he wouldn't
be happy to hear that it was his son who'd taken it upon
himself to do something that might be effective.

If only Charlie hadn't gotten drunk at the Firelight
and said some things that led Stuart to believe he might
be trying to avenge that other rancher's death. That had
started everything. Stuart had admitted as much, right
before James shot him. But the problem hadn't ended with
his death.

Taking a knife from under the seat, he walked over to
what he believed to be the Dunlaps' truck and slashed all
four tires. Whoever it was wouldn't be leaving Charlie's
anytime soon. It wouldn't be until tomorrow. Maybe later.
And then it would be in a body bag.

Rod waited in a storage closet in the hall. He wasn't
sure the driver of the white truck was hostile. Whoever
it was had parked in such a way that Rod couldn't see
him when he got out. He couldn't even guess who it was.
But neither could he imagine too many reasons someone
would need to borrow Charlie's truck in the middle of the
night while Charlie was out of town, unless that person
wanted to be sure he wasn't spotted in his own vehicle.

That led Rod to believe this guy wasn't out doing good
things.

Maybe he was about to confront the UDA killer….

Hearing the creak of footsteps in the kitchen, he opened
the closet door just a little. He'd chosen this particular
hiding place because he knew that whoever it was would
pass him as he—or she or they—headed to the bedrooms.

Then Rod could come up from behind and disarm him. He didn't want to shoot anyone, especially when he wasn't sure he was really in danger. There could be some other explanation for the coming and going of that white truck— not that Rod could think of one.

The heat made it hard to breathe. Squinting to keep the sweat out of his eyes, he tried to discern the slightest glimmer of light. But it was impossible. He'd turned off the lights as soon as that truck had pulled up. With the blinds down, he couldn't even see his own hand in front of his face. He'd expected whoever it was to turn the lights back on. But, so far, that hadn't happened. This person seemed perfectly comfortable in the dark.

Was it Leonard? If so, had he already gotten to Sophia? Was that where he'd been? Out in the desert, disposing of her body?

Muscles clenched, Rod fought to rid his mind of those thoughts. Assuming the worst would make him too eager for a confrontation. And too eager was always foolhardy. *Calm down.*

So who was it? Someone who knew Charlie well enough to be aware of his plans and his schedule. Leonard hung out with him at the Firelight. Leonard knew how to gain access to his house. And Leonard would love nothing more than to hurt Sophia—

Stop it! She was okay. She had to be okay. It didn't *have* to be Leonard who'd taken the truck. It could be whoever was looking after the place in Charlie's absence. Or someone else. Rod guessed Charlie kept his spare key hidden on his back porch, which was why the screen had been cut. Retrieving the keys to the truck would be as easy as walking through the house and taking them from where Charlie kept them, which explained the state of the back door. Why would the perpetrator bother to make sure it was tightly shut if he was locking the screen behind him and planned to come back in just a few hours to return the truck keys?

The creaking stopped at the mouth of the hall.

Come on. Come this way. You haven't found me yet. That means you need to check out the bedrooms.

Fortunately, the person started walking again. He moved cautiously but it wasn't as if Rod could hear hands swiping the walls to keep him from running into something. Somehow, the bastard could see. How?

The answer occurred to him almost as soon as the question did. Night-vision goggles. Of course. The border patrol had them. The ranchers probably did, too. Anyone who hunted in the dark would consider them standard equipment.

Four or five more steps and the intruder would be right where Rod wanted him. He wiped the sweat off his right hand so he could get a firm grip on the butt of his gun. He was ready.

Three more steps…

Two…

Wait for it…not yet….

Suddenly, his cell phone went off. With a violent curse, the man in the hall grabbed the door and tried to yank it open. Rod held it shut, but whoever it was fired, anyway.

As soon as Sophia pulled into the parking lot at the Boot and Spur, the manager walked out to meet her. He asked if she was Sophia St. Claire, then said that Rod had been trying to reach her. Surprised to hear he wasn't in the cabin, she tried to call him again. But he didn't answer.

Waiting in cabin thirteen, she stared out the window at the empty parking lot, as if she expected Bruce to drop him off at any moment, and wondered what to do next. She'd been feeling so relieved when she left Douglas. The doctors had managed to stabilize Starkey, a miracle in itself. She'd even spoken to him and laughed when the first thing he told her was that his acquaintance who dealt in silencers claimed he hadn't sold any to a guy from Bordertown. She couldn't believe that was on his mind at a time like this. It hadn't been for long. His thoughts soon shifted to Rafe, who wasn't pleased to be in his grandmother's care, but had chosen to stay with her at the motel beside the hospital so he'd be close to his dad. Sophia had thought the drama was over for the night, that she'd be able to go to the Boot and Spur and curl up with Rod to get some much-needed rest.

Now she was worried all over again; only this time she was worried about Rod.

Where was he? It was nearly three-thirty in the morning. Was he still with Bruce? If so, she thought maybe she shouldn't keep trying to get through to him. Maybe they were having the heart-to-heart they should've had long ago.

But it was also possible that something else had come up.

Steeling her nerve, she called Bruce's house.

Edna answered. "Hello?"

Bruce's wife sounded sick, fragile. And it was no wonder. She'd lost Stuart today. Sophia felt like the most callous person in the world for disturbing her in her grief, and at such a late hour, but she had to find Rod.

Tightening her grip on the phone, she overcame her reluctance to identify herself. "Edna, this is Sophia

St. Claire. I'm terribly sorry to bother you, but…could I speak to Bruce?"

"Do you know what time it is?" she snapped.

"I do. I apologize profusely. But this is important."

"Not more important than letting my poor husband get some sleep. Call back in the morning if you want to talk to him."

A dial tone hummed in her ear. But Sophia couldn't leave it at that. She called right back. Although Edna had good reason to be angry, Sophia guessed the chill she'd encountered was at least partly attributable to the rumors around town. Rod was Edna's biggest enemy, and Sophia was Rod's biggest ally. It didn't help that Sophia had re-buffed Stuart so many times over the past two years—and then gotten involved with his half brother.

The phone rang and rang. Finally Edna answered again. "What are you doing calling here? Why won't you leave us alone?"

Sophia fortified herself against Edna's anger. "I need to talk to Bruce. I'll drive out there if I have to. This is police business." To a degree, it was. After what they'd discovered at the feed store, Rod possessed information that put his life in danger. But Sophia was terrified about his safety for personal reasons, too; there was no escap-ing or denying that.

"Meaning you've arrested the person who killed my son?" she challenged.

"Meaning I'm doing my best to track down your son's killer and to keep everyone else safe at the same time."

"You mean everyone like *Rod*."

"He deserves the same consideration as anyone else."

"He doesn't deserve *anything*. He—"

Someone in the background interrupted Edna as her

voice crescendoed. Then the phone changed hands and Bruce came on the line. "Who is this?"

Sophia sighed in relief. "It's Chief St. Claire. I can't find Rod, and I'm worried. Do you know where he is?"

"No. He left here at least an hour ago."

"How? I've got his Hummer."

"I lent him a pickup, said I'd send someone for it in the morning."

"Did he say where he was going?"

"I assumed he was going to the Boot and Spur. That's where he's staying, isn't it?"

"I'm at the cabin now. The manager tells me he hasn't been here all night."

"Then I don't know what to think, except…"

"Except what?"

"He might've gone out to Charlie Sumpter's."

"Thanks. I'll check." She grabbed Rod's car keys as she ran out the door. But as soon as she glanced up, she realized she couldn't go anywhere. There was another car in the lot. Her stepfather's pearl-colored Escalade was blocking her in.

"Oh, God…" Hoping to return to the cabin, where she could lock the door, she turned—and ran right into him.

"There you are. How 'bout giving Daddy a kiss?" he murmured and licked her cheek as he covered her mouth with one hand and dragged her between the cabins, out of sight of the office and the parking lot.

Determined to get free, Sophia threw her head back, smashing it into his face. His hold loosened, but the blow had hurt more than she'd expected, stunning her, too. By the time she tried to reach for her gun, she'd lost most of her advantage, especially because her Glock was strapped to her calf, which didn't make it as accessible as she needed it to be. She'd barely lifted her pant leg when he seized her by the hair.

Sophia screamed for help, but there was no response from the office.

"There's no one to hear you." He hit her in the mouth, shocking her with the pain. Then the fight became a wrestling match on the rocky ground—a wrestling match that ended with him grabbing her firearm and tossing it out of reach.

Finally in control, Gary yanked her back to her feet. One hand was still entangled in her hair as he held his gun to the back of her head. "We're going to the truck. Do you understand?"

Covered in dust and sweat, they were both breathing hard. Sophia didn't think she'd ever been so exhausted in her life. This day just wouldn't end. But she couldn't give up, couldn't follow his commands. She knew what he was hoping to achieve. He wanted to drive her out into the desert to shoot her. Then he wouldn't have to transport a bleeding body and could leave her to the elements and the scavengers, like the UDA murderer did with his victims—and drive off. Maybe he *was* the UDA killer.

Briefly, she imagined Detective Lindstrom coming out to take a look at the crime scene and smiling the moment she identified the body. That gave Sophia a fresh dose of determination and strength. She wouldn't be the next victim in Bordertown, wouldn't let herself be killed— especially by her stepfather.

Going limp, she sagged against him, which allowed her to rest, since he was forced to bear most of her weight.

"Walk, damn it." When he let go of her hair to grab her by the arm, she whirled and kneed him in the groin. The gun went off, probably by reflex, but she wasn't hit.

Groaning, he stumbled, trying to recover, which gave her just enough time to slip out of his grasp.

She wanted to run for the office. She'd spoken to the manager fifteen minutes earlier and knew he lived on the premises. But if the sound of that gunshot hadn't brought him out, he wasn't capable of helping.

There's no one to hear you. Did that mean there was no one *alive?*

Just in case, she ran for the barn instead, where she felt she might have the space, darkness and freedom to evade capture.

On her way, she pressed the speed-dial button on her phone for Sheriff Cooper. If he responded quickly enough, she *might* survive....

Rod had been hit in the thigh, which hurt like hell, but he doubted it was a serious injury. Thanks to the solid wood door, the other two bullets hadn't even penetrated the wood. Ignoring the pain, he continued to hold the panel closed. And when whoever had just shot him tried to open it again, he provided enough resistance to tempt his attacker to pull harder—then let go.

The sudden release knocked his opponent into the opposite wall. Knowing he'd achieved one goal, he threw his gun aside. He couldn't shoot blind because he couldn't risk missing. Standing back long enough to fire could enable whoever it was to escape, and there was no way in hell Rod would take that chance. This was going to end here.

Launching himself in the intruder's direction, he flung his arms wide, hoping to catch the guy regardless of whether he ran right or left. He managed to grab hold of the man's shirt and drag him to the floor. His injured leg screamed at the jolt when he went down, but he had enough adrenaline flowing through him to keep fighting.

The shooter fired his gun again, but it wasn't pointed at Rod. Rod had grasped the man's wrist and pushed the muzzle up and away from both of them so the bullet went into a wall. A second later, he wrenched the gun away completely. Then he used his forearm to choke his attacker while putting the gun to his head.

"Who are you?" he demanded.

As soon as the barrel touched his temple, the man stopped squirming.

"I can shoot you and then turn on the light, if you prefer," Rod said when he didn't answer. "It's your choice."

"I… You… I think there's been a misunderstanding," he rasped.

"What kind of misunderstanding?"

"I'm James Simpson. I'm a—a neighbor of Charlie's… supposed to be taking care of the place. I thought you were a burglar…or—or the UDA killer, for God's sake. Everyone's been so…nervous…so afraid of what might happen next. I don't want to see anyone else get hurt. I guess…I thought I'd be able to put a stop to it."

"Nice try," he said.

"It's true!"

"So why have you been driving Charlie's truck?"

"He said I could. He lets me use it whenever I want."

Keeping the gun to his head, Rod yanked him to his feet. But then he had to catch his breath and cope with the pain radiating from the bullet in his leg.

For a moment, he couldn't seem to find his equilibrium. He swayed as if he might pass out but, gritting his teeth, he steadied himself before inching down the hall, where he finally encountered a light switch. Using his elbow to turn on the light, he released James and stepped back. The threat of death by bullet would subdue him now that Rod could see well enough to hit his target.

James's night-vision goggles lay on the floor. He no longer needed them, anyway. His gaze went from the muzzle of the gun Rod held, which was trained on him, to Rod's pant leg. "You—you'd better get some help for that injury. I'm really sorry, man. I didn't mean to shoot you. I swear I thought you were the UDA killer. God, I'm so sorry. Let me call someone, okay?" He lifted his hands. "I'm not trying to spook you. I just want to call an ambulance."

Blood soaked Rod's jeans, making them heavy and uncomfortable. He needed medical attention, all right. But in case the lab couldn't cull any DNA from that cigarette butt he'd picked up at the Sanchez murder scene, or that butt hadn't actually belonged to the killer, he first needed James to reveal whether or not he was the man they'd been hoping to find. If he was, there'd never be a better chance to get answers. The way he'd been sneaking around, using Charlie's truck, certainly implied that he was guilty. Even if he denied it later, Rod would know how to focus the investigation. The Simpsons had plenty of their own vehicles. James didn't need to "borrow" one.

But Rod had been involved in enough criminal investigations to know the D.A. would never be able to make murder-one charges stick without an eyewitness or some hard evidence. Taking Charlie's truck without permission was a far cry from homicide.

Grimacing, Rod began to make a bigger deal of the pain in his leg than necessary. He wanted to appear hobbled, weak and vulnerable. "Hurts like hell," he muttered, and allowed the barrel of the gun to dip, as though he believed James enough to be distracted by his own wound.

"I have a cell phone in my pocket," he said. "If you'll let me get it out, I'll make that call."

He was putting on a good show, but Rod wasn't convinced. He blinked several times as if he was having trouble clearing his vision—which he was, thanks to the sweat rolling from his hair. "Do it slowly," he said.

"I will." While James stuck his hand into the front pocket of his jeans, Rod could sense that his attention was elsewhere. He'd spotted the gun Rod had tossed away as he left the closet. It was lying on the floor within reach….

James pushed three buttons on his phone and held it to his ear. "Hello? Yes. This is James Simpson. I'm at 1184 White Rock Road and would like to report a shooting incident. Someone's been injured and needs medical help right away. Please send an ambulance."

Pretending to struggle with a fresh surge of dizziness, Rod closed his eyes and sagged against the wall. And that was when James made his move. Throwing his phone at Rod, he dove for the gun. But Rod deflected the phone and shot James in the butt.

"Ow! You shot me!" he screamed. "You son of a bitch! You tricked me and then you shot me!"

Unaffected, Rod watched him writhe. "Don't worry. You called an ambulance, right?" Bending carefully so that his leg wouldn't hurt or bleed any more than it already was, he retrieved his gun, which was still too close to James for comfort. Then he picked up James's phone and checked its call history. "Er, scratch that. Looks like you'll have to wait a while—4-5-6 doesn't go to any emergency services that I know."

"You'd better get me some help, you son of a bitch! I'm dying! Do you hear me? I'm going to die if you don't get me a doctor!"

"I'll get us both a doctor. When I'm ready." Sliding down the wall to ease the terrible ache in his thigh, Rod switched to the other gun—James's had to be getting low on bullets—and dug his cell phone out of his pocket. The call that'd come in at such an inopportune time was from Sophia, just as he'd hoped.

Thank God. Keeping an eye on James, who was finally beginning to realize that he wasn't mortally wounded, he called her back.

She answered on the first ring. "Rod, help me!" she whispered. "He's here."

Rod had no idea who she was talking about, but he didn't care. If she was frightened, he wanted to be there for her. "Where?"

"The Boot and Spur."

"I'm coming," he said, but he wasn't sure if she heard him. He didn't get a response; she'd disconnected.

Afraid he wouldn't be able to reach her in time, he called the manager of the ranch. The phone rang and rang without being answered, so he called his boss in California, dragging him out of bed, and told him to get Van Dormer or some other federal agents to the Boot and Spur as soon as possible and to have someone come and take care of James. Then he used a length of rope he found in Charlie's garage to make sure James wouldn't be going anywhere until Van Dormer arrived.

After tying a dish towel above his gunshot wound to staunch some of the bleeding, he limped out of the house—only to find his tires slashed.

Damn it, he had to go back in and wrangle the keys

to Charlie's pickup out of James. But he was on the road minutes later, pressing his hand to the hole in his leg as he drove.

Rod knew it probably wasn't smart to keep pushing himself. He was losing too much blood. But he'd finally won the girl he'd always wanted. No way would he risk losing her now.

32

Leaning against the tackle shed, Sophia tried to peer around the corner. Where was her stepfather? She'd paid a price for answering Rod's call. Gary had been closer to her hiding place than she'd thought. When he'd heard her voice, he'd come after her again. She'd only escaped him in the barn by throwing a bucket at him. He'd tried to bat it away but he'd been running too fast and had tripped over it instead, enabling her to run out of the barn and disappear among the outbuildings before he could recover.

But she'd also lost track of *him,* didn't know how close he was. Fortunately, she'd reached Sheriff Cooper, who was on his way. She only had to evade Gary until he or Rod arrived, which shouldn't take long. But a lot could happen in just a few minutes. And Gary had her gun. If he got hold of her again, it wasn't as if she'd have an equal chance.

In case she didn't make it out alive, she sent a text to Officer Fitzer. Evidence of human smuggling by Gary O'Conner and others in Rod's Hummer. Something happens to me, turn it over to FBI.

A thump near the barn startled Sophia. *What was that?* Obviously, Gary had caused it. But why? Was he hoping to scare her? To flush her out into the open? Or was there something else going on?

Holding her breath, she peered around the corner again but without the porch lights on the cabins up by the office, she could see very little. And she was beginning to worry because she'd told Rod and the sheriff she was at the Boot and Spur, but they wouldn't know to come immediately to the outbuildings.

She had to text them, too, but texting took her attention off what was happening around her.

A horse nickered in the barn, soon answered by another horse. They seemed spooked. Did that mean Gary was searching for her in the stalls?

Probably. That gave her a few seconds, didn't it? Swallowing her fear, she tried to steady her fingers to hit the right keys—but never got the text sent off. Her phone went flying as her stepfather grabbed her from behind and pushed her to the ground.

"It's over. Do you understand?" he ground out, standing over her with the gun aimed at her head. "You run again, and I'll shoot you without thinking twice."

She believed him. He was close enough that she could see him in the light of the moon, and the determination on his face was absolutely convincing.

"Calm down." Raising one hand in a motion of surrender, she used the other to help her sit up. "You'll be sorry if you hurt me. You'll spend the rest of your life in prison. Is that what you want? To lose everything? Don't you care about Mom?"

"You've finally pushed me too far. Why'd you have to do this? You've been out to get me from the very beginning."

Sophia felt as if she had to shout to be heard above the

hammering of her heart. "No. You're wrong about that. I tried to love you. But you wouldn't let me."

"That makes no sense," he said. "I wanted you night and day. I've always wanted you."

"That's not the same," she said sadly. "Anyway, killing me won't save you. I have evidence, evidence other people already know about. It's too late, Gary."

Her words didn't scare him as much as she'd hoped. "You're bluffing."

"I'm not. I made copies of what I found in the feed store. I know about Charlie, Patrick's wife, the mayor. They're making money by investing in your smuggling enterprise."

He laughed. "They don't know that. They think we were importing coffee."

"We'll see, won't we?"

His mouth twisted into a sneer. "You've never been afraid of me, have you?"

"You're wrong. I was afraid of you for years. But now I just see you as pathetic, as someone who's going to prison. So it won't do you any good to kill me."

"I'm not going anywhere," he scoffed.

"You think you can avoid it? That I'm lying about the evidence?"

"The evidence won't matter, sweetheart. Sheriff Cooper will take care of it. For the right price, of course."

Those words hit Sophia like a fist to the stomach. Cooper had been one person she'd always trusted. "What'd you say?"

"I said Sheriff Cooper will handle it." He grinned at her stricken expression. "How do you think he could afford that fishing trip to Alaska last summer? He took his brother and his best friend. A trip like that costs over eight thousand dollars."

"*You* paid for it?"

He winked. "Now you're catching on."

That meant Sheriff Cooper wasn't coming, unless he planned to help Gary. She should've called Van Dormer. But she hadn't even considered it. The deal was that the county provided her backup.

"How many others?" she asked. "Who else do you have on your payroll? Lindstrom?"

"No, not Lindstrom. I don't need her on payroll."

"Because she's easy enough for you to manipulate without money."

"Not me. I don't even know her. Leonard's the one."

"Leonard's involved?"

"I never liked him much, either. But I'm a businessman, Sophia. I work with people who have something to offer."

"What does a chicken farmer have to offer a human smuggler?"

"He hasn't always been a chicken farmer. I hired him when he was a cop to help out at the safe house now and then. The men I brought in to run it are effective but not always trustworthy, you know? I don't want them skimming. Having some insurance helps. Leonard was also my eyes and ears inside the police force. When it looked like he'd become chief, I had it made. But you got in the way of that."

"If it wasn't for the murders, I never would've realized what you really are."

"Everything was working just fine until someone started killing Mexicans," he said.

"You're saying that had nothing to do with the safe house?"

"Nothing. Why would I kill those poor defenseless bastards? Seeing them safely across the border is how I make my living."

"So it must be Leonard, trying to get back at the woman he raped and get me fired?"

"If he *was* hoping to get you fired, it almost worked, didn't it? Then maybe he would've been useful again. But I don't know. The men who run my safe house deal with coyotes all the time. They don't have any idea who's behind the killings, either. No one does."

The hard, rocky ground hurt her palms, but Sophia didn't shift. She wanted to keep Gary talking as long as possible. And he was so proud of what he'd accomplished, of how he'd fooled her and everyone else, he was eager to brag. "Leonard's dead," she told him. "You know that, right?"

"I heard." Gary made a *tsking* sound. "Too bad. Losing the future chief of police will hurt. But sometimes employees have to be replaced. I'll work with it, see what other candidate I can groom. I'm sure Cooper can recommend one of his deputies. With the abysmal salary those guys make, it shouldn't be hard to find someone who's interested in a significant raise."

Beads of sweat ran down Sophia's back and between her breasts, making her T-shirt cling to her. "What about Stuart? Don't tell me he was working for you, too."

"No." Regret glimmered in his eyes. "I don't know what happened to Stu. I didn't have anything to do with that, either."

Apparently, he wasn't enjoying the conversation anymore because he jerked his gun toward the shed. "That's enough. Get inside and take off your clothes."

Sophia's heart began to pump even harder. "What for?"

"I've come this far, I might as well get what I've always wanted. Before it's too late."

The memories of him slipping into her room when she was a teenager came tumbling back to her. Here he was again, after the same thing. It had a sick kind of symmetry, she thought bitterly. "You're going to rape me?"

"I'm going to get what I've always wanted," he said with a grin she'd never seen before.

Where was Rod? How would he find her? Maybe he was here already, searching…. "I'm your *stepdaughter.*"

"That makes us no relation."

"I won't let it happen," she said. "Why would I? You'll shoot me no matter what I do."

"True. But there are two ways to die. One is quick and easy—a bullet in the head. If you pretend to like it, that's how I'll end this. With as little pain as possible. That's how I'd prefer to do it. I'm really not a violent person. But if you refuse…you'll give me what I want, anyway, and then I'll tie you naked to a tree out in the desert and let you die of sunburn and dehydration, which could take days." He studied her. "You choose."

Rod saw the pearl-colored Escalade parked behind the Hummer as soon as he pulled into the lot and exhaled in relief. If both cars were here, Sophia was probably still on the premises. If Gary had taken her somewhere else, Rod knew he wouldn't have a prayer of finding her in time. He wasn't sure he'd find her in time, anyway. He was beginning to tremble and feared he was going into shock from loss of blood.

Ignoring the pain that radiated through his whole body as he got out, he checked the cars, found both empty, then went to the cabin. No one was there, either. It looked exactly as it had when he'd left it earlier.

The terror he'd heard in Sophia's voice seemed to echo in his brain. He'd texted her several times, asking for more information, but he hadn't heard back from her.

Hoping the manager could tell him something, he limped to the office.

Glancing through the window, he saw that the front desk was unmanned, but once Rod stumbled inside, he could hear a television blaring in the back. Someone sat in what appeared to be an office. He rang the bell, but there was no response. Whoever it was couldn't hear him above the damn TV.

"Hey!" Determined to rouse the man, Rod dragged himself around the desk—and found the manager unconscious.

Sophia lay on her back, staring up at a hanging lightbulb Gary had turned on when he'd dragged her into the tackle shed. He was crouched over her, holding the gun. Her blouse lay open, exposing her bra, but she wasn't taking her pants down fast enough to suit him. She was drawing it out, bargaining for more time.

"Hurry up or I'll start shooting your fingers off," he said.

Rod had to be here by now, didn't he? It seemed like so long ago that she'd called him. At this point, he was her only hope. Sheriff Cooper hadn't arrived and probably wasn't coming. He was letting Gary take care of her.

After it was all over, they'd decide who to put forward for her job.

"That's it." Victory rang in Gary's voice as she began to wiggle her pants down over her hips. "How does it feel to know that denying me all those years was only putting off the inevitable?"

Distantly, Sophia imagined him going home to her mother after this and getting into their shower to wash her blood off his skin. Imagined him climbing into bed. Imagined her mother turning to take him in her arms. And felt as if she might throw up. Or maybe the nausea came from all the times he'd had to hit her to get this far....

"Now the panties," he coaxed. But Sophia couldn't do it. She lay without moving, staring mutely up at him.

Surprisingly, he didn't hit her. He was too busy taking off his belt and undoing his pants. "This is what you've been missing," he said proudly, exposing himself.

Sophia knew she had two choices. She could allow her revulsion to get the best of her. Or she could use his sick desires against him.

Determined to survive at all costs, she smiled and motioned for him to lie down beside her. It was almost impossible to suppress her gag reflex when she put her mouth on his, but then the will to survive and her preoccupation with reaching some sort of tool she could use as a weapon took over, and she was able to divorce her mind from her body. She even moaned and was gratified when he moaned in return. He was falling for it, the stupid bastard.

The barrel of the gun cut into her temple, but he was getting so worked up that he wasn't holding it very steady. Praying he wouldn't shoot her by accident, she groped through the hay and the dirt, searching for the pitchfork she'd noticed earlier. Pretending she was as carried away as he was, she writhed and rolled and moaned—and found it.

"See? This isn't bad, is it?" he murmured. "God, you taste good…."

She had a hand on one tine of the pitchfork, but he wasn't watching the gun. She was beginning to believe she might be able to get hold of it. If she grabbed it, twisted and fired simultaneously it could all be over….

Did she want to take that risk? Any sudden movement and he might squeeze the trigger before she could push the muzzle away. But he was trying to remove her panties, and she knew, even if she got hold of the pitchfork, she couldn't use it while she was lying on her back. She wouldn't have enough leverage. Which meant she had no other option.

Arching into him, she groaned and, when he glanced up to see her face, to revel in her supposed enjoyment, she made her move.

It happened so fast, she wasn't sure she had the gun at the proper angle. But she grabbed it—and fired.

Rod had never experienced anything worse than hearing that gun go off—or seeing Sophia lying on that dirt floor with her clothes askew and her face streaked with blood and tears when he opened the door of the tackle shed. It reminded him of the helplessness he'd felt whenever his mother was hurt. He couldn't decide whether to gather her to him and comfort her or kill the man who'd caused her harm.

And then it occurred to him that he could do both, if he started with the man. But maybe he wasn't thinking straight. The room was spinning.

"Rod?"

He heard Sophia's worried voice but refused to take

his eyes off Gary. "Get up," he told him. No way would he shoot someone who was lying on the ground. But Gary couldn't get up. He was rolling around, shrieking in pain. He was the one who'd been shot, not Sophia. The bullet had gone right through his face. Blood streamed down both cheeks, but the bullet had been far from fatal, which meant he wasn't hurt enough.

Rod fired his own weapon, purposely hitting the wall just above Gary's head. Then he fired again and again, inching closer with each bullet to provoke maximum fear. "Pull up your pants," he snarled.

Gary scrambled to obey, but Rod wanted to shoot him, anyway. He might have, if not for Sophia. Having repaired her clothing, she was trying to take his weapon. "Rod, give me the gun."

Rod's head pounded in rhythm with the pulsing in his leg. "I should kill this asshole right here."

"No. I want him to stand trial. And so do you. We're cops, remember?"

"Did he do it? Did he get away with—"

"No. I shot him before he could. And I'm okay. Do you hear me? I'm fine. He'll stand trial. For that and a lot of other things."

Rod pictured Gary in prison and felt some of the terrible anger dissipate. "Yeah, maybe going to prison will show him what it feels like to get raped."

"You're going to pass out. We need to get you some help. Give me the gun," she repeated, and he let her take his firearm and pull him into her arms.

The sun was streaming through the window of the hospital room when Rod began to stir. The doctors had removed the bullet lodged against the bone above his knee and given him a blood transfusion. He'd been asleep ever since. They'd examined Sophia, too, and put some anti-septic on her cuts, but they hadn't felt the need to keep her overnight. She'd stayed to be with Rod.

"Hey, what are you doing clear over there?" he mumbled sleepily.

She offered him a tired smile. "Worrying about you."

"You've been sitting in that chair all night?"

"Since we got here. But that was only about six hours ago. And you were in surgery for an hour of that."

"You didn't have to worry. I can survive anything."

The humor in his voice relieved a lot of her tension. The doctors had told her he'd be okay. Now she believed it.

Shifting carefully to one side of the bed, he patted the spot next to him, and she got up to join him there. His arm went around her as she climbed in and settled against him.

"What happened to Gary?" he asked, toying with her hair.

The warmth of his body enveloped her, making her happy in a love-drunk way. "You don't remember?"

"I remember wanting to shoot him. Did I?"

"No," she said with a laugh. "I called Grant and he took care of the rest. Gary and James are in the hospital in Tucson, under police guard. Leonard's dead."

"So…did I shoot Leonard instead?"

"That was me."

She felt his lips against her temple. "Then I'm sure he deserved it."

"I did it to save Starkey's life." Not to mention her own and Rafe's.

"And did Starkey survive?"

"He was shot twice, but it looks like he'll make it. He's in this very same hospital."

"At least we're making it convenient for you to visit."

"You'll be getting out tonight or maybe tomorrow morning. He'll be in quite a while longer."

"I could go home now, if I wasn't enjoying your sympathy so much."

She snuggled even closer. "Sure you could. You can barely talk."

"I'm lucid."

"Sort of."

"Can you believe it's all over?" he asked.

She knew he wasn't referring to his medical treatment; he was talking about the murders and the smuggling and the risk to their lives. Van Dormer had filled her in, told her it was James who'd killed the UDAs and inadvertently exposed Gary and his operation. "I can't. I'm glad, of course, but I'd be a lot happier if it didn't mean you'd be leaving."

He tilted up her chin so he could look into her face. "What if I were to take you with me?"

She would've liked nothing more. But she couldn't walk out on all the people who needed her. "I wish I could go."

"But…"

"The next few months won't be easy for my mother. And there's a fourteen-year-old boy who's counting on me. He actually reminds me of you at the same age. He's savvy, been forced to live by his wits."

"Where've you been hiding him all week?"

"He's been at soccer camp."

"I'm drugged, but did you just say you have a boy?"

She couldn't help chuckling at his confusion.

"It's Starkey's son. I pretty much raised him for the three years we were together. And I've done what I can ever since. Besides his father, I'm pretty much all Rafe's got. I can't let him down."

Rod ran his knuckles down the side of her face. She had the impression he was thinking, weighing their options.

"Then there's Bordertown," she went on. "With James going to prison for the UDA murders as well as Stuart's death, and the sheriff being indicted for accepting bribes to look the other way—I'm needed here. For all we know, there could be others."

"I see."

"They could use your help, as well," she said hopefully.

"You want me to stay."

She met his gaze. "I'm thirty and I've finally fallen in love."

He kissed her forehead, her cheeks, her lips. "Good thing there'll be a few jobs."

"You'll do it?" she asked in surprise.

"I think I can manage to put up with the place until Rafe turns eighteen."

She held his face between her hands. "I hope that's not the sedatives talking."

He laughed. "It's not."

"How do you know?"

"Because I'm thirty, but I've been in love ever since I was fifteen," he said, and kissed her.

Epilogue

The city council meeting was far more crowded than any Sophia had attended before. She sat nervously in her uniform at the front of the room, facing the five council members who'd fired her. Paul Fedorko gave her a fleeting, apologetic smile, Liz Torres flushed every time their eyes met and Richard Lantus acted preoccupied, as if this was business as usual. But this wasn't just another meeting. In the week since Gary and James had been arrested, they'd buried Stuart Dunlap and Leonard Taylor. She'd removed bugs planted by Leonard from her home, office and vehicle—bugs she never would've known about except for a text message they found on Gary's phone. And the county sheriff and two members of the city council—Neil Munoz and the mayor—had already been named as suspects in a corruption investigation, with others in the works.

Although Neil Munoz was a no-show, Mayor Schilling presided as usual, trying to keep up appearances in hopes of convincing Bordertown's citizens that he'd been falsely accused. And maybe that was true. Too many had been swept up in Gary's "coffee" enterprise to believe they'd all known what was happening. Sophia believed it was just Leonard and the sheriff who were aware of the truth. The others had been duped. Ever since news of what Gary was really doing had broken several other people, including the Simpsons, had stepped forward to say they'd been invited to participate, too, as investors, and had refused for one reason or another. But they all said it seemed legitimate. Gary used other people's capital to grow his illegal business but he paid a fair return, so no one was any the wiser.

The mayor pounded his gavel. "Can we come to order here? Quiet, please. Quiet. We'd like to get started."

Cameramen from ABC News and CNN crouched at the side of the room, recording what the mayor had to say. Sophia could tell the inclusion of such "outsiders" bothered Schilling; he had too much pride to stand there as an accused man. But there was enough going on even without the news media, who crowded into every foot of space not already taken up by a Bordertown resident. Most people had come early to be sure of getting a seat. Recent events had stirred up a surfeit of emotion, and folks had come out to have their say, to complain to their elected officials as well as their neighbors and the press.

Ever since that terrifying night at the Boot and Spur, Sophia herself had spent hours talking with reporters. Mostly she'd told them how glad she was to have it all behind her. The safe house was closed down, and although one of the two men who ran it had escaped, he was an illegal immigrant himself who'd probably returned to Mexico. And she no longer had to worry about James shooting innocent people. But now she was uneasy again. One detail remained. She was about to hear whether or not she'd receive an offer to continue on as chief of police.

Drawing a deep breath, she turned to look for Rod and found him sitting at the back, his injured leg stretched out in the aisle. She knew it hurt him to bend it, but he was getting around and had insisted on coming. He was sitting with Bruce, which made her smile. They'd managed to forge the beginnings of a friendship over the past few days. Yesterday Bruce had taken Rod fishing. Rod had acted as if it wasn't any big deal, but she could tell he was secretly excited. She'd loved packing his lunch, then helping fry the trout he brought home.

Unfortunately Edna and Patrick weren't quite as willing to embrace Rod. Bruce was still struggling to deal with the division in his family caused by their resistance, but at this point a division was to be expected. Patrick's wife was one of the investors in Gary's sham of a business, and she was being investigated along with all the others.

When Sophia caught Rod's eye he motioned to his left, and she shifted her gaze. A few rows away she saw Rafe, who'd come with his grandmother. Starkey was still in the hospital, but his prognosis had improved dramatically. He claimed, as a result of what he'd been through, that he was going to turn his life around and be a better parent to Rafe. Sophia figured she'd believe it when he proved it, but at least he now had the chance.

"As you know, we've had some unfortunate…occurrences in Bordertown during the past few months and weeks," the mayor began when he'd finally managed to call the room to order. "I can't comment on all of it because the investigations are ongoing. But the FBI will get the mess straightened out and those who have broken the law will be punished."

Sophia wondered if that might include him—but again her gut told her no.

"In difficult times a rare few prove themselves to be made of stern stuff," he went on. "We call those individuals heroes." He paused to give his words a theatrical flair. "And tonight we'd like to honor our own hero. Chief St. Claire, will you please stand? We have something we'd like to present to you for your outstanding service on behalf of Bordertown."

Sophia had been hoping they'd reconsider firing her. She hadn't expected an award. She stood to the sound of thunderous applause while Paul Fedorko read a proclamation the council had signed and framed.

"Thank you for service above and beyond the call," he said when he was done. Then he gave her the plaque along with the microphone so she could respond.

"Does this mean I get to keep my job?" she asked.

Everyone laughed, and Paul nodded. "Of course. I'm sure we'll all sleep better at night knowing we have such a capable chief of police, right, folks?"

There was more applause. Rafe even stood to clap. But Sophia raised a hand to silence everyone. "Thank you. I'm truly flattered. By the way, you'll be happy to learn that the ballistics from the spent shell casings and the bullets taken from the victims match the gun found on the suspect."

While she talked, Sophia spotted Detective Lindstrom on the left, toward the middle. She didn't look happy with the accolades Sophia was receiving, but Sophia didn't care. She knew they'd never be friends. Charlie Sumpter, back from his family reunion, was in the crowd, too. He'd been as surprised as anyone by what James had done. Sophia was pretty sure he hadn't realized what he'd invested in, either. And he probably wasn't alone in that. Exactly who was aware of what was going on and who wasn't still had to be sorted out.

Notably absent were James's parents. Sophia had been out to visit them and had seen how much they were struggling with the actions of their son. Because of his attitude toward illegal immigrants and everything he'd had to say on the subject, Kevin felt he was partially to blame.

Anne was absent, too. She was taking Gary's arrest as hard as Sophia had expected; she'd also heard the rumors that they'd been having an affair, which had reached her just a few days ago. But she understood what Leonard had been attempting by spreading those rumors, and she wasn't blaming Sophia for Gary's incarceration, which had come as a complete shock to her. Sophia believed that her mother would work through her loss and eventually file for divorce. She was still an attractive woman; she'd find another man to take care of her, which was what her happiness seemed to hinge on.

"We think we might also have some DNA evidence that places the suspect at the scene of one of the murders," she went on. "We're still waiting for that to come in. But the case looks solid. I'd like to assure you that the worst is behind us. We'll have a difficult time over the next few months as we heal from our collective wounds, but if we pull together we'll make it." Her gaze strayed to Rod, who was grinning proudly. "And now I must admit that I don't really deserve the award the council just gave me. I couldn't have accomplished what was done without the help of Rod Guerrero, one of our own who returned in our hour of need and worked tirelessly, without compensation, to make sure we were safe."

The crowd clapped and stomped, with Rod's father cheering loudest, but Rod interrupted. "Are you kidding?" he said, giving them his cocky, sexy smile. "I got exactly what I wanted."

"What did you want?" someone called, playing along.

"I got the girl," he said, and then the crowd really went wild.

Later, when Rod lay next to her in bed, sliding his fingers up and down her arm and staring out the window, he said, "Tomorrow, will you go somewhere with me?"

"Where?" she asked.

"To the cemetery. It's about time I paid my respects to my mother."

"Of course."

He curled around her. "She would've liked you, you know."

A moment later Sophia couldn't help asking, "Are you okay with staying in Bordertown, Rod? Can you really be happy here?"

"I think this is where I'm supposed to be. All roads lead home—at least for now."

"What will you do about Department 6? I hate to ask you to quit your job."

"I talked to Milt earlier. I'm not quitting my job. I'm going to open an extension office." He winked at her. "And I'll try to recruit the chief of police."

* * * * *

 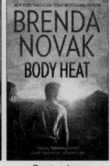 

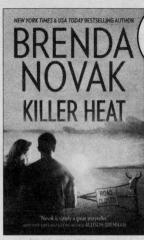

$1.⁰⁰ OFF

MIRA®

Look for the final book in the
Department 6 trilogy from
New York Times and *USA TODAY*
bestselling author

BRENDA NOVAK

KILLER HEAT

*Available September 28, 2010,
wherever books are sold!*

$1.⁰⁰ OFF the purchase price of KILLER HEAT by Brenda Novak

Offer valid from September 28, 2010, to October 12, 2010.
Redeemable at participating retail outlets. Limit one coupon per purchase.
Valid in the U.S.A. and Canada only.

52609392

5 65373 00076 2 (8100)0 11696

® and TM are trademarks owned and used by the trademark owner and/or its licensee.
© 2010 Harlequin Enterprises Limited

HARLEQUIN®
Super Romance®

Celebrate the Christmas season with
New York Times *bestselling author*

Brenda Novak

and fan favorites

Kathleen O'Brien

and

Karina Bliss

A young woman in search of a home…

A prodigal son's return…

A real-life Grinch transformed
by the magic of Christmas…

Curl up in front of the fire with
this joyous and uplifting anthology
that celebrates the true meaning
of Christmas.

Look for
THAT CHRISTMAS FEELING
*available November
wherever books are sold.*

www.eHarlequin.com

HSR71668R

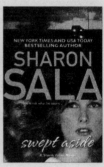

REQUEST YOUR FREE BOOKS!

2 FREE NOVELS
FROM THE SUSPENSE COLLECTION
PLUS 2 FREE GIFTS!

YES! Please send me 2 FREE novels from the Suspense Collection and my 2 FREE gifts (gifts are worth about $10). After receiving them, if I don't wish to receive any more books, I can return the shipping statement marked "cancel." If I don't cancel, I will receive 3 brand-new novels every month and be billed just $5.74 per book in the U.S. or $6.24 per book in Canada. That's a saving of at least 28% off the cover price. It's quite a bargain! Shipping and handling is just 50¢ per book.* I understand that accepting the 2 free books and gifts places me under no obligation to buy anything. I can always return a shipment and cancel at any time. Even if I never buy another book, the two free books and gifts are mine to keep forever.

192/392 MDN E7PD

Name _____ (PLEASE PRINT) _____

Address _____ Apt. # _____

City _____ State/Prov. _____ Zip/Postal Code _____

Signature (if under 18, a parent or guardian must sign)

Mail to **The Reader Service:**
IN U.S.A.: P.O. Box 1867, Buffalo, NY 14240-1867
IN CANADA: P.O. Box 609, Fort Erie, Ontario L2A 5X3

Not valid for current subscribers to the Suspense Collection
or the Romance/Suspense Collection.

Want to try two free books from another line?
Call 1-800-873-8635 or visit www.morefreebooks.com.

* Terms and prices subject to change without notice. Prices do not include applicable taxes. N.Y. residents add applicable sales tax. Canadian residents will be charged applicable provincial taxes and GST. Offer not valid in Quebec. This offer is limited to one order per household. All orders subject to approval. Credit or debit balances in a customer's account(s) may be offset by any other outstanding balance owed by or to the customer. Please allow 4 to 6 weeks for delivery. Offer available while quantities last.

Your Privacy: Harlequin Books is committed to protecting your privacy. Our Privacy Policy is available online at www.eHarlequin.com or upon request from the Reader Service. From time to time we make our lists of customers available to reputable third parties who may have a product or service of interest to you. If you would prefer we not share your name and address, please check here. ☐

Help us get it right—We strive for accurate, respectful and relevant communications. To clarify or modify your communication preferences, visit us at www.ReaderService.com/consumerchoice.

MSUS10R

BRENDA NOVAK

32667	THE PERFECT COUPLE	___ $7.99 U.S.	___ $8.99 CAN.
32725	THE PERFECT MURDER	___ $7.99 U.S.	___ $8.99 CAN.
32724	THE PERFECT LIAR	___ $7.99 U.S.	___ $8.99 CAN.
32885	DEAD SILENCE	___ $7.99 U.S.	___ $9.99 CAN.
32886	DEAD GIVEAWAY	___ $7.99 U.S.	___ $9.99 CAN.
32902	DEAD RIGHT	___ $7.99 U.S.	___ $9.99 CAN.
32903	TRUST ME	___ $7.99 U.S.	___ $9.99 CAN.
32904	WATCH ME	___ $7.99 U.S.	___ $9.99 CAN.
32905	STOP ME	___ $7.99 U.S.	___ $9.99 CAN.

(limited quantities available)

TOTAL AMOUNT	$ _____
POSTAGE & HANDLING	$ _____
($1.00 for 1 book, 50¢ for each additional)	
APPLICABLE TAXES*	$ _____
TOTAL PAYABLE	$ _____

(check or money order—please do not send cash)

To order, complete this form and send it, along with a check or money order for the total above, payable to MIRA Books, to: **In the U.S.:** 3010 Walden Avenue, P.O. Box 9077, Buffalo, NY 14269-9077; **In Canada:** P.O. Box 636, Fort Erie, Ontario, L2A 5X3.

Name: _____
Address: _____ City: _____
State/Prov.: _____ Zip/Postal Code: _____
Account Number (if applicable): _____

075 CSAS

*New York residents remit applicable sales taxes.
*Canadian residents remit applicable GST and provincial taxes.

MIRA®

www.MIRABooks.com

MBN0810BL